THE DRAUGHTSMAN'S DAUGHTER

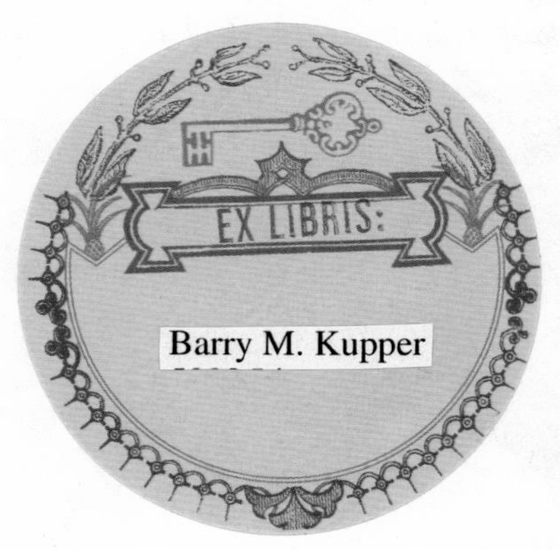

IN THIS SERIES:

In the Court of Kemet
Ancient Egyptian Romances Book #1

In the Temple of Mehyt
Ancient Egyptian Romances Book #2

The Draughtsman's Daughter
Ancient Egyptian Romances Book #3

Lady of the Caravan
Ancient Egyptian Romances Book #4

ALSO BY DANIELLE S. LeBLANC:

Living with Oral Allergy Syndrome: A Gluten and Meat-Free Cookbook for Wheat, Soy, Nut, Fresh Fruit and Vegetable Allergies

Recipes for Unusual Gluten Free Pasta: Pierogis, Dumplings, Desserts and More!

Cooking and Baking with Gluten Free Beer

THE DRAUGHTSMAN'S DAUGHTER

Ancient Egyptian Romance Book #3

By

Danielle S. LeBlanc

www.DanielleSLeBlanc.com

La Venta West, Inc.

For Alex

LA VENTA WEST, INC., 2016

www.laventawestpublishers.blogspot.ca

Print ISBN 978-0-9949751-2-6
eBook ISBN 978-0-9949751-3-3

Table of Contents

Quick Reference
for
Ancient Egyptian Words

Eei-wee em hotep: Welcome in peace, a greeting

Herit: Dung

Heru nefer: Good day, a greeting

Hnrt: Prison complex

Khet: Measurement of distance or land, 1 khet = approximately 52.5 metres, or 172 feet

Mewet: Mother

Nedj kheret: Greetings

Pr-djt: House for eternity, or eternal house, a type of ancient Egyptian tomb in the form of a flat-roofed, rectangular structure with outward sloping sides, also known as a *mastaba*.

Ro: Mathematical term for fraction (of a whole number)

Tayi neb: My lord

Wnwt: Hour

Yet: Father

Chapter 1 – In the Tomb of Amunemhat

Iset dipped her paintbrush into a pot of brownish-yellow ochre paste and, with short strokes, began to fill in the flesh of Amunemhat's face. A small table next to her was littered with pots of paint, brushes made of pounded palm leaves, and linen rags smeared with pigments – evidence of the odd time her strokes strayed outside the lines drawn by the draughtsman.

She stepped back from the tomb's wall to survey the day's work. A few braided wicks resting in bowls of flax oil illuminated the rectangular tomb, alongside the late afternoon sunlight streaming through the mastaba's door. Her eyes were tired from the strain of working in such low light, but she was pleased with the day's work as she'd almost completed the scene of Amunemhat worshiping Osiris. Today, she'd applied the green malachite to the papyrus reeds and lotus leaves along the bottom of the mural, the chalk-white to the skirts of the nobleman and his wife, their orpiment and ochre golden collars and bracelets were done, as well as the dark flesh of their arms and legs. Tomorrow she intended to finish the worship scene and move on to the wall on the other side of the small tomb.

Unbidden, her eyes strayed to the ominous inscriptions above the worship scene:

> *As for any man who steps foot into this tomb which belongs to me and my ka, the gods will protect me. He who offends will be nowhere, as if never having existed on this earth. He and his children and his loved ones shall die from hunger and thirst and will be cooked by the fires. I shall be as an enemy against him, I shall be a lion, a crocodile, a serpent, and shall eat him thrice over. Be forewarned.*

Iset's reading skills were rudimentary, learned only by way of watching her brother as he practiced. But anyone who grew up alongside the Land of the Dead knew the punishments for trespassing in a tomb, both in this world and the next. Given the false pretences under which she'd gained her employment, Iset was particularly troubled by the portents when she'd first begun work in the tombs. Though she tried hard to ignore them, their ubiquitous presence weighed often on her mind.

The air was warm and heavy with late afternoon heat, and Iset slipped a finger under the white linen scarf wrapped over her head, nose, and mouth, tugging at it a little so she could draw in a deep breath. It didn't help that she was wearing so many layers of clothing. One of her father's old vests hung to her knees over top of a full-length, coarse linen robe, beneath which a long strip of linen wrapped multiple times across her breasts, constricting her breath.

Like many workers, she wore the scarf over her face to protect her airways from the sand and rock and dust, and the strong scent of the minerals used to create the pigments she applied to the white-washed walls. But unlike the other workers, the wrappings were necessary to conceal her true self.

Gazing out the door, she decided she was actually looking forward to painting the bright, cheerful flowers of the wealthy man's gardens, even if the small children that played in it caused her sadness. At her age, and with the burdens she had to bear, it was unlikely she would ever marry and have children of her own.

Her mind wandered to the strange man she had seen striding across the Land of the Dead earlier that morning. She'd only glimpsed him from a distance, but even then his looks made it obvious he wasn't from Kemet. The tallest man she'd ever seen, with long braided hair and skin the colour of a smooth chestnut shell. Something in his gait had appealed to her – strong, self-assured, shoulders back and head up. A man like that could impart confidence to those around him.

The light spilling through the door was growing faint, indicating it must be close to the end of the workday. She began to organize her paint supplies for tomorrow morning. In the far corner of the rectangular tomb a black hole gaped in the hard-packed earth – a shaft into the underground burial chamber. She gave it a wide berth. The cavity in the floor yawned like the mouth of an angry god, waiting to swallow her into the underworld. As far as she was concerned, there was no worse death than being buried alive beneath a tomb. And with all the lies she'd been telling lately, there was no way Ammit could weigh her heart and find it lighter than a feather. Her *ka* – her life-force – would be doomed to eternal restlessness.

For the wealthy, a burial chamber was a rich storehouse of the goods required for comfort in the afterlife. For Iset it was the stuff of nightmares.

Iset had her back to the door when she heard sandals scuffing on the hard earth behind her. She was about to turn when a strong, wiry arm wrapped around her waist and something pressed against her throat.

"Don't move," a voice rasped in her ear as the scent of an unwashed body wafted around her, "or I'll slit your throat." Apparently that something against her throat was a knife. Blood rushed through Iset's heart as her breath stopped.

Several more feet scuffled nearby. "Hello, Dedi," a nasal voice addressed her. "I think you have something we need."

Iset grunted in response.

"Oh, don't worry," the nasal voice crooned. "I know you don't speak so good. It's all right. I'll do the talking and I'll be quick. Your uncle was supposed to help us find our way into Pharaoh Wadj's tomb. But he's dead, and now that the tomb is sealed we need to get in there."

If Iset wasn't already pretending to be mute, she would have been struck speechless. *By the gods, what has he done this time?*

"We need you to tell us where to tunnel in," the voice continued. "You see, we're planning to breach the boulder that's blocking the entranceway. And once we're in, we need to know where to break through the floor to get to the bastard's burial chamber where all the goods are. Your uncle was supposed to lead us to the spot on the floor where we need to dig."

The nasal voice got closer. "Do you know where to look, Dedi?"

Iset shook her head as best as she could, given the warm blade pressed at her throat.

"Well then, you got five days to find out where that spot is and tell us. Otherwise we'll be coming for your pretty little cousin. There's a few things I could think of I'd like to do with her."

Iset's legs grew weak. She prayed to her namesake, Isis, along with the goddess's sister Nebet-het. *Please don't let them find out who I am.*

"Five days, boy," said Nasal Man, "And we'll come looking for you again. If you don't have what we need, we'll pay your pretty cousin a visit. Then we'll let it slip how your uncle was involved in robbing that nobleman's tomb a couple of months back. If you're lucky, all they'll do is exile you and your sick old auntie. If you ain't, they'll cut your feet off. Maybe your other little cousin, too. What's 'is name again?"

A distressed noise escaped her throat. If the man behind her wasn't gripping her waist so tight her legs might not hold her up. She didn't need to be told who *they* were. *They* were the royal enforcers. Tomb robbers were the lowest sort of criminals, and the penalty for defiling the peace of the dead could include maiming, impalement on a stake, confiscation of all worldly goods, or exile. Often a combination of punishments was employed. Sometimes if the crime was heinous enough the sentence was taken out on innocent family members as well as the guilty party. It wouldn't matter that she hadn't been involved. And then, of course, there were the ominous warnings on the tomb walls.

"Ahmose," said a new voice from behind her in low murmur.

"Right!" Iset heard the smile in Nasal Man's voice as he repeated the name. "Your little cousin Ahmose. He's kinda puny, ain't he? Wouldn't hold up well to having his body parts cut off. They'd probably dig up the old man, your uncle, too. Just so they could cut off his hands and feet, and wipe his name from the tablets of history so nobody will ever remember his name."

"So!" Nasal Man clapped his hands, and Iset jerked at the sudden sound. "I think you'll be ready when we come looking for you again, right?"

Iset pushed sound up her throat, something of assent.

"Right then! Good! So now I'm going ask you step over to that there hole in the ground and keep your eyes down."

The man holding her began to push her forward towards the chasm in the floor. Iset whimpered and tried to resist, but the man behind her kept stepping forward, propelling her in front of him until her feet were on the edge of the narrow square cut into the bedrock. All she could see was the top of the ladder that led into the pit of darkness.

"There you go, boy," Nasal Man said. "Down you go. This'll help you get a taste of what to expect if you don't do what we're asking. You need to stay there for a few minutes until we make our way outta here."

Noises of protest rose from the back of her throat and she tried to dig her heels into the ground.

"There's only two ways this'll go," the voice near her growled. "You take yourself there, or we push you. I warn you, it'll be harder for you to find the entrance if you break your legs on the way down."

Iset closed her eyes and nodded. She stepped towards the ladder. As her feet found the wooden rungs, she glanced furtively up at the men around her. Four, maybe five of them, all with their faces covered like hers, making it impossible to identify any of them.

"What did I say? Don't look at us!" Nasal Man growled, and a tall, thin man nearby moved swiftly towards her, raising his foot threateningly. Rather than incur a kick to the head, she hunched her shoulders and scurried down the ladder, trying not to think of stepping on a poisonous scorpion or a biting cobra when she touched the ground.

Nasal Man waited until she'd reached the bottom and said, "Step back, all the way to end of the chamber. I don't want to see you down there." Anguish rose in her chest. If she went to the far end of the chamber, she might not be able to see the entranceway to find her way back.

Iset stepped backwards, hands outstretched, keeping her eye on the ladder. Her back hit the wall of the burial chamber and her legs folded. She slid down to the ground. The oil wicks were flickering in the tomb above, casting an eerie reddish-orange glow through the hole in the ground. And then they weren't. Iset gasped. The men had blown out the oil wicks, casting the tomb in total darkness.

"Keep going, boy," Nasal Man called. "Stay there. Don't you dare come out until we've had time to get away from here."

Sandals slapped bedrock, and then all went silent.

Iset couldn't breathe. Panic welled up in her throat as she huddled in the thick blackness, unable even to see her own hand in front of her face. She was living her worst nightmare. Any moment now the roof would cave in and bury her alive. She was sure of it.

She bit her lip hard, focusing on the pain to block out her fear. It was impossible, though, given that she was hyper alert to any sounds of scuttling insect feet, or scaly creatures slithering across the chamber dug out of the bedrock. One day, the coffins of Amunemhat and his wife would be lowered into this room along with vast stores of food, beer, jewellery, combs, and icons of the gods. Then the opening in the ground above her would be sealed over. The main door to the angled mastaba would also be sealed forever. Or at least until men like the ones who'd just threatened her found their way in to loot it.

The nobleman Amunemhat had yet to die, and his tomb was empty now. But not far away hundreds – possibly thousands – of bodies lined the valley at the edge of the desert cliffs. Whether or not they had passed peacefully into the afterlife to serve the gods and the pharaohs interred here didn't really matter to Iset's fear-addled thoughts. She could see the bodies in her mind's eye with their rotting hands folded over their chests.

She tore at the white linen scarf wrapped around her head and over her face, trying to suck in more air. But all she got was the stale, dusty atmosphere of the catacomb clogging her nostrils. It didn't help matters that the linen swaddling her breasts was suddenly too tight, constricting her chest. Even if she could breathe, it wouldn't get past her throat into her lungs. She needed to get *out* of all of it. The tomb, her clothes, this situation. All of it.

Tucking her scarf back around her face, she scrabbled at the hard rock beneath her and pushed herself up against the wall. She stuffed down her feelings of terror and stumbled through the blackness, running her hand along the wall and praying to Osiris to help her find the ladder rather than a nest of snakes or spiders.

Finally, *thank the gods*, her hand touched something wooden. She scuttled up the ladder and ran through the unfinished mud-brick temple built over the crypt. Bursting out into the open air of the dry valley near the cliffs that led out to the desert, she looked frantically around her to make sure the men who'd threatened her weren't waiting for her to appear.

And that's when she ran right into something solid, smacking her cheek against the statue of a god. Or at least, it felt like a statue, for when her hands went up to push back from it she touched something sun-warmed, sculpted, and hard as a marble pillar. She wondered when the workers had placed it there.

Stepping back, she looked up and that's when she realized it wasn't a statue but a real live man. The same tall man she'd seen striding across the valley earlier that day. The most unusual-looking man she'd ever seen. He was broad-shouldered, lean-waisted, and powerful in appearance. Up close she could see that his shoulder-length hair had feathers braided into it and there were blue-black markings on his cheeks: a crescent moon with its points facing downwards tattooed below his right eye, and what appeared to be a thick arrow under the left. He was most certainly not Kemeti.

He gripped her biceps, holding her out at arms' length. "Watch out, boy, or you'll hurt someone." His voice was not unkind. In fact, he sounded amused. Regardless, Iset dropped her eyes as fear rushed through her. She hated to be noticed.

"Sorry," she rasped, pitching her voice low and scratchy so that it was unrecognizable.

The man released her and she kept her eyes lowered to his feet where she noticed that, beneath his knee-length wrap skirt, his calves were also tattooed. Thick black lines spiraled up his legs, and in between them rams and mythical winged creatures roamed.

What in the name of the gods is this man doing here in the Land of the Dead? She glanced up and her gaze stuck. His eyes were shocking with their obsidian pupils set in a blinding white surround. They tilted upwards slightly at the edges, lending him the perpetual semblance of a teasing smile.

His eyebrows lifted. "Everything all right there, boy? You look like you were fleeing Apep, the Lord of Chaos himself." His voice was a deep, accented rumble, but he spoke the language of Kemet without flaw, and not in the crass way many of the other tomb-workers did.

Iset blinked and realized she was gawking. Thank the gods for the wrap around her face that hid her expression. After all, she *was* fleeing a type of evil. She dropped her gaze from his face down to his sandal-shod feet, shaking her head as she passed a hand over the linen that covered her mouth to indicate her speech was impeded.

"Ah, don't speak so well, do you?"

She shook her head again, staring at his muscular calves.

He dropped a heavy hand on her thin shoulder and gave her a gentle little shake, forcing her to look up again. His expression was probing, his brow furrowed. "You sure you're all right?"

She nodded vigorously, trying to school her countenance, no easy task under such close scrutiny, particularly when one had only their eyes to communicate with.

The man's lips compressed for a moment, then he said. "All right then. Off with you boy, but keep an eye out when you're running around here. You could hurt yourself."

She gave a quick nod and did her best to walk past him at a restrained pace, sure that she could feel his penetrating eyes boring into her back. After a minute or two she couldn't resist glancing back over her shoulder, and saw him still standing amongst the rocky rubble, watching her. She turned east, heading towards the worker's village that bordered the edge of the city of Abdju and the Land of the Dead, where she was working. To the west were the grander tombs of the pharaohs, much larger and more elaborate than the noblemen's tombs she worked on. At this time of day Ra pushed the sun across the sky to set behind the gray-brown cliffs that marked the entrance to the great desert beyond the tombs, and the lengthening rays of light caused the stranger's tall dark shadow to stretch out twice as tall beside him.

Iset wondered how long she'd been inside the tomb, as the site was almost empty. She'd missed the drum beat that normally marked the end of the day. Only the foreman, who stayed until the night-shift security guards arrived on-site, was visible from a distance. And the stranger.

Fear hastened her through the dusty, narrow streets of the village, her dread increasing with each minute it took to reach her little hut on the outskirts of Abdju. She needed to make sure her brother was ok, and that the men who'd threatened her hadn't somehow followed through on their threats already. She didn't want to think what they might do if they didn't find 'her pretty cousin' at home.

It wouldn't surprise her if her father – not her uncle – had been involved in the tomb robbing. For the last several years her father had drunk and gambled away most of his earnings. When he'd died last month Iset had experienced a guilty moment of relief that she'd no longer need to hide the sacks of grain and jugs of beer that made up her wages and went to feed her mother and brother.

Although she didn't like to think it, her father just might have been desperate enough to defy the peace of the dead and desecrate a nobleman's burial chamber. And even that of the recently interred Pharaoh Wadj, whose tomb was completed in haste a month ago. The pharaoh had been expected to reign for many decades, so when he died last year during a hippopotamus hunt the tomb was nowhere near done. Her father was the draughtsman who laid out the plans for the burial chamber, along with that of the two hundred or so of the pharaoh's retainers that lay in subsidiary tombs flanking the man.

Iset's difficulty was not in the believing of the story. The difficulty was that she had no idea how to enter the pharaoh's tomb, or how to go about solving the problem. And she only had five days to do it before they destroyed her entire life, and that of her mother and brother.

She almost screamed when, a few short blocks from home, a woman's voice called out, "Dedi!"

Iset whipped around. There, out on the doorstep of her mud-brick hut as always, was the widow Neb-tawy. The old woman sat hunched over on the same little three-legged stool that had miraculously held her fleshy body up for at least the last nineteen years – as long as Iset had been alive. "Dedi," she flapped a hand at Iset. "Come here, boy." Naked from the waist up, the widow wore only a coarse linen *shenti*, her wrinkled breasts resting atop the roll of flesh that bulged over her skirt. Her dusky nipples were the size of a small child's fist.

Iset waved her hand to indicate she was in a hurry to get home, hoping the woman would take pity on her today. *No such luck.* Widow Neb-tawy flapped her hand again. "Come here. I have to tell you that your little cousin Ahmose was running about in the street again with those boys. The stone-cutter's sons. You know how those boys get into trouble all the time. Your cousin Iset needs to be doing a better job keeping an eye on him. She really ought to be watching him more. I swear to Hathor I don't know where she goes during the day, but I am not convinced she is in the home. You ought to speak with her."

Iset's heart thudded but she kept her body still. She bowed her head in acquiescence to the older woman.

Neb-tawy nodded, appearing somewhat pacified. "Well, I know you've all had your hands full since your uncle's passing. I know you're doing your best. Thank the gods they have you here now to help them. I don't know what your cousins or your aunt would do without you."

Iset almost laughed at the absurdity of the statement. *If only Neb-tawy knew.* The older woman flapped her hand again. "Off you go then. Just make sure you speak with your cousins."

A couple of minutes later Iset turned down her lane and pushed open the door to the four room hut she shared with her mother and brother. Reed mats crackled under her feet as she stepped into the gloom of the greeting room. There were no lit flax wicks resting in bowls of oil to brighten the room. They had to ration the precious liquid that made up a small portion of Iset's tomb painting wages.

She called out quietly. "Ahmose?" *Please, please, please Ra let him be safe.* When he didn't answer she slipped through the house to the back yard. "Ahmose?"

Her knees weakened with relief when she saw her little brother's head, bald except for one braided sidelock, hunched over their clay oven. The scent of fresh bread wafted through the air as Ahmose pulled out a stone slab with a loaf of golden barley bread sitting atop it.

Her little brother turned to her with a grin. "Look! It worked this time. I made bread!"

Mindful of the hot slab he was holding under swaths of linen, she slung her arms around him. In a million years she would never tell Ahmose what happened to her at work that day. She was determined to protect him as much as possible from the damage their father had done, to give him at least a few carefree years before the realities of the world settled their weight on his shoulders. Still, she hugged him a little more tightly than usual.

Until he squirmed, that is. At nine, he was no longer as docile under his sister's displays of affection as he once was. "What? Was it that bad last time?"

She laughed, a shaky sound to her ears. The bread *had* been that bad last time, in fact. Rock hard, even. She'd told him that she'd eaten it all when in fact she had soaked it in beer overnight and turned it into a thick stew for their dinner the next day. It had been just barely edible that way. Their mother should have been helping him, but most days it was too much to ask her to get out of bed.

"It's wonderful, Ahmose. I am so proud of you." She beamed down at him. Every day when she returned from work it took her a few minutes to adjust, to allow her voice to take on its normal pitch and to remember that she no longer needed to act like a boy. "I look forward to eating it once I get changed. How was *mewet* today?"

"Fine." Ahmose's mood grew somber with the mention of their mother. He transferred the bread to a thin, convex ceramic plate as he said, "She didn't get out of bed today, but I brang her a bowl of lentils and she ate most of them."

"You mean you *brought* her a bowl, not *brang* her one." She corrected his speech out of habit. Despite his many faults, their father had insisted they learn to speak properly. He was, after all, an educated man who could read and write, and he'd intended for them all to marry well.

"Oh, and Ahmose, the widow Neb-tawy told me you were about the village with the stone-cutter's sons today."

The boy dropped his head, drawing a circle in the sand with his bare big toe. He mumbled, "Yeah. I was out for just a little bit to get some water and I ran into them. I only played one round of keep-the-ball-in-the-air, though, I swear to Ra! We didn't do anything wrong!"

Iset's heart ached, knowing that her little brother hardly had any semblance of a normal life. At his age he should still be allowed to play. Instead, someone needed to stay home and watch their mother. Next year they would have to find a way to apprentice him in some trade, or at least help out in the Land of the Dead, carrying rocks, fetching water, or running errands of some sort. If he could work, they would have a little extra to live on.

"It's fine, Ahmose. Just try not to let the widow see you again. That way she can't berate me for not taking care of you." She winked at him as he looked up through his long lashes at her.

He broke out into one of his charming grins. "She's a nosy old thing who doesn't have anything else to do with her time but sit out on the street and watch everyone!"

"Shhh! Don't let anyone hear you say that." She dropped her voice. "Even if it *is* true." He giggled and she smiled.

Back inside she went straight to her cramped bedroom, unraveling the wide linen strip from her face and head as she walked. She shook out her hair and stuck a hand into the thick, curly masses, massaging her tired head. Her room was furnished only with a narrow reed-stuffed sleeping mat on the floor, a large basket that contained all her worldly goods, and a small statue of Isis. A bowl of jasmine scented water sat atop a stool in the corner. A little window cut into the mud-brick wall overlooked the back garden. Iset drew the threadbare curtain across it, closing out the world.

She tore the layers of clothing off, working her way down to the linen strips that bound her chest. She unwound the strips as fast as she could, clawing at them until finally, *thank Isis*, her breasts were free and she was able to heave in several gulps of air, leaving her almost light-headed. As her heart finally began to slow, she drew in long, slow, deep breaths. *How in the name of the gods am I to find out the plans for the pharaoh's tomb?* To say their father had not left them anything of value was an understatement. His debts were most certainly valuable – but only to those whom they were owed.

Iset knelt and said a quick prayer to Isis before dipping a strip of linen into the bowl of water and passing it over her skin, scrubbing off the heat and dust of the day. Despite being the middle of the season of *Peret*, the coldest time of year, the days were still warm. Just walking through the Land of the Dead kicked up sand and dirt that clung to one at the best of times, never mind when one's skin had a sheen of sweat on it.

A knock sounded at the door. *What now?* "Ahmose? Can you get that?" She called, but only silence answered. She grabbed a long strip of coarse beige linen and wrapped it around her waist and across her breasts, tying it behind her neck into a halter dress as she moved to the front door. She pulled it open and bit her lip to supress a gasp.

Standing in her doorway was the man she'd run into in the Land of the Dead.

Batr's curiosity was piqued the moment he saw the boy with the head wrap scrambling from a nobleman's tomb. At least, he assumed it was a boy given the thin frame and clear, un-wrinkled eyes. Batr had been working in the necropolis near the city of Abdju for three days now and hadn't seen the boy before. While he'd been given the job of an *ikey* – a stonemason – his true purpose was to investigate the plundering of the tomb of a local noble that had recently come to light. As such, he had an eye out for anything suspicious. The panicked look in the boy's eyes was noteworthy.

After their exchange, he watched the boy flee the unfinished tomb before making his way to the foreman, Nedjer, a gnarled-looking man. Nedjer's sun-darkened skin stretched and cracked across his face, wizened like dried-out leather, while grizzled hair curled tightly about his pate. The man looked worse than a group of corpses Batr once dug up by accident in the midst of the western desert. Mummified by the dry heat of the sand, their skin was hard and shiny. Nedjer appeared to have suffered the same fate after a lifetime of working in the rocky, scorched earth of the Land of the Dead.

Batr jerked his head in the direction of the disappearing boy. "I ran into a boy. A mute of sorts, I think. About this tall." Batr held his hand up to his collarbone.

Nedjer grunted. "What about 'em?" The man had the long, dry stem of a papyrus reed in his mouth as usual. He kept his teeth clamped down around it as he spoke.

Batr feigned indifference. "Just curious. Don't meet too many mutes, that's all." He kept his vernacular informal to match Nedjer's slang.

Nedjer grunted again. "True enough. Kid's name is Dedi. Nephew of the last draughtsman."

"The last one?"

"The one 'oo died a month or so back." Nedjer hooked his thumbs into the top of his shenti and drummed his thighs with his fingers. "Kid had some kind of accident when he was little. Crushed his throat and scarred his face. 'S why he always wears the wrap." Nedjer made a circle around his head with one hand. "Came to town a while back. The draughtsman asked if we'd hire him. Kid knows how to paint. Don't cause no trouble cuz he can't talk much. Don't drink or fight like some of the others. Never takes sick time."

Nedjer shrugged and turned over the reed in his mouth before biting back down on it, squinting at the imposing beige cliffs that marked the entrance to the western desert as if they'd somehow offended him by their presence.

Batr took this in, keeping his face carefully neutral. The tomb he was investigating had been robbed sometime in the last three months, after the nobleman was interred in it. So far everyone he'd encountered had worked at the site for many years. Work in the Land of the Dead was ongoing, and when Pharaoh Wadj was buried in his tomb last month, excavation began for Queen Merneith's tomb. It would be another ten years or so before her tomb was completed. Furthermore, several noblemen's tombs were under construction on the eastern side of the site. Tombs like the one the boy had come tearing out of.

While Nedjer had, in fact, been the one to report the tomb robbing in the first place, Batr didn't like to remind the man that he was here to investigate it. The man was quiet, and preferred to keep to himself. He had a healthy distrust of authority and although he'd done his job by reporting the theft after he'd discovered the entranceway tampered with, he'd been unable, or unwilling, to offer up much speculation on who amongst his workers might be involved.

Batr asked Nedjer where to find the boy. Nedjer squinted one eye and Batr thought he almost heard the man's dried-out skin cracking. "Why d'ya wanna to know?"

Batr copied the man's stance by hooking his thumbs into his *shenti* and rocking back on his heels. "No reason. Just wanted to make sure he was all right. He smacked his head against me pretty hard." He chuckled. "Thought he looked a bit stunned."

The old man nodded. "He's kinda delicate looking for a young 'un, ain't he?" Batr thought back on the boy's slight shoulders, slender fingers, and wide, dark eyes, and had to agree.

Nedjer offered no further insights other than where Dedi could be found. And so it was that Batr was standing in the doorway of a hut twenty minutes later when a young woman pulled open the door. For the first time ever, Batr's breath caught at the sight of a woman. Of average height, her full-breasts and narrow-waist were enough to turn any man's eye, despite being a touch on the thin side. But it was her face that made Batr's throat constrict. Oval-shaped, with a narrow chin and high, wide cheekbones. Her fawn-coloured skin reminded him of the soft underbelly of a baby rabbit and her eyes were just as big and wide and innocent as one's. Eyes, he noticed, that were very much like those of the boy who'd run into him not long ago.

She blinked at him, long lashes sweeping those high, regal cheekbones. "Yes? Can I help you?"

Batr had never had difficulty talking to women. He *loved* women. And usually women loved him back. He was a charming man with a mysterious past, and he knew just how to play that to his advantage. But for a moment he stood like a fool, staring at the woman before him. He rubbed the back of his neck and cleared his throat.

"I-uh, forgive me. I did not mean to intrude like this. But I am looking for a boy, Dedi?" He found himself falling in to the slightly more formal dialect of the court. He wondered if he was trying to impress her. Something about her presence bespoke a woman of class.

Her lips, plump and dark and well-defined, spread into a smile, though he thought her eyes were wary. "I am sorry to disappoint you, but he is not home from work yet. What did you say your name was?"

"Batr, *nebet-i.*" It wasn't necessary for him to call her *my lady*, but she seemed to command it of him somehow, perhaps because her own speech was more formal and eloquent than that of the other villagers he'd encountered. "My name is Batr. I ran into Dedi today on the site and wanted to stop by to make sure he was ok."

"Oh?" She raised one delicate eyebrow. "Did something happen? Is he well?"

"Nothing to fear. We just bumped into one another and I feared he was a little rattled by it. I inquired of him afterwards and learned that we are both newcomers to the Land of the Dead. I thought to introduce myself."

"I'm sorry, but I don't know when Dedi will return. Sometimes after work he meets with some of the other men to play games, or drink beer. We were just going to sit down for our evening meal."

Batr inclined his head. "I apologize again for intruding."

He was about to say more when a boy, about seven or eight years old, came rushing into the greeting room, calling out, "Look, Iset! The buns worked, too!"

The boy was carrying a stone slab, layered with a thin ceramic plate laden with small loaves of bread on them, but moving so fast he tripped on the edge of a reed mat on the floor. The buns flew up in the air and the beautiful woman reached out for them. Distracted by her, he didn't notice the ceramic plate soaring off the edge of the slab towards him until it was almost too late. He tried to duck but slipped on the smooth, worn stone of the doorstep. Stumbling forward, the plate struck his temple as the floor rushed up to meet him.

Chapter 2 – A Memorable Dinner

Batr's head rested on something hard but comfortable. A soothing hand stroked the side of his head and the scent of jasmine wafted over him. He opened his eyes and there, hovering above him, was the face of the goddess he'd met moments ago in the doorway. Her skin glowed in the dim light, framed by a mass of wavy black hair so long it brushed his shoulders as she leaned over him. A delicious tickle ran straight down to his groin.

The beautiful woman removed her hand from his head but he reached up to enclose her wrist and pull it down, trapping it against his chest. "By the gods," he murmured. "You are stunning."

Her eyes widened but she recovered quickly. "Are you feeling well?" She asked. "I'm so very sorry about Ahmose hitting you with the plate. He feels awful."

Batr released her wrist as her words called attention to his aching head. Pounding head, really. First the plate had hit his head, then his head had hit the floor. It hadn't *quite* knocked him unconscious, but it had certainly made him groggy, and he didn't recall the woman taking his head up onto her lap.

He fingered around his hairline. He could feel a bump forming already. He chuckled but stopped when that caused the pain to worsen. "Do you know, nebet-i, I have fought in numerous battles and that little man with the bread was the first ever to knock me senseless?"

"Truly?" The boy's voice cut in. "You've fought in battle? Have you killed many men?" There was a rustling beside him and the boy crouched next to them, an eager look breaking through the worry and fear written on his face.

"More than my share," Batr responded, and the boy's mouth gaped. Above him the woman tsk'd her tongue. Chastised, he added in a grave voice, "But killing is not to be taken lightly, boy." Then he winked and Ahmose clapped a hand over over his mouth to cover his grin.

"Now excuse me, uh," he shifted his head to get a better look at the woman, "how long was I insensate? I hope I didn't say anything incriminating." He flashed his most powerful grin. It never hurt to have a beautiful woman on one's side. She was somehow connected to Dedi, and Batr wanted to know more about him. He sincerely hoped the woman wasn't Dedi's wife. Or anyone else's for that matter. While often entertaining, other men's wives could also be a lot of trouble.

Disappointingly, the woman slid out from under him, forcing him to sit up. "Just for a moment or two," she said. "How are you feeling now?"

He ran his fingers along the growing bump on his head again and winced.

Ahmose blurted out, "You should join us for dinner."

Batr didn't miss the hard, sideways look the woman threw the boy, the flattening of her full lips into a thin line. But Ahmose was already grabbing her hand. "Please? Please can he stay for dinner? It'd be rude not to ask, wouldn't it? Especially after knocking him out, and all that. You always say if someone arrives at mealtime it's our… whaddaya call it? Our *obligation* to invite them in, in case they have even less than we do. That *is* what you say, isn't it?" As soon as the boy turned his pleading eyes her way, the woman's expression softened.

She gave a slight nod, as if resolving to do something unpleasant, and turned to Batr. "I am sure you must have somewhere else to be, but if not, you are welcome to join us for dinner. It's the least we can do. There isn't much to it, but we did manage to salvage a couple of Ahmose's buns. Even if it was at the expense of your head."

Aside for a slight twitch of her lips, her placid expression didn't change. Batr was now thoroughly intrigued. He inclined his head and smiled. "I am here in Abdju alone, and would be most glad of the company."

The woman turned to Ahmose and asked, "The rooftop has been set for dinner?"

Ahmose danced from foot to foot, unable to contain his excitement. "I swept it already. And the rest of the meal is done. I'll take it upstairs now. Oh! Can I make some of the carob tea afterwards also?"

"I don't know, Ahmose, *can* you?" Her eyebrows rose in question.

The boy huffed a loud sigh. "*May* I make some tea? You said if we had a special occasion we could use the carob that Senebtawi gave us. It *is* a special occasion now, isn't it? We *never* have guests over."

"Hmmm, you pay more attention to the things I say than I thought, don't you?" The woman asked wryly, before reaching out to stroke the boy's head. "Yes, of course you may make tea afterwards."

Ahmose gave Batr an eager grin before turning and running out of the room. Batr wondered why it was that a young boy was so involved in the dinner process and decided the woman must work during the day. Perhaps she sold trinkets or pottery at the market, or brewed beer. He pushed himself to his feet and leaned against the wall.

The woman turned to him and asked, "Are you quite sure you want to join us?" Her sly smile beguiled him. He didn't think he'd ever gotten an erection just from seeing a woman's smile, but he was in danger of it now. Her lips were incredibly expressive. She continued, looking up at him through her thick black lashes. "I should warn you that if you stay you'll likely be forced to endure all kinds of wildly inappropriate questions about where you come from and what you're doing here now."

She spoke as if she were sharing a secret with him, and it felt deliciously intimate. She could be talking about sifting grain and sound sensual, her voice was that warm and rich. He pitched his voice low and smooth to match hers. "I am familiar with all kinds of wildly inappropriate things, nebet-i.

And you may ask me anything you like about them, especially if you are curious about trying any of them."

Her eyes widened and she took a step back. "I did not… I was not implying…"

Fascinating, he thought. Could she really be so artless? He took pity on her and said, "If you wouldn't mind, I've come straight from work. Before dining I should like to freshen myself a little."

She relaxed. "Of course. Please, have a seat." She indicated a wide stone bench on the other side of the room. "I'll fetch you some water. I have a few things to finish before I join you on the rooftop anyway."

She came back a moment later with a large basin of water and some linens and he said, "I'm sorry, but you have the advantage of me, nebet-i."

"I do?"

"Mmmm. I still don't know your name."

"Oh! Yes. Of course. Isetnofret. But most just call me Iset."

"Isetnofret?" *Isis is Beautiful.* "A fitting name, if I may say so." He gave a slight bow, though it pained his aching head to do so.

"Right. Thank you." Her voice was clipped as she turned on her heel and left him alone in the gloomy room.

Dipping a strip of linen into the water, he quickly washed the worst of the day's grit and sweat from his body, smiling at the handful of jasmine flowers floating in the bowl. She might be uncomfortable with him being in her home, but she'd been kind enough to add the little white flowers to scent it.

While washing, he peered around the darkening room, taking care to move slowly and not jostle his throbbing head. No oil wicks flickered and, given the sparseness of their greeting room, he suspected they were unable to spare the extra oil. The room had a low square table, carved out of a block of the stone readily available this close to the cliffs of the desert, along with the wide bench he was sitting on, and two stools. It was apparent they were poor in the extreme, yet Iset spoke with refinement, and encouraged

Ahmose to do the same. He wondered again who they were in relation to Dedi, and to the deceased draughtsman.

Whoever they were, he decided his best approach would be to charm the lady and regale the boy. He had no taste for terrorizing women, but he was not at all against seduction as a means of garnering information. A vision came to mind of Iset laid out on a bed, those spectacular black tresses spread out around her in shocking contrast against her light skin. From there, it was natural to envision her sitting up with her hair tumbling down her back, her long, fawn-coloured legs wrapped around his dark waist, and his hands sliding under those sable locks to skim her naked back.

No. He smiled to himself. He was not against seduction at all, if it came down to it.

Iset checked in on her mother but the woman was sleeping so she didn't bother waking her. From her mother's room, however, she took a vial of jasmine scented oil from a small side table and dabbed it on her wrists and neck. *Just to get rid of the scent of sand, paint, and sweat.* Her hands shook slightly. The events of the day were a jumble of fear and excitement coursing through her, a sensation pulsing in her body rather than any coherent thought. *What next?* The words repeated themselves over and over in her mind. She prayed that she had managed to get any paint stains and dirt from her hands during her quick wash before Batr's arrival.

He certainly aroused her suspicion. He admitted to making *inquiries* about Dedi, and his excuse for showing up at their home seemed flimsy. She wondered if he might be one of the men who'd threatened her. She didn't think so though, as she didn't recognize his voice or his great height, and she was sure the other men already knew where she lived whereas Batr had seemed genuinely surprised by her when she'd answered the door. The other men also knew Dedi had a female cousin. *Thank the gods* they didn't know that cousin and Dedi were one and the same.

She realized she also didn't really *want* to believe Batr could be involved in a plot to rob the pharaoh's tomb. Despite his unusual appearance, he had kind eyes and a ready smile, and his self-assuredness was appealing. She set that thought aside. She needed a strategy for dealing with him. Ahmose obviously liked him, and she felt awful that he'd been left with no men in his life to take him in hand. But she couldn't let this stranger get too close or too comfortable tonight. If her secret – well, *secrets*, now – were discovered they would be utterly ruined. Luckily, her little brother was an accomplished liar when he needed to be. He'd kept the secret of her work for the last six months, and he understood the necessity of it.

Sounds of movement in the other room indicated that Batr was making his way to the rooftop. She waited a few moments before going to join him and her brother. Mounting the steps alongside the hut, she tried to keep her breathing in check. She needed to appear relaxed.

Like most people, they ate their meals on the flat roof where there was more space and the heat was not as oppressive. Although the sun had set, the sky was not quite dark yet and the moon was bright, so there was no need for oil wicks. The night was cooling off, and she'd thrown a shawl over her shoulders. Ahmose and Batr were seated on cushions arranged over reed mats. Between them on the mat were the buns and bread Ahmose had made, bowls of lentil and barley mash, and dried dates, along with a jug of wine and three mugs.

As she neared Batr stood and bowed – a formal gesture that brought a flush to her cheeks. "Nebet-i," he greeted her in a soft voice.

"I – uhm, thank you." *What is required of a lady when a man bows?* No man had ever been so decorous with her before. She'd never been to court, never seen a proper noblewoman, and had no idea how they behaved. "Please. Sit down." She waved her hand at the cushion he'd been seated on, then tucked her bare feet up under her and sat in a circle with the other two.

Ahmose watched the whole exchange with an open mouth, and Iset almost laughed, hoping she hadn't looked the same way when Batr bowed to her. Ahmose needed only a moment to process the scene before his questions began anew. "Have you been to court, Batr? Was it here in Kemet or was it somewhere else? Like where you're from? Where *are* you from?"

In spite of herself Iset did laugh this time. "Please forgive Ahmose. As I'm sure you've noticed we don't get many foreigners in the Land of the Dead. Perhaps in the court of Abdju, or in Thinis where the queen greets the foreign dignitaries, but the tomb workers have mostly been here for generations. Nobody leaves and very few people move here."

Batr reached out and tugged Ahmose's braided lock of hair, chuckling. "It's all right. And yes, as you said," he turned to her and an odd tingling spread across her chest as his gaze rested on her. "I *do* get a lot of looks, but most people are too afraid to ask. It seems, however, that Ahmose here is not intimidated by me."

Reticent under the compliment, Ahmose ducked his head, and once again Iset ached with sorrow for him. It was all well and good for her to say nice things to him, but she knew it didn't replace the approval of a man, such as a father or older brother. She knew first-hand what it felt like to need a kind word from someone now and then. She only regretted that Batr's kindness would make the absence of men in their life that much more apparent when he left after dinner.

Iset scooped some lentils and barley into a bowl and handed it to Batr. As he reached for it his fingers brushed hers and she started at the contact. She met his gaze briefly, and flushed to see that he'd noticed her shock, his eyes creasing at the edges with amusement.

Dropping her gaze, she looked at Ahmose as she addressed Batr. "I apologize for our simple fare, but of course we weren't expecting anyone to join us tonight. But you *will* have the chance to sample some of Ahmose's bread. He's been perfecting it for some time now."

Batr shook his head, holding up a hand in protest. "Please, this is just perfect, and far better than I would manage on my own." He settled back on his cushion and said, "But to answer your question, little man, yes. I have been to court."

The hand that held Ahmose's wooden spoon stopped in mid-air on its way to his mouth. "Truly? What for? Did you see the queen? Was it the court in Thinis? That is – what – how long away from here?" Ahmose held up fingers as he counted. "It is about a two or three *wnwt* walk from here to the Iteru. We've never been that far, of course, but I've heard it's about that distance. Then you take a boat north… a few *wnwt* I think? Five or six? So altogether it is a whole day of travelling, right? That is very far!"

Batr chuckled. "That depends on your sense of distance. It is very far for some, not so much for others. But indeed, I did see the queen. She is a very gracious lady."

Ahmose's eyes widened. "Is that where you got your tattoos? Do they do that in the court of Thinis?"

Iset thought she detected a slight hesitation before he said, "No. The ones here," he indicated his cheeks, "were given to me as a small child by my tribe. They're for protection from evil spirits, like you do here by placing amulets around infants. The others are to help my family find me in the afterlife, provided by a traveller from the far north."

Iset wanted to know more about his family, but Ahmose continued in his way, "Have you travelled much, then? How far is it from where you're from to here?"

Batr sipped some wine. After a pause he said, "Well I used to travel quite a lot. I come from the lands in the desert to the west of Kemet, from a group of peoples known as the Libu, split into different tribes. Most of our tribes were nomadic, and moved around quite a lot between the oases. I think if you were to walk all the way from where we use to roam to Abdju it would take you, oh I don't know, maybe one *abd* – one month – to cross the desert."

"One whole *abd*?" Iset cocked her head. "My goodness, how would you survive in the desert so long?"

The skin around his eyes crinkled in a smile. "My people lived *always* in the desert. But it doesn't matter, because the smart way to travel here would be to go north to the great sea. From there you can either walk or sail to the mouth of the Iteru, then sail down along it. It's much faster to travel by ship."

"So you've traveled by ship on the great sea?" Ahmose leaned forward. "Was it a large ship? I've only ever been on the reed fishing boats along the little stream that runs through Abdju, about a half hour from here. I'd love to see the large ships the merchants take along the big Iteru up to the sea."

"Indeed, I've traveled quite a lot by ship." Batr nodded once. "I have seen the island north of my homeland, with its cities of Knossos and Phaistos. That's where Kemet sometimes gets wood, such as cypress, to make furniture, as it's stronger and easier to carve than the date palm here. They grow a wonderful little fruit there that they call *olive.* It's small and black and tangy, and they press it to make oil, much like you press flax here." Batr held up one finger and measured the length of the olive fruit on it.

Ahmose was staring at him, mouth gaping, and mischief lit Batr's eyes as he said, "The island is hard to reach, and you must know how to find your way by the stars and the sun, as there's no land between the coast of Kemet and the island. So don't go trying it in one of your fishing boats now." Ahmose giggled and Iset's heart warmed at the sound.

Over the course of their dinner Batr continued to tell them stories of his travels and weave *hekka* – magic – over them. Or at least Iset felt that he was spinning something around them. Perhaps it was the glowing cast of the twilight sky behind him, coupled with the images of exotic places she'd never imagined, for in spite of her initial misgivings, Iset found herself entranced by his words, his movements, his facial expressions, as he spoke. He comically waggled his eyebrows for Ahmose's delight, his face lit up with warmth and good-humour, and both Iset and Ahmose laughed more than they had at least since their brother Sharek passed away.

Batr put down his now-empty bowl of food. "I've also been east to Byblos and Ugarit where they worship Ba'al and Dagon. They make some of the best wine in all the living world in that area. Wine so good that even your queen imports it from the region. Some of the furniture in the homes of noblemen here is made of wood from that area. Wood such as cedar and pine. They grow in enormous forests of tall, strong trees with trunks so wide around you need three or more men with arms outstretched to span them. And the smell – ah – the smell is like nothing you can imagine. Fresh and crisp and so relaxing. One feels themselves to be wholly at peace in such a place." He gave a wistful smile and Iset found herself longing to see what Batr saw.

"You must miss traveling now that you are here in Kemet," she said.

He blinked and became serious. "Not so much anymore. Here in Kemet I have the chance to build a life for myself. To have a home, not just a shared cabin on a ship, or a room in some filthy port city. I don't always have to watch my back and wonder who might try to rob or kill me." His hard mood shifted and he winked at Ahmose

"Do you mean you had to watch out for pirates?!" Ahmose sat up straight. "Have you seen them?!" Batr's only response was a slight curving of his lips, and Ahmose leaned forward. "Noooo. You have? Truly? Were they dangerous? Did you fight them off? Were they amongst the men you've killed? Do they really steal maidens away in the night? Have you ever been captured by them?"

Batr shifted on his cushion, adjusting it, and Iset thought that for once he looked uncomfortable. "Well, I wouldn't say that I *fought* pirates or that I was captured by any. They also don't *usually* steal maidens. Some think it bad luck to have a woman on a brigand's ship."

"You sound quite familiar with them. Are you saying you *were* a pirate?" Iset meant to tease, but as soon as the words were out she knew them to be true. The tattoos, the powerful manner, the travelling, his charm. It made a strange sort of sense. It struck her that this man could be very dangerous. Even if he wasn't with the men who'd threatened her, he might also be looking for a way into the pharaoh's tomb. Iset realized she hadn't taken one bite of her food yet and she set her bowl aside.

Batr didn't answer her question, he just watched her intently. Silence hung heavy in the air. She mustered a cheerful tone. "Ahmose won't sleep for days now thanks to your jesting. He'll be up thinking about pirates and queens and such." She turned to her brother and said, "I think now is a good time for you to go and make that carob tea, darling."

"But I want to –," Iset gave one shake of her head and the boy huffed. "Fine. I'll go."

He gathered up the empty bowls and moved across the roof. When he was down the stairs and out of earshot Batr said, "He's a good young man. You've done well with him."

Iset spoke softly, though her heart thumped heavily in her chest. "We have nothing worth stealing."

His mouth hitched up on one side but there was no humour in his voice. "I'm not interested in stealing anything from you. Or hurting you, for that matter."

"Then why are you here?"

"The same reason I told you. To inquire about Dedi's well-being."

"And why was that again?"

He sighed and spread his fingers, palms up, as if to show her he hid nothing in his hands. "Exactly what I said. Your husband…?" His voice trailed off in a question.

"Dedi is my cousin."

"And Ahmose is?"

"My brother."

"And you all live here…"

"With my mother. She is…ill. Bedridden at present. My *yet* passed away a month ago." He could find the answers to his questions by asking almost anyone within a twenty-minute walk from her home. She saw no reason to create secrets of them. But her mother's condition was not something she discussed with anyone.

He nodded and something flickered in his eyes before he said, "I'm sorry to hear about your *yet*. As for your cousin, like I said before, he literally ran in to me at work. He looked like a spirit had chased him out of the tomb he was working in. I just wanted to make sure everything was all right. But you say he went straight out from work?"

"If he'd come home, I would have seen him." She breathed deeply, keeping her face impassive and her gaze steady. Her hand only tremored slightly as she raised her wine mug. Was he trying to catch her in a lie?

"Is that common? What sort of man leaves such a young woman here all alone at night?"

"Why not?" Her voice sounded sharp to her ears, as his words called to mind the threats the men had uttered in the tomb. "Are you trying to imply I'm in some sort of danger?"

His brow furrowed, and she feared she'd revealed something in her haste. He shook his head slowly. "You are in no danger from me. But I know if I were in your cousin's place I would vastly prefer to be by your side than in a tavern full of men."

"Perhaps *I* prefer to be left alone."

He shrugged his powerful dark shoulders. "Then I'm sorry if my coming here has disturbed you. That is the very opposite of my intentions. I can leave if you'd like."

He didn't look like he wanted to leave and Iset wasn't sure she wanted him to either. It would be horribly rude to ask him to go after Ahmose nearly took his head off with the bread slab. She sucked her lips in, biting down on them. Other than his coincidental arrival on her doorstep, she had no tangible reason to distrust him. He could have lied about his past. It would have been easy. And he could have overpowered herself and Ahmose already if he wanted to hurt them. But he hadn't. Perhaps the fact that she had so many secrets to keep was making her paranoid. Perhaps he was just an accomplished flirt, and she need only be wary of his advances.

She smoothed her dress over her knees. "Why Abdju? Of all the places to go, why are you here in the Land of the

Dead? This is not a place that people seek out, especially not foreigners."

In the distance a chorus of crickets took up a song. He paused, and his words were measured and thoughtful. "I'm here because I've put my past behind me. I won't deny I was once a brigand. Life in the desert is hard, our tribe was at war with others, and…" he paused and she sensed a darkening of his mood. Whatever it was, though, he brushed it off and continued. "I wanted a different life. Sometimes people do things they are morally opposed to in order to survive and take care of their family. But that was some time ago. For the last four years I've toiled here in Kemet in the military. I had a connection in the queen's court and they recommended me to the position here."

Batr leaned forward and took her hand between his two calloused ones, trapping it on the mat between them. There were many reasons she should pull away; there might still be flecks of paint on her hands; the gesture was too familiar; he might get the wrong impression about her; she didn't trust him. Any one of those was a good enough reason to snatch her hand from his. But she didn't. His words had struck deep with her. *Sometimes people do things they are morally opposed to in order to survive and take care of their family.* Could she of all people fault him for that?

Amusement hovered in the corners of his mouth, contrasting his serious tone. "It's not often that I concern myself with whether or not a woman, or anyone else for that matter, finds me trustworthy. But I would very much like for you to believe that I am. I have no intention of hurting you or your brother or your cousin. And if there is ever anything I can do to help you, I would be honoured if you considered asking me for it."

"Tell me," she slipped her hand from his and immediately missed the contact and warmth. "Are you smiling because you're a bad liar, or because you think I'm some gullible village girl who will succumb to the charms of a man with court manners?"

He blinked, then a deep rumbling rose up from his chest and he laughed. His teeth flashed startlingly white against his smooth chestnut skin and the darkening night sky. He laughed so long that Iset finally gave in to her inclination and smiled, covering her mouth with her hand in a poor attempt to hide it.

Batr liked Iset all the more for her cleverness. She might not easily surrender to his charms, but getting close to her was the best way he could think of to probe what she knew about the theft. It wasn't his fault if it also happened to be the most pleasurable way. He sincerely hoped she wasn't involved in the tomb robbing. He'd hate to have to arrest her when he could think of much better things to do to – and with – her instead. But her guarded answers to his questions raised doubts about her innocence.

"I'm smiling because it's rare to find someone both beautiful *and* smart. But I see how it is, nebet-i." Batr stretched his long legs out to the side, propping himself up on one elbow with his head resting in his hand, close to her crossed knee. He gazed up at her. She was lovely from this angle with her face inclined down at him, her beautiful breasts in profile. "You'd prefer me to behave like a callous criminal. I suppose if I *was* such a beast of a man, and was interested in an attractive woman such as yourself, I would simply throw you over my shoulder and take you home to my bed. There is no one here who could stop me."

Panic flared in her eyes and he was reminded that, although she was both stunning and smart she was also, apparently, inexperienced with flirting. "I'm sorry to disappoint you, though," he gave her his best wide-eyed innocent look. "My maiden-stealing days are over. If you find yourself in my bed, it will be because you want to be there."

She waved her hand in dismissal. "Now really, don't you think that's a bit much? I have a perfectly good mattress here, I see no reason to go elsewhere – or *share*, for that matter." She added the last in a stern voice just as he was about to tell her that any mattress she wanted was fine by him.

"And please," she reached for her wine and said, "for now I would prefer that Ahmose not hear tales of your maiden-stealing and plundering days. I have enough to manage without worrying that he will run off to join a pirate ship." He thought he could discern a smile curve her lips just before she sipped her wine.

Any retort he'd have made was cut off by Ahmose's head appearing alongside the roof. A moment later he shuffled towards them, a tray with mugs balanced in his hands. All talk of pirates and mattresses stopped for the remainder of the evening. Ahmose asked questions with a rapidity that prevented Batr from asking more about their cousin Dedi. He did find, however, that he enjoyed both the boy's lively mind and the sweet – albeit guarded – smiles of Ahmose's lovely older sister. The woman he assumed must be the daughter of the now-deceased draughtsman.

The horizon was a midnight blue and the stars twinkling in the sky when Ahmose began yawning and his head nodded into his chest. Despite his protests, Iset sternly told him the time had come to take himself off to bed, and that he shouldn't keep Batr up all night when he had work in the Land of the Dead in the morning. The trio made their way down the stairs and back into the house to say their goodbyes. Ahmose shook Batr's hand in a rather manly fashion and thanked him quite courteously for taking the time to share his stories. Batr bit back a smile at the boy's attempts at court manners and thanked him in turn for his hospitality.

Ahmose blushed and, falling out of his attempt at formality, mumbled, "I s'pose it's the least I could do for almost knocking your head off."

The boy left them alone in the greeting room then and Batr realized how very dark the room was without any oil wicks lit. Iset's fawn-toned skin was luminous with the moonlight that shone through the door left slightly ajar behind them. Batr had a rather delicious vision of her clothed in nothing but silvery moonlight, that black hair streaming down her back and curling around her breasts.

She tucked a strand of onyx hair behind her ear and darted her tongue over her lush, pink lips. This did little to help the growing tightness in his groin. She said, "Yes, well, I do apologize again for the incident with the bread slab, but I *did* warn you that Ahmose would ask you a million questions if you stayed."

Batr laughed softly. "And so he did. But truly, I didn't mind. The company was particularly pleasant."

"I suppose you should be going." Her gaze darted up to his. The hesitancy in her voice was enough to indicate her interest. The part of him that had intended to try and bed her was keen to pursue that design. But over the course of the evening he'd discovered that Iset was not just some sensual village girl, but a lady of quality. And actually *wanting* this woman would complicate matters if she was somehow involved in the tomb robbing. For the love of Ba'al, it would complicate matters even if she wasn't. It was one thing to seduce *her*; it was another to allow *himself* to be seduced.

"Yes. I suppose I should be going," he said, but instead of moving towards the door he reached out and folded his fingers around hers.

Desire coiled in Iset's core like a brick warmed in a stone oven. She knew she should resist this complex man, as her life was much too problematic to accommodate another challenge. But he'd also been kind to both her and her brother, and his touch was warm and gentle, yet firm. Her heart fluttered in her chest and drawing breath became difficult. She wondered if he would try to kiss her, and if she might just let him.

When, instead of drawing her towards him, he only lifted her fingers to brush his lips across the back of her hand, she found herself both relieved and disappointed. The breath she'd been holding came out in a small puff.

She stuttered, "I – uhm – thank you for your company tonight. I will tell Dedi you stopped by to see him."

Amusement hovered in the corners of his eyes as he said, "Thank you, nebet-i. I do hope to see you again soon."

"I – perhaps. *Senebti.*" *Be well*, she answered.

"*Senebti*. Sleep well." And with that he was out the door and into the night. Iset closed the door behind him and leaned her back against it, shutting her eyes and pressing the back of the hand he had kissed to her cheek. She tried not to smile, even as she shook her head. She felt like crying and laughing at the same time. What a surreal day it had been, as if she'd been the victim of someone's *hekka*, some kind of magic that made the worst and the best of things happen. Batr had told her to sleep well, but she doubted she'd be able to sleep for days to come.

Chapter 3 – The Lady Landholder

2 days before

Raia heaved a frustrated sigh and gathered the stacks and rolls of papyri up off her father's desk, trying to bunch them all in the circle of her arms. She didn't understand how it was that her father's taxes were so much higher this year than they used to be. The harvests were smaller than the previous year, and her father hadn't acquired any more land that she knew of, at least not in the two months leading up to his death when he'd been too ill to even leave his bed. Based on the quick calculation she'd done a few months ago, Raia had an idea of how many sacks of grain his taxes should be. However, the scrolls in front of her told a different story.

Then again, it had been seven years since her last thorough walk-through of her father's estate, right before she'd married. She'd been too busy with her children and her own landholdings to get involved in her father's affairs, especially after her husband's passing. Hopefully her father's scribe would be able to explain it all to her tomorrow. She'd never been much for reading, having only a rudimentary knowledge of the craft, though she was more than capable of tallying the lines and symbols that made up their numerals.

Managing numbers was what she'd been raised to do, after all. And she knew them well, not that it helped her much now. In her mind, she once again ran through the figures that kept her awake at night. Seven children to manage, three of her own and her four younger brothers and sisters. Two landholdings – her own and her father's – and therefore two sets of taxes, to oversee. Twenty-one days before the tax collector came. And one twenty-three-year-old woman to take care of it all.

Yes. She knew the math well enough. It was a good thing that her father had also imbued her with an aversion to failure. If she let herself dwell too long on statistics, if she'd been the sort to gamble and read the odds, she'd know there was no point in getting out of bed in the mornings.

But Raia wasn't the sort to gamble. With so many numbers to take care of, she couldn't afford to place bets. The waters of the little iteru would soon recede, leaving behind their rich silt, and she must begin organizing the planting of the fields for the next season. Her and her father's farms supplied much of the wheat and barley that served as wages for the people who worked in the Land of the Dead. Without her crops, hundreds of people would be without food.

She stepped around the great desk, turning away from the door that led to the back of the manor. Raia squatted down to arrange the papyri in a woven, reed basket when two more numbers made a surprise appearance. Her younger brother's hunting dogs, tall, thin, long-bodied white animals with grey spots and long snouts, came bounding into the room. Since she was crouched at their level they proceeded to leap about and, hopping up on their hind legs despite her orders, they pushed at her shoulders in aggressive play until she lost her balance and fell on to her behind, scattering papyri everywhere.

"Oh! Get off me! Semer! Get in here and take care of your dogs." Raia yelled for her brother, twisting her head to avoid the enthusiastic, lapping tongues that came perilously close to her mouth. She *hated* it when they licked her mouth, panting in her face with their hours-old meat breath. The fact that one of them had firmly planted his paws on her chest, his nails pressing painfully into one breast through the thin fabric of her linen robe, did nothing to further endear the animal to her. Normally she didn't mind dogs, but Semer's two hunters never listened to her, or even to Semer most of the time. He let them run wild, no matter what she said.

Raia pushed until she was able to get back to her knees, the dogs still springing up and down around her. Discovering the papyri, they lost interest in her and began nosing at the pieces, pushing a few rolls across the floor and pawing at them. "No!" Raia scrambled across the floor on her hands and knees to reach for the records.

"Nebet-i, there's someone here to see you." Her father's manservant addressed her from somewhere behind her, likely standing in the doorway that led to the front of the house. *Can't he see I need help?* She thought. *If he had any sense, he would.* But she knew her father's old manservant was just waiting for the day Semer took over her father's farms and he wouldn't have to answer to a woman any longer.

Well she couldn't wait, either, but that would require her younger brother to actually sit down long enough to learn to manage his own affairs, something he seemed incapable of doing.

Exasperated, Raia addressed him over her shoulder, "Not now, Peret, can't you see I need Semer to get rid of his dogs? They'll eat the scrolls before I can sort out my *yet's* taxes!"

Before she could turn, she heard a new voice; a man's rumbling speech pitched in a low, commanding tone, "Down."

Raia rested back on her heels in shock as her brother's dogs both sat down on their haunches, staring past her shoulder.

"Now out," the man said, and after a moment's pause, the two hunters obeyed, brushing past Raia as if she were no more exciting than a statue they'd sniffed a thousand times before. Then a man squatted next to her, reaching for the scrolls and bits of papyri, and Raia blinked in astonishment. Even in profile, he had to be one of the oddest men she'd ever seen. Dark-skinned and leanly muscled, he had long braided hair, half of which was pulled back in a knot at the back of his head. A wide, curved blade hung from a braided sash around his waist. She surmised he must be a soldier as she'd never seen a Kemeti man outside the military walk around armed like that. But what was most unusual were the blue-black tattoos on his brown cheeks and the larger, thicker ones that spiraled up his calves, trailing up, up under the bottom of his pure white shenti.

She tore her eyes away as she realized she was staring at his generously muscled thighs, the thought flitting through her mind that it had been too long since she'd been this close to a man's legs – *three years and four months* – but it was too late. He'd looked up from the scattered tax reports and caught her regard. His eyebrows rose half a finger's width. *Just a ro's length* – a fraction of a whole number.

He broke the awkward moment by asking her, "I take it those are not your dogs?"

In spite of her loyalty to her family, she couldn't stop her eyes from rolling in annoyance. "Hardly. They are my brother's. He is mad for hunting and he refuses to keep them outside, no matter how ill-behaved they are."

Then, embarrassed with herself for sharing so much with a stranger, one who happened to still be crouched next to her with their knees almost touching, Raia seized the scrolls from his hands. She dropped them into the basket before pulling herself up to stand above him and smooth out her robe.

The stranger stood from the ground like a scroll of papyri unfurling to full length, a smooth motion that revealed a man much taller than expected. A man taller than Raia herself, if it could be believed. And she *did* have a hard time believing it, despite seeing it with her own eyes. Raia had never met a man taller than herself. The closest any man came was eye level, something she'd grown accustomed to, and even appreciated. During business negotiations men were less likely to attempt intimidation tactics on a woman with the advantage of height. It was almost a mathematical formula, the greater the height in finger widths, the greater their discomfort.

"Yes? What is it?" Her tone was more clipped than she'd intended, but his presence disconcerted her.

"My name is Makae, nebet-i. I'm here on the queen's business, on a matter pertaining to your *yet*." The man bowed and, when he stood, flicked his eyes over to the manservant still standing in the doorway. Raia had forgotten his presence and she quickly dismissed him, ordering him to have warmed jasmine tea brought to the room. She couldn't turn away one of the queen's men, however much he might unsettle her, and now he had her attention.

While she waited for him to settle onto a narrow, stone bench with his back to the wall and for Peret to bring tea, she inquired after the health of the queen and her infant son. But Raia had a difficult time focusing on pleasantries. Knowing the man had something to tell her about her father made her restless. She didn't think she could handle any more bad news at present. She'd only just begun to get back some semblance of a rhythm to her life after her father's death three months ago.

And so she paced the room from her father's desk to the door leading to the front entrance hallway. In the back of her mind she counted her steps – six medium-length strides each way, starting on the right foot and ending on the left each time, she couldn't seem to break the pattern.

In answer to her question, Makae said, "When I left the queen was well. And our next pharaoh is a strong lad with lusty lungs."

Raia gave the expected smile. "That is wonderful news, I am glad to hear of it." Meanwhile, she continued to tally her steps in silence.

Finally, Peret brought in the tea, serving them with a narrow glance at Makae. Raia knew what he was thinking; the man would accept no other master but her father's son and heir, never mind a foreigner. There was no point in telling Peret he needn't fear the queen's man, that Raia had no expectations of marrying again. Few men could serve as her equal. She did not lack for money, power, land, children, or intelligence. As far as practical reasons were concerned, she needed nothing from a man.

She shut the door behind Peret, not caring what the manservant thought of it, and turned to the foreigner.

"Nebet-i," he began, leaning forward to rest his elbows on his thighs and clasping his hands together between his spread knees. The compassion she saw in the depths of his dark eyes set her heart pounding. That he brought bad news was a certainty. "I am here in Abdju because your *yet*'s tomb was broken into and robbed sometime in the last few months, after his interment. We don't yet know who the perpetrators are, but I have been sent to investigate."

Having stopped her pacing near her father's desk, Raia was so shocked she leaned heavily back against it. Her bottom hit one of the small icons of the gods used to hold scrolls down flat, knocking it to the floor. She was vaguely aware of Makae kneeling at her feet to pick it up, his bent head near her legs, before he placed it back on the desk mere finger-widths from her thigh. None of it mattered. The eternal peace her father had worked so hard for was destroyed, taking her own peace on the earthly world along with it.

Makae sat back on the bench, his back to the wall, watching as the woman once again began to pace the long, bright, white-washed room. Back and forth she strode, twisting her hands in her long linen robe. Without a doubt, she was furious. That was fine. He could handle that. At least it wasn't the hysterics he'd anticipated encountering when he'd first stood on her doorstep, waiting to be let in to the wealthy manor home, knowing himself to be the bearer of bad news. Telling a woman her father's tomb had been desecrated was not something he'd looked forward to. Makae was a peaceable man who preferred to avoid the exaggerated, emotional scenes some women seemed to enjoy putting on. Thankfully, Raia did not appear to be one of those women.

He studied her as she strode back and forth in the small space, a frown furrowing her brow. She was not at all what he'd been expecting of a lady landowner. Then again, he wasn't sure just what he expected of a woman who managed the farms that fed the hundreds of workers in the Land of the Dead. Perhaps he thought she'd be older, more mannish, and most certainly less striking.

Incredibly tall, Raia had broad shoulders, prominent cheekbones, the most delicately contoured nostrils, and a feline grace of movement. The thick gold collar around her neck and the gold hoops over her ears contrasted strongly with her lustrous, brown-black skin. If the circumstances were different, if he'd met her at a banquet or in another setting, he imagined she'd be quite attractive.

But at the moment she looked capable of doing violence, and he wondered idly if she'd turn her ire on him.

She fulfilled his expectation when she whirled around and snapped out, "Well? Are you always this silent? What are you doing to find the men who did this? I presume you *are* doing something?"

In response, Makae crossed his arms over his chest and rested his head back against the wall, lifting one eyebrow in the process. He might be the queen's servant, but he was not this woman's. *And yes,* he thought, he *was* often this silent. It was precisely why he'd been the one chosen to stay at court, while his more gregarious brother insinuated himself amongst the tomb workers. Raia wouldn't be the first woman to disparage that particular trait of his, and there was every likelihood she wouldn't be the last. So he waited.

After a moment spent glaring at him, some of the fury appeared to melt from her shoulders. Her full, dark lips skewed slightly to the side as she nibbled the inside of her cheek before she spoke, this time with less haughtiness and more sincerity. "I am sorry. I should not have bit out at you like that. Whether or not I am distraught, it does not excuse rude behaviour. Please, will you tell me what your plans are, and what exactly they did to my *yet*'s mausoleum?"

Makae appreciated her humility. She looked like a smart woman and he decided to be honest with her.

"First, I must ask that you not share this information with anyone else. If we are to find the men involved, it is paramount that nobody knows we are investigating. It might send the thieves into hiding. Second, you can trust me when I say the queen takes tomb robbing very seriously. It is not only an offense against maat, but one against the queen's authority and the gods themselves. We will do everything in our power to find out who did this. My brother and I only arrived from Thinis last night with the queen's orders. He has gone to the village to begin an inquiry there, while I'll be staying here in the court."

"Here? Why? It had to be someone who works there, does it not?" She waved a hand towards the west, in the direction of the Land of the Dead. "Who else would rob a tomb but a peasant?"

He cleared his throat, choosing not to take offense at her choice of words. She didn't know his background and, given the expensive imported wood furniture and large style of her father's home, she'd probably never even spoken to a village labourer in her life. Obviously, it hadn't occurred to her that the nobility could be just as corrupt as a common peasant, sometimes far more so given their resources and connections.

"It's not that simple," Makae said. "Burial thefts usually require co-ordination at various levels. In all likelihood, you are right and some tomb workers were involved. They're the ones who know when a new tomb is completed and filled, and a few might know the secret entranceways, as well as the goods stored within.

"In the case of a larger tomb, like your *yet*'s, the chambers are dug out from the rocky ground of the Land of the Dead." Makae made a cupping gesture with his hand to indicate digging at a great depth. "Once completed, a boulder placed behind the door blocks the entrance from the inside, then the roof slabs are laid overtop," he smoothed his palm over the imaginary, ground-level rooftop, "and a mastaba built above ground over it all." His long fingers traced the angled sides and flat roof of the above-ground structure.

"For a lesser nobleman," he continued, "a hole large enough for a coffin and a few worldly goods is cut into the ground and then the mastaba built over the hole. Either way, to gain admittance thieves need to know the exact location of the entranceway, or the main chamber, in order to break through the roofing slab, or drill through the boulder blocking the entrance. They also need access to the tools and the manpower required to dig or cut through the entrance. These men are all probably tomb workers who are familiar with the guards' schedules and the tombs themselves. However, in order to get rid of their goods and cover up their crime, a contact amongst the wealthier classes – or in some cases, the nobility – is vital."

Therefore, Makae and his brother had strategized, along with their long-time friends Bey, the Captain of the Royal Guard, and Ebrium, the queen's lead investigator, that it would be best for the brothers to separate and send one to work in the Land of the Dead while the other worked amongst the topmost of Abdju's society.

She frowned. "But what if someone recognizes you here and then sees your brother in the village? You do not exactly *blend*." She made a hand gesture to indicate his overall appearance, a look of disapproval on her face. "Do you and your brother look alike?"

A slight smile tugged at the corner of his mouth as he prayed to Ba'al for her not to fly into a rage again. "Identical twins, actually." Her mouth gaped, but he cut her off before she could protest. "The village is at least a half hour walk away and there is little interaction between the tomb workers and the court. *Ikey* – stone cutters – don't exactly frequent the court, and most nobles do not walk all the way out to the village. It is unlikely anyone will see us both."

"But how can you be so sure?"

"How do your crops get to the tomb workers?" He asked her.

A crease appeared on her brow. "I have a man of labour, one who oversees the crops. He deals with one of Lady Ahaneith's officials. Why do you ask?"

"And who does the official deal with?"

"A man who organizes the labourers who cart away the crops to the village. What is your point? What does this have to do with anything?"

"Do you *know* any of the tomb workers?" He turned one palm up in question.

"Me? Of course not. Why would I?"

He tilted his head, letting her work it out on her own.

"I…" She stopped, as realization dawned and her eyes narrowed at him. Then her lips flattened and she closed her eyes, breathing in as if mastering herself.

Makae bit back a smile. He'd made his point. Even though her farms grew the crops that fed the tomb workers and many of the villagers in the Land of the Dead, she didn't know a single one of them. Even if someone in the court was involved in the thefts, they were probably working through a third party, someone living on the fringes of both the village and the court, and who was unlikely to see both himself *and* his brother and make the connection between the two. And unless they actually saw his brother Batr at work in the tombs, they would likely just assume the brothers were one and the same man. Makae's cover story – that he was in Abdju assessing Lady Ahaneith's defenses – could easily include exploring the village and the entrance to the desert east of the city.

When Raia opened her eyes again, Makae made sure there was no trace of a smile on his face. Instead, he took the opportunity to turn the questioning to his advantage. "Nebet-i, I need to ask if you know anyone who might have wanted to disturb your *yet*'s peace. The nature of the crime indicates that it might have been personal."

She blinked at him, that crease furrowing her brow again. "Personal? I don't understand."

Makae unclasped his hands, holding them palm up. He hated to be the one to explain these things. "It is only one possibility, and an unlikely one, but there has been the odd case of a tomb being robbed out of spite. What better way to seek revenge on someone than by disrupting their eternal rest? Did your *yet* have any enemies? Someone who disliked him enough to want to forever destroy his peace?"

"My *yet* was a good man," her voice was tight with controlled anger, as if affronted that anyone would even suggest he wasn't. "People liked him."

The woman clearly had a sense of loyalty and respect for her father. Both were traits he found admirable. However, they were also ones that could hinder his investigation.

"Nebet-i," Makae pitched his tone low and soothing to set her at ease, "I did not say otherwise. But even the best of men can unintentionally incite another to anger. Perhaps he did nothing wrong, and yet someone believes he did."

"No," she shook her head. "He had no enemies, I am sure of it." But even as the words were out of her mouth she paused, drawing in a sharp breath, looking thoughtful.

"Yes?" Makae leaned forward, his forearms resting on his thighs.

A heavy sigh escaped her as she inclined her head. "No, it is probably nothing, it was so long ago and I do not even know if it is anything worth mentioning." He inclined his eyebrows to urge her to continue and she did.

"Well, as you can see, the homes here are rather closely built. Though our home is large and the property spacious enough, our farms are about a thirty-minute walk from here," she gestured to the east, in the opposite direction of the Land of the Dead, "closer to the Iteru where we can more readily control the water flow. My farmland is adjacent to my *yet*'s. The other side, however, belongs to Userkare." She pronounced the name *Uuuser-karr-aay*, dragging out the sounds as was typical of the Kemeti language.

"Or at least, it belongs to Userkare now. As I said, I really do not know what happened, but when I was growing up my *yet* managed those adjacent lands. After I married, Userkare returned to Abdju from a long absence and took control of the lands. My *yet* warned us all to stay away from the man, that he was not right in the head.

"It is the only thing that comes to mind, but again, it was almost ten years ago and perhaps it means nothing at all. The man has done nothing since, he keeps to himself and I have not encountered him. I never even see him at court."

Makae pressed her for more, but Raia was either too reluctant to implicate her father in any wrong-doing, or did not know more. He decided to look into the matter of Userkare as soon as he was able. Makae moved to take his leave, but Raia stopped him as he unfurled from the bench to stand in front of her. He marveled once again that she was so near to his own height. He'd never known a woman as tall as she, and he found that he liked not having to dip his head down to see her face.

"Please," her dark eyes turned to him and his stomach tightened at the plea he discerned in them. He sympathized with the blow she'd received. He knew what it was to lose family, and to have their bodies desecrated. "You said the nature of the crime indicated it was personal. What exactly happened to my *yet*'s tomb?"

His jaw tightened. She would not want to hear this, but she deserved to know the truth. He said, "We know it was robbed and most of the valuables taken, including the jewellery he had on his body. Then the thieves set fire to the tomb. I'm sorry, but they destroyed your *yet*'s remains."

He watched as the small muscles in Raia's forehead contracted, causing her eyebrows to lift slightly as her chin softened in an expression of forlorn sorrow. For the briefest of moments, Makae saw a beautiful, lonely woman, burdened by loss and responsibility. Her lips, he observed as they parted slightly to exhale a slow, shaky breath, were of the same rich, brown-black colour as her skin, lightening to a deep plum colour in the centre, hinting at ripe, juicy sweetness. Or wooden tartness, he reflected, if plucked too soon. And the way her lips were tightening in indignation again, he imagined there was much more tartness than sweetness in her.

After a few moments she lifted her gaze to his. A hard expression settled in her jaw, replacing the emotion that had momentarily tempered her strong features, although her eyes were glassier than before. She said, "I don't care who did this or why. They have destroyed the eternal peace of my *yet*'s *ka* – his life force – and all the worldly goods he worked so hard to acquire. He may never rest easy now. When you find the men involved I want them all to suffer. Then, once they are executed, I want their names and the names of their families wiped from the tablets, so they will never find rest or be remembered, just as they've done to my *yet*."

Makae nodded. It was no less than he'd expected, and a reasonable request. "Fear not, nebet-i, it is precisely the punishment they will receive." Makae intended to do everything in his power to make it happen.

Chapter 4 – Discoveries

The morning after Batr appeared on the doorstep and stayed for dinner, Iset brought her mother a breakfast of leftover bread and a bowl of lentil mash from the night before. "Good morning, *mewet*," she set the tray of food on a stool next to her mother's bed. "Did you sleep well?"

Her mother opened bleary eyes. "Isetnofret." She reached out a hand, but dropped it before she could grip Iset's. "I'm sorry. I'm so sorry. I heard you on the roof last night. There was someone here, wasn't there?"

"Yes, mewet." Iset moved about the small, dark room. There was only one narrow window to illuminate the bed, dresser, and two stools. Iset wondered if there might be a hiding place she'd missed. After her father passed away she'd gone through his belongings, as her mother had been unable to look at them without crying. There hadn't been much anyway. A couple of robes that she'd taken for herself – to wear as Dedi – and a few scraps of papyri that didn't seem to have much of value on them. As it was, she could only read a few words of the scrolls she'd found, and that was only thanks to her older brother Sharek who'd begun teaching her to read while he studied to become a draughtsman like their father. It was time to search again; if her father had a copy of the plans for the pharaoh's tomb, it would be hidden somewhere in their home.

The thin woman on the bed pushed herself to a sitting position. Iset thought her mother's eyes looked hollower, and her cheeks even more gaunt than usual. Despite that, and the white that heavily streaked her hair, Ankhesenamon retained a shadow of the beauty she'd once been known for. It was her mother's beauty that had attracted her father, a man considered something of a catch due to his education and the fact that he moved amongst higher-ranking scribes, such as his friend Senebtawi.

Iset knelt and looked under the bed, just to be sure, even though she already knew there was nothing of value there. The floor was simply hard-packed dirt, populated by a basket or two of clothing that she'd gone through more than once before.

She explained to her mother as she stood up, dusting her hands off. "There was a man here. He stayed for dinner."

"Oh?" Ankhesenamon patted her hair down. Her voice came as if from far away. "Is he a suitor? Will he be asking for you?"

"No. He knows Dedi from work and came by looking for him. That's all."

"Oh. Dedi. I see." But she didn't. Iset's mother had rarely left her room for over a year now. Confused as she was, Dedi seemed to exist only in the periphery of her mind. A person that came and went that she didn't really know. Though she felt awful for thinking it, Iset knew it was better this way. If anyone asked her mother about Dedi, she wouldn't be able to accidentally let something slip. Iset had tried once or twice, when she'd first taken up the façade, to explain to her mother who the strange "nephew" in their house was, but somehow her mother's mind tangled things up and became more confused than ever about who Dedi was. Rather than ask, she just accepted his shadowy presence in their lives.

Iset opened the dresser cupboards, moving around the few thin robes and shawls her mother owned and reaching under them. It felt mercenary doing this while her mother sat right there, but what other choice did she have? She needed to be certain she hadn't missed a drawing, or perhaps even a note, anything that might have the location of the entrance to the Pharaoh's tomb.

"I'm sorry." Ankhesenamon said again, oblivious to Iset's searching. "I'm sorry I wasn't feeling up to joining you. I'm just so tired."

"I know, mewet. It's all right. Don't worry about it."

"I hope you fed him well and were polite."

Finished with her futile search, Iset sat on the edge of the bed and put the bowl of lentils into her mother's hands. "We did our best. Ahmose made him some of the carob tea that Senebtawi brought us a couple of weeks ago. Don't you remember? Ahmose brought you a cup last night also. If you ask him today I'm sure he'll be thrilled to tell you all about it."

"Senebtawi," the gaunt woman frowned. "Your *yet*'s friend."

"That's right, mewet. Have some of your lentils." Iset put a finger under the bowl to urge her mother to eat.

"There was something I was going to tell you about him…"

"I'm sure you'll remember it later. Don't worry. Anyway, mewet, I'm very sorry but I must get ready to go out now. Ahmose will be up shortly to stay with you today. I have the day free tomorrow, though. Perhaps if you're feeling better we could go out to the market, or you could join us on the roof for dinner, and then sit with some of the other ladies in the evening."

"Oh. I don't know about that." She must have seen Iset's pained look because she shifted the bowl to one hand and gripped Iset's thigh. "I'm sorry, sweetie. I'm just so tired. But maybe I'll try tomorrow." She gave a weak smile and Iset mustered a cheerful look.

"Of course, mewet. Have a good day. I'll see you tonight."

"Thank you, dear. And say hello to your cousin Dedi for me."

Iset pressed a hand to her chest, trying to prevent the pain that spread there from bursting forth. "Of course, mewet. I love you." She had to flee the room before her mother saw the tears well in her eyes.

Back in the living room, she took a few deep breaths. Ahmose, blurry-eyed with sleep, pattered into the room. "'S everything all right?" He mumbled, rubbing his cheek with his palm.

"Yes, of course." Iset turned away, pretending to fumble with the many layers of clothing she'd donned in preparation for work. "Ahmose, listen, I need you to do me a favour. I think *Yet* may have hidden something in the house before he passed away. While I'm gone, I need you to look around." *Awful.* She was awful for asking him to do what she herself wasn't able to do. But at least he didn't know *why* he was looking.

"D'you mean like that time *Yet* got a sack full of fresh figs and hid them around the house and you 'n' me 'n' Sharek searched all around until we found them all?" Ahmose's voice was alert and hopeful now.

"Yes. Like that. Except that it probably won't be figs this time. It is more likely to be a drawing, or a piece of writing, or… or something of that nature. Something we have not seen before. You know I have all of his things in a basket in mewet's room, so it will not be there. And it might be hidden in a very obscure place. Inside, or even in the yard, perhaps."

"That's all right. I'll find it. It'll give me something to do today!"

"Thank you." Having mastered herself, she was able to give him a long, hard hug before heading out to work. It was only when she was halfway to the Land of the Dead – as her stomach growled and her head acquired a light, buzzing sensation – that she realized she'd once again forgotten to eat breakfast.

Iset was just moving on to paint Amunemhat's garden when the horn to mark the midday meal blared out. Today, thank the gods, she wasn't working in the tomb alone and needn't fear being ambushed by the tomb robbers. Weni, the man she worked alongside, had been sick of late with a lung issue and took the odd day off when he had trouble breathing. Hence his absence the day before. Iset didn't mind Weni. Aside from regular bouts of racking coughs, he was quiet and didn't ask her questions.

"C'mon, boy," Weni wheezed. "Let's get ourselves some bread and beer."

Iset nodded and gestured that she would follow along in a few minutes. As soon as the man left the building she set aside her paints and slipped out of the tomb. It was hard to go unnoticed in the open desert landscape, but Iset was slight and the rest of the men were focused on getting their meal, a sip of water or beer, and a spot in the shade. The tall mastaba tombs in the eastern side of the cemetery afforded her some cover as she made her way to the inventory hut.

Inside the hut, Teos the scribe kept the inventory used each day to decorate and build the tombs. Each morning the workers lined up to pick up the tools of their trade from the man. Whenever anyone needed more pigments to make paint, or a new chisel to cut stone, they acquired it here as well. At the end of the day, most tools were returned here as well. Teos kept a careful log of everything that came and went and who'd taken it, to ensure that nothing was stolen.

It also happened to be where the lists of work crews were kept. In order to determine who'd been working under her father on Pharaoh Wadj's tomb Iset needed to find the list. She wasn't exactly sure what good it would do, but if she knew who worked with her father she'd have a better chance of determining who threatened her. Perhaps they were involved. If not, there was also a small chance that one of the men on the work crew might be able to tell her where the Pharaoh's burial chamber was located. She had no idea how she'd get the information once she found the men, but knowing who they were was a start at least.

Iset snuck around the side of the building and pressed her back against the wall, wondering if Teos had already gone for lunch. After what was surely only a minute or two but felt like far too long, with heart hammering, she tip-toed towards the narrow window cut into the wall of the main front room where Teos usually sat behind a small desk stacked with papyri scrolls.

A foot from the window the toe of her sandal caught a rock. The stone clattered and skittered across the bedrock. Iset froze, holding her breath, fear buzzing in her ears.

There was no way anyone who saw her would think she was up to anything but bad things. Too late she realized it would have been smarter to just walk up to the front door and step inside, as if she expected Teos to be there. Too bad she wasn't an accomplished thief, as well as a liar, she thought. Another pause and she forced herself to peer into the room, looking in on an angle so she'd be less likely to be seen from inside.

After walking for several minutes in the blinding sunlight, it took her eyes a moment to adjust to the darkness of the hut. Dust motes sifted through the air inside. She saw the desk, the wall of shelves behind it that held papyri scrolls, and the door on the far side of the room that led to the inventory room. But no Teos. Iset crept around to the front of the hut, swiveling her head from side to side to make sure no one was about.

Once in front of the building, she opened the door and slipped inside, yanking it shut behind her. *Too hard*, she winced as the door banged. Holding her breath, she waited. Nothing happened. So she went for the wall of scrolls. Her older brother had told her about the room, several times in fact. He'd been awed by the careful tracking of the crews, what they were paid, and exactly how much was required to build the tombs. How many slabs of granite for the roof, how many paintbrushes, how many stone picks and chisels, all that and more was recorded in the script that Iset found so difficult to discern. Her brother had aspired to be one of the men who kept these records, if unable to work as a draughtsman.

She pushed thoughts of Sharek aside and focused on determining which stack of scrolls contained the information she needed. The shelves were organized chronologically, but where did they start and which ones pertained to the Pharaoh's tomb? She pulled one out at random and squinted at the strip of linen tied around it. She managed to make out the date – *Nehebkau* – the first day of the second season – in the third year of the reign of Pharaoh Wadj. Wadj had reigned for ten years, so she'd need to move ahead seven years to find the dates she sought.

She brushed her fingers along the scrolls, occasionally tugging one out to check the date. One for a nobleman's tomb, another for his wife, a pharaoh's uncle, and so on and so forth until she almost despaired of finding anything useful.

Her stomach rumbled loudly, but she ignored it. She hadn't eaten last night either. Her exchange with Batr had left her nervous and confused, her stomach in knots. His questions put her on edge, and she feared he suspected something. But when she'd closed her eyes to sleep, she could feel his lips on her hand, and see his sultry smile and white teeth flashing. The baffling urge to smile back was interspersed with a fluttering panic at what might happen if she didn't find the Pharaoh's burial chamber. It'd made for a jumbled, fitful sleep and a sickening feeling deep in the pit of her stomach.

There. Iset blinked at the thick scroll in her trembling hand. It would only be one of many scrolls that pertained to Wadj's tomb. The making of a pharaoh's tomb was unlike the noblemen's tombs that Iset worked on. Many of the noblemen's tombs were primarily above-ground structures. Beneath them a small burial chamber was dug out, just large enough for a coffin and a few necessities for the afterlife. It was just such a chamber that she'd been forced down into the day before.

For a pharaoh, however, a massive amount of earth was excavated many metres below the ground over the course of several years. Leaving the tomb exposed to the light of day made it easy for the workers to build walls, paint them, place in carvings and statues, etc. Once the pharaoh passed – and the retainers selected to serve him in the afterlife had been sacrificed – they were all placed inside their respective chambers and the workers built a ceiling over the entire thing. Afterwards, mastaba tombs, or sometimes mounds of sand – that which had been excavated to build the tomb – were piled over top of it all to hide the entrance.

Over the ten years it took to build Wadj's tomb, numerous scrolls would've been filled to record all the workers' wages and the necessary supplies. Almost two hundred retainers were sacrificed and buried in individual chambers around Wadj's burial room, each with a long list of items required to serve them – and the pharaoh – in the afterlife. It was no small undertaking to assist a pharaoh's passing to the peaceful fields of the other world.

She was just reaching to pluck out another scroll from the shelf when she heard voices along the side of the building. "No, no. Don't worry. Teos'll be gone for another fifteen minutes or so. The lunch break ain't over yet. But you can't just show up here like this again, or my wife'll find out." A woman's voice murmured inaudibly in response. Iset's heart leapt in her chest and her eyes darted about the room. There was nowhere to hide except for the inventory room. If she was caught in there she'd be as good as dead. They'd assume she was stealing. But what choice did she have?

She closed the door to the inventory room behind her, careful not to disturb any of the tools and equipment that lined the floor, tables, and walls. She heard the front door opening, feet shuffling, and the door clicking closed.

"So what is it you want today, wench? I don't have much time." The man's voice was a rough, deep rumble, of the sort that could never whisper discretely. Iset detected something lacing the edge of his voice. Lust, perhaps?

The woman's response was too low and breathy to make out, except for the tone – wheedling and provocative. Iset caught the words "love" and "necklace". The man gave a menacing chuckle. "Don't be silly, woman. Of course I love you, but I'm not just going to give it to you for nothing. You want me to bring you something extra from the pharaoh's tomb you need to show me why it's worth my time."

Iset's hand flew to her mouth, pressing against the scarf that wound about her face. *Oh gods, one of the thieves is on the other side of the door. Probably with a prostitute, or a concubine.*

Another quiet mumble and the man said, "All right then, come here, sweetheart," his rough voice urged. 'That's right. I just want a little taste of you before I go back to work." There was a woman's giggle, then a wet noise that

Iset recognized as two people kissing, causing her to recall her first kiss.

She'd been fourteen, and it was a festival day. Alongside the little river that cut through the city of Abdju people had set up a bonfire, and dancers and musicians played along the banks. In the shadow of a merchant's hut, her betrothed had grabbed her hand and pulled her into his embrace. Then he'd kissed her. It had been awkward, yet thrilling. Until the moment he'd slipped his tongue past her lips and she'd recoiled in shock. He hadn't tried to kiss her again.

From the moans she heard on the other side of the door, however, she judged that those two were enjoying that blending of tongues. The woman's voice became more audible, as she urged the man on. Iset's fingers clenched around her mouth until her jaw ached as she listened to the woman moan and the man mutter, "Mmm, I love you. Once we get this loot, we'll go somewhere else. I promise." Iset squeezed her eyes shut and tried to block out the sounds from the other side of the door.

Almost too late, she realized she was missing an opportunity to identify one of the robbers. She tucked the scroll she'd been clutching into an inside pocket of her father's vest, tying the strings of the vest to prevent the scroll from slipping out. Then, with one hand pressed against the door to stop it from swinging open or squeaking, she gently tugged on the door handle.

Able to pull the door open a slight crack, she peered out into the hut. The couple were on the far side of the room. The woman was seated on the desk, while the man had his back to the inventory room door, his bulk hiding the woman's frame and face. He wore a full-length robe, yanked up over his hips and held up by the woman's hands, scrunched tight against his bare, thrusting buttocks while her ankles rested on his shoulders.

Iset blinked, trying not to stare. She'd grown up in a village where people kept animals in their yards, and was familiar with the mating of goats and donkeys and other creatures. She had girlfriends who'd married and shared their stories. Twice betrothed herself, her mother had prepared her for what she could expect in her marriage bed. But the display of wild, sweaty, grunting lust that shook the desk beneath the couple was something else altogether, a grotesque and rather comical scene.

Just then, the man jerked a few times and threw his head back. Iset lurched back into the room, gently pushing the door to the frame, afraid to close it completely in case it made a noise, but afraid to leave it open lest they see her.

There were a few moments of heavy panting, and then the man growled, "I gotta get back to work, but tonight I'm coming by, and we're doing this again." The woman giggled again and Iset heard feet scuffling in the dirt, the door opening and closing, then silence. Her heart beat in her ears; her breath came in short gasps. That sickly buzzing took up residence between her ears again, the light-headed feeling almost overtaking her. She dug her fingernails into her palms until it hurt, forcing herself to think clearly; she had to get out before Teos came back from his lunch break and found her. She'd have no excuse for being here. She couldn't even pretend to need pigments or brushes, as she'd received fresh supplies that morning.

Iset waited another half minute before yanking open the inventory door and sprinting across the room. In her haste she almost pulled open the main door without stopping to check. At the last second, though, she came to her senses and peered outside the window. Seeing no one, she stole out the main door and dragged in a breath of dry desert air.

She'd missed her second meal of the day but she had one scroll for her troubles. And she had heard the voice of another tomb robber, one she might be able to recognize by its deep, rumbling tones. It wasn't much, but it was better than nothing.

Batr was on his way back to the stone quarry when he saw a man and woman slip hand in hand out of the inventory hut. Batr flattened himself against one of the nearby tomb walls and watched as they said their goodbyes.

The woman, wearing a wrap that left her pendulous breasts bare but covered her legs to the knee, pressed her length against the man. In return, he squeezed her bottom, then patted it and released her. They parted, and the man walked around to the other side of the building Batr was standing against, giving him a good look at the man's profile. He had a flat, crooked nose that had likely been broken more than once on an otherwise unremarkable face.

Two people out for a lunchtime tryst. Batr chuckled to himself, envying the man's audacity. He thought of Isetnofret, Dedi's beautiful cousin, and the kiss they'd almost shared last night. While she might well be innocent in the ways of flirting, she was a bright, intuitive woman and he had little doubt that she possessed enough passion to bring him to his knees. In fact, he'd *love* to be on his knees in front of her. Or *between* her knees. Or, the gods help him, her on *her* knees in front of him.

His groin tightened and he moved to adjust himself. He ought to get back to work, but the turn of his thoughts made it awkward for him to leave the shadow of the hut for another minute or two. Just as he was forcing himself to think about poisonous snakes, scorpions, jackals or anything else that might take his mind off of seducing Iset, the door to the inventory hut opened a second time. A head peered out the door before a slight figure slid through the gap. Head swiveling to glance around, the figure hurried in the opposite direction from Batr over the rocky surface.

Batr couldn't be positive, due to the head scarf wrapped around the figure's face and head, but given the thin build and vest, he was fairly confident it was Dedi. What in the name of the gods was Iset's cousin doing inside the inventory hut during the lunchbreak? And what did it have to do with the couple having a noon-time rendezvous? Perhaps their meeting hadn't been romantic after all. He couldn't just pull the boy aside and question him, it might raise suspicions amongst the workers and Batr needed to be discreet until he was certain he'd identified the thieves. Furthermore, the small, nagging desire to please Iset also made it difficult to offend her by interrogating her cousin.

Still, Batr was determined to find out more about the couple who'd been inside the hut. And he'd already formed a plan to find out more about Dedi…

"You there! Foreign one. Yes, you. Come here." The widow Neb-tawy flapped a fleshy hand in Batr's direction. He feigned confusion, but in truth he was hoping for just such an opportunity when he'd chosen to walk this way.

Batr had finished his work day and hoped to see Dedi on his way out of the Land of the Dead. Instead, he'd ended up spending the twenty minutes back to the village with a group of workers, one or two of which seemed like the sort to be involved in gambling or other less savoury activities. He'd gotten himself invited to a tavern tonight to drink with some of the men and he'd decided to stop by Isetnofret and Dedi's hut on the way there, by route of the widow's hut.

"Hello there, little mother." Batr pressed the older woman's moist hand between his rough, dry palms. His term of respect brought an approving gleam to her eye. He'd met the woman his first day in the village, as she'd stopped him on his way to the market, and he couldn't help but like the nosy old lady; she reminded him of one of his grandmothers. And it never hurt to make friends with the village gossip, as long as one was careful what information they shared in return.

"Where are you off to now? Out to spend your earnings at the taverns, drinking and playing games, are you?" The old lady's eyes narrowed and she shook one chubby finger at him.

He grinned and gave her a bow. "What do you think I should do instead, little mother? Should I spend the evening by your side, basking in your fine company?"

The old lady's lips tightened, but he discerned the smile lurking in her eyes. Then her big, half-naked body waggled as she broke out into a chuckle. "By the gods, no. I would never expect a young man like you to spend all night keeping company with an old lady like me. Besides, what would the neighbours say?"

Batr put a hand over his heart. "They would say that you wooed me with your attractions, little mother, and that it was to be expected from one so captivating as yourself." He remembered how Iset had accused him of trying to charm her with court manners last night. By the gods, he certainly intended to try that again tonight.

The widow rapped him on the arm. "Nonsense, silly boy. Besides, you aren't my type. You're well-mannered and handsome enough, I'll give you that. But you've got too many odd tattoos, and all that hair." She tsk'd and shook her head. "But I'll let you sit beside me for a few minutes." She flapped her hand at the ever-present stool next to her. Batr knew she kept it there for any passerby who might stop to chat.

He folded his tall body down onto the stool – a strip of leather slung between three weather-beaten wooden legs. He leaned his back against the side of the hut. The bricks, still warm from the heat of the day, soothed the sore muscles of his shoulders. Working as a quarryman was back-breaking work. Not since his days as a rower on the great pirate ships had he done such exhausting labour.

Neb-tawy asked him, "So who've you met now that you've been here a few days?"

Batr shrugged. "Well there are the men on my crew of course." He listed their names and the widow nodded or shook her head, giving him brief backstories when necessary, or warding him away from ones she thought might "lead him astray". He stifled a laugh when she said that. As if he weren't a grown man. As if he hadn't spent three years of his life as a pirate, and another four a soldier. He'd encountered much worse men than the grave-diggers in this little village. But he was attentive as well, those men who could lead him astray might also lead him right to the tomb robbers, and he intended to seek them out, even as the widow warned him away.

"Oh, and I bumped into someone yesterday," he finally came around to his purpose. "A boy. Dedi, I think his name was? I stopped by his house last night and met his cousins, Isetnofret and Ahmose?" He hoped the lift in his voice implied the questions it would be too inappropriate to ask outright.

The widow's sharp eyes looked him over with renewed interest and a touch of what might be caution. "I see." She nodded slowly. "And?" He understood her hesitation. Despite her willingness to talk with him he was still an outsider, and she was protective of Iset's family.

Batr lifted one shoulder. "They seemed quite nice. The boy was excited about some bread he made. He tripped and hit me in the head with a bread slab and almost knocked me out. Afterwards, we shared a pleasant meal. The bread really was quite good."

The widow's large body jiggled with mirth, and she slapped her knee. "Oh! Oh!" She laughed so hard she started a coughing fit. She leaned forward, hands splayed on her outspread thighs while she hacked up phlegm. Batr tried to comfort her just as an older couple walked past and stopped to help, but Neb-tawy waved them on. When she caught her breath she brushed off the coughing fit. "This is nothing, just the ailments of an old lady. But oh! That is just like Ahmose to do something like that. Ahhh well," her voice sobered. "There is some story with that family, I tell you."

"Oh?" Batr kept his face impassive, not wanting to arouse her suspicion. For all he knew, if he wasn't careful, tomorrow rumours would be circulating that he was openly pursuing Iset and a village marriage was pending.

"Oh yes. That poor girl, Isetnofret. Her poor mother." Neb-tawy shook her head and Batr wanted to shake her in frustration. The woman was going to force him to ask, just so she could *appear* reluctant to tell some sort of scandalous tale.

He gritted his teeth, then asked politely. "How so? Isetnofret and Ahmose were very kind last night and it would sadden me to know they've fallen on difficult times. Although now that you mention it, I do recall they said their mother is a little ill. She didn't join us for dinner. Neither did Dedi."

"Oh indeed." Neb-tawy's chins wobbled. "Difficult times indeed. You see, the mother, she's very unwell. Has been for some time. It's been going on for years. She's lost so many babies, it's made her mad."

Batr's gut twisted, as if a sharp fruit pit stabbed his abdomen. He understood what the loss of a child could do. He'd seen it with his own mother. He'd had twelve brothers and sisters at one time, and multiple others that never survived past the first month or two. Now there were only two – himself and his brother. He wasn't sure if one of his younger sisters was still alive, but he liked to think so.

If his expression changed, Neb-tawy didn't notice, as she continued talking. "She'd had a few losses before Iset's older brother was born, ones that never came to birthing. Then the oldest boy came along, oh, I'd say he would've been about twenty-one now. So there was him, then Iset a couple of years after. Then another few losses, and then a girl. Pretty little thing. She lived a few months before she passed away, Ra rest her little *ka*. It looked for a while like there wouldn't be any more but then along came Ahmose. When he was, oh I think maybe five – this would have been about four years ago – there was another boy. He lived about eighteen months but then got the diarrhea and that was the end of him. That's when the poor woman really started to have problems. She'd cry for days, wouldn't leave her bed."

Neb-tawy began to rock back and forth, her large breasts stretching and scrunching against her belly as she rubbed her palms on her thighs. "Poor, dear woman. She was just starting to get better last year when their oldest one, Iset's older brother, had an accident and died. That was the last reed stick in the bundle, so they say. She doted on that boy something fierce and his death really took the life out of her. She's hardly left the hut since. And now with Iset's father gone, too…," Neb-tawy shrugged one shoulder, shaking her head slightly. "Some of the women try to see her, but she won't take visitors anymore. There's a sickness in here," she tapped her head, "and here," she tapped her heart, "that's got a hold of her now."

No wonder he'd been confused about whether Ahmose was Iset's son or brother. The task of raising the boy had fallen to her. "But, wait," he said. "What about their *yet*? Wasn't he a draughtsman in the Land of the Dead?"

"Mmmm." Neb-tawy's mouth thinned. "He *was*. But I can't say he was ever much help. Now I don't like to speak poorly of some people, especially those that have seen hardship. I know what it's like. I've lost a few of my own babies. We all have, of course. And that woman's lucky she's survived at all, what with how difficult childbirth is. But that man," Neb-tawy tsk'd her tongue. "He could've been better all right. From what I hear he spent most of his nights at the taverns, betting on games. But after a time his debts got too big and some of the taverns wouldn't even let him in anymore. And I don't know what it's like where you come from, but here you don't want to be one of those men that're gambling in the alleyways at night."

Batr didn't think it necessary to tell her that the closest thing they had to alleyways in the desert – *where he came from* – was the shadowy space behind one's family tent. You were more likely to be killed in a raid from a neighbouring tribe than for gambling with your own cousins. But he understood the sentiment. The gods forbid he ever be stupid enough to bet in an alleyway in any of the port cities he'd spent time in. You didn't wind up in debt that way, you wound up dead.

The widow shook her head and tsk'd again. "And that poor girl Iset taking care of it all."

"But they have Dedi now to help, right?"

"Mmmm. That boy. I just don't know what to make of him. He came around, oh, about six months ago?" Neb-tawy scratched her bald pate with one thick finger. "Iset's *yet* said the boy was in need of work, and because of his thing," Neb-tawy gestured to her mouth and throat to indicate Dedi's semi-muteness and scarring, "he was having difficulties. Don't know much about the boy, but I suppose he means well enough. Don't know how much he can help, though. I know what the wages are for those painters, and for a new one like him it's not much, that's for sure. And he's always out at night, leaving Iset alone with it all."

With each new revelation about Iset, Batr's interest – and suspicions – grew. When Dedi had run into him yesterday he'd looked scared witless. Not like a hardened criminal. Could it be possible the boy was just trying to help his family and gotten tangled up in something? Batr was beginning to wonder if something more than just a single tomb robbing going on. Perhaps another theft, or something else of a criminal nature.

He stretched his long legs out and crossed his ankles. "And what of Isetnofret? Are she and Dedi planning to marry?" They were cousins, after all. It was normal to marry someone close, and familiar, to the family.

"Oh, not that I know of. Not that Iset hasn't had her offers, though."

"Oh?" Batr was suddenly aware of the beating of his heart in his chest, and a pressure on his breast. *Interesting*, he observed. He knew Iset had made an impression on him, but he was surprised to discover that the thought of her marrying someone affected more than just his groin. Could he actually be experiencing jealousy? He pursed his lips, considering this new sensation.

"Mmmm." Neb-tawy coughed and spat before continuing. "From the time she was little she was engaged to the son of one of the scribes, Senebtawi, a close friend of her *yet*'s."

Batr recognized the name, but it took him a moment to register it. Last night Ahmose mentioned that the carob tea had been a gift from Senebtawi. This must be the same man whose son Iset had been engaged to.

Neb-tawy sighed. "But the boy died just before they were due to marry. I think Iset would have been about fourteen or fifteen then. Then there was that nobleman who came through here a couple of years ago. He'd been looking for a location for his own tomb. He was quite taken with our Iset, he was. Saw her in the market and offered for her right away. Her father agreed, but then the man's wife came to town. She didn't take kindly to the idea of him taking a second wife, and refused to let him marry Iset. Can't say it was the worst thing to happen, though." Neb-tawy's eyes narrowed. "I never liked his look, I tell you."

"Did Iset want to marry him?"

Neb-tawy shrugged. "It would have been a step up for her, all right. The man was well-off, but at least thirty years her senior. I can't say whether she wanted to or not, as her *yet* didn't worry himself much about her and she's always been a quiet girl. He liked his sons all right, though."

"And Iset has had no offers since? I would think that a marriage would help her family's situation somewhat." The questions were out before he could stop himself. It wasn't his business, and it shouldn't matter. But it did. Just a little bit.

Neb-tawy began rocking again, with her thighs spread and bare, dirty toes dug into the earth. "She's had interest. Of course she has, she's a pretty girl. But she won't leave her mother or brother, so a man would have to take care of them, too. That and she's getting older now. She's what, nineteen? Twenty? Men want a wife to have babies, except if he's already got a pack by someone else. So unless she gets out of this village, maybe goes to Abdju and the big city, she's not got many more options. Or she becomes some man's second or third wife, a lesser wife."

The widow lowered her voice and leaned towards Batr, who turned his ear to her. He was pleasantly surprised to find that she smelled of cloves and cinnamon, rather than stale sweat and unwashed-body, as he'd been expecting from one who sat out in the sun all day, even in the cooler winter months.

She murmured, "I sometimes wonder if Senebtawi, the *yet* of the boy she was to marry, might be getting ready to offer for her. He's got a group of children from his last two wives and needs a mother for them. I wouldn't blame her if she rejects him, though. Raising eight children by two other women?" She shook her head as if to say *no thank you.* "Although he *was* a close friend of her father. I imagine he's trying to do right by the girl, and he's alone now too, since his second wife died in childbirth last year and the first one a few years back from the diarrhea."

Batr's mouth thinned as he absorbed all this. He wished he could remember how Iset had reacted to the mention of Senebtawi's name last night. The fact that he couldn't angered him, and that also surprised him. Who she married ought to be no concern of his. "Little mother," he cleared his throat. "How did Iset's *yet* pass away again?"

"Oh! That was an odd one, all right. He fell down the cliffs in the Land of the Dead. They say he was out drinking one night and wandered off alone. He climbed up the cliffs out there," she flapped her hand in the direction of the tombs, and the cliffs beyond that marked the entrance to the depths of the desert. "And lost his footing and fell. Cracked his head right open."

Batr hoped his sharp intake of breath would be taken as shock at the story, rather than a reaction to a revelation. What if Iset's father had involved Dedi in something before he died? Something dangerous that had gotten the man killed?

Perhaps he was jumping to conclusions, but it all seemed too coincidental, didn't it? First, Dedi arrives in town. Then, sometime in the last few months, a nobleman's tomb gets robbed. The boy's uncle – a draughtsman in the Land of the Dead who would easily have access to information about the tombs – also dies in a rather odd fashion. Odd indeed, considering the cliffs were at least a half-hour walk from the edge of the village and no easy climb for a drunken old man. Why bother going there? And finally, his own encounter with the terrified-looking boy and, upon going to look for the boy, finding his cousin, a too-thin, suspicious woman who refuses to marry despite living in a state of near-poverty with a sick mother to tend to.

Batr frowned down at the sandy earth, hard-packed from years of the widow's feet resting on it. He didn't think Dedi could be the leader of the tomb-robbers, but it seemed more and more probable he was involved. And Batr needed a weak link to exploit to find out more about the robbers. If he could get Dedi or Iset to cooperate with him he might be able to find a way to help them while they helped him.

Iset's situation sounded dire. Even given his brief time with her, he got the impression she was loyal enough to her family that, if Dedi was involved in criminal activities, she would protect him at all costs. Unless, that is, Batr could convince her that protecting Dedi would actually harm them rather than help.

And he was finding that his inclination to assist Iset grew with each new disclosure about her. Last night she'd been wary of him, but she'd also had an innocence to her, a kindness – considering the jasmine flowers in the water she'd given him and her shyness about their simple fare – a gentleness evidenced in her tender touch on the growing lump on his forehead when he'd come to in her lap – and a sly sense of humour that appealed to him. To think that she'd endured so much hardship and yet had such sweetness of character… that made her an interesting woman, indeed.

He chatted with the widow a few more minutes on mundane matters to avoid rousing her suspicion, though he was impatient to see Iset now. When he finally rose to leave, the widow reached out to grasp his wrist and pull him close.

"Iset's a beautiful girl. But she's also smart and good. I hope you'll do right by her. She deserves someone to take care of her and she's been hurt plenty enough already."

Batr blinked. Had he somehow revealed something? It seemed the widow Neb-tawy was more observant, more like his own grandmother, than he'd given her credit for. "I assure you, little mother, that I have no intentions towards Iset."

A crease formed in the flesh of her forehead. "Well why not? You haven't brought a wife along with you. You've already said you like her brother, and her mother is quiet enough, and less tiresome than most since she keeps to herself. A man needs a wife sooner or later and you don't strike me as the type of man to dilly-dally about what he wants."

"But I never said I wanted Iset." Batr marveled that he actually felt heat creeping up his throat and thanked the gods for his dark complexion and the setting sun.

"You didn't have to." The widow's eyebrows lifted, a knowing look twinkling in her merry eyes. She rubbed her thighs as she took up her rocking again. "Yes. I think you will do well by her. She probably won't mind all that hair of yours, as long as you keep the lice away."

"I don't have –," Batr chuckled when the old lady grinned at him and he realized she'd managed to fluster him. He shook his head. "Thank you, little mother, I'll take your advice into consideration." He made his escape from what was fast becoming an uncomfortable situation.

But as he wound his way through the dusty streets to Iset and Dedi's hut the widow's words echoed in his head. *Why not? A man needs a wife sooner or later.* Circumstances had made marriage impossible in the last few years. Years ago he had promised himself he wouldn't become too attached to anyone other than his one surviving brother. A family was an unnecessary entanglement doomed to cause pain and hardship. But a woman like Iset would make a fine mistress if she was willing. And if she was cleared of involvement in the tomb robbing, well why not indeed?

Chapter 5 – Senebtawi

"Isetnofret, you really ought to know better than to invite a strange man into the house. People will talk." Senebtawi placed his hands on the curve of his narrow hips, rolling them forward, which only served to emphasize his protruding abdomen. It didn't so much hang over the top of his shenti as jut straight out in front of him, like a hard, round ball. Like the pregnant belly of a young woman. However, Iset knew some women found that particular attribute attractive, as it served as an indication of prosperity and good health. In Senebtawi's case, it proved to be true. He was very wealthy, his shentis were always of the finest, whitest linen and, despite his somewhat advanced years, he never complained of sickness.

In fact, by the standards of most village women Senebtawi was not an unattractive man. His jaw was strong, the braided side-lock of his hair still jet-black, and his shoulders were broad and straight in defiance of the many hours he spent hunched over papyri scrolls, keeping the accounts of the wealthy and tracking the tomb workers' wages.

Due to Senebtawi's unexpected arrival, once again Iset barely had time to transform after work when someone knocked at her door. Once again that knock had caused a hard knot of anxiety to grow in her stomach. Ahmose had said his hellos and chatted for a few moments – the boy knew Senebtawi usually came bearing a gift of some sort – and then Iset allowed him to go play with his friends before dinner, leaving her alone with Senebtawi. After exchanging a few pleasantries in the main greeting room, her father's friend began pressing her for details regarding Batr's visit. Iset was reluctant to share much with him. The less she talked about Dedi, and anything pertaining to Dedi, the safer she felt. A small part of her also feared that, if she spoke about Batr, her conflicted feelings about him would become apparent.

And now she was irritated by the implication of wrong-doing, and that Senebtawi seemed to think himself in a position to chastise her. Of course she'd known last night when Batr dined with them that the neighbours would see them on the rooftop. Everyone sat on their roofs at night, and Iset had even waved to a few of them over the course of their meal. She had many secrets, but there was no reason to hide a man on her roof. She realized it was natural for the neighbours to be curious and to talk about her. But what bothered her was that Senebtawi had found out so quickly, and then felt the need to come immediately to castigate her.

"I'm sorry, Senebtawi," she said, "but I hardly see the problem. There was nothing at all improper about it. It's not as if I were here alone. Mother was in the house, and Ahmose sat with us the entire time. Dedi came home just after the man left. And besides, even if I were alone with him, I am a grown woman, twice engaged to be married. There is no shame in having a man as a dinner guest."

"But *that* is the problem, Isetnofret. You don't see any problem." Senebtawi rubbed a long, thin finger along the side of his nose, then tugged at the braided loop of hair on the side of his otherwise bald pate. His eyes, long-lashed and kohl-rimmed, gave all the appearance of one speaking with a naïve child. "It is not safe for you to be alone with a foreigner. Clearly Dedi isn't doing a very good job of protecting you."

Iset's lips thinned. "Protecting me from what, exactly? Ahmose was by my side and the man works with Dedi. We were on our rooftop where practically the entire village could see us. I was hardly in any danger. He was looking for Dedi when Ahmose nearly took his head off. He could have been killed, for Ra's sake! It would have been horribly rude to turn him away after that."

Senebtawi stepped towards her, taking her hand up between his in a gesture she knew was meant to be kind. She reminded herself that he meant well, that he was generous with them, and had just brought over a bowl of fresh figs. Such a delicacy was difficult to come by this time of year, what with the harvest season being over. Of course, grain, or beer, or meat would have been more practical and filling, but he'd said the figs would be a treat for them. He was only trying to help the family of an old friend, and a woman once meant to be his daughter-in-law.

"Isetnofret," he leaned in and she caught a wisp of his scent – strong clove oil that made her nose wrinkle. "It is a sign of your innocence that you don't realize what your beauty can do to a man." His grip tightened on her, his voice took on a rough undertone. "Not every man will ask you politely to marry him. Less honourable men just take what they want."

Iset's hand became a fist in his grasp but still she didn't pull away. "Then it is lucky that both you and Batr are honourable, is it not? For I am here alone with you, also."

An indulgent smile spread across his face as he released her and held his hands out, palms upwards. "Come now, there is no need to be querulous. I am only trying to warn you to be careful since you no longer have a man to watch out for you."

His scent was dizzying and a pressure weighed on her chest, making it difficult to breathe. She was not being *querulous*, she thought, but rightfully annoyed. "Then I thank you for your concern, Senebtawi. However unnecessary it is. I *do* have Dedi, after all."

Senebtawi looked as if he was about to move closer again, but a knock at the door interrupted them and Iset slipped around him to answer it. She blinked, wondering if she was imagining things. There in her doorway stood Batr.

His eyes swept over her and she thought she saw concern in his appraisal. "*Nebet-i*," he murmured.

A feeling of lightness washed over Iset. She was actually *relieved* to see him. "Batr. This is a surprise." She stepped aside and he ducked to enter. A split second of guilt washed over her as she comprehended that she was encouraging his presence to stave off further conversation with Senebtawi.

Batr's arrival would only anger the older man further, and probably confirm his suspicions.

"Dedi isn't here right now, but…" She trailed off. Her conversation with Senebtawi causing her to wonder if it was Dedi he'd come to see or if, perhaps, Batr might be stopping by to see her instead.

"No matter. I will leave my message with you." Batr waved it off. His gaze had gone straight for Senebtawi, a hard look in his eyes she hadn't seen before. He tipped his head at the older man. "I'm Batr."

Senebtawi's cheek twitched as he took in the powerful-looking man. Batr had drawn himself up to his full height. A good several inches taller than Senebtawi, his head almost brushed the ceiling of the small hut. His shoulders were squared and although his calloused hands hung loose at his sides, his firm, muscled body radiated a potent force. Taking that in, along with the set of his jaw and slight flare of his nostrils, Iset caught a glimpse of the formidable pirate he must have been.

Senebtawi must have seen something of that as well, as his lips stretched in a semblance of a smile. "Senebtawi. A close friend of the family. Their well-being is of my *utmost* concern."

Batr grinned, but with the hard glint in his eyes he looked more wolfish than good-humoured. "I am sure they are grateful for it."

Iset's arm ached and she realized she was still holding the door open. She widened the gap and said, "Thank you again, Senebtawi, for your concern, and for the lovely figs. It was very kind of you to think of us." She prayed to her namesake that he would take her hint and not press to stay.

Senebtawi drew his shoulders back as his thoughtful gaze lingered on Batr. The older man was not one to be easily intimidated, particularly given his elevated social status and wealth. Rather than answer Iset, he addressed Batr, "Isetnofret was just telling me about your visit last night. What is it, exactly, that you are doing here in the Land of the Dead, and where do you come from?"

With his inimical smile still in place, Batr answered. "Quarrying, at the moment. And as for where I come from, I have been all over." He shrugged one large, muscled shoulder.

"I would expect that a man of your years would move around a bit less. That all sounds rather capricious." The older man's eyes narrowed as he cocked his head, still assessing Batr.

In a soft voice that gave Iset shivers, Batr said, "Does it now?"

Last night Iset had questioned Batr's roving, but to hear Senebtawi do it provoked her. He was trying to prove his point that Batr was untrustworthy, as if she couldn't reason that out herself. She forced a light laugh and said, "Well I suppose circumstances are not always so kind to others. We cannot all be lucky enough to be born in the Land of the Dead."

Senebtawi's eyes narrowed a fraction before his attention snapped to Iset and he smiled. "Of course, my dear, you are right."

"Thank you for stopping by, Senebtawi." She pulled the door open as far as it would go. "I am sure if my mother were feeling better she would also thank you for the figs, and wish you a very pleasant evening." If he didn't take her hint now it would be disrespectful not only to Iset, but to her mother.

The older man turned from Batr and nodded his head in acknowledgement. "My dear, it is always a pleasure to see you." He strode to her and took her hand in his. "And you know, Isetnofret, that if there is ever anything I can do for you, you must tell me. I hate to think that you are in here," Senebtawi gestured around the room but still hung onto her with one hand, "with only your brother and mother to keep you company all day."

"But there is also Dedi here at night." Iset murmured. She could feel Batr's penetrating gaze shift to her, and she questioned once again if letting him in to witness – and take part in – this exchange had been wise.

A scowl flashed across Senebtawi's face. "Dedi. That boy isn't doing enough to take care of you, Isetnofret. You're getting skinny."

Indignation flared in her and her free hand gripped the door tightly, until the edges dug into her palm. "Thank you, Senebtawi. I'm sure your bowl of figs will help with that."

His head wagged but he said, "Good night then, Isetnofret. Give my regards to your mother. *Senebti.*" *Be well.*

"*Senebti.*" She closed the door behind him and another wave of light-headedness washed over her. This time black dots appeared before her eyes. She kept her palm on the door for support and dropped her head, trying to draw in breath.

"Iset?" Batr's voice came from close by. A large hand closed over her shoulder and a spicy, masculine scent wafted around her. Unlike Senebtawi, there was no nauseating potency to Batr's redolence, just something warm and reassuring.

"I'm fine." Her voice sounded far away in her ears. She tried drawing in strength from Batr's scent, breathing deep, but that just caused a bewildering, tingling surge to sweep through her and over the surface of her skin.

"Iset," she heard the concern as he gently tugged her around to face him.

She turned her face up to him, but the black spots in her vision made his face fuzzy. "I'm fine. Truly." She shook his hand off her shoulder and took a few steps into the room. "I just need to…" But she didn't get to finish her sentence. Her vision went dark and the floor slipped out from under her.

Batr caught the woman just before she collapsed to the ground. Even as he feared for her well-being he noticed how very light she was. Lighter than a shift of wheat. He laid her down on the wide bench at the far end of the room then went in search of water.

A minute later, having found the kitchen area, he was back with a bowl of lentil mash, a mug of barley beer, a bowl of water, and strips of linen. He dipped the linen into the cool liquid and gently swiped around her forehead. "Nofret." *Beautiful*, he used the latter half of her name. "Nofret, wake up."

Batr knelt by the bench and dabbed at her neck, letting his gaze trail over her in her unguarded state, checking to make sure Senebtawi hadn't left a mark on her. He'd overheard her arguing with the older man as he approached her hut. Batr was not, as a rule, one to sneak around women's windows. But he'd heard his name, and then the tone of Iset's voice had reminded him of the last time he'd left a woman alone with a dangerous man.

It was during his early days as one of the queen's guard. He'd been ordered by the pharaoh himself to leave him and the queen alone in a room, and then the bastard hit her, knocking her down and almost causing her to lose her unborn child. Batr was on hand a few days later to assist his close friend Bey, Captain of the Royal Guard, in killing the pharaoh in order to protect the queen. Batr had no love for men who took what they wanted from women by force, and he'd listened just long enough to know that Senebtawi was the type of man a woman ought to be wary of.

Last night he'd thought Iset an exceptionally beautiful woman. The liveliness in her eyes and the expressiveness of her lips had been fascinating to watch. Now unconscious, her slack face appeared much younger. Sweeter, even. Batr brushed a lock of curling hair from her face, letting it slide through his fingers, soft as the downy fur of a kitten. A last ray of sunlight coming through the window highlighted reddish tints in her hair he hadn't noticed before. He imagined it would look almost fiery at daybreak, as Ra pushed the sun up onto the horizon.

The one thing the old bastard Senebtawi was right about earlier was that Isetnofret looked too thin. He wondered if she was sick, or just not eating. She'd hardly touched her food last night, and if she was going without it would explain her falling unconscious. Dark circles marred her under-eyes, bluish-purple against her smooth, fawn-coloured skin. Batr swept a thumb over her cheekbone, cradling her pale face in his dark-skinned palm.

Her full lips were slightly parted and their delicate pink colour reminded him of the kair fruit that grew in the sand of his homeland. The trees grew up strong, thriving without water in the heat of the desert where little else survived. Their flowers were a spectacular bright coral-orange on mostly leafless green stems, and the small fruit matured into a soft pink, sometimes a red. From all that he'd gathered about her, he likened Iset to a kair tree. With little to nourish her, a useless father, a sick mother, and lost siblings, she had grown up resilient. And yet there was a vibrant sweetness to her.

Batr's analogy almost stopped when he recalled that kair fruits were actually incredibly bitter in their natural state. They had to be skinned first, then soaked in water with something to sweeten them. The fruits were also difficult to pick, thanks to the sharp thorns. Then he decided the comparison was rather apt. Iset was beautiful to look at, but thorny and a little dangerous. He hoped that, perhaps with a little assistance on his part, the innate goodness he sensed in her would have the opportunity to overcome her adversities. He wondered what his brother Makae would say if he knew that Batr was thinking this way about a woman. No doubt he'd be amused to no end.

Clearing his throat, he tried again. "Iset. Wake up." He shook her shoulder gently. She made a soft noise of protest and rolled on to her side towards him. She tucked one fist near her face, and her other hand reached out. When her fingers brushed his bare chest, she splayed her palm across it, sliding her hand over his skin. His groin tightened, and he shifted a little, trying to relieve his discomfort even as his gaze hooked on the sensual swell of her mouth.

He had the urge to fold the woman back up into his arms and bury his nose in her jasmine-scented hair. Then force her to do nothing but eat and sleep for a week, preferably in his bed. Whatever was going on in this family, he was going to find out.

Batr folded his hand over hers on his chest.

"Nofret." He whispered, leaning towards her. "Come on now, please wake up." If she didn't wake up soon he'd either have to force-feed her or leave her to go find a healer, an option he wasn't keen on.

She opened her eyes just a crack. "Mmmm," she mumbled. Her lips curved in a sweet smile, and the tightness in his groin spread up into the pit of his belly. He cursed himself for still finding her so appealing, unconscious as she was, even as he feared for her well-being.

"Nofret, *please* wake up." He gave her another gentle shake.

"Mmm?" Her eyelids fluttered, then opened wide, startled. As if she'd just realized he was actually there. She held his gaze for a moment before looking down to stare at her hand, still splayed over his chest beneath his fingers. "Oh!" She exclaimed, "I…" she trailed off, flushing prettily and biting her lower lip. But she didn't pull away.

At that moment, the door burst open and Ahmose burst into the room like a sandstorm. "Iset, you'll never believe how fun it was! We were playing with – oh, hullo Batr! What're you – oh! Everything all right there, Iset? What's going on?"

She snatched her hand from Batr's chest and pushed herself upright while Batr instinctively twisted away from her.

"I – uhm – nothing, darling." Iset smiled at Ahmose. "Everything's fine. I was just feeling a little tired and, ah, Batr was keeping me company. Why don't you go get yourself some dinner, and I'll join you – oh, say in a few minutes? I just need to finish up here with Batr."

"Batr's not staying?" Ahmose deflated a little.

"I – I don't think…" Her glance flitted between Batr and Ahmose, a trapped look on her face.

"I cannot stay, little man." Batr interjected, recovering his senses. "I'm sorry. I only stopped by for a few moments to invite Dedi out tonight. I'm going to meet some of the other workers at a tavern, the House of Hent, and thought he might like to join. *However,*" he stressed as Ahmose's expression shifted from deflated to crestfallen, "I *also* wanted to invite you all to join me tomorrow for the Horus Festival. Work on the tombs will be halted for the next two days for the festival, and I thought you might like to go down to the water and watch the god being transported along the little iteru."

About a twenty-minute walk from the village there was a small offshoot of the great river. There, men fished and bathed and rowed along the waters. Once a year, in honour of his birthday, the Horus god was transported from the temple along the water and back again. If anyone in the household came along with him, and he was hoping at least one of them would be Iset, it would be an opportunity to learn more about whatever was happening in this house, and perhaps in the tombs as well.

Ahmose's face lit up like the sun breaking through the clouds after a desert windstorm. "Oh, by the gods! Yes! Iset, please say we can go!" He hopped from side to side. "I've never seen the Horus god transported. I've heard they send oil wicks in boats along the waters, and it is all lit up. And there will be food, Iset, so much food, and you know the governor and the Lady Ahaneith provides it so we can eat all we like. Just think! And singers and dancers and so many things to see. Please say we can go. Please, please, please. Pleeeeease."

Iset blinked. She spread her fingers wide before pressing them on her thighs. Batr could see she was still weak and trying to get her bearings, although she'd valiantly lied to her brother a moment ago about her well-being. "Just – let me think about it a little, Ahmose. All right? I'll let you know before you go to bed. But please, right now, I just need a minute with Batr, okay?"

The boy made a long, wet blowing sound through his lips. "Isseettt, come oonnnn."

"Enough, Ahmose. Go get something to eat and I'll talk to you when I'm done."

"Okay, in a minute. But I wanted to tell you, you know how you asked me to look for something of *Yet's* this morning? I found something in the back..."

"That's enough, Ahmose!" Iset's voice was sharp, cutting the boy off before he could tell them what he'd found. Ahmose looked stunned, and Iset's voice softened, "That's enough for now, Ahmose. You can tell me later what you found, all right? Please, just give me a few minutes."

Batr, curious to know what the boy had found that could upset Iset so much, decided it was best to bide his time rather than pushing for answers. He winked at the boy, who mustered a small smile in return before turning and huffing out of the room.

Iset moved to stand but Batr pushed her back down with a hand on her shoulder. "No. When was the last time you ate a full meal?"

"I don't know." Impatience crept into her voice. "Last night, maybe? I've been very busy."

"You hardly ate last night. I watched you. Try again."

She puffed out an irritated noise. "Maybe yesterday at lunchtime, then. I had some bread and barley beer at lunch. I don't know." She shrugged, frowning in annoyance. "Why?"

Why in the name of all the gods was she not eating? He stifled a growl of frustration, wishing he knew more about her, but knowing enough to understand she had much to occupy her mind. "You need to eat something, or you won't be able to keep up with us tomorrow at the festival. Here." He handed her the bowl of mash he'd brought in earlier.

She took the food but raised an eyebrow. "Who says we're going to the festival with you?"

"I do. But you're only allowed to join us if you eat something." He placed his fingertips under the hand that held the bowl and nudged it towards her lips. "Go on, have a spoonful. Let me see you do it so I know you're going to eat."

She gave him a mutinous glare, but he just folded his arms and jerked his chin at the bowl to urge her on. She scooped up a spoonful and stuck it in her mouth. Then, with lips wrapped tight around the wooden spoon, she had the audacity to smirk at him.

He chuckled and shook his head. "Woman, you are something else. But if you don't consume that bowl of mash, I promise I will sit here all night and watch you until you do." He wondered if he would actually risk losing the opportunity to uncover the tomb robbers for the sake of making this woman eat. He suspected he just might.

"Well, in that case I better get eating, or I'll never get rid of you."

"You wound me deeply with your words, Nofret." He put a hand solemnly over his heart and shook his head. "But I'm man enough to take it. I understand that you're just trying to cover up your deep and burning desire for me. You needn't be shy with me." He placed a reassuring hand on her knee and gave her his best innocent expression. Relief that she seemed to be well enough to be snarky made him giddy. He said, "You needn't fear rejection, Nofret. I am willing to accept your advances."

She brandished her lentil-laden spoon at him even though he detected a blush creeping into her fair cheeks. "Be careful, Batr. Right now my burning desire is to see you wearing this mash you so desperately want me to eat."

He grinned. "I'll wear anything you like if you come tomorrow, Nofret." He liked calling her by that moniker. It suited her well, and he savoured the intimate feeling of being able to refer to her as *Beautiful* at any time. For good measure, he added, "Or, if you prefer, I can wear nothing at all."

Her lips pursed in a parody of anger, and his grin widened. "Come. I'll behave. I promise. Mostly," he shrugged one shoulder and winked.

Her expression shifted. "I don't know… my mother has been ill…"

"Come. Your mother will be all right for a few hours. She can come if she is feeling well, or invite one of the neighbours to watch her. The widow Neb-tawy, perhaps."

Iset's spoon stopped mid-way to her mouth as her head jerked up. "You know her?"

He beamed. "Is it possible for anyone to pass through town without that woman stopping them to talk?"

She snorted softly, a hint of a smile playing on her lips. "No. I suppose not. Perhaps you are right about tomorrow."

"Of course I am." His palm still rested on her leg, just above her knee. She seemed not to notice and he was reluctant to move it. "I'll just be there to ensure that you enjoy yourself and don't fall unconscious again. Not that I mind holding you in my arms, nebet-i, but I think we'd both prefer you to be conscious next time I lay you on a mattress."

Her cheeks flamed a fetching shade of pink that made her appear younger and more alert. She made an exasperated sound in her throat as she finished chewing a mouthful of food. "If I promise to finish this bowl of food, will you leave me in peace?"

"Do you promise to come tomorrow night?"

"Are you always so insistent?"

"Are you always so stubborn?"

"Yes. Yes, I am."

Batr broke out into laughter. "Honesty. I like that in a woman."

The smile in Iset's thick-lashed eyes faded and her gaze dropped to the bowl in her hands. "I'll come with you tomorrow." She said quietly. "But if you don't mind, I'd like to finish this on my own now."

"Of course." Batr rose and walked to the door. He pulled it open, but turned back to her and said, a little more formal than he'd intended, "Please tell Dedi he's welcome to join me tonight in the House of Hent, the tavern near the edge of the village. And I look forward to seeing you tomorrow before sunset." He gave her a stiff bow before stepping out into the sunset and closing the door behind him.

Just before he shut the door, he thought he saw her eyes narrow and her jaw take on a determined set. He wondered what in the living world was going through her mind. Whatever it was, he was fairly convinced that Iset was hiding something, and he wasn't going to stop until he found out what.

Chapter 6 – In the Court of Abdju

Two days earlier

Makae studied the tall woman on the other side of the performance square. He had a good view of her from his position in front of the raised platform in the centre of the palace courtyard. It was the evening of Lady Ahaneith's banquet, a pre-celebration for the Horus Festival set to begin in three days' time. Now that the meal was over, a hundred or so nobles milled about the palace courtyard, twining their way past coils of burning incense and flickering torches pressed into the hardened earth. Everyone was dressed in their finest. Both men and women wore chains of gold or strings of coloured beads draped from their heads, necks, arms, and legs. Wigs, braided in elaborate loops and adorned with precious stone beads, perched atop shaved heads, while fresh, white linen shentis and robes glowed against the deepening sky.

Raia had caught Makae's eye more than once throughout the entertainment portion of the evening and subsequent dinner. She stood out amongst the shorter, more narrowly-built people of Kemet the same way Makae and his twin brother Batr often did. Clothed in a long white linen robe with a shawl draped over her shoulders, she wore a thick gold collar around her neck and gold hoops over her ears. Earlier in the evening, her jewellery had reflected dazzling rays of dying sunlight, and now threw back glints of fiery red and orange from the torch flames. When she smiled, her teeth flashed a bright white against her smooth, brown-black skin.

It was as he'd suspected yesterday. On such a night as this, surrounded by her friends, she looked more relaxed, happier, and even more striking than when he'd seen her the day before. Other women might be cowed under such a burdensome height as hers, but she did not hunch to hide it. She stood as straight as one of the columns ringing the palace courtyard, shoulders back, chin up high. Graceful and powerful in appearance, she dwarfed those around her not just with her size, but with the strength of her presence. She was, in a word, magnificent.

His official duties with the Lady Ahaneith – the deceased Pharaoh Wadj's second and lesser wife, and the woman who ruled the lands to the south of Thinis – had kept him occupied with other business since he'd last seen Raia. But tonight, now that the feast was over, he was free to move about, and to speak to Raia. He wanted to ask her if she recalled anything more about her father's dispute with the neighbouring landholder and if she'd thought of anyone else who could be involved. But Makae was not one to fool himself either; he knew well that he was looking for an excuse to talk to Raia simply because he found her a fascinating woman, one worth knowing better.

"I cannot decide if he is handsome or just intriguing because he is so strange. But he must be some sort of foreign nobility, is he not?" Twosre mused, looking past Raia to the man standing at the base of the dais. Short, sturdy, and full-breasted, her friend Twosre had been staring in a less-than-subtle fashion across the courtyard for some time now.

Raia didn't need to turn to see who Twosre spoke of. She'd seen him plenty over the course of the evening already. Makae was hard to miss, seated as he was on the raised platform next to the Lady Ahaneith throughout the meal. In fact, Raia was trying to avoid looking at him. Each time she did, a discomfiting sensation rose up in her stomach. Once, he'd caught her gaze, and his eyebrows raised just a fraction of a finger width, as they did when he'd first noticed her looking at his thighs yesterday. The initial shock of meeting his eyes slammed through her with all the strength of a staff wielded by Sekhmet, the lion-headed goddess of war, and she'd looked away in haste, pretending to be scanning the crowd.

Lucky for her there were people enough milling about now, and everyone had had plenty of wine and beer to drink. Most were pre-occupied with discussing the gifts Lady Ahaneith had passed out earlier, as well as the fine wine imported from the northern lands. Few would notice her eyes straying to the stranger by Lady Ahaneith's side, nor would they stop to overhear her friends' chatter about him.

"Mmmm," Merti – a lovely, slender woman with wide innocent eyes – nodded, her lips compressed in thought. "He must be royalty. He has that bearing." She made a majestic gesture with her hand. "Perhaps some sort of tribal prince. That gold cuff on his arm did not come cheap, I am sure. And he's wearing *a huge knife* on his belt." Here she made a gesture with both her hands to indicate a great length.

Twosre chuckled, giving the other women a sly look through lowered lids, "I wonder what else he has that's huge?" She copied Merti's hand gesture, and the women burst into laughter.

"Oh, oh, oh! That tiger skin he's wearing around his shoulders," Merti whispered in a voice of awe, "Do you suppose he killed it with his bare hands? Or that great big knife of his?"

Raia bit her bottom lip and tried not to roll her eyes as the women giggled again, but Twosre caught the look and turned on her. "Come now, Raia, do not tell me you aren't at least a little bit curious. After all, it is *you* he's been watching all night."

Raia cleared her throat. Makae *did* look more regal than she'd first given him credit for, and it gave her quite the start. Although she'd found him unsettling yesterday, she hadn't been convinced she found him truly attractive. She'd also imagined him to be little more than a messenger. But given the gold jewellery he wore, and his seat of honour next to the Lady Ahaneith, he was probably more powerful, higher-ranking, and wealthier than she'd assumed. It shamed her to know that not only had she been less than genial to him yesterday, regardless of his station, but that she'd done it based on poor assumptions. Furthermore, he was not to blame for the desecration of her father's tomb; he was merely the bearer of bad news.

"Well?" Twosre jostled her with her shoulder. "You must be at least a little curious who he is."

"No," Raia shook her head. "I know who he is."

"You what?" Twosre, a little tipsy after several mugs of wine – six by Raia's count – leaned towards Raia too quickly and lost her balance. Taking a step forward to right herself, she knocked her forehead against Raia's shoulder. "Whoops! Sorry there, darling," Twosre patted Raia's arm while Merti stifled a giggle. "Raia, what are you not telling us? Why does he keep looking at you?"

"He's working for the queen," Raia paused. Numerous times over the course of the evening she'd been tempted to tell her friends about the defilement of her father's tomb. She had no one else to share the awful secret with, not even her brother Semer, the closest in age to her but still young and volatile. Semer would fly into a rage and swear to murder whoever was involved, but in the end he'd do nothing, and Raia would be exhausted with the effort of calming him down.

No, Makae had asked her not to speak of it and besides, Twosre was not exactly the soul of discretion, especially not when she'd been drinking. Raia recalled the cover story Makae had given her, a true one based on recent events, and said, "I believe he is assisting the Lady Ahaneith with her defences, given the recent incidents with the tribes."

"Wait," Merti cut her off, squinting as if thinking hard. "Which tribes?"

Twosre gave an exaggerated sigh. "Merti, do you not pay attention to *anything* that happens outside of Abdju? Some of the clans to the south are acting up. A few of our stupid soldiers were drunk, and accosted some tribeswomen down there. There was a fight, and men were killed, Merti, on both sides. It is rather important, since there've been raids on the southern towns ever since, some not very far from here. Really, do you mean to tell me if a group of painted tribesmen showed up in your back courtyard threatening rape and murder, you'd have no idea why they were there?"

"I pay attention," Merti muttered, looking injured. "I always know what's going on in Thinis."

"Pfft," Twosre scoffed. "Only because you want to know all the court gossip and hear what the queen wore so you can copy it!" She turned to Raia, slurring her words slightly. "So tell me, what does that fine piece of military man over there have to do with all this, and with you?"

Sympathizing with Merti for Twosre's harsh, yet somewhat justified, tirade, Raia wasn't pleased that the conversation turned back to her again. She doled out details sparingly. "I… there's not much to do with me, really. I just met him briefly yesterday."

"Oh?" Twosre grinned and waggled her eyebrows suggestively. "Do tell."

"It was nothing," Raia waved a hand. "He only came by my *yet*'s to ask if I felt my farms were in any danger of raiders."

Merti gripped her forearm and blinked up at her. "Raia! He's perfect for you! He's like a… a great big giraffe!"

Raia snorted at the inference. "Thank you, Merti. That's kind of you to say."

"Oh!" Merti's hand flew to her mouth, but it didn't cover the reluctant smile that grew behind her fingers. "I didn't mean it like *that*, only that you are so tall and he is so tall, and would it not be nice to find a man taller than you?"

Twosre scoffed. "Or just a man at all?"

"What is that supposed to mean? Are you saying I cannot find one?" Raia's eyes narrowed at her friend, who stood a little unsteady on her feet. The long braided loops of Twosre's wig swung slightly as she swayed forward and back to an uneven beat. Raia herself had had a few mugs of wine and was not as steady on her feet as usual. It couldn't be helped, as it would be rude to turn away the servants when they came to refill one's glass. Drunkenness was a sign of appreciation of one's host. And after the shock of yesterday, she could certainly use an extra mug or two of wine.

"What I meant, Raia, is that you have not been with a man in ages." Twosre lifted her wine mug and took a long sip. "I mean, have you even had a man since Imhotep passed away, what is it now? Three years ago?"

If Raia were the sort to blush, now would be the time for it. Instead, she said shortly, "No. And I do not want one."

"Mmm, mmm, mmm," Twosre swivelled her head in an exaggerated shake. "I always thought Imhotep was a little on the dull side. If he'd been any good in bed, you would know what you are missing."

"Twosre!" Merti gasped. "You cannot speak ill of Raia's husband like that."

Raia opened her mouth to defend Imhotep, and then thought better of it. Their love-making had been… *functional.* Emotions did not factor into their marriage, one arranged almost from birth. She and Imhotep were companionable enough, she supposed, but Raia had to admit – albeit with some guilt – that Imhotep had never inspired any strong emotions in her, or she in him.

Twosre was unrepentant, "No. I am not speaking ill of Imhotep. I am sure he was a fine husband. But he evoked all the passion of a bowl of yesterday's mashed barley left out on the rooftop overnight. If Raia had ever had a good strong man between her thighs she wouldn't be saying right now she doesn't need one." Twosre gyrated her full hips for emphasis.

Her words made Raia recall how she'd been caught staring at Makae's thick, dark thighs yesterday, and before she could stop herself, the words slipped out. "They're tattooed."

"What are?" Merti frowned at her. "Your thighs? Since when? Is that a new fashion?"

"No! His. Makae's. His calves have tattoos on them. So do his cheeks."

"Oooh," her willowy friend stuck her chin forward and squinted past Raia at Makae, as if Merti could see his tattoos through the evening gloom and all the way across the courtyard. "Do they mean something?"

Leaning closer to Raia, the voluptuous Twosre jostled her again. In a loud, conspiratory whisper, she said, "I think you should sleep with him."

Merti turned to Twosre, a little wine sloshing over the edge of her mug, not giving Raia an opportunity to negate Twosre's suggestion. "Really? But isn't he here just temporarily?"

"All the better!" Twosre declared, toasting her mug into the air for emphasis. "She needn't worry about his will imposing on her life. You, Raia, can take lovers as you choose. I know that if I were in your situation, darling, and a man who looked like *that* was looking at me the way he has been looking at you, I would not be standing here now. I would be in a dark corner of this courtyard with my hands down his shenti by now." Merti gasped and Raia couldn't help but let out a bark of laughter. Twosre continued, declaring, "He looks like a lion, ready to mate."

"By Ra, I hope not!" Raia snorted. "I have seen cats mating, it does not look pleasurable. At least not for the female."

"You know what I mean!" Twosre waved her free hand dismissively. "Listen to me, Raia, you really ought to have intense sexual encounters with *that* man before he leaves Lady Ahaneith's court." Her arm shot out awkwardly behind her and waved a finger in Makae's direction. Or at least, where Makae *had* been before the talk turned to feline copulation.

Merti giggled before asking Raia hesitantly, a touch of concern creeping into her voice, "Would you? I mean, maybe it would make you feel better. You work so hard and never take time to enjoy yourself. Sometimes a woman needs to *feel* like a woman, not just someone's mother or sister or daughter. Maybe it *is* time you considered taking a lover."

"Herit!" Dung droppings, Twosre swore softly, her gaze fixed behind Raia. Merti gasped, muttering another of her "Ooohs," and Raia twisted around to see what they were looking at.

In doing so, she smacked the back of her hand against something hard. Her fingers were caught up in a firm grip, and it was her turn to blink in surprise. Raia's natural inclination was to look down at the shorter people around her, and therefore as she turned her lowered eyes rested on a set of burnished, brown collarbones. Lifting her gaze, she found Makae looking down at her.

Still holding her hand, he bowed low over it and, when he stood, she was sure she saw amusement hovering in the corner of his dark eyes. "Nebet-i," he murmured in a voice as smooth and rich as date syrup. "It is a pleasure to see you again."

Raia remained speechless for a moment as her heart took up a heavy pounding in her chest and an unfamiliar heat flooded down to the space between her legs. Then, unwilling for him to see her in yet another embarrassing situation, she drew herself up to her full height and inclined her head in a cool greeting.

"Good evening, *tayi neb,*" Merti was the first to speak, drawing Makae's attention and giving Raia a moment to collect herself. Merti called him *my lord*, and Raia wondered if he merited the title. She wished she had been less haughty in her welcome, but something about him made it difficult for her to behave herself around him.

Makae introduced himself to the other ladies and Merti – with her typical eagerness – said, "Tayi neb, we were just discussing your work with Lady Ahaneith and the tribes in the south. Raia tells us you are doing… interesting things. What is it, exactly, that you are doing again? With the tribes?" Merti trailed off, her eyebrows drawn together in confusion.

For her part, Raia wished she could sink into the ground and let the sands of the desert close over her head. Makae's eyebrows had, once again, lifted just a fraction of a finger's width, and his gaze turned to her. There was little doubt he'd made the connection between the conversation he'd interrupted and Merti's quick mention of his work. Never mind sinking into the sand, she'd like to throttle her dear, silly little friend. Raia couldn't look at Makae. Instead, she bit down on her lips and focused on a pair of women walking across the performance square.

Makae took up Merti's question, answering in his rich voice, though Raia could hear the hint of a smile in his words. "Yes, there are *interesting* things happening in the south. I have been in conference the better part of yesterday and today with Lady Ahaneith and her advisors to discuss security matters and, in particular, the safety of the people here in Abdju."

He spoke this with a pointed look at Raia, as if by way of explanation for not updating her on his investigation into her father's tomb raiding. The implied intimacy sent a thrill through her, and she pressed her thighs together, the sensation between them growing uncomfortable.

Catching the silent exchange, Twosre leaned towards him with a suggestive smile. "Tell me, tayi neb, what exactly qualifies you to advise our Lady Ahaneith in such matters?"

Makae inclined his head good-naturedly, acknowledging her question and ignoring the innuendo. "I have some experience with sea and desert warfare, nebet-i. I was a nomad – a tribesman – in my youth, and during my time as a soldier in the military here I've spent quite a bit of time in the desert. I was also a sailor, and travelled along the great Iteru and the great northern sea."

"My, that *is* impressive. But do you not think we are safe here?" Twosre asked. "What about the garrison in Ta-Senet? The governor there controls the traffic and the trade coming north. Surely he can stop any attacks long before they reach Abdju."

Nodding, Makae said, "It is true the governor there is excellent, and very loyal to the queen. I met with him last year when it became necessary to remove the queen there for her safety."

It was a well-known story by now, how Sekhrey Bey and his group of loyal pirates had saved Queen Merneith from a kidnapping plot. Knowing Makae had been a part of that group of trusted men gave Raia pause. Clearly he was even more capable and high-ranking than she'd suspected.

He continued, "Queen Merneith has every confidence in the governor. However, there are other ways to reach Abdju, and a skilled trekker might still find a way around those massive cliffs that separate the Land of the Dead and the city of Abdju from the desert. We have been trying to determine where we might need extra guards – and whether another desert outpost might be necessary."

Merti, who had been fixating on the large, curved blade at Makae's hip, now asked him, "Would it not be best just to go to war with the tribes? Surely we are the stronger, and could best the savages."

Makae's swift intake of breath didn't escape Raia. Merti, Raia thought, had probably offended the former tribesman with her unintended slight. When he answered, his voice was calm and even, but she sensed his stiffness. "I understand how the tribesmen feel. Their autonomy and their women have both been dishonoured. Slaughtering people who have become enemies through one's own error does not bring peace or submission, only furthered resentment and renewed aggression. We must find a way to negotiate without compromising our own security. It is the honourable thing to do."

It was a surprisingly compassionate, level-headed opinion, and in response Twosre pushed her lips out and raised her eyebrows in a rather comical expression, nodding to indicate she was impressed. Then, knowing how important loyalty and honour were to Raia, Twosre turned her look to Raia and exaggerated it further, as if to say *Did you hear that?*

Raia responded by narrowing her eyes at her friend, before saying to Makae in a kinder tone than she'd used before, "You speak like a true tactician. I see why the Lady Ahaneith might find you useful here. Not all of our nobles have such an understanding of these matters."

He turned his dark eyes to hers and a long moment passed, during which she was held captivated by his probing gaze. Finally, his expression softened into a smile so slight it was little more than a shift in his eyes and a marginal upturning of one corner of his mouth. That slight smile was enough to cause her stomach to flutter and heat to pool between her thighs. She found her own lips turning up in response.

Merti's voice cut through the moment. "Tayi neb, you have recently arrived from Thinis, correct? Might I ask you a question about the current court attire? Do you happen to recall what the queen wore the first day she introduced the court to our new baby pharaoh?"

Over the next several minutes Raia found it amusing, and more than a little appealing, to see how Makae effortlessly navigated around Twosre and Merti's questions. At no point did he scorn Merti's trivial comments, or rise to Twosre's thinly veiled innuendos. Instead, he remained politely agreeable. But every now and then his eyes would meet hers, and that breathless sensation swept through her again, until she began to fear there was something wrong with her. Heat flushed her cheeks despite the chill night air, and she was sure the wine was making her giddy.

After some time had passed and there was a lull in the conversation as Merti sipped her wine, Makae stepped near her side and said, "Nebet-i, I hoped it might be possible to speak with you alone again soon."

As soon as the words were out of his mouth, Twosre, who was facing the other way, twisted her head around in an owl-like gesture, and remarked, "Why not walk her home after the banquet? Gods forbid some of those southern tribesmen attack while she is on her way home *all alone*."

Raia wanted to kick her well-intentioned and less-than-subtle friend, but settled for a quick glare in her direction.

Inclining his head, Makae said, "It would be my honour."

While his face remained neutral, Raia was sure she saw something flicker in his eyes as he held her gaze, something warm and meaningful and unreadable, causing that uncomfortable-yet-pleasurable sensation to start up again. Raia realized she didn't want to ignore it. For once in her life, she did not want to do the practical thing. She wanted to do exactly what Twosre suggested she do earlier. She wanted to take this man to her bed.

Raia reached for her wine. She was quite sure she would need another mug or two. Perhaps three.

They took their time walking back to Raia's home, winding through the dark streets with the muffled voices of other meandering revelers filtering around them. Being less familiar with Abdju, Makae let Raia lead him through the lesser-used routes where the streets were darker and less populated so that they could speak uninterrupted and unheard. The night was filled with the scent of myrrh and cardamom incense, wafts of perfume from passing nobles, and the braying of donkeys. More than once they caught sight of a drunken nobleman, perched unsteadily on the back of an unfortunate donkey led by a young servant, the hooves making soft thumping sounds on the hard-packed earth.

"I intend to question Userkare tomorrow." Makae inclined his head towards Raia as he mentioned the neighbouring land-owner; the man Raia's father had warned his children away from.

Slowing her step, Raia placed her hand on his forearm, bringing him to a halt. "I should like to come with you." It wasn't so much of a query as a statement.

Makae paused as his gaze searched her face, considering whether to relent or insist she remain removed from his investigation. Her fingers were warm and soft on his skin, and she was just beginning to pull her hand away when he caught it up, tucked it into the crook of his arm, and resumed walking.

He nodded, looking ahead. "I think it is a good idea if you come, actually. We can tell him you are managing your *yet*'s affairs and wanted to clear up any business that might be left unfinished between them."

They spent a few minutes working out the details of their excuse for speaking to Userkare and then moved on to discuss Raia's father. Makae said, "I have heard that you are very capable with your lands. How is it that you came to be in control of not just one, but two properties?"

A smile flickered across her normally stoic face, and she raised one eyebrow. "You are not investigating *me*, are you?"

He found this playful aspect of her to his liking, and he grinned. "Of course not. But it is not in the common way for a woman." He held up one hand to fend off her anticipated argument when she turned to him. "I have no problem with it. I could not do it half so well; I have no knowledge of farm management. I am only curious about how you came by it."

He steadily held her regard until the suspicion in her eyes died out and she yielded. "My mother," she said, "was unable to bear any more children after my birth, and she passed away when I was seven from a lingering sickness. After she died, my *yet* taught me everything about running a farm, how to keep the accounts, how to manage the workers and the crop cycles, how to oversee the digging of the ditches to ensure even silt coverage during the season of the flood. He didn't know if he would have any sons to inherit his farms, and he wanted to ensure that I would be capable of managing the estate one day. When I was an infant he arranged my marriage with the son of the neighbouring landholder. My *yet* wanted me to be a useful partner to my husband, one who could run his estates alongside him."

Makae glanced over at Raia. She spoke matter-of-factly, but he could see the quiet pride in the lift of her chin and the steadiness of her gaze despite the note of sadness in her voice. She clearly had a considerable amount of respect for her father.

Her younger brother, Semer, she explained, did not have the same knowledge of estate management that she did. At fourteen he was almost at an age to take over his father's estates, but her father had been too ill over the past year to teach the boy much. Instead, Raia had taken over most of the work, and she feared her brother lacked the initiative to learn.

"Perhaps it is time he married," she mused. "I do not know how else to make him see the necessity of putting aside his hunting hounds for a time and pay attention. He is hunting mad, and cannot seem to think of anything else."

"Your *yet* re-married and had Semer, then?" Makae asked.

Raia nodded. "Yes, but his second wife had little to do with my upbringing. As a child, I spent my time in the fields and my *yet*'s work room, and then when I turned thirteen I moved to my husband's house. We were married almost seven years before Imhotep's accident. He fell from the top stairs of the granary one day and did not survive long after that."

While Makae registered the melancholy in her voice, it did not strike him as the lasting mourning of a lover. Her marriage sounded more like a business arrangement than a love-match. Not at all unusual, but he wondered how Raia felt about it. He couldn't help but notice that she had drawn nearer to him as they spoke. Her fingers still rested comfortably in the crook of his arm, and occasionally as they walked her hip bumped against his, or his arm brushed the side of her breast. She didn't pull away when that happened, but seemed to press a little more closely. He didn't think she was conscious of her actions, or the effect it could have on a man, but beneath her tightly controlled exterior he sensed a deep well of emotion, one he'd caught a glimpse of yesterday, and then again tonight when their eyes met across the courtyard. What would it take to excite her passion, to engage her emotions?

Rather than ask such a private question, however, he pursued the matter of her father. "Do you suppose the tomb theft could have anything to do with your *yet*'s fields? Could it be possible that a disgruntled slave or servant was somehow involved?"

"No." Her answer was firm, without hesitation. "My father was a good man. He had no enemies."

Makae took in the firm set of her jaw, the tight line of her lips, and the challenge in her eyes, and decided not to press his point. He doubted the truth of her words, but he didn't doubt that she, at least, believed what she was saying. The best of men could unwittingly make enemies. A man in

Ra-hotep's powerful position undoubtedly had more than one or two.

For all he knew, tomorrow's meeting with Userkare might prove her wrong. If that happened then Makae, at least, would not be the one on the receiving end of her disapproving glare. And so he once again turned the conversation back to the one thing she seemed most comfortable talking about – her farms.

"So tell me," he said, resting his hand on hers on his arm, "what does a lady-landowner do with her days?"

As she answered, Makae listened with growing interest. It was not so much the details of farm management that drew his attention, but the way in which Raia spoke of them. He hadn't imagined a woman like Raia spending time walking the fields, ensuring the crops were planted properly and the ditches dug for watering, taking part in the day to day toils of running vast farmlands. But she spoke of her lands in detail, as one intimately familiar with them. While she might not know the names of any of the tomb workers who received her grain, she knew how many of them did. How many seeds were harvested, how many debens of grain were in her granaries, such details were of import to her. She didn't see him smile when she spoke of these numbers, but he was impressed. He liked the pitch of her husky voice reciting sums and figures. Numerals, apparently, were another thing that incited her passion.

Raia was surprised that she found it so easy to speak to Makae about her situation. She supposed the wine had, in part, loosened her tongue, though she wasn't as tipsy as she'd been earlier – time had helped her to sober, as had the cool night air. She welcomed the opportunity to talk about her father, something she dared not do with any of her friends, or even her much-younger siblings, out of fear that the reality of her burdens would overwhelm her if she spoke them out loud. She also couldn't bear to hear inane, quasi-sympathetic murmurings directed her way. However, despite being so tall and striking, Makae was calm and unobtrusive.

His presence eased her qualms and she found herself sharing her most pressing concerns.

"And you have all the children now, as well as managing both estates?" Makae asked, his forearm strong and muscled and warm beneath the palm of her hand.

"Yes," she answered. "And I have my two youngest brothers and one sister with me. Six children in total with my own three. Semer lives on my *yet*'s estate, but I am there most mornings to deal with his affairs. My younger sister Abar is twelve now and she helps quite a bit with the children. But she is destined to marry soon when her monthly cycles begin. My *yet* arranged it before his passing. We have slaves and servants who help, of course, but I would prefer to have more time with the children."

Although Makae did not say anything, she took his raised eyebrows and slight nod to indicate his understanding. When they arrived at the gate to her courtyard, she found herself asking him in for a glass of wine. A sense of giddiness washed over her when he smiled down at her and said, "I would like that very much."

Before she'd left for the evening, she'd told the servants to take the evening off after they attended to the children. Knowing she'd be out late, she'd also told the children not to wait up for her, promising to provide them with all the details of the banquet in the morning. Raia was well aware that they would be entering a dark, quiet room when she opened the door and let Makae into her home.

He stepped past her into the main greeting room, and she shut the door to the outside behind her. Rather than moving into the room she stayed where she was, her back to the door, taking a moment to set her nerves in order. It had been a long time since she'd slept with a man, and then it had only ever been her husband. She had no idea how to go about making it happen. Would he know that was what she wanted? Would he find her lacking in some way?

As her eyes adjusted to the pitch blackness of the room, she sensed rather than saw Makae's tall, broad form in front of her. She reached a hand out and her palm found his naked chest, beneath the leopard skin that draped his shoulders. He stepped closer, and her heart took up a painful thumping in her breast while she held her breath.

His face materialized before her, and she could see that the slightest of smiles played across his lips. He covered her hand on his chest, wrapping his fingers over hers, and she let herself be pulled to him until he circled an arm around her waist. The house was cool, the night air blowing under a gap in the door, and he tucked her against his body, heat emanating from his hard, bare chest that warmed her down to her toes.

She inhaled his spicy scent and her body melted a fraction more against his. Makae's eyes gleamed with intensity as he held her gaze, lowering his head and slanting his mouth over hers. Then she closed her eyes and gave herself up to the tingling sensation that coursed through her. His lips on hers were sure, yet soft; softer than she'd imagined from a man like him. She wanted *more*, to be closer, to feel his warmth against her skin, his arms around her, his strong thighs against her.

She ran her hands over his muscled biceps as he gripped her waist and pulled her tighter to him. Her head fell back to allow her to press alongside him and not lose contact as their kiss deepened. He flicked his tongue over her lips and she opened her mouth to him, tasting him in return. One of his hands slid up her side, coming so very, very near to the edge of her breast. When he stopped a hair's span too soon she was frustrated enough to turn into his palm. Abandoning all practical considerations, her body seemed to want him to know how much she wanted him.

As if the slow undulation of her body against him wasn't clear enough, Raia made her desires much more obvious when, taking his hand, she led him to her room and reached back to undo the tie of her robe, letting the fabric slide off her shoulders to puddle on the floor at her feet. She proceeded to prove to herself that for once in her life she could forget about the numbers and focus on something that brought her pure enjoyment.

Chapter 7 – In the House of Hent

Iset stood in the darkness outside the House of Hent, adjusting the scarf around her face to ensure it draped over her nose to conceal her face yet hung loose enough to enable her to slip a mug of wine or beer beneath it to sip on. Furthermore, she needed a moment to steel herself. It wasn't her first time in the tavern. She'd been there once before with her father, not long after she'd first taken on the role of Dedi. As a woman, she'd never go to a place like the House of Hent. It simply was not something women in her village did, except for those who worked there, of course, and Hent herself. But her father had said it would be unnatural for a young man such as Dedi, who was "new in town", to not socialize with the other tomb workers and village men. In a small community like theirs it would be suspicious if Dedi was never seen on the rooftop for dinner, or out drinking and playing board games with the other men. And so she'd gone out with her father from time to time to other men's homes, or to various places where they gathered. However, since her father's passing a month ago she had hardly been out at all, and never had she been to the tavern alone.

The thought of pulling open the door and entering by herself was terrifying, but it had to be done. Batr's invitation provided an opportunity not only to find out more about him – and what his intentions were – but also an opportunity to find out who might be threatening her family. Time was running out and she had to take every chance she could, no matter how dangerous or uncomfortable, to learn what she could about the thieves and the tomb they intended to break in to.

Iset made sure her scarf was tucked tightly around her face before smoothing her sweaty palms over her father's vest, flattening out non-existent wrinkles. Short of what the thieves had already threatened her family with, she could think of little worse than having her identity discovered in the midst of a group of rough, drunken men. She glanced down, checking to make sure that her chest was sufficiently wrapped so that no noticeable bumps from her breasts protruded under her robe.

Satisfied all visible traces of Iset stayed hidden, and that she was prepared to be Dedi for the night, she took one last deep breath before pulling open the door to the House of Hent.

Stepping inside, the tavern assaulted her senses. There was the cloying scent of incense mingling with barley beer and strong wine, the general din of men drinking, a female *hnr* – a musician – playing a string instrument, dim lighting, and jarring glimpses of men's faces in the flickering oil wicks. She caught sight of a few men grinning and leering at the serving women, winking behind their backs, and that was all she needed to cause all her fears to return. *Oh gods, what if they found out who she was?*

Her heart raced, and for a moment panic almost overwhelmed her. The same light-headed feeling she'd had earlier that day, before she'd fallen unconscious, washed over her as dark spots threatened her vision. She forced herself to breathe and remember that as long as she didn't speak, no one would know who she really was. She'd sat with men in broad daylight on her lunchbreak, worked in the tombs with them, drank beer – not many, of course, she was a slight woman unaccustomed to drink, after all – but in all those times no one had known her to be anything other than Dedi, a young man with a speech problem. After a few moments she was able to assume a casual stance as she searched the room for a glimpse of Batr, or any other familiar face.

Just as she was beginning to fear she'd arrived too late and missed Batr, a hand clapped on her shoulder, startling her. "Dedi, there you are!" Batr's cheerful voice boomed next to her ear. She inclined her head in a nod and he grinned. "Glad you could make it. Come, join us! You're just in time, we've ordered another round of wine."

With one hand on her shoulder, Batr propelled her towards a group of men seated on cushions arranged around a low table. The tables were divided by grimy strips of linen stretched over wooden frames. She recognized some of the men, and as she neared she did a quick assessment to determine which available spot would put her in the most shadow, rendering her less noticeable.

Although she always tried to avoid attention when dressed as Dedi she had, however, noticed that people tended to ignore her presence anyway. For some reason people often took Dedi's muteness to also indicate deafness, as well as simplicity of mind. As if the accident that had supposedly damaged Dedi's face and throat had also rendered him incapable of critical or independent thought. From the first time she'd transformed into Dedi, Iset had become much more aware of her own actions around others. She never wanted to inadvertently hurt someone else the way that others hurt people like Dedi – by ignoring their very existence, or making them feel insignificant. However, in this instance she hoped that her silent presence might afford her the opportunity to listen and observe. If she was lucky, she might just learn something about those who threatened her.

When Batr took his hand off her shoulder, she chose a spot next to Addaya, her brother's best friend before he passed away. Addaya nodded in greeting and Iset nodded back, a pang of sadness and loss flashing through her belly. Addaya always reminded her of her brother, Sharek. There had even been a time last year when she thought Addaya might offer for her.

A serving woman, wearing nothing but a shenti wrapped around her waist and a string of cheap beads hanging over her ample breasts, brought a tray full of wine mugs. Iset took one and drank deep to fortify herself. Over the rim of her mug, she saw Batr watching her, and she quickly looked away. The warm, playful interest that filled his gaze when he looked at her as Iset was now replaced by something sharper, more probing, and possibly much more dangerous.

Of course, she should have known Batr would be altered in this setting. In the time she'd spent as Dedi around other men, she'd come to see that they behaved differently without the presence of their mothers, sisters, or children to tame their conduct. They drank to excess, touched the serving women in a too-friendly manner, and spat and snorted frequently. She'd learned that the way a man acts when he thinks a woman he wants isn't watching speaks much about his character.

On more than one occasion she'd thought that if she were to ever take a husband she'd like to see him unawares in a tavern first. She couldn't help but wonder what Batr would be like tonight.

Addaya nudged her arm with his elbow. "How's your family, Dedi? How's Isetnofret? Is she doing alright?" Iset's brother had passed away before Dedi came into being, but in her role as Dedi she'd encountered Addaya a couple of times around town. They'd also passed one another in the Land of the Dead, where Addaya worked as a brick-maker. He'd introduced himself, but there'd been little interaction between them.

Iset nodded, clearing her throat. What else could she do?

"Whassat?" One of the other men rounded a blurry eye in their direction. "Talkin' about Dedi's pretty little cousin?" His mug sloshed wine, a few red drops spilling into his lap and staining his shenti.

One corner of Addaya's lip quirked up. "Yes. Isetnofret."

The drunken man leered. "Mmmm, that's worth talking about all right. Dedi, boy, how come you haven't taken that girl yet? Something the matter with you?"

Iset blinked. Even if she wasn't feigning muteness she'd have been hard pressed to find an answer to that.

Addaya looked to her. "Yes. She *is* still unmarried, isn't she?"

Iset's belly gave an uncomfortable flop, wondering if he might still be interested in her. She gave a nod, even as an image of a hot summer's eve long-since passed came to mind. Addaya had walked her home one night when her brother had chosen to stay out later. He'd come right to the front door, placed a hand against the wall behind her, and stroked her cheek with the back of his hand. He told her he'd always thought she was pretty. Her heart had thumped, and a thrill coursed through her. From the time she was a young girl she'd found Addaya handsome, and he'd always been nice to her.

She'd spent the next month hoping something more might come of it. She'd gone to bed at night thinking how wonderful it would be to marry a man she actually liked, rather than someone like the old man her father had tried to marry her off to a few years before. Each time *that man* looked at her, she'd had to try not to grimace and hide herself from his lecherous gaze.

Her brother had died a few weeks after the night with Addaya. After that, Addaya stayed away, and Iset often wondered if the aura of sadness that settled over her house had something to do with it. She could hardly blame him if that were the case, although she ached at the thought.

The blurry-eyed man leaned closer to them and Iset caught a whiff of his fetid breath. He had a few missing teeth, and a couple in the process of rotting to black. "Did your accident damage yer cock as well as yer voice? No way I'd be living in the same place as that pretty little cousin of yours and not be givin' it to her every chance I got. Married or not." From his seated position, the man shifted his hips about in a disgusting, gyrating motion.

Addaya and some of the other men laughed. Another man chimed in, "Married? By the gods, no! Not if one has to inherit that mother of hers. I hear she hasn't left her bed in months. And her little brother doesn't even have a trade yet. I tell you what, though, I'd be happy to pay the girl to share her bed for a night or two! She's prettier than the girls that work here, that's for sure."

"Better that than paying for her family for the rest of your life, eh?" The men laughed and continued to make jokes at Iset's expense.

Mortified, her eyes flew to Batr's. He was watching her with narrowed eyes and pursed lips. She became aware that her hands were fisted at her sides, bunched into the folds of her many layers of clothing. She was shocked to find that she was wishing for a weapon, while at the same time she wanted to cry. Humiliation, anger, and betrayal burned in her. How could Addaya laugh? They were talking about his best friend's sister.

Her mind raced as she forced herself to question how a cousin like Dedi would respond to this. She wasn't strong enough to fight a single one of these men, even if they'd had a hand tied behind their backs. She wished she'd stayed home. She didn't want to want to know about Addaya, or hear the things the men said about her. She didn't want Batr hearing them either, it made her feel even worse about herself and her life.

Then Batr's voice cut smoothly through the lewd remarks. "I doubt Dedi here appreciates the way you're talking about his cousin." His lips were twisted upwards, but his eyes were a warning, and Iset saw the dangerous brigand in him again. The other men must have noticed it too, as an uncomfortable silence fell about the table. Addaya and a couple of other men threw resentful scowls at Batr, but kept their mouths shut.

Only one man snorted and grumbled, "What do you know about it, anyway? You don't even know the girl."

"As a matter of fact, I do." Batr's face was arranged in a pleasant expression, his body relaxed, but any man would be a fool not to recognize the signs of a man well-versed in fighting. Although Iset had never thrown a punch, even she could sense it in the way his shoulders rolled back and his chest expanded.

After a moment, Batr eased the tension around the table by relaxing his expression into a sly smile, and he said, "Besides, I suspect Dedi must do quite well with the ladies. We all know women appreciate a man who will listen, and it's not like they can force him to repeat back what they said. They're unlikely to ask him to talk about his feelings, either."

A few of the men chuckled, murmuring their assent.

Batr continued, "I don't see how a man could afford to marry anyway. Not with the way wages are often paid so late in the Land of the Dead, and the recent cuts." Iset breathed in relief as the men turned to griping about their rations. She shrunk back into the shadows and sipped her wine, listening to them talk.

The harvest season had been poor this past year, thanks to a low flood. Their rations of grain and beer were reduced just over a month ago. Iset resorted to giving Ahmose and her mother the larger shares of their evening meals. Coupled with stress and lack of appetite, her belt fit looser than it used to. Senebtawi's earlier remark about her skinniness had stung, but she knew it was true. If things didn't improve, she'd have to take to digging papyri roots out of the earth just so her family might have enough to eat. She could think of little more embarrassing than everyone knowing her family was starving and desperate, as people only ate papyri in times of famine. The only way she'd be able to bring herself to do it would be to sneak out under cover of darkness to run down the little iteru on the outskirts of the village. It would be time-consuming and dirty work, with little rewards.

"It's gotten so a man can't even buy himself a sweet bun anymore," one man muttered, referring to the date-sweetened buns that, although cheaper than honey buns, were still pricier than the coarse bread made from ground barley.

"Can't even get himself a wench, neither," the blurry-eyed man who'd insulted Dedi's prowess gestured to one of the serving women. The women at the House of Hent were known to do *other* sorts of business in the tiny bedrooms behind the main tavern area.

The serving woman brought two more mugs of wine over and Batr handed one to her. She hadn't seen him call for more, but he must have done it somehow. She held up her hands, shaking her head, but he was insistent. In a voice too low for most of the men to hear, he said, "Your cousin was kind to me yesterday, allowing me to intrude on their dinner. The least I can do is buy you a few drinks."

Unable to argue, she accepted with an inclination of her head. After all, it had been a difficult couple of days and work stopped for the next two days for the Horus Festival.

Batr addressed the men, "So what does a man do around here if he wants to make a little something extra?"

A familiar voice cut into the din, causing Iset to stiffen. "Depends on what a man's willing to do to get it." She darted a look at the man who'd just arrived and now stood over Batr, his brow furrowed. She didn't recognize his face, with its large, crooked nose, but she knew the loud, rough voice; it belonged to the man who'd been fooling around in the inventory hut that afternoon. She thanked the gods that she'd chosen the darkest spot at the table to sit at, and that his attention was focused on Batr, not her.

Batr raised one eyebrow and drawled, "Well I guess a man in need is willing to do just about anything to get what he wants."

"Anything, eh? Sounds like you aren't too concerned about the pharaoh's law, or disrupting *maat.*" *Maat,* the peace and order of Kemet, and the living world, might not be of interest to a group of thieves, but it was of great concern to Iset. It was one of the reasons she was so ashamed of her father's involvement in the tomb robbing. Had there been no physical punishment for the crime, she'd still fear the disruption of the order of the living world. The tomb inscriptions depicting punishments in the afterlife were no idle threats, as far as she was concerned.

"A man can't concern himself with the law when he has mouths to feed, now can he?" Batr's tone was serious and Iset blinked in confusion. He certainly didn't sound like the same man who'd told her last night that he'd left his pirating days behind. It didn't sound like the man who'd forced her to eat today, and hadn't taken advantage of her while she was unconscious. This man in front of her sounded like an opportunist. And what mouths had he to feed? He'd said he was here in Abdju alone.

"Hmph," the robber man grunted, and gave a slight nod. He kept a suspicious eye on Batr, but sat down, and the conversation amongst the group turned to other things.

Given the men's interaction, it was clear to Iset that Batr wasn't working with the tomb robbers. She wondered what his intentions towards her and Dedi were, if he somehow knew about her father, and if he wanted to find a way to get into Pharaoh Wadj's tomb on his own. Perhaps he thought he could be more persuasive with kindness, rather than threatening her. She hadn't expected a pirate to charm and confuse his prey into giving him what he sought. She'd expect him to just take it.

Iset kept hidden in the dark corner, tucked slightly behind Addaya and across from Batr, sipping at a third mug of wine. From where she sat she was able to watch him interact with the men and the serving girls. When a woman came by to bring them more drinks, Batr winked or grinned at them, and in response they cocked their heads towards the back rooms in invitation. But despite his flirting, he'd shaken his head each time until the women moved away, disappointment written on their pouty lips.

If Iset were in their line of work she wouldn't blame them. Batr was a good deal better-looking, and fitter, than any of the men in the tavern, save Addaya. Addaya was still an attractive man, but up close Iset could see that the whites of his eyes had taken on the yellow tinge of a man who drinks too much. While still strong, his belly now protruded over the top of his shenti.

Batr was much more cordial towards the serving women than the others as well, who were mostly just crass – Addaya included. At one point her brother's old friend smacked a woman on her rump as she was turning away. When she looked back with a sly smile in her eyes, he excused himself from the table and followed her into a back room. The men chuckled as he left them.

One of them shook his head and said mournfully, "That boy don't even need to pay for it sometimes, eh? Must be nice to still be young and handsome, with a strong back."

"You were never handsome, Narem." The blurry-eyed man with the missing teeth taunted Narem.

"Shut your face. At least I had all my teeth once. You've been a toothless bastard since the day you first suckled at your mother's teat," Narem shot back.

Iset slugged back the last of the wine in her mug. As she did so, her gaze strayed again to Batr. He leaned back on his cushion, resting on one elbow. His eyes were inscrutable, but steady, as he met her glance. The fear that she'd somehow betrayed herself tonight overcame her, and she decided it was time to leave. She had, at least, found out the identity of one of the tomb robbers. She also knew now that she must be on guard around Batr. He'd hinted he'd do anything to gain fortune, and she had to protect herself and her family from him.

She moved to stand from the cushions, finding them plusher than she anticipated. She made an ungraceful roll to the side, propping herself up on her hands and knees before she was able to push herself up to standing. From there, she wavered on her feet, suddenly discovering the three mugs of wine had been much more than she could readily handle. Normally it would be no more than she could manage, but lack of sleep, food, and her recent weight loss had taken their toll on her. In that moment it was as if all the blood rushed from her head to her feet, and dark spots obscured her vision.

Wanting to make a quick escape before she did something stupid and revealed herself, she motioned with her hand to indicate her exhaustion to the other men. As she did so, she lost her balance, got a foot tangled in the pillows and, with legs and arms flailing, she crashed to the floor amongst the cushions, smacking her shoulder painfully on the edge of the table and jostling the mugs of wine.

The men around her laughed and hooted. Disoriented as she was, Iset didn't immediately realize that her scarf had slipped down around her face. For a brief moment her nose, along with her eyes and forehead, were exposed. Luckily, she was facing away from the table so none of the men behind her saw, and her hands flew to fix it even as she rolled to the side to get up. Most of them were too busy cackling, and calling out, "Good boy, Dedi!" "Finally got drunk, did you?" "About time you let loose!"

A strong hand reached down and, gripping her bicep, helped pull her up. "Steady there." Batr's scent enveloped her. She shook him off, but as she tried to step around him her damnable feet tangled around themselves, and he caught her arms once more, holding her up in a firm grip.

Iset cursed herself for a fool. She was a stupid girl who'd drunk too much and thought she could get away with pretending to be a man. A stupid girl who would never marry. She wished herself home, curled up on her mattress, so that she might cry alone in peace until there was nothing left inside.

Turning to the men, Batr chuckled. "I think someone better make sure the boy gets home safely. I was on my way out anyway; I'll take him back."

"Hold on a minute," the crooked-nosed man barked, getting to his feet. Iset's heart raced. Oh gods, Batr was still griping her arm and now the man in league with the tomb robbers wanted them to stop. She wondered how far she'd make it if she tried to break free and run. *Not far*, her thoughts chimed, considering Batr was very strong and she couldn't make her feet work properly.

The other man came to stand next to Batr and said in a low voice, "I want to talk to you for a minute. Alone."

Batr nodded. With her arm firmly in hand, he led Iset to a nearby corner, then propped her against the wall. His face was tight as he growled at her, "Wait here. I'll be back in a minute. And *don't* try to move."

It was all she could do to keep herself standing. She prayed to the gods she wouldn't get sick. If she did, she'd have to remove the wrappings around her face, and that could mean the end of everything.

Batr moved a few paces away and the crooked-nosed man followed, leaning in close. Batr got a whiff of stale sweat, and he balled his hands into loose fists at his sides. He hoped the man hadn't had the same revelation that he did a moment ago when Dedi tripped. If the man knew Dedi wasn't who he appeared to be, they'd almost certainly come to blows.

The man said, "Were you serious about what you said earlier? About doing anything for work?"

Batr shrugged and hooked his thumbs into the top of his shenti. "What have you got?"

The man rubbed a palm over his jaw, glancing around him with cagey eyes. "Could maybe use a strong arm to break through some rock, and an extra arm to dig something. Something not many others know about. Understand what I'm saying?"

"Maybe. But what's in it for me?"

"Oh, it'll be worth your time. More than you'd make in a year in the Land of the Dead at least."

"All right. What's your plan?"

"Tomorrow. Meet me at the inventory hut when Ra has the sun at its highest. I'll tell you there. There's too many ears about tonight."

"All right then. Tomorrow." Batr nodded.

Either they'd be breaking into another tomb, Batr figured, or this man needed help burying a body out in the cliffs that led to the great desert. Whatever it was, he'd have to wait until tomorrow to find out. He was glad, at least, that the lure he'd cast out had worked. If he was lucky, by tomorrow he'd have hooked himself a tomb robber or two.

Batr had invited Dedi to the tavern tonight in the hopes of learning something about the tomb robbing. Instead, he'd learned something completely unexpected. And now he had to get them both out of the tavern before anyone else figured it out, too.

Outside in the cool night air, Batr tried to put things straight in his head. It was late, or rather, early in the morning, and the narrow streets were empty. The only light came from the stars above, and a sliver of moonlight. He hooked an arm around Iset's narrow waist and half-dragged, half-propped her up to help her walk. He was inclined to lift her lithe body into his arms, but if anyone *did* happen by them it would appear he was carrying a young man in an intimate fashion. He could throw her over his shoulder, but in her condition he didn't want her getting sick down his back.

Batr was both infuriated and impressed by Iset, and the conflicting emotions left him confused as to how to proceed. It all made sense now. Or at least most of it did. Batr had watched Dedi's expressive eyes all night long. First he'd marveled at how similar they were to Iset's, thinking they must be closer cousins than he'd previously thought. He'd seen hurt in those eyes when Dedi looked at Addaya, and then when the men made lewd jokes about Iset. There'd been fear, too, when the crooked-nosed man appeared. But the man had ignored Dedi, and Batr thought it unlikely they were working with one another. He'd wondered at that, and at what secrets Dedi's family was keeping. Then, when Dedi had fallen, and his scarf shifted briefly, things became clearer. There was no Dedi, only Iset.

He couldn't help but admire the woman. She'd managed to fool a village full of people who knew her well. She'd defied expectations and taken up a difficult job to support her family. She was either incredibly brave or very, very stupid. He didn't think her lacking in wit, though. He admired her tenacity. She was tough all right. But how dangerous of her to impersonate a young man in the first place. And then there was the wine; while she hadn't drank in excess, in her condition it was clearly too much.

For tonight, he decided it best to pretend he didn't know who Dedi really was. Perhaps after his secret meeting tomorrow with the tomb workers he'd be in a better position to confront Iset. At the moment, for all he knew Iset was just a lone woman struggling to help her family survive. It was possible she didn't know anything about the thefts at all. Unlikely, he thought, but possible.

Once they were a safe distance from the tavern, Batr slipped his arm out from around her and asked, "Can you walk on your own?" He peered down at the reedy figure swaying beside him.

She lifted one finger and waved it in the direction of her house. Her raspy voice slurred from under the white scarf wrapped around her little head, "S'okay." Okay, until her first solitary step resulted in her stumbling and Batr catching her in his arms again.

He sighed and hooked an arm around her, slinging her light body over his shoulder.

"Mmmph!" Her protest was blissfully muffled by the scarf around her face and Batr couldn't help but smile. He felt her chest brush against his back, and realized that she must have bound her breasts in order to hide them. Breasts that were, he'd noticed the other day, quite full despite how thin she was. Binding such beautiful body parts was a travesty, he decided. If ever there was a violation of *maat* that was it.

Once again, he thought about tying her to his bed and compelling her to do nothing but sleep and eat for a few days. By the gods, with the way she was going, she'd need a couple of weeks of rest at the very least. And once she'd done that, if she stayed willingly in his bed, well… there were other things he'd like to do as well. Things that most decidedly *did not* involve her dressed as a boy. Or dressed at all… He shook his head, pushing such thoughts aside. He chuckled to himself, knowing his brother Makae would find it terribly amusing that he was thinking this way about a girl who happened to be dressed as a boy.

A few minutes later he was standing in front of Iset's door. Although his eyes had long since adjusted to the darkness, he still had a hard time seeing the handle in the shadow of the doorway. She stirred, pushing herself a little upright against his back while he fumbled trying to open the door. He slipped her off his shoulder, helping steady her as she put her feet on the ground, and she slumped against the door frame, mumbling something that sounded like "'M fine." She flapped a hand at him, but whether it was meant as hello or goodbye he couldn't tell.

He shook his head, chuckling, and reached for the handle. But it twisted under his grasp and pulled open, knocking Iset off balance and causing Batr to grab for her waist and pull her to his side.

Ahmose stood in the darkened room, rubbing an eye with the palm of his hand. "M'hello. Whas'appened?" He mumbled.

"M'hello," Iset parroted in a muffled voice, her cloth-swaddled head lolling against Batr's chest.

Batr cleared his throat and thought fast. "Sorry to wake you, little man. Dedi drank a little too much tonight. Which room should I put him in?"

"'S all right. He sleeps on the roof. You can take the stairs on the side of the house if you can manage it."

"On the roof? By the gods, it's the coldest season of the year. Why is he sleeping on the roof?"

"Nightmares. But…" he paused, licking his lips and squinting at Iset. "Nevermind. I probably shouldn't have mentioned it."

"Mmmm mmmm," Iset's head rolled emphatically from side to side.

Batr smiled. "Don't worry. I promise I won't make fun of him. Strong men have nightmares, too, you know."

Ahmose looked up with bleary, but hopeful eyes. "All right. I'll grab his sleeping mat, if you can carry him to the roof." Batr watched Ahmose shuffle in the darkness towards the room he'd earlier suspected was Iset's. Then he scooped up Iset in his arms. After a moment's mumbled protest, she went limp and let him carry her up the stairs along the side of the house.

A moment later Ahmose ran up the stairs with a narrow, thinly-stuffed mat and a thick blanket in hand. He laid it out near the space they'd dined the day before, and Batr gently set Iset down. As he was sliding her body down her hand slipped from around his neck, and her palm trailed down his arm. His skin prickled with the contact, and he found himself very much wanting her to trust him, to tell him what he could do to make things right for her. But given what he knew of her, he deemed it better to find a way to bring her about willingly, rather than forcing her to tell him the truth. She'd very likely resist and resent any coercion.

Ahmose arranged the blanket over her, glancing up at Batr and taking care to make sure the scarf still covered Iset's face.

Iset murmured something, and Batr heard his name. "What's that you said?" He asked her, squatting next to her.

She reached out a delicate hand and placed it on his thigh. Her eyes were closed as she said in a soft, sleepy voice full of remorse, "'M' sorry. Thank you."

"You're welcome." His voice was gruff. With reluctance, he removed her slight hand from his thigh and tucked it under the blanket.

He led a frightened-looking Ahmose back down the steps and they stood beside the house. Batr asked again, "Why is he sleeping outside? It'll get cold before dawn." While the days were still warm, at this time of year the nights could drop down to almost freezing. Sometimes children put out bowls of water overnight in the hopes they *would* freeze. For most, it would be the only time they'd see ice in their entire lives.

Ahmose wrapped his arms around himself and shifted his weight back and forth. "I probably shouldn't tell you. Iset… and er, Dedi, wouldn't like it." Her rubbed his arms, then said in a rush, "Sometimes he has nightmares. Bad ones."

"But why sleep outside? What are they about?"

"Our brother – I mean mine and Iset's – our brother died in an accident in the tombs." Ahmose glanced up at the rooftop, as if afraid Iset would overhear them. "He was working on a – a whaddaya call it? A *pr-djit?" A house of eternity*, the type of mastaba tombs they built in the Land of the Dead. Batr nodded and Ahmose continued, wrapping his arms tighter around himself. "He was underground, and the ceiling caved in. He was alone when it happened, so they didn't find him for a couple of hours."

A tear glimmered on Ahmose's cheek and the boy swiped it away, but didn't stop talking. "They say he ran out of air down there, that he didn't just get hit on the head and die right away or anything. So, uh, Dedi, hasn't told me or anything, but I think he dreams about it. He started having nightmares right after our brother died. I heard him mumbling about it, about not being able to breathe. I think that's why he moved up to the roof." Ahmose rocked back and forth on his heels.

Batr's heart felt like it was being crushed in his chest. How much worse could it possibly get? Not only had their brother died in an awful fashion, but Iset dreamed about it. To top it off, she had to work in the tombs.

Batr also noticed that according to the widow Nebtawy's story, Dedi hadn't even come to town until six months ago. That would be six months *after* Iset and Ahmose's brother died, so it didn't make sense for Ahmose to say that Dedi started having the nightmares after their brother's death a year ago. Clearly Ahmose was just as brave as his sister, but he didn't have his story quite as straight.

Letting the slip pass, Batr clapped a hand on the boy's shoulder and gave it a rough squeeze. "Thank you for sharing this with me, Ahmose. I promise I'll keep this confidence and not let Dedi, *or Iset,* know you told me."

The boy looked up at him with watery eyes and a grateful smile. Then he looked down and drew a circle in the sand with his big toe. "What about Iset? Will she be all right? There was something wrong when you were here earlier, wasn't there? I could tell when I came in even though she lied about it and said she was fine." His next words came out in a whoosh of air. "I know I'm not supposed to say anything, she made me promise not to talk to anyone about this stuff, but I don't have anyone else to tell. She works too hard and I don't think she's eating enough. I know she's giving my mother and me more than our share of food and I don't know what to do if she gets sick or anything bad happens to her. There's no one left, and my mom's real sick and I'm not old enough to do anything to help." Ahmose angrily dashed tears off his face and looked away, the moonlight illuminating his distraught profile.

Batr drew in a deep breath. He knew how Ahmose felt. He'd lost almost his entire family thanks to one awful night, and he'd felt just as helpless as the boy did now.

"I tell you what, little man," he said, "I want to see you both happy. I'm going to find a way to fix this for you and make sure you and your mom and your sister are safe. I promise I'll find a way." Even if he had to fight every last man in the Land of the Dead to do it, Batr meant to keep his promise.

Chapter 8 – Userkare

The day before

When she woke the morning after Lady Ahaneith's banquet, Raia was not surprised to find a man in her bed. She'd brought him there, after all. She rolled over to face Makae's broad back, blinking against a shaft of bright light slicing through one of the narrow windows in her bedroom. What surprised her, though, was that she felt no regret, other than that caused by a slight headache and fuzziness from too much wine. Furthermore, her body was deliciously sore in a way she couldn't recall it ever being before. Stretching and arching her aching limbs and torso brought back visions of a night spent under and over the man next to her.

A night of sensual decadence, she thought. That's what it felt like. Like savouring a bite of a fresh, juicy fig dipped in lavender-steeped honey, followed by a sip of wine imported from the lands to the north of Kemet.

And that kiss that had started it all... The memory brought an involuntary smile to her lips, still plump and tender from a night of love-making, and she found herself licking them, biting on her lower one as she closed her eyes. Starting out with a firm, yet gentle, meeting of the mouths, their kiss had grown into something much more. Raia hadn't realized how much hunger she'd had in her all these years. She told herself it was because it had been so long since she'd been with a man, but a small, guilty part of her acknowledged that she'd never had such a want for her husband.

Thinking back on it, she couldn't believe that she'd actually led Makae to her room. That she'd been the one to reach for the ties of his shenti, to undress herself and bare herself to a man who was almost a complete stranger. *And a very silent one at that*, she thought wryly. He was wise in that regard. If he'd spoken too much, or uttered one wrong word, she'd probably have lost her nerve and thrown him out without hesitation.

No, she couldn't regret it. Not after what he'd done. He'd *worshipped* her. That was the only way she could think to describe it. Makae had traced his fingers over her curves, and his touch sent wracking shivers racing through her, hot and cold at the same time. He'd kissed every inch of her, as if her height and size was something to be treasured. He'd brushed his fingers over the shiny, finger-length marks on her abdomen made when her belly had stretched with childbearing, and he'd kissed those, too. That simple action alone almost caused her to weep, a shocking discovery. She had no idea that such recognition could ignite so much emotion in her.

And then when his mouth trailed further down, between her legs, he swept all her thoughts away. She'd become a writhing mass of need and want and excruciating pleasure, until he moved back up over her and gave her the release she craved. And then she'd moved over him and done the same for both of them all over again.

Opening her eyes to stare at his back, she wanted to reach out to waken Makae, to run her hand over the strong, sinewy muscles of his back and shoulders. Raia wanted to fold herself up in his warmth, to make love to him again in the morning hours. But she didn't. She was well aware that she'd inadvertently exposed much more of herself to him last night than she liked to admit. More than she'd revealed to anyone else. While she wasn't sure exactly *what* she had exposed, she'd been raised to believe desire equated vulnerability, something to be stamped out.

Her father had taught her that need and self-indulgence were weaknesses others could exploit. On the other hand, discipline and perseverance engendered triumph over adversity. Such a philosophy had served her well her whole life. But something had shifted last night, she'd allowed herself to succumb to a mindless whim, and now that she'd given in once she wanted to do it again and again.

She didn't need this man again. She simply couldn't. Once he'd finished his work in Abdju, he'd be on his way back to Thinis, in the queen's service, while she still had children to care for and her own work to do. It would be foolhardy to continue this past one night. Instead of reaching for him, she balled her fist near her breast.

Soon she would wake him and tell him to leave, before the children rose and came clamouring for stories of last night's banquet. For now, she shifted a little closer, just enough to breathe him in – a faint hint of wood smoke from last night's fires and burning incense, mingled with his own rich, masculine scent. She closed her eyes, warning herself not to fall back asleep.

Makae felt the bed shift as the woman beside him moved nearer. Years at sea and campaigning in the desert had taught him to sleep lightly, in the event of a raid, a thief, or worse. As soon as Raia woke so, too, did he. He remained still, curious to see what she would do. At one point, he was sure he felt the heat from her palm near his shoulder blade. It hovered for a moment before it was gone, accompanied by the sound of rustling bed sheets. Finally, tired of waiting, he rolled over to face her.

Knowing she was awake, though her eyes remained closed, he stroked the back of his knuckles along her smooth, high-boned cheek. Her eyes fluttered, and he leaned in, brushing his lips over her shoulder, taking in her fragrance – cardamom tinged with last night's incense. Sliding the sheet down over her arm, he appreciated the goosebumps that rose on her skin, as well as the view of the tops of her full, dark breasts, and the deep crevice created between them by the weight of her arm. A soft gasp escaped Raia, her body arched towards him, and Makae smiled.

He felt no compunctions about making love to her last night, and hopefully again this morning. She was no innocent virgin, nor was she a suspect in his investigation. Raia followed her own will, she'd made that abundantly clear last night when she'd led him to her bedroom and stripped down in all her glory before him. Furthermore, she had no man – no father, husband, or older brother – to answer to. Nor did she appear to need or want one, either.

Except that there had been want last night, hadn't there? For both of them. And again, now, as his fingers grazed the long, elegant column of her neck, down over her collarbones, trailing towards the edge of the sheet and the cleft between her breasts. Her eyes remained closed, but she bit her bottom lip as her swelling flesh rose towards him. Raia shifted and her leg slipped between his, her thigh pressed against the base of his hardness, causing him to utter a curse as his hips bucked towards her of their own volition. That brought a smile to her face, though he saw her try to stop it, and he snorted, whispering, "Torturous woman. You aren't sleeping at all."

Her thigh pushed more firmly against him, and when her eyes opened her assent was clearly written in the heat he saw there. He was about to flip her over on to her back and drive himself into her when he heard a flurry of soft thumps on the bedroom door. A second later, the door slammed open and a pack of children whirled into the room, giggling and talking all at once.

"Rai, you promised to tell us…" "What were the *hnr* like, *mewet*?" "What did Lady Ahaneith wear?" Voices came and died as each child registered Makae's presence in Raia's bed.

As soon as the knocks sounded, Raia had twisted and sat bolt upright to face them and, perhaps, to hide Makae, but he was in their direct line of sight. There was no reason for Raia to cover her nakedness. Women often went topless in the summer heat, while peasants went naked to work in the fields, as did most children until puberty. But Makae tugged the sheet over himself a little to conceal the rapidly wilting evidence of his anticipation for another round of love-making.

"Rai, I am so sorry to wake you, they would not wait…" A pretty girl, presumably Raia's younger sister Abar, was the last to enter the room. She stopped when she saw the five mute children staring at the bed. "Oh," Abar gasped, a mortified blush creeping over her olivine cheeks.

One of the other girls, a slender thing about seven years of age, shyly stepped forward and held her hand out in greeting. "*Eei-wee em hotep* – welcome in peace. My name is Tawaret, and this is my sister Tarset." She indicated another girl, presumably her twin. Both sisters had shaved heads and, although their skin was a few shades lighter than Raia's, there was something of her in the lofty set of their chins.

Makae smiled. "*Heru nefer* – good morning. I am Makae." He reached past Raia's naked waist, enjoying the look of shock on her face, to take Tawaret's hand. Two boys, near in age at around eleven and ten years old – Raia's brothers – also greeted him. Then the youngest, Raia's son and a boy of about four, came forward with his proud, rounded little belly jutting out over his short legs.

"Why are you in mewet's bed?" His fists rested on his hips, but he appeared more curious than angry.

"That is enough now, Basa," the oldest girl hurried to take his wrist, drawing him away from the bed. She addressed Raia, "I will take them to the rooftop for our morning meal."

"Thank you, Abar. I will join you shortly."

"Will Makae come, too?" The oldest of Raia's brothers was scrutinizing him with interest, his gaze lingering over the tattoos on Makae's cheeks.

Raia made a noise of protest in the back of her throat, but Makae cut in smoothly, "I'd be happy to join you with your mewet." Lacking another term in their language, *mother* was simply the term applied to all near female relatives, whether Raia was the boy's sister, aunt, or grandmother. It didn't really matter, though; she was all those things to these children anyway.

Herding the children before her, Abar threw a look back over her shoulder, one eyebrow raised, before sweeping out of the room and pulling the door shut behind her. The moment the door closed, Raia crumpled, dropping her face into a cushion on the bed, covering herself so Makae couldn't see her expression.

"Oh gods," she moaned, her voice muffled by the cushion. "They were not supposed to see you here."

Makae smiled and, laying back down beside her, laced his hands behind his head. "Why not? They didn't seem to mind."

She finally turned to him, her face still half hidden by the fabric, though her woeful expression was apparent. "They didn't mind because they do not know any better! How will I explain this to them?"

Makae grinned, pleased to see that something could rattle her practiced composure. "What's there to explain? Tell them you got tired of sleeping alone."

"And then what do I say when you are not here tomorrow?" She propped herself up on one elbow, bringing her breasts into view, catching his attention and wiping the grin off his face.

He let his gaze linger over her the luscious curves of her body for a moment before raising his eyes to hers and asking, "Who says I will not be here tomorrow, if you want me to?" Then he reached out and cupped the back of her head, pulling her down for a hungry kiss that sent all the blood rushing from his head, right back to where it was before the children broke into the room.

Despite the rising heat in her core, Raia forced herself to pull away from Makae's heated kisses, before she lost herself and left all her children waiting for her on the rooftop.

She disliked the uncertainty she heard in her voice as she said, "You do not have to… that is, it was only one night." Not many men would be interested in a woman with such a brood of children to take care of. While her wealth meant she had more than enough to support a man in high style, with all his honours and the queen's favour Makae had no need for it. She had little that might appeal to him.

Yet Makae just shrugged one shoulder. "It doesn't have to be that way."

"But I have…" she made a sweeping gesture to indicate the door and all the children that just piled out of it.

Makae smiled, though she detected a note of sadness in his voice as he said, "I had many brothers and sisters and clan members once. I miss them very much and it would please me greatly to feel a part of a family again. Even if it is only to share a morning meal."

His raw honesty caused something deeper than just physical desire to flicker in Raia's core. It rose up into her chest, filling her with a shivering warmth that threaded under her skin. She pressed her lips together to prevent the unexpected flood of emotion from somehow escaping her in verbal form.

After a moment spent mastering herself, she rolled from the bed, stretched, then bent down. Standing, she tossed his shenti at him, and said lightly, "Good. Then you may join us for our morning meal before we go to meet Userkare and find out why he and my father did not get along. But first, you must cover yourself." She threw him a grin over her shoulder before reaching for her own robe, preparing to face the pack of curious children awaiting her.

Two hours later, in a neighbourhood not so very far from her own home, Raia stood in the dimly-lit entranceway of Userkare's crumbling manor. Makae was by her side, waiting for the servant to return and tell them if Userkare would receive them. For some indiscernible reason, her heart fluttered in her chest and her hands were clammy. When Makae's hand brushed hers by accident she started, and he glanced at her with a question in his eyes.

She shook her head. She couldn't explain why she felt so anxious. Instead, her eyes roved the entranceway, counting. Two columns marked either side of the stairway that led up to the rooftop through an open space in the ceiling. Three dusty, medium-sized icons were clustered in the far corner – Isis, Ra, and Horus. Six large slabs of stained, un-swept limestone made up the ground on which they stood.

Just as she'd begun straining her eyes to count the cracks in the plaster that covered the brick walls around them – twelve so far – the elderly, bent servant returned, leading them through the home into a small courtyard behind the house. Ringed with a low brick wall, the enclosure consisted of multiple tall, leafy doum trees left to grow unpruned, along with jasmine that crept up uninhibited over the walls. Like the fractured wall of the entranceway, an air of neglect clung to the garden, as evidenced by a pond in the centre filled with murky water and only a few sickly-looking lotus pads. The day had grown cool and overcast and, despite her warmer attire, Raia shivered, pulling her shawl together in front.

The servant gestured to the far corner, near the door in the courtyard's wall, where they encountered Userkare. A man somewhere in his late forties but much-older looking, he sat propped on a long bench with a back that curved up behind him. Bony fingers rested atop a blanket tucked up under his armpits. His face, bearing the signs of having once been handsome, had a sunken appearance, as one long-suffering from a wasting illness. Raia knew the look. Despite his excellent health just a year and half ago, her father had that same look during his last few weeks in the living world.

However, when Userkare's gaze rose up to hers, the intensity in his eyes forced Raia back a step. They were burning, as if with a fever, and he looked upon her as if he *knew* her.

"Raia," he reached out a skeletal hand and she had no choice but to take it, to let him enfold her hand with fingers more papery and fragile than a scroll of decades-old papyrus. His voice rasped, "I have waited so long for this moment."

She felt Makae's curious gaze on her, but she was just as surprised as he. "I – I'm sorry, Userkare, I do not know what you mean."

"Of course you do not, child. Your parents never told you about me, did they?" He gestured to a set of wooden chairs nearby, indicating they draw them near. Raia acquiesced, knowing she could hardly tell him her father had warned her that Userkare was mad, and that she should keep away from him.

Once seated, Makae began to explain the reason for their visit, but Userkare brushed off their story with a wave of his hand. "My lands are safe enough." He said when

Makae told him he was working for Lady Ahaneith to ensure the safety of the crops and the nobles who managed the lands. Userkare coughed, a dry sound that came from deep in his chest. When he touched a square of linen to his mouth, Raia noticed the cloth was stained with dried blood.

"It does not matter now, anyway," the older man wheezed, a small and bitter smile playing on his lips. "I do not think I shall live long enough to worry about next season's planting. But tell me, Raia, what brings you here?" The man all but ignored Makae's presence, focusing all his energy on Raia. With the unobtrusive manner she'd come to associate him with, Makae leaned back in his chair and allowed Raia and Userkare to interact unimpeded.

"I…" Raia searched for the words she'd practiced with Makae, but instead found herself asking, "What do you know about me? Why do you believe my parents would not tell me about you?" Her fingers curled over the arms of her chair. Something told her she didn't want to know what Userkare had to say, yet she had to hear it.

That small smile played over his thin lips again, wistful, angry, and sad at the same time. Instead of answering, Userkare said, "Do you know you look just like her?"

"Who?" Raia leaned forward.

"Your mother, of course. So tall, so elegant. You have her eyes, her cheekbones, her shoulders. Your skin is even the same hue. So beautiful. Perfect, really. It has been so long I thought perhaps I had imagined it…"

"You knew my mother? When?" Her mother had never mentioned Userkare, she was almost certain of it. In the years following her mother's death, Raia had tried to commit to memory everything her mother had ever said. It wasn't easy, of course. She'd been only seven years old, and many a time she'd cursed her memory for not allowing her to see her early years with her mother. She mostly remembered her mother's sickness, the horror of failed childbirths and miscarriages, and the frightening exhaustion in their aftermath. After her mother's last failed birthing attempt, Raia had vowed aloud never to have children. But her mother made her promise otherwise, assuring her that the strength required to be a good mother would help her to endure all sorts of trials.

Userkare leaned his head back against a cushion tucked behind his neck. "I knew your mother most of her life. I watched her grow up. Her mother was a slave of sorts in the home next door." With a slight motion of his long, slender fingers he indicated the home to the east that loomed on the other side of the wall.

"No," Raia shook her head. "That's not right. My mother was a nobleman's daughter."

Userkare chuckled, but it resulted in another wracking cough, and a fresh spot of blood on his linen square. "Is that what Ra-hotep told you? Just like him. It's a wonder he was able to keep it a secret from you all these years. A true testament to his power and influence, I suppose."

As if from a distance, Raia observed that she was not as shocked as she ought to be by the revelation that her father might have lied. Even as a small child, Raia had known her mother was not the same as many other Kemeti noblewomen. Though her manners were never out of place, she always seemed to stand alone, rather than within a crowd. Thinking back on it now, Raia recalled uncomfortable moments when she and her mother would enter a room and the servants would stop talking and stare at her. On the streets there had been looks as well, hadn't there? He must have been powerful indeed, if her father had managed to hide that truth from her all her life. What kinds of promises – or threats – would it require to stop people from telling her?

"Please, Userkare," Raia leaned forward again and placed one hand on his thin arm. "Please tell me what you know about my *mewet*. I have so few memories of her and father was unwilling to speak of her after her passing. My brothers and sisters came later, from his second wife."

He looked down at her hand on his arm and placed his own hand tentatively over hers. He nodded. "Of course. You must want to know." In his wheezy voice, he told her, "Your grandmother was brought up from the south during a campaign. She was captured from some tribe down there by a Kemeti militia. Your grandfather," Userkare shrugged a frail shoulder, "I do not know. Your grandmother was pregnant when they brought her here, though it wasn't apparent at the time. She lived for only a few short years after your *mewet* was born, and never really learned to speak our language. The family next door raised your *mewet* as a…" Userkare searched for words, "a companion of sorts for their older daughters. When she came of age, they sought to marry her off."

"Is that when my father married her?" Raia had been led to believe that her parents' marriage was a love-match of sorts, or at least that it had not been arranged from birth.

"No," Userkare was about to say more, but another fit overcame him, and it took him several moments to regain his composure. Raia waited, mentally cursing the ill-health that made it difficult for him to tell her what she wanted to know. When he regained his composure, Userkare shook his head. "No. He did not marry her right away. I was to."

"You what?" Raia pulled her hand from Userkare's arm, sitting back in shock. Makae took her hand and she did not stop him, letting him warm the back of her hand with a slow, circular motion of his thumb

"We were meant to marry," Userkare said. "She and I. I was a few years older, and my family disapproved. They wanted me to have a more – ah – advantageous marriage. Your *mewet* was not exactly a slave, but her origins were unknown, and she had no wealth of her own. But I did not care. From the time we were young, I knew I wanted to marry her. As a boy I would come sit out here sometimes, and you she always loved to watch the fish," he gestured to the scum-filled pond in the center of the garden. "So she would come over and we would talk. She was always easy to sit with, and when I asked her to marry me she agreed. I offered her family a good bride price to purchase her hand. I was very wealthy once, despite what you see now." He gestured to the decaying garden.

Raia frowned; dazed that she had never heard this story before. "What happened?"

Userkare gripped the arms of his chair, his bony fingers straining as he sat forward. His dark eyes glittered like hard bits of obsidian as emotion twisted his face. Raia wasn't sure if he was about to have a fit, or if her question had angered him. Then, after a few breaths, he recovered himself and sat back, still holding the arms of his chair.

"What happened," his voice was brittle, like a dry twig ready to snap, "is that my family was sent into exile indefinitely. Right before your *mewet* and I were to marry. I could not ask her to come with me, to bear such an existence. We did not know where we were to go, how we were to live. We could take only what we and a few servants could carry."

Makae interjected smoothly here. "I am sorry to bring up painful memories, Userkare, but I must ask why you were exiled."

The older man waved a dismissive hand. "A misunderstanding. My family was pardoned by Pharaoh Wadj and Queen Merneith when they came to power, and we returned. But by then it was too late. Your *mewet* was gone."

Raia's voice was hoarse as understanding dawned on her. "That's when you and my father quarreled."

"Yes," Userkare nodded. "We did. I came to see you as soon as I learned she'd borne a child."

"But why?"

Userkare looked away to the far corner of the garden, hands twisting in his lap. Raia waited, impatient but not wanting to press him too much in case he stopped talking. Finally, he turned back to her with watery eyes and a sad little smile. "I wanted to see you, child. To have a glimpse of your *mewet* again, to see if there was any of her in you. But your father refused. He told me you were grown and already married. He and I had been friends once, you know, when we were young. I never knew he wanted to marry your *mewet*, or that he was upset that she'd wanted me over him. But I guess that was the way of it, as he offered for her right after I was sent into exile. I do not blame her for marrying him. I never would. She had no choice in the matter, really. A woman in her position does not have options."

Another coughing fit wracked his thin body, and this time blood flecked his lips. He licked them absently, as if used to this, and Raia winced. She knew he was right when he'd said he would not remain much longer in the living world.

"I am sorry," he said, passing a hand over his face. "This has brought back many memories for me. I do not think I can continue this today…" his voice faltered, fading off as emotion choked him.

Raia was disappointed; she'd wanted to hear more about her mother. Then again, perhaps she did not want any more revelations today. It was enough to know that her mother's life was not what she'd envisioned it to be. She'd never questioned if her mother had been happy with her father or not, but she was beginning to recall subtle things, things perhaps as a child she'd noticed unconsciously. Such as the way her mother turned away when her father entered the room, as if she'd rather not look at him, or the way she'd smiled sadly at Raia sometimes, like she was thinking of something else.

Other, more disturbing memories flashed through her mind as well, ones she couldn't be sure of. Her father sneering, the sound of her parents' voices through the mud-brick walls of their home, raised in anger. She remembered hearing a name once, something foul that she hadn't understood then, but that made sense now knowing her mother was born a slave of sorts. Raia pushed the thoughts aside. She didn't believe her father could have said such things. He was a good man who'd never spoken ill of her mother. In fact, since her mother's death Ra-hotep never spoke of her at all…

Makae watched as Raia slumped back in her chair, emotions flitting across her face. Clearly she was overwhelmed. Userkare was also tiring, but Makae needed more information from him before he could be satisfied.

"I am sorry to press you, Userkare," Makae leaned forward with his elbows on his knees, "but I need to ask you a few more questions. Just how angry were you with Rahotep for marrying Raia's mother?"

Userkare's thin face tightened. "Of course I was angry. But what could I do?" He shrugged one shoulder. "As you can see, I have barely managed to keep my lands profitable. I had no friends when I returned from exile, and most of my family died during those hard years we were away. I was able to reclaim my house and some of my lands, but otherwise I had nothing."

Makae inclined his head and asked, "Were you angry enough, perhaps, to wait ten years?"

"I do not understand," the older man frowned.

Deciding to gauge Userkare's reaction, Makae said, "Rahotep's tomb has been robbed."

The shock that passed across Userkare's face did not appear feigned. The older man scrubbed a hand over his cheeks as his mouth hung slack. "Robbed, you say? By the gods. When did this happen?"

"Sometime in the last couple of months. Do you know anything about it?"

The man's head wagged side to side, even as his mouth stayed open, as if unsure what to say. Finally, he rasped out, "No. Nothing. I am afraid I cannot help you."

Makae pressed him for another couple of minutes, but Userkare's condition worsened, and soon his answers came in gasps. Raia looked less-than-well herself, and Makae decided it was time for them to take their leave. They wouldn't get anything else out of Userkare today. Or perhaps ever. As they left, the older man begged Raia to come back again soon, and to bring her son and daughters so that Userkare might meet them. She promised to consider it, but Makae thought she looked doubtful.

On their way back to Raia's, he marveled at her rigid back and the proud, unyielding tilt of her chin. She was battling emotions yet refusing to let them show, at least not in public. He waited until they were in the privacy of her home, sitting on a wide stone bench in her greeting room with a jug of wine before them and the children playing in the back courtyard, before he asked how she was holding up.

Sipping wine from a mug held with a shaky hand, Raia said, "Fine."

Makae raised an eyebrow. Seeing his scepticism, she sighed and amended her answer. "Not so fine, perhaps. I… I have some memories of my *mewet*, but I feel as if I never really knew her. And now I begin to wonder how well I knew my father."

Makae slid his arm around her shoulders, and drew her closer against him so that she could lean against his chest. It gratified him that she allowed him to provide this small measure of comfort.

She tilted her head up to look at him. "Do you believe him? That he had nothing to do with my father's tomb?"

Makae mused aloud, "I don't know. He certainly is in no condition to break into a tomb himself, nor even walk to the tombs, and neither is that old manservant of his. But who would he be working with? He said he has few friends here, and you said you never see him at court. If he was involved, why tell us so much about your *mewet*'s history? He admitted to being angry with your father, providing us with his motive before we even asked. Or perhaps he is just a very good liar."

The two turned the matter over for a few more minutes before Makae said, "I will look into it further, I promise. Perhaps I can find out if Userkare has come into any wealth suddenly. Surely if he had, he would use it to improve his condition. If you are able, perhaps you can see if any of the servants recall him arguing with your father when he returned from exile, or if they know of anyone else who might wish to rob your father's tomb.

"In the meantime, your brothers were quite adamant this morning that you take them to the Horus Festival this year. Do you intend to?"

Sighing, Raia shook her head against his shoulder. "It is so much work to manage all of them, and I cannot ask Abar to watch them again. She deserves to have one year at the festival to herself before she marries."

"Take me with you, I'll help."

"Truly?" She cast him a skeptical look. "You *want* to take that many children to the festival?"

"Why not?" He asked, wanting her to share her doubts with him. Makae had had his share of liaisons with women, and did not lightly offer to spend his time with them outside of the bedroom. If she doubted his intentions, he expected the opportunity to explain himself.

Before Raia could answer, however, the front door thumped open and for the second time that day someone interrupted them.

Raia was just pushing herself upright off Makae's chest when a young man came striding into the room. Spotting the two of them on the bench, his hands clenched at his sides. He appeared to be on the verge of an angry outburst.

Instead, he inclined his head stiffly. "Raia," he said.

Beside him Raia went still, but Makae sensed the tautness of her muscles. She greeted the young man with equal formality. "Semer."

Ahhhh, thought Makae. *So this is the younger brother*. He studied this boy on the threshold of manhood, his lean body clad in a fine, long-sleeved linen robe, a fox skin draped over his shoulders. He was tall for his age, though nowhere near his sister's towering height, and with his paler skin, thin lips, and wide jaw he looked nothing like Raia. Gold hoops adorned his ears, and a gold chain draped his bald pate. Makae thought his style a trifle overdone, given the time of day and that he was only visiting his sister. But then again, he thought many wealthy young men had a tendency to unnecessary adornment, not recognizing the distinction between elegance and ostentation.

Raia introduced Makae and, after a brief acknowledgement, Semer turned to his sister and said, "Rai, I need to speak with you in private."

"Right now? Can it wait, Semer? I have had a rather difficult day."

"No," the young man flicked a meaningful glance at Makae. "It cannot wait."

Expelling an exasperated breath, Raia pushed herself off the bench. To be polite, Makae followed suit. Raia turned to him with an annoyed expression and said, "Please, wait here. I will not be long."

Raia led her brother out into the hallway adjacent to the room and Makae, moving just a few steps nearer to the doorway, was able to overhear them. Makae preferred not to make a habit of listening in, but it was obvious whatever Semer had to say had to do with him. The boy did little to conceal his aggravation; he didn't even bother to lower his voice much although the two were standing just on the other side of the wall, a few steps from the doorway.

"Rai, how could you?" Semer chastised his older sister. "How could you bring a stranger into your house and let him spend the night in your bed? What sort of example is that for Abar and your daughters?"

Raia's voice was a furious whisper. "Who told you he spent the night? And besides, I do not see what business it is of yours, Semer."

"I came by earlier looking for you, and the boys told me about it. You did not really think you could bring a man *like that* into the home, around my brothers and sisters, and I would not have a problem with it?"

"How dare you, Semer? This is my home. I can bring who I like into it. If you have a problem with that, perhaps it is time you grew up and took some responsibility for your brothers and sisters. Did you think I would go on alone forever, just taking care of everyone else, and never give a thought to my own desires?"

Makae detected the emotion thickening Raia's voice. Anger, and a great deal of indignant pride.

She continued with her hushed tirade. "Since *Yet* passed away all you have done is hunt and fish. It is enough to take care of one family and one farm, never mind two of each. I have asked you repeatedly to take an interest in the property, but since you do not seem to care perhaps it is time I found someone who did."

Makae could imagine the expression on Raia's face, her eyebrows raised and her plum-coloured lips pursed in annoyance. The same look she'd given him the first day they'd met and she accused him of not doing his job well. He pictured a young man like Semer chafing under that haughty gaze.

"What's that supposed to mean, Rai? Are you telling me that *that* man in there will help you run the farm?"

Raia snorted. "No. That man, as you call him, is one of the queen's guards, a respected man who sat next to the Lady Ahaneith at last night's banquet. So you would do well to show some respect, little brother. And what he is doing here is irrelevant. I have been alone for over three years, Semer. I am not some chaste priestess that I can go without any companionship or affection forever.

"I doubt he has any interest in *Yet*'s farms. I'm talking about hiring someone to manage the farm, or rent it out. And I promise you, if I have to resort to that, I *will* cut your allowance, Semer."

"You can't do that!"

"Keep pushing me. *Yet* made the provision for it when he wrote his last wishes. I can do it if I must."

"I'll apply to *Yet*'s scribes for my inheritance, then." A desperate note crept into the boy's voice.

"That would be pointless. They will not give it to you until you can prove you are running the farm without my assistance. You know that. He made arrangements for them to watch over you, to ensure that you were learning how to manage the farm. I'm sorry, Semer, but I have had enough. The last few days have been very trying for me. If you were around you would know. Either you learn to take care of things, or I will have to hire someone else who will. And I'll not bother asking why you came by this morning. I have little doubt it was to ask for assistance in funding another hunt."

Semer gave a passable imitation of a grown man's growl, given that his voice was still changing, and said, "I will not let *Yet*'s farm fall into the hands of some stranger. Even if he *is* one of the queen's men."

Sighing, Raia said, "I told you, Semer, it is not like that. But if you dislike the idea of leasing the land, and you want your inheritance, you know what you need to do."

Makae raised an eyebrow as Raia's little brother burst out with a "Fine!" that sounded more like a petulant child than a boy on the cusp of manhood.

"Fine?" Raia goaded him. "Fine what?"

"Then I *will* find a way to manage the farm and get my inheritance! With or without your help!" A moment later the front door slammed, followed by the sound of the door creaking open, and Raia's voice, coming more from the window near the front courtyard rather than the hallway, calling out, "Get back here, Semer!"

The siblings continued their argument in more muted tones further from the room he was in, and Makae could no longer make out their words. Stepping away from the doorway to stand with his back to the door, Makae pretended to study the banquet scene painted on the white-washed walls while he waited for Raia to rejoin him. He smoothed a hand over the braids of his hair, tugging a little on the ends, thinking over what he'd just heard. Hunting trips for nobles did not come cheap. They required trackers, boats, dogs, food, supplies, and servants, as well as priests to pray to the various gods of the animals for a profitable hunt, and so on. The best location in Abdju for game was nearer to the great river, almost a two hour walk away, and many nobles camped there for days, taking along dozens of retainers and assistants at great expense. While a peasant could hunt with a spear in order to provide sustenance, a noble hunted for the sport, and that cost far more than it gained.

A young man with a penchant for such sport could easily run into trouble with debtors. Raia had mentioned Semer's obsession with hunting more than once, and was clearly concerned by it. And a rash young man in need of funds might be pushed to do something unsavoury – like rob his own father's tomb – in order to pay for his pleasures. It was clear Semer frequently applied to his sister for funds, and was frustrated by the restraints on his inheritance.

What a change from this morning, Makae ruminated, when he'd imagined things with Raia to be relatively uncomplicated. He'd been attracted to her, and she to him. He admired her greatly, and although he'd only known her a short time, she was the sort of woman he might want by his side.

However, over the course of a few short hours, two suspects with close ties to her and her family had arisen. Despite Makae's growing respect for Raia, his loyalties lay first and foremost with the queen. If Raia's brother – or her mother's former betrothed – had taken to tomb raiding, Makae would have no choice but to see them punished to the fullest extent of their laws. And there was little doubt in his mind that if he were to have Raia's brother executed she'd never forgive him.

Chapter 9 – The Festival

Iset hated the nervous fluttering of her stomach. But there it was, fluttering away nonetheless, no matter how many times she willed it to stop. It wasn't sickness from drinking too much last night. No, she'd gotten over that hours ago, not long after she'd woken on the rooftop in the bright morning sunlight with the enthusiastic chirping and twittering of the finches, sparrows, and weavers in the nearby palm trees a cacophony of sound vibrating against her ears. She'd been stiff and horribly uncomfortable, her mouth as dry as if she'd been swallowing sand all night long.

If ever there was a time for nightmares that would've been it. She'd woken with her chest still bound, making it hard to draw in a full breath. Unable to recall exactly how she'd gotten on the rooftop, she had vague memories of the soothing scent of Batr's skin, the hardness of his chest and back, and his arm under hers, propping her up against him. She knew that, for a brief time last night, she'd felt safe with Batr by her side. And that sense of safety in itself was distressing. Had she revealed too much somehow? Ahmose had affirmed Batr knew nothing about her true identity last night, but she wasn't so sure.

Whatever she'd said or done last night, no one had yet come to take her and her family away to the *hnrt* – the prison complex – and she supposed that was something to be thankful for.

She'd been too ill from drink and worry to eat breakfast, managing to hold down only a mug of thick barley beer. When she was feeling a little better, she tried perusing the scroll she'd stolen from the inventory hut, but understood very little of it. It appeared to just be a listing of the amount of stone picks used by the workers in the fifth year of the tomb's construction. A useless document, really. After all the risks she'd taken, she was still no nearer to finding the entrance to the pharaoh's tomb than the day before, and just thinking of it made her queasy all over again.

Standing in her bedroom now in the late afternoon, Iset picked up the bronze disc that served as a mirror and checked her reflection one more time. She'd carefully applied thin lines of kohl around her eyelids, and smudged a bit of red ochre onto her cheeks and lips. She hoped the makeup was enough to cover the fact that she looked utterly and embarrassingly much worse for her night at the tavern.

Batr was due to arrive any moment to pick them up for the Horus Festival, and Iset couldn't be more conflicted. He'd spent time last night talking to the tomb robber with the crooked nose, she remembered that much. Was he trying to insinuate himself with them? And why? He'd been so kind to her – as Dedi – last night. He'd defended both Dedi and Iset when the men made lewd jokes, and he'd ensured she got home safely without trying to pry for information about the entrance to the pharaoh's tomb. He hadn't gone off to the back rooms with any of the serving women like Addaya did, even when the women appeared more than willing. He *seemed* like a good man. But she feared she was being lured into a false sense of security.

She put down the bronze disc and picked up the necklace that Ahmose found yesterday. Before she'd gone to the tavern last night Ahmose had shown it to her. Although he'd searched the hut like Iset asked him to, he'd ultimately found their father's hiding place inside the stove by accident. He told her he'd been baking bread again and gone to take out the stone bread slab. As he did so, the slab slipped and burned his fingers. He dropped the stone and it knocked a brick loose on the side of the stove. When he'd gone to fix it, he'd found the necklace tucked inside, wrapped in a bundle of linen. Iset gave a prayer of thanks to her namesake Isis for her assistance in their time of need. She couldn't imagine any other reason for the timing of Ahmose's discovery. For once something had gone in Iset's favour.

The necklace was a stunning piece of craftsmanship, a large beaded collar with thick chunks of dark blue lapis lazuli and red carnelian. A gold and ivory pendant of the eye of Horus hung from the centre. Iset couldn't even begin to guess how many sacks of grain it would cost to commission such a piece of jewellery, but she was certain it was more than she would make painting tombs over several years.

At first, she'd considered trying to sell the necklace. It was worth more than enough to get them far away from Abdju. But she had no such connections and if anyone discovered how she'd come by the necklace she might as well turn herself into the authorities. Besides, if she sold the piece it would be almost no different than if she'd robbed the tomb herself. While the laws of Kemet might not differentiate between a thief and his family, her own conscience couldn't stomach the thought of profiting from the destruction of a man's eternal rest. A small part of her clung to the irrational desire that she'd find an honourable way out of the mess her father had left them in.

"Why do you think he had that necklace, Iset?" Ahmose's voice came from the doorway, interrupting her thoughts. She put the necklace back on top of the bundle of linen, folding the fabric up around the piece.

How could she tell him that the necklace was irrefutable proof that their father had robbed a nobleman's tomb? Given the circumstances, it was the only explanation for his possession of the piece. If Iset had harboured any hopes that her father hadn't really been capable of such a crime, they'd been dashed last night when she saw the necklace.

She turned to her little brother, who was fidgeting in the doorway, his hands twisting on the ties of his shenti. He looked up at her with big, scared eyes and she could see that he suspected there was something not right about the situation. She hated to lie to him, but she couldn't tell him the truth. It would ruin any good memories he might have of their father, and only worry him needlessly.

Iset said, "I'm not exactly sure. Perhaps he was holding on to it for someone. Or perhaps he meant it as a gift for *mewet.*"

Ahmose's lips thinned. She knew her brother was more observant than she sometimes gave him credit for, but it was easier to pretend her lies were effective at making him feel better. She couldn't stand to think that he was worrying just as much as she was.

"So if we don't know for sure," he reasoned, "then maybe we shouldn't give the necklace to *mewet* just yet."

Iset blew out a relieved breath and gave a weak smile, "No, perhaps not quite yet. I think it best not to tell anyone yet. Until we know for sure."

Ahmose nodded, his eyes on the ground. Iset mustered a cheerful voice. "Are you excited about tonight? Just think of all the wonderful things we'll see! I haven't been to a Horus Festival in years, either, you know. But I remember how much fun it was. There will be sweet buns, and grilled fish, and all kinds of nuts. And acrobatic dancers."

A smile crept across Ahmose's face. "And there will be roasted goat and sheep, won't there?"

"Indeed there will!" She tapped him on the nose. "They roast them on a big spit over a fire, and you can watch them do it. Then we'll make sure you get a nice big slab and you can fill your tummy."

Ahmose rubbed his bare, skinny belly, a wistful look on his face. "I hope Batr comes soon."

Iset forced a smile. Whatever feelings Batr elicited in her, she was going to make sure that her brother had a good time tonight. He deserved that much. Then a thought struck her. If Batr was being nice to her – possibly even trying to seduce her with his flirting – in order to find out what he wanted to know about Pharaoh Wadj's tomb, then perhaps she could do likewise to him to find out what he knew about the thieves.

If he'd befriended the tomb robbers, or was in league with them somehow, maybe she could find a way to make *him* want to help *her*. If he liked her enough, if she could make him care for her and Ahmose, then perhaps he would want to stop the robbers from hurting them. He could convince them that she – and Dedi – didn't know anything. He'd made it clear he found her attractive. Perhaps if she were to respond even more favourably to his advances he'd be more inclined to assist her. Spending the evening at the festival posed the perfect opportunity for her to get closer to Batr.

She'd never tried to entice a man before, but how hard could it really be? She'd had plenty of practice at pretending to be someone else; perhaps she could pretend to be something totally opposite from Dedi, and be a temptress as well. All she had to do was make sure she didn't get her own feelings tangled up in the process…

It was precisely as Batr suspected. Or almost so. Earlier that day he'd trekked out to the inventory hut in the Land of the Dead. As he'd made his way over the stretch of rocky sand between the noblemen's tombs on the edge of town and the crypts of the pharaohs, he'd felt more vulnerable than he was comfortable with. There was a vast swath of space, about a ten-minute walk, in which he had nothing in the way of cover. He was visible to any and all who might be watching. He wondered if the potential tomb robbers had chosen this spot intentionally – so they could verify he was coming alone – or if they were incredibly stupid and didn't care if the entire city of Abdju saw them meeting by the tombs.

After all his years of pirating and soldiering, he was used to the weight of a large blade hanging from his hip. But he'd been forced to leave it off when he began work in the Land of the Dead. It would be too obvious, as most men didn't carry weapons on their person. That afternoon, however, he had strapped a small blade to his thigh beneath his shenti. If he had to, he could easily access it. There were always his hands too, of course, which were vicious weapons in their own right.

He'd been greeted inside the inventory hut by the man with the crooked nose, and there he'd been introduced to two other men. He recognized one of the men as Teos, the man who kept the inventory. The other man had a high, nasal voice, and was a security guard who worked nights in the Land of the Dead. The very nature of their work made them obvious suspects for a tomb robbing, Batr thought, although the choice of men was also smart. The security guard could allow men into the Land of the Dead at night, Teos had access to the tools required to break into the tombs, and the crooked-nosed man was brute force labour, a stone cutter with a strong arm.

Pamiu, the security guard with the nasal voice, eyed Batr with suspicion. "What brings you to the Land of the Dead? You're new here. How're we supposed to trust you?"

Batr hooked his thumbs into his shenti and tipped his head back, looking down the length of his nose at Pamiu. The man was tall, but reedy and a little nervous, though he hid it fairly well. Batr had dealt with much worse in his years at sea, and he wasn't easily intimidated. "Your friend invited me." He jerked his head towards the man with the crooked nose. "And until I know what I'm here for, I couldn't care less if you trust me."

The reedy man took a few steps around Batr, looking him over as if he were a goat he might consider buying. Finally, he said, "Maybe there's work in it for you. We need a strong arm in exchange for more gold than you're ever likely to see in your life. Think you can handle that?"

"My arm is strong enough, I'm a quarryman. But what's the job?"

"Don't you worry about that. You just need to show up when we tell you, where we tell you."

Batr snorted. These men were idiots. While the nasally man might be the leader of this little group, he couldn't possibly be the orchestrator of a successful tomb robbing. Whoever that was, that man had a network of people to help cover up his crimes, and connections to others who would buy the stolen items. The man in front of him was just a self-important lackey.

Feigning disinterest, Batr leaned back on his heels. "So that's all you're going to tell me? You expect me to take some unknown risks to do an unknown job for an unknown amount of pay?"

The security guard narrowed his eyes at the crooked-nosed man. "You said he was willing to work. What's this garbage now?"

Batr interjected smoothly. "Tell you what, friend, I'm not unwilling. Just give me some clue about the job and the risks. That's all. I like to know what I'm getting myself into."

Pamiu sneered, then relented a little. "Fine. We'll be breaking in to one of the tombs soon. You don't need to worry about which one, or when. You just need to show up when we tell you. If we're caught," he shrugged one shoulder, "well, that's it for all of us. But if we aren't, there'll be plenty to go around to make up for the risk."

Batr nodded. It was exactly as he'd expected. "Who else will be there when we do it?"

"Just enough people to make it work. Myself, Teos, Ra-Eai," Pamiu jerked his head towards the crooked-nosed man who'd invited Batr here, "and another man, some muscle to help dig. That's all we'll need."

"Hold on," Batr held up a finger. "Who sells the stuff? How do we get what's coming to us?"

The guard gave Batr a suspicious glare and gave one slow shake of his head. "Never mind about that. It isn't your business. You'll get what's coming to you. We done this before and no one's had reason to complain. Understand?"

Batr smiled and held his hands up in a gesture of amiability. "Understood."

"Good. Then we got a deal?"

"Indeed we do." Batr and the guard gripped one another's' forearms in agreement. Batr was fairly certain he'd found at least some of the men involved in the initial tomb robbing and, if all went well, he'd be able to catch them in the act of robbing another one.

Iset quite took Batr's breath away when she opened the door a few hours later. Her long black hair hung loose around her back and shoulders, with small red beads woven into thin braids throughout. A matching necklace with several strands of red beads hung about her slender neck, setting off the lovely fawn tint of her skin. She wore make-up, which he was unused to seeing on her. As a result, her sultry, kohl-rimmed eyes and ochre red lips were even more alluring than usual. He felt a swell of desire, and a sense of hope that she'd taken extra care with her appearance was for his sake.

He hooked his thumbs in the top of his shenti and leaned against the doorframe. "Nebet-i," he pitched his voice low in what he trusted was a sexy murmur. "You look absolutely stunning tonight. If you've done this in an effort to seduce me, I am more than happy to oblige you by succumbing to your charms. You may have your way with me if you please."

She blinked, her ripe mouth forming a charming "o" of surprise, before her lips thinned and she said in exasperation, "Can't you even *try* to behave yourself for a few minutes? If not, I promise you'll find yourself walking through the fair alone with my little brother."

Batr shook his head sadly. "Once again you cut me to the heart, Nofret. It's a good thing you look so very lovely tonight, or I would be sorely tempted to leave you here all by yourself."

"I – excuse me?"

"Come, don't worry about it, I'll not leave you behind. You look beautiful and I promise to behave myself. Well, at least around your brother. *Mostly*," he added with a wink.

"Oh for the love of the gods, you are incorrigible."

"It's all part of my boyish charm, nebet-i, trust me. It drives women wild."

"Oh I bet it drives them wild all right. It's positively maddening."

He grinned, and was just about to yield to the desire to pull her into his arms and kiss her senseless when Ahmose bounded into the room. "Batr! You're here! I'm ready. We're ready, aren't we, Iset? We can go now, right?"

Iset smiled and patted the boy's head. "Yes, we can. You said goodbye to Mewet?"

Ahmose nodded vigorously.

Batr was still lounging in the doorway, blocking the way out, when he asked casually, "But what about Dedi? Will he be joining us?"

Ahmose looked swiftly to Iset. Her face was impassive as she said, "No. He's gone ahead with some other friends. Perhaps we'll see him there and come home together. But he thanks you for helping him home last night."

Batr held Iset's gaze without responding. He watched her long enough to see a flush creep into her cheeks and her eyes flit away. She scrunched the fabric of her dress at her thighs in her fists before smoothing it down with her palms. She had a remarkable capacity to lie on the spot, but he saw it was an effort to maintain her calm demeanour under his scrutiny.

"Well then," Batr broke the silence, "let's hope we find him in the crowd. I enjoyed his company last night."

And so they all made their way out the door into the late afternoon sun. Over the course of the half-hour walk down to the bank of the small river that ran through the city of Abdju, Ahmose asked Batr close to a hundred questions about his travels and life in the desert with the Libu tribes. Batr carefully navigated the questions, attempting to keep his answers as truthful as possible without coming too close to the reasons how and why he was now working in the Land of the Dead.

"I saw Queen Merneith in Thinis several times when I served as a soldier," he said when Ahmose asked how many times he'd seen the queen. "She's a very kind lady."

"But you are no longer a soldier, correct?" Iset asked. Her pretty eyes were turned to him, her nostrils flared slightly. He'd seen that look before. Once, when his tribe was camping near one of the many oases they stopped at, he'd woken early with the need to relieve himself. He'd completed his business and then, enjoying the quiet sunrise over the desert, knelt to scoop some water from the oasis over his face. Looking up, water dripping down his cheeks, he spotted a slender young gazelle across the pool, watching him with wide, hunted eyes. It held perfectly still, as if hoping not to be seen, but needing to know if its life was in danger. Batr had slowly sat back on his haunches and, after a minute or more of observing one another, the gazelle lowered its graceful head and lapped at the pool, keeping one wary eye on him.

For a short time, they shared a peaceful space – a lush, colourful, and fertile oasis in the midst of a savage, barren desert. Just two beings trying to survive. That is, until a noise startled the animal and its eyes snapped upwards, staring at him in alarm before taking fright and bounding off. But he'd forever carried that moment of tranquility in his memory as something special. And now here was Iset, looking at him the same way as the circumspect gazelle.

He sighed. "No. I'm not a soldier anymore. I was just a temporary conscript, and have since left their ranks." It wasn't a total lie; he wasn't precisely a soldier anymore. He was an honoured member of the guard, one who'd received special recognition from the queen on several occasions. He'd helped to save her life more than once, and a few months ago he'd helped his friend Ebrium during an investigation into a double murder in one of Thinis' major temples. For his service, both he and his brother had received rather fine mansions in Thinis, replete with several servants and various bits of jewellery. So no, not a common soldier anymore. Something much more than that.

He wondered if he told her who he really was if she'd let him help her. Watching her face in profile as they walked – her tight jaw and lips pressed into a flat, stubborn line – he didn't think so. It would take much more than just the truth for her to open up to him and let *anyone* help her. She didn't trust him, and he had to find a way to make her see that she could, just as he'd tried with the gazelle in the oasis.

Iset was relieved when they reached the bank of the river, and the grounds designated for the festival. Here the earth was lusher than that of the village on the outskirts of the Land of the Dead. Whereas the village was the monotonous beige of the desert, the city of Abdju had rich, fertile soil thanks to the river. Date palms, willows, and sycamore trees grew in abundance, as well as the tall papyrus reeds that sprouted up in the marshy areas near the water.

Here also the air was different. In the village fine dust from the hard-packed sandy earth weighed down the air, leaving it heavy and dry. Here it smelled of moist leaves, the river, and meat roasting on spits around the grounds. Rather than the sounds of people shuffling to and from work in the Land of the Dead, and vendors calling out the names of the wares in the sacs on their backs, here there was a general buzz of excitement from the hundreds of people, possibly thousands, who milled around the grounds and marshy soil.

Iset needed the distractions the festival provided. She'd been sick with worry for days, and Batr's near-constant presence in her life since then only confused her more. Knowing that he'd been a soldier, one trusted enough to be allowed in the queen's presence on more than one occasion, made him a dangerous man indeed. But she wondered if there was some way she could use that to her advantage. If she could determine who the tomb robbers were and what their plan was, could he help save her family?

She'd intended to try to charm him tonight, but he'd been so cocky when he arrived at her home that he'd thrown her off-guard. As if he'd known exactly what she was trying to do, he'd stripped away the veneer of her defences. Perhaps she should re-group and try again, to find a way to stop him from probing into their lives. If she was going to enlist his assistance, she wanted it to be on her terms.

Dozens of stands with patchwork animal hide and linen shade covers were set up around the grounds. Those sporting long line-ups offered free food provided by the governor of Abdju and the Lady Ahaneith, Pharaoh Wadj's second wife and the woman who ruled over Abdju. Other stands sold trinkets, icons of the gods, and jewellery. Ahmose immediately set about searching for the shortest food line, while assessing his other options for later.

Iset's heart warmed to see her little brother so delighted by the variety of goods to be sampled. She warned him to eat slowly so he wouldn't make himself sick gorging on rich delicacies like grilled fish and roasted sheep, the types of food they only sampled on festival days and could never afford for themselves.

Batr urged her to eat also, and she managed to pick at a few things. Her stomach seemed to have shrunk lately, however. That, coupled with the anxiety that had taken up residence in her abdomen, caused her belly to quickly rebel, and she let Ahmose finish the leg of a pheasant she'd been nibbling on. Batr, she noticed, ate heartily and with gusto. She laughed and told him he must have eaten enough to feed ten teenage boys. He grinned and said that working in the Land of the Dead required a man to eat like an ox to keep his energy up.

After they'd tasted their fill and Ra was beginning to push the sun behind the dunes of the desert to the west, they made their way to the make-shift theatre. A few dozen people sat on stools close to the stage, while others stood behind them, watching the play. A group of *hnr* – singers, dancers, and actors – were re-enacting a battle between Horus and his uncle, the god Seth. Horus was avenging the death of his father Osiris, whom Seth had killed out of jealousy. Two men wielded long thick sticks. One was a well-built man wearing a tall mask made in the likeness of a falcon's head to represent Horus, and another wore a jackal's head mask, the symbol of Seth.

The two gods moved around one another in a well-choreographed dance, jabbing, twisting, jumping, and spinning their sticks. The crowd gasped, hissed, called out, and finally cheered as Horus dealt his uncle Seth a killing blow. Four men ran out and carried the dead god off-stage, where he was no doubt to be dismembered and his bits cast to the four corners of Kemet in the same punishment he'd dealt his brother Osiris.

Then the actors took up a story about the birth of the new pharaoh, Den. Queen Merneith had given birth to the baby boy four months ago, and this was the first time his birth was enacted at the Horus Festival. All pharaohs were associated with Horus, as both were divine beings with dominion over Kemet. Therefore on stage, as the baby Den – represented by a small bundle of clothing stuffed with rags

– was born, the Horus god entered him – through the strategic manipulations of fabric – and the pharaoh and the god became one and the same.

Ahmose turned to Batr, wide-eyed. "Did you see the new pharaoh being born, Batr? Was it like that? Did the Horus-god's spirit enter him?"

Batr chuckled then sobered when it became clear Ahmose's question was a serious one. He coughed. "I… uhm… I *was* in Thinis when Pharaoh Den was born, but no. The queen did not give birth in the open for all the court to witness. I presume Horus entered the boy in the privacy of the queen's bed chambers."

He caught Iset's eye over Ahmose's head and she smiled. He *was* so terribly good to her brother, indulging all his questions and enthusiasm. She couldn't help but like him for it, even as she tried to harden her heart to stop herself from truly caring for him. It wouldn't do for her to start fantasizing about what a life would be like with a man like him, a man who treated her and her family with such consideration and respect. A man who would be a kind and loving father of the sort she herself never had.

Batr's skin tingled at the warmth he saw in Iset's eyes, but in the next moment her expression shuttered and she turned away. He drew in a sharp, exasperated breath. Damn if she wasn't the loveliest and most confusing woman he'd ever known.

Re-grouping, Batr tilted his head towards the river. "Come, let's go down to the water. I believe they'll be moving the Horus god back to the temple soon. If we hurry, we'll be able to see him." Batr tucked Iset's hand into the crook of his arm. She stiffened and he held his breath. He rested one hand over hers lightly, allowing her enough leeway to pull away if she chose. After a moment she relaxed and her fingers softened on his forearm. Glancing down at her, he winked. She rolled her eyes and shook her head, but he saw her lips curve upwards. It wasn't much, but he felt he'd won a small triumph.

By the time they reached the river's shoreline, night had settled in. Torches set up along the banks of the water cast long shadows on the faces of the people spread out amidst the trees and reeds. Ahmose spotted some friends and asked if he could go watch the procession of the statue of Horus with them. Iset acquiesced and Batr was pleased to find himself alone with her in the semi-darkness.

Within a few minutes, they could see the procession of boats drifting up the river. Each year on the day of his birth, the statue of Horus was taken from his temple nearby and transported along the river during the day. This allowed him to visit other gods, as well as celebrate his birthday festivities. Now it was nighttime and he was making the return trip back to his temple. Bowls filled with oil had been lit on the deck of the large boat, as well as on those of the boats around Horus's. Temple slaves crouched in the front and back of the barge, pushing long poles into the soft mud of the river to propel the boat forward.

Iset shivered and rubbed her arms against the chill air, and Batr shifted so that he was behind her. He slipped his arms around her, pressing his chest gently against her back to let her feel his warmth. Her body went rigid, but she didn't break away. He dipped his head towards her and nuzzled the scented hair around her ear. He whispered, "Don't worry, Nofret, I'm behaving myself. I'm just trying to keep you warm."

He felt her take a deep breath and wondered if she'd bolt. Or twist around and kick him. He wouldn't put that past her for a second. She shifted, lifting her hands to rest them on his forearms and he wondered if she might push him away. Batr was pleasantly surprised when she exhaled and relaxed back against him. Her fingers were still tense on his arms, but she seemed to be overcoming some reluctance to let him touch her. He was even more gratified when she went so far as to rest her head against his shoulder, her soft, curling hair tickling his skin in the most sensual manner.

A tingling sensation shot straight down to his groin, and he stoically forced himself to think of every non-sensual thing he could imagine. He thought of the crocodiles in the great river, and deadly snakes slithering through the reeds, he thought of the widow Neb-tawy sitting on her stool, which once again brought him back around to thinking of Iset, which didn't help matters. He shifted slightly, trying to give himself some space from the woman leaning against him. Gods forbid he make this much progress with his pretty little gazelle, only to scare her off with his hardness rubbing at her rear.

They stayed that way for several long minutes as the boats floated north upstream past them. Miniature rafts with small oil bowls bobbed along the length of the narrow river and alongside Horus' entourage. Their little orange flames twinkled like fiery stars on the water's surface, mirroring the silvery stars in the night sky, encasing them in shimmering light. Like some kind of *hekka*, weaving magic around them. All around the grounds, bowls with cones of greasy incense burned on stands, scenting the air with myrrh. On the bank on the other side of the river, musicians beat a slow rhythm, accompanied by the sensual lilt of double reed flutes.

Batr felt something profound shift in him. This was one of the most beautiful, peaceful moments he'd ever experienced and he didn't want it to end. Being here, with Iset snugged up against him, keeping one eye out for her curious and bright little brother, Batr felt an unfamiliar, yet welcome sense of calmness and *rightness*. He'd never really considered settling down with a woman, his life-style had never allowed for it. But then again, he'd never met a woman like Isetnofret either.

His arms were still wrapped around Iset's waist, and her slender hands had slid to his wrists. Looking down at them, he marveled at the contrast of his dark arms against her white dress and light, olivine skin. He leaned his head down and inhaled the scent of jasmine from her skin and hair. His groin stirred at the thought of all the things he'd like to do to her under cover of darkness. By the gods he'd love to lay her down on a bed of soft leaves and press himself between her smooth thighs. Or lean her against a tree and kneel at her feet, hiking her dress up to her slender hips and tasting the sweet warmth of her most sacred of places.

In a voice husky with desire, he asked her, "Are you enjoying yourself?"

"I am, in fact. It is a magical evening, is it not?" She turned a little, tilting her head against his shoulder to look up at him. Their faces were so close they almost bumped noses, but he didn't move away and neither did she.

He smiled, holding her gaze. "I was just thinking the very same thing." His eyes dropped to her mouth, where a hint of a smile turned her lips upwards, beckoning him.

Just as he began to tilt his head to close the gap between their mouths, she turned her face away and gestured to the river and the grounds. "Thank you for this. It has been a wonderful reprieve from – well, everything else. And Ahmose is having the time of his life."

"Did you need a reprieve?" His voice was calm and low. He envisioned how, if he'd wanted to pet that gazelle near the oasis all those years ago, he'd approach slowly, palms up. With that in mind, he stroked her bicep in a soothing gesture. "Why haven't you been eating these past few days?"

She didn't answer immediately; looking out over the water instead and watching the boat procession fade in the distance. He feared he'd gone too far, too fast, and he couldn't backtrack now.

Iset didn't look at him as she said, "I have… things… that I worry about. Our *mewet* is sick. We don't – that is – Dedi doesn't make a lot working in the Land of the Dead, and our *yet* recently passed away. Soon I'll need to find a trade for Ahmose to apprentice in. I would like something better for him than to be a painter, like Dedi. Our *yet* was a draughtsman, and our older brother studied to be one as well. If either of them were alive, they could train him. But now there is just us. If Ahmose isn't home to help take care of our *mewet*… well I would miss him terribly." Her last words came out clipped, as if she'd meant to say something else and thought better of it.

"And is there no one who can help you with that? Surely you have some other family, or friends?"

She kept her eyes trained on the water as she shook her head. "No. My *yet* made it… difficult sometimes, and he alienated what was left of the rest of our family, they want nothing to do with us. Senebtawi – the man you met briefly – was my *yet*'s friend, and he's offered to find Ahmose an apprenticeship. But…" her voice trailed off and her grip on his wrist tightened. "I would prefer not to be in his debt."

"But please," she twisted in his arms so that she was half-facing him. "I would rather not talk about him tonight. I find I've been enjoying the evening more than I'd expected, and I don't want to think about my other troubles."

Batr decided not to push her too far; he didn't want to lose what little confidence she had in him. He tried to lighten the mood, and smiled down at her. "Were you not expecting to enjoy my company? I promise you, I'm not as dangerous as you think me to be."

"No? But you are dangerous nonetheless, aren't you? Even if you aren't still a pirate." Her eyes were intense as they searched his face, as if trying to read him, or see inside. It was a sensation he wasn't at all comfortable with. It reminded him too much of the way his brother Makae looked at him sometimes, boring through his cheerful veneer.

He said lightly, "Come now, let's be honest, Nofret. Why do you think me so menacing? What have I done to make you think I pose any sort of threat?"

"Absolutely nothing. But you strike me as the type to leave heartbroken women in your wake, and I have no interest in being one of them."

Batr blinked. While impressed by her candour, she had, perhaps, struck a bit too close to the heart of the matter. She continued, leaning against him and warming his chest with her body. His natural reaction to her nearness was arousal but her words, though delivered softly, were cutting.

"You see, Batr, I don't believe you have any intention of staying in Abdju. You have already confessed to growing up a nomad, travelling the seas for years as a pirate, working temporarily in Kemet as a soldier – which I presume would require you to travel a considerable amount – and now you have landed here. You have only been here for, what, about a week now? And yet here you are attempting to trifle with me.

"I don't know how or why you came to Abdju, but I can hardly trust your attentions to be anything but transient. That is if, in fact, you have any true regard for me, as you have yet to express any beyond admiration for my appearance. And that in itself is fleeting, for soon enough I'll age like everyone else. My breasts will sag and my skin will wrinkle."

He wondered if it was odd that her words didn't dampen his arousal at all. Yes, her breasts were fantastic, but it wasn't just that he was interested in. In fact, the more she spoke, the more he wanted to take her up into his arms and silence her with his mouth.

But he didn't, and she went on. "Furthermore, I'm generally considered to be a respectable woman here in my town. It won't help my reputation one bit to be seen with you if your intentions are simply to take me to bed and then move on. I'll be a laughingstock and my chances of a decent marriage will become even thinner than they already are. There are plenty of women who offer their services without you needing to waste time on me."

Batr opened his mouth to say something, *anything*, he knew not what. He was used to all types of women, and he was especially fond of women who were honest and didn't play games, but this was something else altogether. Had he really thought he could charm her into sharing information and yes, ideally his bed as well, and then walk away from her? Or what? Take her and her family to Thinis and install her somewhere as his mistress? Knowing her now as he did, he realized how foolish that was; she'd never accept such a situation. He'd wanted to help her, but his plans to do that hadn't really extended much beyond untangling her from whatever trouble she was in *right now*. Batr wasn't used to thinking about long-term things; his life had been too transient and unpredictable.

"To be frank," she turned her face up to him, "I *do* find myself attracted to you. I appreciate your kindness towards myself and my brother. But I fear Ahmose will soon become attached to you, and when you leave he'll suffer one more in a series of painful losses. I don't know what exactly your intentions are, but if it's me you're after, I suggest that from now on we meet in a more private setting, where Ahmose won't be affected. You don't need to curry favour with him to win me over. Particularly if our relationship is to be cut short when you move on again in the near future."

Was she offering him an affair? Batr frowned. But before he could formulate a response for her, he caught sight of something that made him pause. *His brother*. A ways in the distance, over the tops of the flickering torches, Makae was watching him with eyebrows raised and head cocked. *Dammit*. Batr couldn't have Iset seeing his twin. If she did, she'd have good reason to be suspicious of him. He jerked his head to let Makae know he'd spotted him, and for him to move away. Then he swiftly put his hands on Iset's waist and twirled her around to face him.

He held her tightly and leaned his face close to hers so she wouldn't turn and see Makae. "Nofret, you have every right to wonder these things. I don't blame you. And I *want* to continue to discuss this with you." He paused to lick his lips, taking the time to choose his words. By the gods, this was the worst possible time for Makae to find him. But he couldn't ignore his brother. Communication had been difficult given the distance between the village and Ahaneith's court, and they couldn't share everything through messengers they didn't fully trust. "I have to leave you for a few minutes. I wouldn't go if it wasn't very important. Wait for me here, I'll be back. I promise."

"Huh." Iset's arms crossed under her breasts. Her foot was tapping on the grass and he winced. He knew that stance. It was the universal posture of an angry woman. Her voice was tight as she said, "I think leaving in the middle of a conversation about you leaving says something, doesn't it?"

He needed to salvage the situation somehow. He didn't have the answers she was looking for, but he didn't want her angry with him. Still holding her waist, he pulled her to him and, ignoring her stiff arms, nuzzled her ear with his lips.

She tensed under his hands, but he heard her sharp intake of breath. There was desire for him in her, buried deep.

"Perhaps it does say something." He whispered. "But perhaps it means nothing at all." He let his lips brush her earlobe and she started, but didn't pull away. "I have no intention of walking away from you right now and not coming back."

He released her and gave her one last meaningful look before stalking off in the direction he'd seen his brother go, feeling Iset's eyes boring in to his back every step of the way.

Chapter 10 – Festival's End

Iset watched Batr go, every inch of her body rigid and tight. Heat coursed through her body, aching in the very depths of her core. When his large, ambling figure disappeared into the crowd she finally remembered to breathe. *Damn him.* Never had a man confused her so much. She wanted to trust him. Very, very much so. When he'd held her in his arms she'd felt safe and secure and cared for. For once in her life she thought it possible that someone else might be willing and able to support her, to prop her up the way the sturdy wooden beams of a home held up the slab of the roof. She wanted to fold up those few enchanted moments with him and hold that feeling in her heart always.

But given Batr's nomadic history and his ability to smash through her defences and insert himself into her and Ahmose's lives, she knew something wasn't right. Batr *would* leave, and there was good reason to suspect he planned to leave with the treasures of the pharaoh's tomb in tow.

She stared out over the water for some time, watching the torches on the opposite bank flicker and dance. The music from the *hnr* drifted back down the river, their tune now a cheerful one so at odds with her conflicted feelings.

Her thoughts were interrupted by a slurred voice from behind her. "Ishetnofret. Ish been so long."

Iset turned, her arms crossed over her breasts, rubbing her chilled biceps. Addaya lurched out of the shadows towards her. *Drunk.* Addaya was flat out drunk. "Ishetnofret," he repeated in a sing-sing voice, waggling his fingers at her. There was a goofy leer plastered on his face. "How're ya? Haven't seen you out in a pharaoh's age."

Iset's skin prickled in warning. From her hazy memories of last night at the tavern, she remembered Addaya following the serving woman into the back rooms of the

House of Hent. She remembered him laughing when the other men made crude comments about her. Anger welled up in her. Her fingernails dug into her arms, and she stepped back from him, widening her stance for better balance.

She drew herself up to her full height, almost as tall as him, and lifted her chin. "I've been rather busy, actually. A few things have happened this past year. You may recall that my brother died, my *yet* died, my *mewet* is ill, and I'm raising my little brother all alone." She cocked her head, her lips twitching in a tight, sarcastic smile.

"Aww, c'mon now Iset. I'm sorry 'bout all that, ya know? Always liked your brother." He came closer and she could smell the alcohol from his breath in the air. "I've been thinking 'bout you, Isetnofret. 'Bout that time I walked you home."

"That was a long time ago, Addaya. And you never came around after that." Despite her efforts, her voice shook with emotion. "You never said *anything* about it, and you never came to see how we were doing." How had she ever thought him attractive? Already at twenty-one, his jowls sagged, his paunch hung over his shenti, and the braided loop of his hair was unkempt.

She kept her eye on him as she took another step back, but her foot slipped on a rock and she stumbled. He lunged forward and caught her up, his hands fisting in the back of her dress as he pulled her to him, trapping her arms at her sides.

She struggled, but even intoxicated he was still incredibly strong. His voice became a clear, sharp hiss in her ear. "C'mon, Isetnofret. We had a little something, didn't we? I hear your cousin Dedi hasn't been making much in the Land of the Dead. We could work a little something out, couldn't we? I'm willing to pay for it."

With one arm gripping her tightly against him he slid the other over her bottom. "You're a little skinnier than you used to be, but I'd give you enough to buy some extra beer and grain now and then to help out. Isn't that the deal you've got going on with Senebtawi and that foreign one I hear you've had over at your place now? I heard Senebtawi brings over fancy fruits shipped up from the south."

"What?" Iset was almost shocked into stillness. Except that Addaya's hand was still roving, and as she squirmed he tried to move his fingers up her side. "Get off me, you swine." She reared her head back and spat at him, hitting him under his eye with a glob of saliva.

Addaya cursed and released her. He lifted his hand as if to strike her. But he didn't get the chance. Batr loomed beside him and grabbed his wrist, twisting it around and up behind his back. With his nostrils flared, eyes narrowed, and muscles corded and tight, Batr looked murderous. He growled at Addaya, "You owe her an apology."

Addaya tried to twist from Batr's grip, but Batr was bigger, stronger, and battle-hardened. Iset could see that he was perfectly in control, despite the fierce look on his face. He ratcheted Addaya's arm further up his back, and Addaya came up on his toes to alleviate the pressure.

"Owowowow! You're going to break my arm! I'm sorry, alright?" Pain seemed to have cleared the haze of drink from his eyes as they bulged and rolled wildly around. "I'm sorry, Isetnofret! I didn't mean it. Just let me go."

Batr released him and Addaya shook his arm to work out the pain. Batr glanced at her, a question in his eyes. She ignored it and stalked up to Addaya. She didn't care that people were starting to look at them. "You *ntiu*," *worthless one,* she hissed. "How dare you? You were my brother's best friend and you didn't even care that he died. You are a man without honour. Your name should be wiped from the slates of history when you die so that no one will remember it. And yet here you are, drunker than the goddess Sekhmet herself, and you have the nerve to accuse me of prostituting myself. If I were to sell my favours I promise you it would be for a lot more than a bowl of figs from Kush. I know my own worth."

And just like that the frustrations of the last several days, the exhaustion, the confusion, the terror, everything bunched up inside her and her hand flew out and cracked across Addaya's face. He stared at her with a stupid look of shock, so she did it again. And then again. The smacks were hard, open-palmed, and brought about with all the force she had in her thin body.

A loud whoop arose from nearby, startling Iset. "Get him, Iset!" Iset jerked her head and saw Ahmose standing at the front of a crowd that had grown up around her, Addaya, and Batr. "Hit him again, Iset! He's a dog! Worse than a jackal's ass!" Several people, faces she recognized from her village, had begun to cheer her. Others were laughing and murmuring words of support.

In horror, Iset turned from Addaya to grab Ahmose's arm and steer him away. People offered her their appreciation as she passed. Apparently many were familiar with Addaya's debauchery. She realized she'd been too secluded and self-involved this past year to even hear the gossip about him. But she was also embarrassed that she'd let her emotions get away from her, and she dragged Ahmose a good distance before stopping. When she did, she saw that Batr had followed along behind them.

She huffed out a breath and held up a hand. "I don't really want to talk about it. I shouldn't have done that in front of Ahmose. And you, sir," she turned to her little brother and shook a finger at him, "Just because I lost my temper doesn't mean you have a right to swear like that. I shouldn't have hit him in the first place."

"Oh no, you definitely should have." Batr deep voice rumbled, laced with amusement. "That was really quite impressive. Remind me *never* to get on your bad side."

"Yeah, Iset! You whacked him a good one!" Ahmose mimed her smacking motion, cutting through the air with first one hand, then the other. "And you tore him up with what you said! To curse his name into oblivion like that! I didn't know you had it in you! I've never *seen* you mad like that, Iset. He must have said some awful things to deserve it. I hope everyone hears about what a jackal's ass he is tomorrow."

"Hey! What did I say about your language, Ahmose?"

Ahmose settled down somewhat, looking chastened.

"That's right, little man," Batr winked, "You better be careful. Now that you've seen what your sister can do, you'd best have the fear of the gods in you."

Ahmose gave him a sly smile and Iset couldn't help the slow grin that spread across her face. "I did get him pretty good, didn't I?"

"Nebet-i, you would make a formidable enemy on the battlefield." Batr gave her a mock bow with a courtly flourish. Ahmose giggled and Iset finally allowed herself to laugh. She felt light-headed and light-hearted. A part of her had come loose and been set free when she hit Addaya. And now, sharing this moment with her brother and Batr, she felt especially close to them both. She reached out to Ahmose and her little brother wrapped his arms around her waist, giggling.

She looked up and Batr caught her glance. He was smiling, and nodding at her. She saw something startling in his eyes, something she'd never seen directed at her. Open admiration. Her breath caught at the sight of it. She'd told him earlier that he'd never expressed admiration for anything other than her looks, but she could see in his eyes that there was more to it, even if he hadn't said the words. A small voice in her head pointed out that Batr *had* been there when she needed him. He'd come back for her, just like he promised he would. And that had to mean something, didn't it?

Ten minutes into the walk home Batr offered to sling a sleepy Ahmose up into his arms and carry him. Batr didn't mind one bit. The boy was light enough and the look of appreciation on Iset's face would have made him happy to carry ten times more all the way to Thinis and back. Ahmose dozed off within minutes, his little bald head rocking gently against Batr's shoulder.

They were mostly quiet on the way back. Batr had time to mull his meeting with Makae. The two brothers had met in a small stand of shadowy trees. They'd clasped one another's forearms in greeting and spoken quickly, in low tones. Makae hadn't expected to see him, but the meeting was fortuitous as it gave them a chance to update one another on their findings.

Makae told him that he'd been working alongside the daughter of the nobleman whose tomb was robbed. He'd slipped away from her and her family at the fair when he'd caught sight of Batr. He had a lead or two that he was following up on, and hoped to have some names in the next day or so.

Batr told his brother about how he'd been recruited to rob another tomb. He intended to find out who else was involved, and if they were the same men who'd robbed the nobleman's tomb last month.

Makae jerked his head in the direction Batr had come from, where he'd left Iset waiting for him. "And the woman? Who's she?"

"She – ah – that's complicated. She might be involved, but I believe it's against her will."

Makae gazed impassively at Batr with hooded lids until Batr shifted his weight around on his feet. He hated when Makae did that. Makae had always been the quiet, observant one, and Batr the loud, gregarious one. Looking at Makae was like looking in a bronze mirror at a version of himself that wouldn't let him get away with being superficial, or ignoring certain truths.

Batr puffed out a breath and glared at his brother. "You know you're a donkey's ass sometimes, right?"

Makae held his palms up and shrugged once. "What did I do?"

"You know what."

Makae raised an eyebrow. "What aren't you telling me?"

"Fine. Fine, but you're still a donkey's ass, you know." Batr proceeded to outline what he knew about Iset and her doubling as Dedi. He left out the intimate conversation they'd been having moments ago – right before Makae's appearance interrupted them – and the fact that her little brother Ahmose reminded him of one of their own departed brothers.

Makae crossed his arms and leaned back on his heels. "Are you trying to tell me that your confidence in her innocence has nothing to do with her being a rather stunning beauty? I can't recall the last time you had your arms wrapped around someone you were thinking of arresting."

Batr rubbed a hand over his jaw. "I'm not having this conversation. I need to get back."

"Right. To that pretty woman who dresses like a boy and who is involved in a tomb robbing but isn't."

"I love you, brother, but you're in danger of catching a fist in the face right about now."

Makae grinned. "I love you, too."

Batr snorted and shook his head, but clasped his brother's outstretched arm as they had when greeting one another. Makae said, "But seriously, Batr, I don't know what you're doing with her, but I hope you've given it serious thought. And I hope for your sake she *is* blameless."

"What's that supposed to mean?"

One corner of Makae's lip twitched upwards. "That she sounds like a woman of some substance. And if she can make you look all silly-eyed like you have been the last few minutes then perhaps it's time you considered settling down."

"I'm not interested in settling down."

"Do you ever think it might be time you got over what happened with the tribe and start a family of your own? If you can't, you'll end up spending the rest of your life alone. And those pretty looks of yours aren't going to last forever, you know."

Batr didn't like to be reminded of the night they'd lost their family, but it was always hard for him to get mad at Makae. Instead, he said wryly, "Huh. Well I guess I could say the same to you, brother, since you look an awful lot like me, you know."

Makae gave him an enigmatic smile. "Hmmm. But I'm not the one against having a family, am I?"

The brothers had parted then, promising to keep in close contact over the next couple of days, employing messengers and encrypted missives to share new developments.

Now, as he walked with Iset by his side, Batr's thoughts roamed back to her proposition. Was she serious about having an affair? And if so, was it because she wanted *him*, or because she wanted to distract him from finding out more about her involvement in the tomb robbing? In the past, he wouldn't have bothered to make a distinction if it included sex with a beautiful woman. Whatever a woman's reasons, be it for fun, money, or other more calculating motives, in the end he wouldn't have become entangled. Now, though, he found that it mattered. He wanted more than just Iset's body - he wanted her to *want* him.

When they finally reached her home, Iset pushed open the door and Batr ducked inside, still carrying Ahmose. He came up short, realizing there was somebody there. A few oil wicks were burning on stools, and a woman sat on the bench at the far end of the room.

"*Mewet*!" Batr registered the shock in Iset's voice. So this was the sick mother. He looked at her more closely, and saw the resemblance. She looked very much like Iset, although older, tired, and even gaunter. But still, he could see the vestiges of a beautiful woman. Her hair, although streaked with grey and unkempt, was black and thick and carried tints of red, like her daughter's.

The woman stood and gave a thin smile. "Iset, dear. I woke up and I – I wanted a cup of tea. You were all gone and it was dark, so I… well I was going to make some, but I couldn't quite recall where…" She trailed off as her eyes travelled over to Batr. "Hello. I'm terribly sorry. I wasn't expecting guests." She patted her hands over her hair then smoothed her palms down her dress.

Ahmose stirred in his arms so Batr set the boy down and strode over to the woman. "It is a pleasure to meet you." He took her hand and bowed over it in a formal gesture.

"Oh! Yes. And you also. I am Ankhesenamon." Her eyes flicked to Iset, who happened to be staring open mouthed at her mother. Batr could see the glimmering of tiny flaming oil wicks reflected in the unshed tears filling Iset's eyes. He saw hope and joy as well.

Iset started, though, when Ahmose said in a sleepy voice, "*Mewet*? You're up?"

Ankhesenamon had left her hand in Batr's, and he could feel her fingers tighten even as they trembled slightly. She drew herself up taller. "Yes, dear. I'm feeling better tonight."

Ahmose ran over to her and threw his arms around her waist. "Oh, *mewet*, we had so much fun tonight! There was so much food, and there were plays, and so many boats and the Horus god, and then Iset beat up Addaya, and oh! It's all thanks to Batr because he took us and it was the best night ever. I wish you'd been there, too."

The woman smiled and she and Ahmose sat on the bench while he chattered about their night.

Batr decided this was a moment that shouldn't include him, and he whispered to Iset that he would leave them now. He said his goodbyes to their mother and Ahmose, and Iset followed him to the door. Stepping outside after him, she pulled the door shut behind her and put her back to it.

She gave him a wobbly smile. "Thank you, Batr, for *everything*. Tonight has been… well it's been memorable. And I don't think you can understand just how wonderful it is to see my *mewet* out of bed. It's been some time since that happened."

A tear slipped past her lower lashes and Batr reached to brush it away, cupping her cheek in the process. Her soft, plump lips parted and she lowered her gaze to the ground but nudged her face against his palm. The gesture warmed him and he stroked the soft skin of her cheek with the rough pad of his thumb.

Batr rested his other elbow on the door next to her head. He leaned forward and heard her breath catch in her throat as he grazed her lips with his. Her breath was sweet, like honey buns, her lips warm and supple. He nudged her neck with his nose and was pleased when she began to pant short, shallow breaths, her breasts angling up towards him in a subtle, presumably unconscious motion. Inhaling her alluring scent, his groin tightened with the need to press her against the door, lift her dress, and thrust himself up into her.

Drawing in deeply of her jasmine scented hair, he whispered next to her ear, harkening back to her earlier words. "You're a woman to be admired, Nofret. For so many reasons, I admire you. And it's not just for your appearance. You are strong, kind, smart, selfless, and good. You're a better person than I am. I don't think I've ever held a woman in higher esteem than you. I have traveled the world and met many women, and I can assure you there is nothing transient about my deep respect for you."

She turned to him with a startled expression, once again almost bumping his nose as she had earlier that evening. He smiled, tilted her face upwards, and brushed her mouth with his. Then, when her tongue darted out nervously to moisten her lips, he followed it with another kiss, covering her mouth with his. She rose up on her toes to push back against him, her supple breasts pressing against his chest, her torso stretched against his. When her delicate fingers wrapped around his shoulders, her small nails digging into his skin in the most agonizingly pleasurable display of her desire, Batr thought he'd happily let her draw blood if it meant he could sate himself with her.

He fitted his palm against her lower back, holding her tight against him as their mouths met with a growing intensity, a fierce give and take in which he was no longer sure who was directing the kiss and who had the greater need.

Tightening his grip on her, a covetous need to touch her everywhere thrummed through him – a need to taste her, to be deep inside her. He wanted to shatter her defences and leave her thrashing, panting, and moaning under him. He wanted *her*, in his bed, every night, every morning, all the time. If he didn't stop this soon he'd lose control.

With his hands pushing on her hips, Batr held Iset back a distance while he struggled for breath and sanity. Her hands slid from his shoulders to drag through her hair, shaking her head slightly.

"I…" Iset's voice faltered, a confused expression flitted over her beautiful face.

She looked incredibly luscious, her lips kiss-swollen and parted, eyes dark with desire, breasts rising and falling with each heavy breath. Batr bit down hard on his bottom lip to keep himself from giving in to temptation and taking her in her doorway. Perhaps she'd even let him, given her passionate response, but he knew he couldn't do that to her. She deserved more than that. At least for their first time together. Later – when she knew just how much he respected her – there might be opportunities for other, more adventurous things.

The fact that he was even considering such things bewildered him, and he released Iset's hips, dropping his hands by his sides in loose fists. Through ragged breaths he ground out his farewell. "*Senebti, nebet-i.* I hope you sleep well tonight."

"*Senebti,*" she murmured, leaning back against the door and covering her mouth with one hand.

With that, he forced himself to turn and stride through the night, back to the dark empty hut he currently called home. A cold night breeze blew over from the dessert, and he wished he were in the far north, where he could throw himself into the icy waters of the great sea and drive out all thoughts of making love to a woman who was more enigmatic than any other he'd ever known.

Chapter 11 – Archers and Ladies of the Night

The next day

In the days leading up to the Horus Festival Makae had been too busy with preparations, and ensuring that Lady Ahaneith could move safely through the crowds, to find the time to investigate Raia's brother or Userkare. But his brief exchange with Batr the first night of the festival impressed upon him a sense of urgency to find the men responsible for the tomb thefts, lest they get away with yet another robbery. Makae had little concern for the eternal peace of the deceased Pharaoh Wadj – the man's ka could rot in the underworld for all Makae cared – but each break-in would make it increasingly difficult to hide the crimes from the people of Kemet. And once they learned of it, they could take it as a sign of the queen's inability to rule and maintain maat. Her regency was tenuous at best, and both Batr and Makae owed her greatly for placing her trust in them, and bestowing her favours upon them.

Makae could not live with himself if shame befell Queen Merneith because he hadn't done his job properly. And so it was that the day after the first day of the festival, with Lady Ahaneith's security no longer in question, Makae set about determining the innocence, or guilt, of Raia's brother.

First he sought out Lady Ahaneith's head huntsman, the man who organized her hunting expeditions. Under the pretense of arranging a hunt, he asked who a nobleman might speak to about gathering a team of hunters.

The huntsman, a stocky fellow somewhere around forty years of age, with a barrel chest and a wide stance, tucked his thumbs in the top of his shenti and said, "I can organize what you need. But you better tell me what you're looking for."

"Ahhh, yes," Makae hedged, "I have no doubt you'd do the best job of it. But the thing is, I am trying to impress a lady. It so happens her brother is an avid hunter, and I thought if I arranged a hunt for him it might put me in the lady's good graces. Thought I'd use the fellow the boy normally uses so it's all just the way he likes it. It seems her brother has, ah, taken a dislike to me."

Makae thought it best to play the humble lover, and keep his story as close to the truth as possible. If Semer was innocent then Makae intended to go ahead with the hunt and invite the boy along. It couldn't hurt matters, considering Semer really didn't seem to like him.

He hadn't seen Semer since the day the boy invaded Raia's home after they'd questioned Userkare. For that matter, Makae hadn't seen much of Raia, either. Although they'd attended the festival together with the children – it had been his suggestion, after all – Makae had yet to spend another night in her bed. Given his suspicions regarding her brother he couldn't help but feel it would be very inappropriate to continue their intimacy until he'd cleared up the situation. Although she hadn't asked him to stay again, he had sensed her disappointment that he didn't offer to. He hoped to rectify the matter as soon as possible.

The huntsman gave a snort that could have been a chuckle as he looked Makae over and nodded knowingly. "Had the same problem with my second wife and her useless brother. Luckily, he up and died before he got in the way. What kind of game you looking for? That makes a difference."

Foreseeing this question, Makae had asked Raia the other day what sort of hunting her brother preferred and so was prepared with an answer. "Deer."

The other man's eyes narrowed in thought. "What'd you say the kid's name was? Might be I know who he uses."

"Semer, son of Ra-hotep who passed away recently. His sister is Raia, the landowner."

Nodding again, the huntsman said, "I know 'im. Come across him in the plains to the south of Abdju where the deer are most plentiful. The kid's out there all the time.

Likes the foxes, too, as I recall." He gave Makae the name of the huntsman and a couple of the archers that Semer often used and where they might be found.

Makae went to the huntsman's home, a medium-sized mud-brick hut on the edge of the wealthier neighbourhood of Abdju, but there was no answer at the door. So he continued on towards a nearby field, a place Lady Ahaneith's huntsman said was often used by archers for practice. There he found three younger men competing, shooting across a long stretch of sand and low-growing scrub at human-sized dolls – linen robes stuffed with rags and straw – propped up against stone slabs.

Giving them the same story he'd given the huntsman, the men reacted with varying degrees of suspicion. At first, Makae didn't understand their hesitation to tell him if they'd hunted with Semer, or their unwillingness to let him hire them for a hunt involving the boy. That is, until one of them asked who was paying for the hunt.

Makae frowned. "The responsibility lies with me. And I can assure you I am good for it. I'll even pay you up front if you need it. But what's the problem?"

Finally, one of the men confessed that Semer had been known, from time to time, to not pay his hunters accordingly. "I don't like to speak ill of the nobility," one of them, a tall, lean man with a scar across one cheek, said. "But sometimes he's erratic."

"Erratic how?" Makae crossed his arms over his chest and affected a casual stance. "Look, friend, I'm trying to make nice with his sister and if the kid is having problems, it's best I know of them now, before I get in too deep with the family. If they're in debt, I'd like to know." This was more true than the archers could possibly guess. If Semer was involved Makae had best know now before things became more complicated with him and Raia.

The archers exchanged looks before the one with the scarred cheek shrugged one shoulder and said, "Sometimes he's generous and gives us something extra up front, and other times it's like he forgets. When we complain to the huntsman he says Semer doesn't always pay him on time, either. We don't have much recourse if the nobility doesn't pay up, you see. If we complain, we risk getting a bad name and losing our jobs altogether."

A sinking feeling settled in the pit of Makae's stomach as he wondered how in the living world he would tell Raia that he'd have to execute her little brother.

Then another of the archers, a reedy fellow with large ears and a nose with a bump as high as a desert sand dune, chimed in. "I don't always trust Djer, though. It's the huntsman who's supposed to pay us, you see, after the noblemen pay him. He says he's just as bad off as the rest of us, but he's always got enough to buy himself a drink, sometimes even a woman." A wistful expression came over his face.

With a mischievous gleam in his eye, the scarred archer accused him, "You're just saying that 'cuz you're jealous he paid for the whole night with that pretty girl from the House of Tiy you've had your eye on."

Makae remained while the two archers made fun of the third for his longing for the lady for hire. When their raillery died down, he asked, "Any idea where I might find the huntsman? I went by his place but there didn't seem to be anyone home."

The large-eared archer snorted. "He was probably there, still sleeping off last night. I saw him at the festival last night, partaking in Her Majesty's fine wine. You'll likely find him there again later tonight, or maybe at the House of Tiy, spending all our deben of grain."

Makae hoped it was the latter. If the huntsman – a man he'd never laid eyes on before – was at the festival, Makae would have about as much luck finding him as he would finding a grain of wheat in a silo full of barley.

While waiting for nightfall, Makae set about investigating Userkare, the man formerly betrothed to Raia's mother. Back at Lady Ahaneith's court, he sought out the lady herself, to see if she had any idea why Userkare's family was sent into exile, and if it had anything to do with Raia's father.

He managed to catch Lady Ahaneith while she was taking a light repast on the palace rooftop. Served as she was by a multitude of servants under a white linen canopy, a slave announced Makae and he ducked his head under the low-lying fringe of the sunshade.

Seated on the ground amongst an array of cushions, the young ruler raised her white-blonde head and smiled at Makae when he entered. Tipping her unusual green eyes up to him, she lifted a delicate hand for him to grip and bow over. "Makae," she murmured in lightly accented Kemeti.

"*Hem-etj*," he greeted her as *Your Majesty*. As Pharaoh Wadj's second wife, Lady Ahaneith was second only to Queen Merneith in prestige.

Once seated near her on the cushions and dispensing with the pleasantries, he asked what she knew of Userkare.

"Userkare," she frowned. "His farms supply some of the food for the tomb workers in the Land of the Dead, correct? No, I do not believe I have met him."

Makae shook his head. "Likely not. He's elderly and very ill and does not attend court. I do not think he has much time left in the living world. He was exiled some twenty years ago. No, a little more than that, about twenty-four years past." He corrected himself, recalling it was shortly before Raia was born.

"Long before my time," Ahaneith pursed her lips, a wrinkle appearing in her smooth brow.

Her words called to mind the first time he'd met Ahaneith five years ago. Reasonably new to Kemet himself then, he'd been part of the group of soldiers to escort her when she'd first landed on the northern coast. Back then, she'd been the pretty daughter of a wealthy Sumerian merchant who'd sent his youngest daughter as a gift – a wife – for the Pharaoh Wadj, in the hopes of building trading ties. Makae easily recalled the image of the frightened, reed-thin, thirteen-year-old girl standing on the deck of a war vessel, and her valiant attempt to maintain her dignity in the face of a group of armed men speaking an unknown, foreign tongue.

Thinking on it, Makae was once again glad Pharaoh Wadj was dead. The selfish bastard had left his innocent child-bride to fend for herself in Abdju while he entertained himself elsewhere in Kemet, rather than taking the time to school her in the ways of ruling. However, Makae could see that the young woman was now beginning to break away from her advisors and think for herself. In the past few days he'd watched her differ with her advisors more than once on matters pertaining to the security of Abdju, deferring instead to Makae's expertise in both sea and desert warfare. With the right guidance, Makae believed she had the potential to be a capable leader of the southern towns.

"I seem to recall some rumour about the man," Lady Ahaneith said, hooking a finger under the beaded turquoise collar that rested on her alabaster skin and lifting it, as if the necklace weighed too heavily on her slender neck. "He returned from exile before I came to Kemet, is that right? There was some land dispute. I do not know the details, only that it was mentioned in passing not long ago by Ammon, my land official. It is coming time to collect the taxes on the farmlands, you know, and he made some remark about Ra-hotep's death and some long-standing argument about the land adjoining their fields."

She gave a small, apologetic shrug and said, "You will have to speak with Ammon, or perhaps the scribe who manages Ra-hotep's and Userkare's lands. One of them might recall something and be more useful than I. But since I have you here for a moment, Makae, I would like to speak with you about our security without the others around."

She told him she'd received word that morning that another town in the south was raided two days ago and wanted to ask his advice. "You are yourself of a nomadic tribe, and have an understanding of how to negotiate with them," she'd said. "Some of my advisors have never stepped foot outside of the big cities, whereas you have campaigned at sea and in the desert. I would like to hear how you perceive the matter, and how best to keep Kemet from going to war. You know better than most how Queen

Merneith would handle something like this, and I have always admired her wisdom."

They spent the next hour or so in discussion before Lady Ahaneith surprised him by saying, "I should tell you that I intend to ask Queen Merneith for your indefinite continuance here to oversee our security. I would prefer to have your consent first, if you will give it."

"It is a great kindness for you to ask, Hem-etj. I am truly honoured." Ahaneith could have easily asked the queen's consent and then ordered him to stay. That she'd asked him first was a mere formality, but a polite one that showed her consideration.

Accepting the position would mean that, for the first time in their lives, he and his brother would be separated, perhaps permanently. Makae regretted it deeply. As far as he knew, Batr was the only close family he had left in the living world. At the same time, he'd always imagined they'd have to part ways at some point. Refusing Lady Ahaneith's offer was not an option, it would be far too disrespectful and anyone else would think he'd suffered from madness for snubbing such an honour.

Three days ago he also would have been pleased that such an arrangement would enable him to pursue Raia freely, with the knowledge that their relationship need not to come to an abrupt end when he left town. However, once Raia learned that her brother was a suspect in his investigation, he doubted the news of his continued presence in Abdju would be in the least bit welcome.

Makae said all that was appropriate to thank Ahaneith. Once their business was complete, he took his leave and called for a messenger boy, charging him with the task of running to the village on the outskirts of the Land of the Dead. Not knowing what he might meet with, Makae preferred to have his brother at his side when he went in search of Semer's huntsman. From what the archers told him, he gathered the House of Tiy was a less-than-savoury little place on the edge of the city, and he didn't like the idea of walking in alone. Furthermore, if the huntsman was unwilling to talk to him, or was in the company of friends, it wouldn't hurt to have Batr with him. It was unlikely the huntsman would know anyone that had come in contact with his brother in the Land of the Dead. Tomb workers had no need of a huntsman; their food was mostly provided by Raia's and Userkare's farms, and they usually fished, rather than hunted, to supplement their sometimes meagre rations. Villagers hunted and fished to survive, not for sport.

Sending the messenger boy off with a note encrypted in the language of their homeland, Makae requested Batr meet him on the edge of the city after nightfall. Batr had arranged for a boy in the village to accept any messages sent between them. That way, neither messenger would know that the recipients on either end were twins. Makae had told his messenger that he had a sweetheart in the village, while Batr had told the village boy he had a sweetheart at the palace. Running swiftly, a messenger could make it between the city and the village in under an hour. As long as Batr could be found, he ought to be able to make it to the city in time to accompany Makae to the tavern.

This accomplished, Makae made his way through the dusty streets of the town surrounding the palace grounds to the home of the official Lady Ahaneith suggested he speak with. There was little hope the man would be home, given that the Horus Festival was in its second day, with most of the nobles in attendance. But Makae had time to spare before he sought out Semer's huntsman at the tavern and it was worth the attempt.

When he knocked on the heavy wooden door of a large, white-washed mud-brick home, and stood waiting for several heart beats, he knew he'd surmised correctly. It appeared even the servants had the day off. Returning to the palace with a restless mind, he had little to do but wait for nightfall and his brother's arrival.

The House of Tiy was not built for people of Makae and Batr's height, as evidenced by their need to duck their heads – and remain hunched – upon entering the ill-lit tavern. Makae had been in any number of dingy, sleazy taverns over the years, and this had to be one of the worst of the bunch. As his eyes adjusted to the heavy gloom, he observed that the cushions scattered across the broken reed mats on the floor, serving as seating for the patrons, were frayed and torn in places, stained with years' worth of beer and wine spills and other indefinable brown and yellow splotches. The sick scent of vomit hovered in the stale air, and tattered privacy screens drooped between clumpings of cushions, their effectiveness questionable given that they dangled from splintered bits of wood.

The brothers exchanged raised eyebrows, and Makae thanked the gods that his days of frequenting such places were in the past. The tavern was fairly empty, given that the Horus Festival offered a certain amount of free beer and wine for festival goers and it was still early in the evening. The House of Tiy wouldn't fill up until the most seasoned of drinkers had exhausted their allowed amount and come in search of more alcohol.

Makae and Batr ordered a couple of mugs of beer from a serving woman and settled themselves in to wait for the huntsman. After a short time, a woman approached them. She wore a poorly made wig that should have been put to rest years ago, and an excessive amount of red ochre rubbed into her cheeks and lips. The one thing not tawdry and aged about her, Makae noticed, was a wide, beaded collar in blue about her neck, skillfully designed to look like the goddess Isis taking flight. Of an indeterminate age, given the amount of makeup and the poor lighting, Makae guessed her somewhere in her forties. Her forceful carriage indicated that she must be Tiy, the owner of the establishment.

"Nedj kheret," greetings, she said, openly assessing them. "I am Tiy, welcome." As she took in the fine quality of their clean linen shentis and their well-fed, muscular appearance, her overdrawn red lips stretched in a wide, hungry smile. Her look told Makae that the men who patronised this place were as shabby as the furnishings.

"New in town, are you?" she asked, clapping her hands and rubbing them together, looking them over with eagerness, as if hoping they might open the small sacks tied to their belts and let gold spill out over her floor.

"Something like that," Batr grinned at her. His more gregarious nature served the brothers well when they needed to charm women. While a woman might open up to a quiet man like Makae over time, it was rarely an immediate thing. Batr said in his smooth, intimate voice, "Some acquaintances recommended your tavern as one of the finest in town."

"Oh, wasn't that kind of them," she twittered, flapping a dismissive hand but with an appreciative gleam in her eye. Even she had to know no one could say such a thing about this dilapidated hut, but she quickly took to Batr.

With a suggestive lift to her drawn-on eyebrows, she added, "I also have some of the finest girls in town, if you happen to be in need of a little *entertainment*."

Makae noticed Batr's smile tighten and tension stiffen his shoulders. The posture was so unlike his typically laid-back brother that Makae wondered what had got him so pent up. The image of Batr with his arms around a pretty village girl the day before at the Horus Festival came to mind. He hoped his brother wasn't getting too involved with a suspect. Then, recalling that his own position was not much better, he set his thoughts aside and answered their hostess.

"Thank you," Makae said. "As a matter of fact, we're looking for someone. We heard Djer the Huntsman comes here often. We're looking to arrange a hunt and were considering hiring him."

"Ha! That *nti hati?*" *That senseless wretch*, Tiy scoffed. "Trust me, you don't want to deal with him and you won't find him here again any time soon. That *libe*," *that fool*, "owes me a deben of grain for one of my girls, and he's not allowed to come back in here until he pays up and can show me that he's got enough for the night. I gave him credit and what did he do? Tried to pawn some story off on me about how the rich young nobleman he hunts for didn't pay him, and so he couldn't pay me. As if I cared whether or not he got paid, as long as I'm compensated for what he takes."

This did not bode well for Raia's brother. If the huntsman really *wasn't* getting paid, it was a good indicator that the boy was having pecuniary problems.

Batr shook his head and said to the woman, "That's a shame. Wouldn't want to work with a fellow that doesn't pay his debts."

"Pffft," Tiy parodied a spitting motion. "May a donkey take him from behind. He spent the whole night with my best girl so she couldn't take any other clients, and if *I* don't get paid, the girls don't either. And I can tell you, the things he likes to do don't come cheap."

Successful women in Tiy's profession generally attempted to cultivate the appearance of discretion in order to make their customers feel that their visits and their particular tastes would be kept secret. Tiy was clearly not one of those women. However, her loss was their gain, and the procuress's words sparked Makae's memory.

He asked the woman in a casual manner, "The fellow who told us about you is an archer. He's got some ears on him," Makae cupped his hands over his ears and gave them a little flap, like an elephant's. "He mentioned you had a pretty girl here that he liked. Would that, by any chance, be the same girl you're talking about?"

Tiy gave a disdainful laugh, the frizzy wig perched atop her head shaking precariously. "Ha! *That* man. Comes in here all the time, bleating around after Akela like a baby calf. She won't have him, though, I tell you. Wants her to quit working so he can take care of her, but if he can't afford to keep her for the night, how in the living world is he going to afford to keep her for life?"

"So what do you gentlemen say?" Tiy asked with a greedy glint in her eyes. "Shall I send some girls over, or would you like to visit one of the back rooms right away?"

Finding her pushiness and overt offers distasteful, Makae cleared his throat and said, "Actually, I'd like to meet that girl, Akela. I've heard so much about her now I feel we ought to see her."

Tiy clicked her tongue. "I'll have you know if there's two of you in the room with her it's still double the cost, even if it *does* cut back on the time you spend with her. But I'm sure I can convince her to accommodate the both of you."

A shiver of revulsion wracked Makae's body. While the two brothers had shared many things over the years, taking one woman at the same time had never held any appeal for them. Especially not one that needed to be "convinced".

"No, uh, thank you," he said a little unsteadily as, out of the corner of his eye, he could see his brother's shoulders shaking with suppressed laughter. "I'd just like to see her alone, if that's alright. My, uh, brother can wait."

It was a slim chance, but perhaps the prostitute knew something about the huntsman's business dealings with Semer. A combination of alcohol, darkness, and clandestine meetings had a tendency to prompt men to wag their tongues.

"You sure, hon?" Tiy looked between them, obviously hoping for the extra charge. "I'll bring you another girl. What kind do you like? Young? Dark? Light? Big or small breasts?"

Batr said shortly, "No. I'll wait."

Instead of the glib, joking response typical of him, there was an uncharacteristic hardness in the set of his jaw. Makae had to wonder if that village woman had Batr more twisted up than he'd first imagined.

Tiy led him to a room in the back of the tavern. Knocking on the door, it swung open to reveal a woman so young and pretty that she startled Makae into taking a step back. He'd expected a woman of no more than average comeliness, hardened by years of tavern life, but this was a true beauty in the making. She possessed the softly rounded face of a girl not yet reached maturity, full lips, and wide, upturned eyes set in smooth dark skin the colour of cinnamon. Her dress – a strip of frayed linen that, while clean, was faded from countless washes – revealed her slender form, wrapped as it was around her waist and over her right shoulder, leaving one breast bare. Around her neck rested an unusual, elegantly beaded collar similar to Tiy's, this one in shades of red and gold.

Introducing the girl as Akela, Tiy said, "Your friend, the archer with the ears," here she mimicked Makae's motion by cupping her hands around her ears and flapping them, throwing him a sly smile as if they'd just shared an intimate secret, "he talked so much about you Makae here had to come see you himself."

Trepidation flitted across the girl's face as she looked him over, but still Akela held out a hand, taking Makae's large one in her soft little one. "Come," she said, pulling him into the room.

"Wait!" Tiy held out her hand, her shrewd eyes narrowing. "You have to pay for her first. I won't give nobody credit again, no matter how fancy they might look."

Reaching into one of the leather pouches tied about his waist, Makae pulled out a small, bright blue ring made of faience, which Tiy snatched up. It disappeared quickly into the folds of her dress. No small wonder, as the ring was worth at least two full nights with the girl.

Once the door was shut behind them, the girl – who didn't quite reach Makae's shoulder – asked him what he'd like her to do. Loathing that he was even in this situation, he just wanted out of the room as fast as possible. Although he had no intentions of doing *anything* with the girl, guilt assailed him. He and Raia had made no promises to one another, and she was sure to hate him for investigating his brother, yet it was her face that came to mind when he looked down at this lovely young woman.

"Nothing," he said. "I don't want you do anything. I just want to ask you a few questions."

"I – I don't understand." If Akela had looked Makae over with hesitation in her large dark eyes before, she now looked like she wanted to make a dash for the door behind him.

Makae held up a hand and took a step back from her, not that there was much space to do so. There was barely room for a threadbare sleeping mat, a stool with a woven basket beneath it – in which the girl had stacked a neatly folded shawl and a strip of linen, her only articles of clothing most likely – and a small icon of Isis in the corner. More of the ornate, beaded necklaces hung from sticks tied to the walls. That appeared to be all the worldly goods the girl possessed.

"It's okay," he said, "I'm just looking for some information. I just want to know about the huntsman who visited you the other night."

The girl licked her lips and her eyes flicked to the door again. Makae wished his brother were in here instead of him. Batr would have had her charmed within moments, convincing her that trading information, rather than sex, was a good thing.

Gesturing to the collars hanging on the wall, he asked. "Did you make them?"

Still unsure, Akela ventured to answer, "Yes."

"They're exquisite. Did Tiy teach you that?"

Her eyebrows shot up and a pretty little smile tilted her lips upwards, as if he'd said something terribly amusing. Given what little he knew of Tiy, even he could guess the woman incapable of such painstaking, fine work. "No. I taught myself. Tiy buys me the beads from my profits, and lets me sell them. I had hoped to make enough to stop doing this work," she gestured towards the sleeping mat, "but I don't get many customers here.... Sometimes a man buys one for his wife, or a sweetheart, but not often." Her smile faded.

Makae seated his tall frame on the precarious, three-legged stool, leaving a couple feet of distance between them. He suggested, "What about a space at the day market in the city?" Many women made a small profit laying out their wares on reed mats at the market, selling items to some of the noblewomen, or even going door-to-door.

"Oh, Tiy has me working here during the day. I help with washing the sleeping mats and sweeping the floors and baking bread. I've learned to brew beer as well." Following his example, the girl sat on the edge of the sleeping mat, pulling up her knees and wrapping her arms around them.

"What about the Horus Festival?" He asked. "You could have applied for a free stall."

She shrugged one thin shoulder. "Tiy wanted me here, working."

Suspicion niggled at him, and he asked, "How long have you been here, at the House of Tiy?"

"About six months. I – I wasn't always like this. I didn't have a choice, really. I lived with my grandmother until she passed away last year. I had nowhere else to go, and Tiy found me on the street. She took me in and gave me work, and a room and food."

Realization dawned on Makae at the same time anger rose in him. Tiy must realize what a jewel this pretty, unknowing girl was for her wretched business. She'd snapped the girl up and was preventing her from earning any of her own income, making it impossible for her to get out from under Tiy's heavy thumb.

He stuffed his revulsion down in order to maintain his calm exterior. For now, at least. "Well, it's quite the talent you have. I haven't seen finer beading either here in the court of Abdju or in Thinis."

"Truly? You've been to Thinis? Have you seen the Lady Ahaneith and the queen?" The girl's eyes grew even larger, and she sat forward.

Knowing he'd hooked her interest, Makae relaxed a little. "Indeed, I have seen and met both ladies."

He let Akela ask him a few questions, mostly about the adornment of the nobles. While Makae was not one to pay much attention to such things, his sisters, cousins, and aunts had made their own jewellery. When sharing a tent with five or eight or ten girls as he had growing up, one heard more than they cared to about necklaces, bangles, and earrings. It was inevitable that he'd learn a thing or two, enough at least to be able to appease some of her questions. Furthermore, he'd had some recent practice discussing such matters with Raia's friends at Lady Ahaneith's banquet the other night.

Finally, he turned the inquiry to his favour, telling the girl that she would be doing him a great service if she could divulge all she knew about the huntsman's state of affairs.

"Oh," her shoulders hunched at the reminder of her present occupation. "I don't know much. He was in here the other night and didn't pay his debt. Tiy won't let him back again until he does."

"Is that a common occurrence? Has he ever *not* paid his way?"

She shook her head, "No, he usually pays."

Makae sensed her hesitation and, wanting to reassure her, reached out and took her hand. "Listen, I don't want to see anyone get hurt. What I'm interested in has little to do with the huntsman, and more to do with those he works with. I just need to ask a few questions."

"But why?"

"I can only tell you it's a matter of great importance pertaining to the queen and the Lady Ahaneith. If you could help me, I would be very appreciative." He hoped that, given his appearance and the details he'd already given her about court life, she wouldn't press him for more information.

Her mouth formed an "o" shape as she drew in a sharp breath. "I see," she looked him over again in curiosity, as if she'd only just seen him for the first time. Determination glinted in her eyes.

"I *do* remember him saying something once, when he was very drunk. He was joking about how he was making some rich young man pay him extra for things, like bringing tents and food and such, things that would normally be included in his trips. He charges him for all kinds of little things he shouldn't. He was bragging about how smart he was for getting away with it."

"Did he say anything else about that young man? I heard from your friend the archer that sometimes the huntsman doesn't pay them. He used the excuse that the nobleman didn't pay him, and therefore he couldn't pay the others."

Akela scoffed. "He gets paid plenty. He's just lying to them, like he did with Tiy. He tells people he didn't get paid so he can put them off, and hopes they forget about it, which they sometimes do. Oh!" She covered her mouth with one hand. "Please don't tell Tiy I said that. She'd really go after him if she knew he was lying on purpose. She'd have him beat up or something and I'd hate for that to happen."

"Really? But he didn't pay you last time." Makae cocked his head, one eyebrow raised.

Her expression turned sheepish, and after a moment she said in a shy voice, "Sometimes he tips me a little extra, and I hide it under my sleeping mat where Tiy won't find it. He's not always *that* bad of a man."

Makae nodded. He didn't blame the girl for wanting to protect her benefactor, however lacking in morals the huntsman might be in other respects. He pressed her again, "So you're sure this rich young man always pays him on time? That's never been an issue?"

"No. He pays all right, there's no problems with that. I know because the huntsman usually comes here right after a hunt. I know some of his hunters suspect what he's doing. I – I feel bad because I know it upsets Shoshenq because he can't afford to see me then, and he's a nice man and I know he wants to marry me, but," she twisted her hands in her lap, "I *can't* tell him the truth, you know? He'd be so mad and then maybe he'd get into a fight with the huntsman and then he'd have *no* work at all."

Makae frowned. "Shoshenq?"

"The one with the ears," she cupped her ears like he and Tiy had done.

"Ah!" Makae grinned and she returned his smile. "One more question," he held up a finger. "Do you know the name of the young man he's been cheating?"

"No," she bit her lips, squinting in thought. "But he did say that the man's sister was very wealthy, she's a landowner or something?" She looked up, a question in her eyes, and he nodded for her to continue. "So the boy applies to her for what he needs to pay for the hunt. And the boy never plans a hunt unless he has the wealth ahead of time and pays up front, so the huntsman said it isn't really cheating, since the boy's family is so rich anyway."

Makae scrubbed a hand over his face, on the one hand wishing he'd never taken the time to investigate Raia's apparently innocent brother, as it would only cause him more problems. On the other hand, he might be able to do some good at least, now that he *was* here.

"Listen," he told Akela, "I would appreciate it if you didn't tell Tiy what we discussed, or anyone else for that matter. I don't want it getting out that I've been looking into the huntsman, or his clients."

"Of course," she nodded. "It's for the queen."

"Right. And, uh, here," Makae reached into one of his pouches and pulled out a small lump of gold and, taking her hand in his, placed it in her palm.

She gasped. "What's that for?"

"Your time."

"That's… no, that's too much. You already gave Tiy too much." She held out her hand for him to take the gold.

Appreciating her honesty, he persisted. "Then it's for that necklace, there." He pointed to one of the necklaces on the wall; a red one he thought would look particularly striking against Raia's dark skin. "It should be more than enough to get you out of the House of Tiy. If you trade it in, you could pay for several months in a small hut, and enough beads to get your business started. Or you could marry the archer, if you like, and this can help support you for a time. If you come find me tomorrow at Lady Ahaneith's court, and bring your necklaces, I'm sure I can find a lady or two who would be interested in becoming your first clients."

"But…" the girl gaped at him. "Why?"

He lifted one shoulder. "Because you have helped me more than you know. And because I can." It didn't seem necessary to tell her that she also called to mind the sisters he'd never see again in the living world. The thought of any one of them in her situation made him angry enough to commit violence.

The young woman's eyes filled with hope, and she stuttered, "I – thank you. Thank you so much. Tomorrow, then."

A thought struck him, and he asked, "Will Tiy cause you any problems for leaving? You can come with me tonight; I'll find you a place to sleep."

She shook her head. "No, I – I ought to tell Tiy I'm leaving first. She did take me off the street. I don't think it would be very kind of me to run off without talking to her first."

When he frowned, Akela said confidently, "She might not appear kind, but she has never mistreated me. She'll let me go."

Makae was doubtful – the girl seemed too good-natured and innocent to even recognize if she *was* being mistreated – but he couldn't very well kidnap her. He'd just have to make sure he and Tiy reached an understanding before he left.

"All right, then." He unfurled from the stool. "If I'm not there when you arrive, wait for me at the palace."

Feeling enough time had passed to let Tiy think he'd made use of the girl's services, Makae took his leave. Jerking his head in his brother's direction, he indicated he was ready to go. Just before they left the tavern, Makae sought out Tiy.

The older woman gave him a knowing grin, and said, "So, was she all you'd hoped for?"

"Indeed." He drawled. The woman's leer was particularly repugnant, and if she'd been a man he'd make sure she was violently punished for trying to keep a poor young girl in her debt. Instead, he said, "I would like to pay for the girl to have the week off, to do as she pleases." He drew out another faience ring and held it up.

"Oh?" Tiy kept her greedy eyes on the ring.

"Yes. But if I find out that you've put her to work, or prevented her from going out at all, I will come back. And I can assure you if I have to do that you will not be happy to see me again."

The woman's eyes snapped to his face and, seeing the hard look there, she blanched beneath the layer of red ochre on her cheeks. Recovering, she gave him a stretched smile. "Of course, *tayi neb*, whatever you desire."

He gave her one last hard look before handing her the ring and exiting the tavern. Outside, Makae drew in a deep breath of cool night air, shedding the cloak of disgust that had shrouded him since they stepped into the tavern.

Lost in thought, he started when Batr clapped him on the shoulder and said, "That was quite something, brother! I've never seen you frighten a woman before. I take it you learned something from the prostitute?"

"Yes. Sort of." Makae had been worried about telling Raia her brother was guilty. Now he was worried about telling her the boy was innocent. And how to explain that he'd paid a lady of the night for the information?

"Good," Batr cracked his knuckles and looked around at their surroundings. With most of the people at the festival, the streets were quiet and empty. "Then why don't we find a *real* tavern, have a decent drink, and you can tell me all about it?"

"An excellent plan. I could certainly use a mug or two of wine, and your sage advice."

Batr chuckled, shaking his head, "And I yours, brother."

Chapter 12 – Threats and Necklaces

The following day

When the Horus Festival had run its course, Iset was back at work. Once again her painting partner was too sick to accompany her. She wouldn't be at all surprised if it had to do with the Horus Festival. The festival lasted two whole days and it was always the case after such an event that some people pled illness, taking an extra day to recover from the excitement – or over-indulgence.

Ra pushed the sun across the sky towards the cliffs that lined the desert, and the work day was almost over. She'd spent most of the day trying to keep her face towards the door, and her person away from the gaping hole in the floor that led to Amunemhat's burial chamber. Although she still had one more day before she was supposed to meet with the men who'd threatened her, she didn't want to give anyone an opportunity to sneak up on her.

She bent over her small table of pigment bottles and dipped her reed brushes back and forth between the red ochre and white gypsum. Mixed together on a granite slab, they created the right shade of pink for the lotus flowers of Amunemhat's garden.

Her fear of the tomb robbers aside, Iset didn't mind being alone all day. It gave her time to think. Yesterday – the day after they'd gone with Batr to the festival – her mother had spent the day out of her bed. She'd breakfasted with them on the rooftop, commenting on how soothing and healing the sun felt on her face. Then they'd walked around the village. As it was still a festival day, the town was quieter than usual, but the widow Neb-tawy sat outside, of course, as did some other women her mother knew. They'd stopped to chat here and there and it felt like old times, back before her brother Sharek passed away.

Ankhesenamon even felt well enough to bake a batch of sticky, date-sweetened buns. Iset loved those buns, and try as she might she could never make them as good as her mother. Ahmose danced around the backyard, pulling a steaming bun apart with his fingers and stuffing it into his mouth despite the women's pleas and cries of laughter that he would burn his fingers and his tongue. Their mother laughing, *really laughing*, had been such a heart-warming moment. Iset tried not to hope too much, knowing that at any moment her mother could crawl back into bed and never get out again.

For the first time in a very long time it felt like they were a family. A happy, normal family. She'd found herself wishing Batr were there with them to see what they could be like in their good times, not just in distress. As if he might be more inclined to stay in Abdju if he knew that Iset could be happy and fun, that she'd once been carefree. Oddly enough, she'd felt a similar sense of contentedness walking home with him from the festival. Batr had held Ahmose in his arms, while a comfortable silence lay between them. She'd caught herself thinking once again that he would be a wonderful father if he ever had children of his own.

And then of course he'd kissed her. She hadn't been able to get that moment out of her head. Try as she might, she'd laid on her sleeping mat on the roof, half-awake all night, thinking of him. But for once, that dream-like state had been a pleasant one, one filled with visions of Batr's warm eyes, strong hands, and sensual mouth. Every time she thought of him, she couldn't stop the silly smile that tugged on the corners of her lips.

She'd gone so far yesterday as to seek out his hut to bring him some of the sweet buns her mother had made. A reckless thing to do and she knew it. She'd gone because she wanted to see him again, and because a part of her sought the comfort his arms offered. Even now, her breasts tingled at the memory of his nearness in the doorway when he'd told her how much he admired her, the way the fine hairs on her skin stood up when he'd brushed his lips past her neck. So much overwhelming need and emotion had welled up in her with the simple press of his mouth on hers. She feared that if he ever laid his hands on her in earnest, if he ever truly tried to seduce her, she wouldn't be able to deny him anything.

Her inability to resist him was precisely what made him so dangerous. She'd thought she could seduce him to get him to help her, but this wasn't a game she could safely play. Her emotions were already too tangled, her life too complicated.

When she didn't found Batr at home yesterday, she'd gone on to Senebtawi's. Once there, a servant led her inside to the sitting room and while she waited for her father's old friend she'd fallen into musing. Senebtawi's large mud-brick manor had a small courtyard, a porch with columns to bolster the roof, and white-washed walls. Inside, the bright and spacious home was furnished with expensive chairs and benches made from imported wood. Cheerful scenes much like the ones she painted in noblemen's tombs covered the white-washed walls. The mansion was a far cry from her little hut.

It seemed a hundred years ago, in a different life, that she was engaged to marry Senebtawi's son and destined to live in this house. She rarely wasted time thinking about what her life could have been like if she'd married either of the men she'd been engaged to, but now she wondered if she might have been happy with Senebtawi's son. She closed her eyes and tried to recall the boy's face, and the way it felt when he kissed her for the first time. But instead of seeing a boyish face on the verge of manhood, she saw the manly face of a chestnut-skinned foreigner with exotic tattoos. And for some reason that made her heart ache and tears spring to her eyes.

Clearly, she decided, the lack of sleep and the stress were affecting her. She was becoming irrationally emotional, and she rarely allowed herself to indulge in emotional displays.

Finally, Senebtawi came to greet her and save her from her morbid thoughts. He accepted the sticky buns and expressed his delight that her mother was feeling better. She was thankful for the excuse of the buns to stop by his house and, after some pleasantries, she tried to bring the conversation around to her real purpose. She'd spent a considerable amount of time thinking of the best way to approach her father's old friend. In the end, she had to find out if he knew anything about her father's involvement in the tomb robbing. She was running out of time, and she was both nervous and relieved that she hadn't heard from the men who'd threatened her. It made her wonder all the more if Batr had been tasked with watching her - and Dedi.

"Senebtawi, I was wondering if my *yet* might have mentioned any new friends he was seeing before he passed away?"

Senebtawi laced his fingers together and rested them on the mound of his rotund belly. "Well now, I cannot recall. Why do you ask?"

"No reason, really," she waved a hand dismissively. "Only that Ahmose found a trinket while playing in the garden. I don't believe it belonged to either my *yet* or my *mewet*."

"Oh? What sort of trinket?"

"Oh, it's just a necklace, an eye of Horus. It's nothing special, really, but I thought perhaps there was someone I could return it to."

Senebtawi's lips thinned as he leaned back on his heels and assessed her. A discomforting chill ran up Iset's spine, like the cold, scaly feet of a lizard. She'd gone about this all wrong, she knew, but there was nothing for it but to see it through.

"I'll tell you what, Isetnofret. Why don't you bring that necklace to me and I'll find who it belongs to."

It felt like a hand tightened over her chest, though she couldn't fathom why. Senebtawi was only trying to help, like he always did. She forced a smile and said, "Thank you, that's very kind of you. But I think I'll hold on to it for now.

I should ask my *mewet* before I give it away. I just didn't want to trouble her, or bring up old memories of my *yet*."

Senebtawi rubbed the side of his nose with the length of one index finger. "I think your *yet* would have mentioned a missing necklace. You know, Isetnofret, maybe it would be easier for me to find the owner than you. Why don't you let me take care of it for you? You have enough to worry about."

Ignoring his well-meaning insistence, she put on an innocent air and asked, "Do you suppose it could have been someone who worked on Pharaoh Wadj's tomb with him? I suppose he must have spoken with you about the building progress?"

Senebtawi's broad shoulders rose and fell in a shrug. "Isetnofret, you know your *yet* wasn't allowed to discuss the details of the tomb with others. I was not involved in the building of the pharaoh's tomb. My scribal duties involve keeping the inventory for some of Abdju's finest noblemen, not the tomb builders." His eyes narrowed. "Did he speak with *you* about the tomb? Is that why you're asking?"

"No," she shook her head. "I just… I thought you might know something more about… well, what he'd been doing or thinking about in the weeks before he died. He must have been in an awful state of mind, or terribly drunk, to have gone all the way out to the cliffs the night he died. I just don't understand why he was there in the first place." She finished in a rush.

It was the first time since her father's death that she'd given voice to a vague suspicion about the night of her father's death – a seed of suspicion that finally took root when she'd been threatened the other day.

But Senebtawi only lifted his palms and sighed. "I am as in the dark as you, Isetnofret. But please, put this out of your mind. You will drive yourself mad trying to understand what was going through his mind. And I'm sorry to say it, but your *yet* wasn't well. He drank too much and he gambled too much. You would be best to forget about what he might have been thinking."

He clasped a hand around the back of her arm, drawing her one step closer to him. "But while you are here, my dear, I want to talk to you about what happened the other night at the Horus Festival. I heard about what happened with Addaya. I have already sent someone around to warn him to stay away from you."

Iset blinked, tugging back a little but he held firm to her arm. "You didn't need to do that. I took care of it."

He wagged his head, and she read the patronizing tilt of his eyebrows and the quirk of his lips. "Isetnofret, what did I tell you the other day about some men just taking what they want? You shouldn't have gone to the festival with that foreigner. If you'd wanted to go, you should have come to me. I would have been happy to escort you. Nobody would have tried to touch you if I'd been there with you."

"Actually, I believe I did a fairly good job of dealing with Addaya myself. And Batr *was* helpful. He helped stop Addaya." Once again she found herself defending Batr to Senebtawi, a position she was growing increasingly resentful of.

Senebtawi's fingers tightened on her arm. "I'm telling you Isetnofret, that man isn't to be trusted. I don't think he'll be in Abdju very long. Men like him leave as soon as they get what they're after."

"And what *exactly* is it you think he's after?" She disliked being treated like an ignorant child. If he was going to imply vulgar things, she'd rather he just come out and say it.

"I don't know. But he's working on the tombs with all that wealth, and I don't trust that his intentions are honest. If you were married, you wouldn't have to worry about these things, about men like Batr, or men speculating on your virtue, like Addaya. You'd have a husband to get rid of them for you."

His breath was too close, his grip too tight. Iset yanked her arm from his hold and stepped back, closer to the door. "I'm not interested in marriage right now. To *anyone.* And Batr has done nothing uncourteous, so there is no need for concern, but thank you anyway, Senebtawi. I know you mean well, and I hope you enjoy the buns. *Senebti.*" She'd pulled open the door and let herself out.

Remembering Senebtawi's presumptuous warnings now, as she worked in Amunemhat's tomb, her hand shook with anger and she smudged the pink line of the lotus petal she was working on. She swore softly and turned away from the door to grab a rag to dab at the paint.

And that's when the hairs on the back of her neck prickled.

Feet scuffled behind her and she whirled around, her paint brush clenched in her hand like a weapon. Four men blocked the doorway. Low in the sky, the sun glowed reddish-orange behind them, casting them in shadow. She squinted against the light even as she took a few steps back, brandishing her useless paint brush in front of her.

"Hello, Dedi."

The breath froze in her throat. It was Nasal Man, the one who'd threatened her the other day.

"How are things?" His tone was pleasant, as if they were old friends just catching up on the doorstep. He cocked his head and the other three men fanned out around her. All of them wore scarves wrapped around their heads again so she couldn't see their faces. She wondered if the broken-nosed man was amongst them.

An edge crept into the nasal man's voice as he asked, "I don't suppose you're ready to tell us where the entrance is?"

Iset lifted her shoulders in a slow shrug, as if to say she didn't know anything.

"In that case, I'm here to remind you that tomorrow is your last day to cooperate. If you don't have what we're looking for, we'll be paying your cousin a little visit."

One of the men to Iset's right chuckled and said in a rough voice, "And I'll be looking forward to that. She owes me after what she did at the festival." Iset's head jerked in the man's direction. *Addaya.* Her breath left her lungs in a whoosh. *How could he do this?*

Nasal Man snapped out, "Shut up, you idiot." But it was too late. Now she knew who two of the robbers were.

After what happened with him the other night she didn't harbour any illusions that Addaya was a decent person, but she hadn't expected *this*. Sharek would be furious if he were alive. And so much for Senebtawi "taking care of it" and sending someone to warn Addaya off.

Nasal Man advanced on her. "I guess it doesn't matter, anyway. You won't say anything, will you?"

She shook her head furiously, flicking her eyes around at the men, trying to figure out who the others were.

Beside her Addaya bounced back and forth on his feet. She could see his smirking eyes, squinting just above the wrap that covered his face. He chuckled softly and said, "And when this is all over, I'm going to take care of that foreigner, too. He's a son of a dog who deserves to suffer. I don't see why we even need him."

Nasal Man growled over his shoulder at Addaya, "Would you shut up already? I told you we need an extra arm to break through that rock. Unless you think your puny little sticks will hold up all night?"

Addaya snorted in disgust, but looked away.

Iset's heart stopped, then gave a painful lurch. *Batr is one of them.* But she didn't have time to think about that now; the men were closing in on her. She had the absurd urge to brandish her paintbrush at them, anything to defend herself. The only direction she could go was towards the underground burial chamber behind her. Her head swiveled between the men frantically. She couldn't go back in there. She'd die if she did. Her chest was bursting for air just thinking about it, her heart skipping and thumping against her ribs. Black spots threatened her vision, and suddenly her body felt fragile and too light, like she might float away.

Nasal Man said smoothly, "You know how this goes. Back on up there."

She shook her head so hard it hurt. *No*, she mouthed the word but they couldn't see it under the scarf wrapped around her face. *No, please.*

"Now look here, boy, if you don't get in there now I'll have to get one of these men to throw you in. You don't want break to nothing now, do you?"

By the gods she couldn't let them see her cry. Closing her eyes, she fought back the hot liquid welling behind her lids, willing her breath to flow back into her body. She could do this. She *had* done this. She forced her feet towards the black hole in the ground, and then one after another down the rungs. Images of scorpions, mummified fingers, spiders, snakes, and bodies buried alive flitted through her mind. She tried valiantly, but unsuccessfully, to counter them with thoughts of clear blue skies, trees wavering in a breeze, and, stupid as it was, even thoughts of Batr's arms around her the other night as they watched the Horus procession float up the river.

Whether or not there was air in her lungs she didn't know. After an eternity, her feet touched solid ground and she stepped back from the ladder as she was told. Anything the men said after that point she didn't hear. Her heart beat too hard too loud, a roaring in her ears. She wanted to tear at the bindings on her chest and around her face, but she couldn't let the men above see her. The smell of stale air and dry earth choked her, filling her lungs and mouth with the taste of sand and death. Her head buzzed and spots filled her vision. An image of her brother buried under a ton of bricks came to mind, inside a chamber just like this one, gasping for air as rubble fell down around him. And then darkness filled her sight and she knew no more.

Iset knew she was dreaming. She'd seen this scene before, almost every night for the past year now. Torchlight flickered across the white-plastered walls of the underground burial chamber, revealing the raised-relief – yet to be painted – battle of the falcon-headed Horus and his jackal of an uncle, Seth. Two hands in front of her held a chisel. Not her hands, but a man's. This didn't bother her, though, as she watched the strong, skilled fingers smoothing away the plaster to etch out the shape of Horus's mighty arm.

The hands were familiar and so very dear. So much so that tears and emotion swelled up just watching them. If she weren't in the peculiar position of being inside the body that belonged to those hands, she'd pick one up and hold it to her cheek. It was a cruel trick of her dreams that she could never do that.

Even though she knew what would happen next her gut clenched, nausea sweeping over her. In her head she heard a distant voice – her voice – trying to force its way from the throat of the body she was in, *"Sharek, get out!"*

But the body continued working, oblivious to the struggle of her dream-self trying to warn him of the imminent danger. Dust and sand sifted down from the ceiling-floor above. The body she was in glanced up, shrugged, then went back to the relief work. A minute later more dust sifted down, enough to blow out two of the torches, casting the other end of the chamber – the side with the ladder to the above-ground world – into darkness. The body gave a huff of annoyance and turned, moving towards the torches.

Iset tried screaming again, tried to master the dream body she was in, to force it to run for the ladder. But it was worse than screaming under water, worse than screaming into sand. It was screaming with no sound whatsoever, with an aching, useless throat. No matter how many times she dreamed this dream, she always tried to warn him. Her efforts had only increased over time, even as her awareness of her inability to change things had grown.

The body moved to the torch nearest the ladder, plucking it out of the ground. Just as he turned to re-light it, a loud creaking noise came from overhead. The body held still, listening. Another creaking noise and an ominous cracking spread from directly above to the far end of the chamber.

A curse came from the dream body – not Iset's doing. The beloved hands dropped the torch to the ground and reached for the ladder. A creak overhead warned of more to come, and then a chunk of rock came down, smacking the hand off the ladder. The body scrambled to gain purchase on the ladder, but rocks fell hard and fast now, knocking the body down to the ground. Iset shrieked soundlessly as, once again, she was about to live through her brother's death.

But just as she was steeling herself for the moment when she couldn't breathe, a voice cut through the rumbling of cracking rock. Calling her name, shaking her body. *Her body*, not her brother's dream body.

She sat bolt upright, immediately searching for the night sky she was accustomed to seeing when she woke from her nightmare. She dragged her sleeping mat to the rooftop every night, no matter what the weather, so that she could see the stars and breathe deeply of the fresh air, to know right away that it wasn't really *her* that was dying in her dream.

But this time, instead of the night sky, she saw Batr's face.

Chapter 13 – The Feud

Earlier that day

Once again, Makae stood between the white-washed columns on the doorstep belonging to Lady Ahaneith's official, Ammon. Once again, Makae feared the man would not be home. The official was the only lead Makae had for information on Userkare. Having dismissed Raia's brother last night after meeting the young prostitute in the House of Tiy, Userkare was the lone suspect Makae had left, and the sickly old man was an unlikely one at that. But the time he'd spent with his brother last night left Makae with a sense of urgency. He'd detected an unfamiliar restlessness in Batr, and knew they needed to act fast to find out who else was involved in the raids. Not just to prevent another theft, but to protect the young woman that Batr was convinced was somehow involved.

He knocked a second time, glancing towards the window cut into the mud-brick wall nearby. A white linen curtain fluttered in a light breeze. It was a cool, overcast day, and if he'd been anywhere else in the living world Makae would expect a few drops of rain to fall. But here in the south of Kemet it almost never rained, rarely more than once a year and no more than a few minutes at most.

Just as he was about to turn and leave, a surly-looking servant with closely cropped, curly white hair hauled open the door and glared at Makae.

"Yes?" The white-haired man asked, as if Makae had offended him in some way.

Knowing the man likely objected to his unusual appearance, Makae supressed the urge to goad him, and instead asked in polite tones, "Is your master home?"

"Who's asking?" The man looked Makae over with disdain, but when his gaze rested on the large, curved blade belted at his hip the older man's eyes widened and he looked up in shock.

Makae inclined his head, amusement pulling at the corners of his mouth. "Makae. I come with the Lady Ahaneith's sanction on a mission for Queen Merneith."

"I… ahem… one moment, *tayi neb*." Suspicion lingered in the lines around his squinting eyes, but the servant was all obsequiousness now. The man bowed deeply and was about to call for his master when another man's deep voice came from within, "Let him in, Paser, it's all right."

The older man widened the gap in the door to allow Makae to step in. Blinking against the sudden shift from the grey-skied brightness outside to a darkened entranceway, Makae was able to make out the figure of a powerfully-built man with the wide-legged stance of a seasoned sailor standing a ways back from the door. As his eyes adjusted, he discerned this must be Ahaneith's official, Ammon. His shenti was spotless, shining bright whiteness in the gloom, and his gleaming pate was freshly shaved and oiled.

Makae introduced himself and, after being led upstairs to the rooftop where they seated themselves in the shade of a canopy, he explained his purpose. The Lady Ahaneith's official was sworn to secrecy when it came to her business, so Makae had a measure of faith that he could tell the man the truth about his mission.

"Ahhh," Ammon ran a hand over his smooth head when Makae asked about Userkare's history. "His exile was well before my time."

Makae bit back his frustration. Of course it wasn't the man's fault. On closer inspection Makae guessed Ammon's age to be somewhere in his late twenties; he would have been no more than a boy when Userkare's family was sent south.

"However," Ammon held up a finger, "I *do* recall his return. Or at least, the commotion it created. It all happened just before I came to my position here in the court of Abdju, and it was quite the kick-up. The palace scribes were still talking about it when I began my work for Pharaoh Wadj."

Ammon paused while a servant brought up a tray laden with mugs, a clay teapot, and an array of bowls filled with nuts and seeds to snack on. He frowned and glanced over at Makae.

"Perhaps something a little stronger than tea?" Ammon asked, a knowing smile hitching up one corner of his mouth. "You look like a man who could use a reprieve."

"Gods, yes," Makae chuckled, shaking his head and not bothering to ask how Ammon knew. Lady Ahaneith's official had the air of an observant and capable man, one well-travelled and knowledgeable in the ways of the world. The sort of man Makae could come to respect, given time.

Ammon sent the servant back downstairs with orders to bring up two mugs of wine. When he returned a few short minutes later and the men were settled back against a couple of cushions, wine in hand, Ammon resumed his recollection.

"When Userkare was a young man," he said, "his entire family was exiled for trying to steal land from Ra-hotep, and for lying about their crop yield. This was back during the reign of Queen Merneith's *yet*, Djer. After Djer passed away and Pharaoh Wadj and Queen Merneith came to power Userkare petitioned for forgiveness, which they granted, gods bless their graciousness. Apparently, upon his return, rumour spread that Userkare made some accusations about Ra-hotep, saying that he had contrived to have Userkare's family exiled so that he could seize control of their land."

Cocking his head, Makae asked, "So Ra-hotep took over Userkare's lands when he was in exile?"

"Mmm," Ammon lifted one eyebrow over the rim of his mug as he sipped wine. "He did. But Userkare got them all back when he returned. Well, at least in theory. He claimed that, even though his family's lands were returned to him, Ra-hotep had extended the bounds of his property, moving the strings that delineated their properties. He swore Ra-hotep's scribe had records to prove that his land had been smaller before Userkare's exile, and that his own lands were greater than what was restored to him."

Makae knew what Ammon was referring to. Land measurements were recorded by scribes for tax purposes. To demarcate the land, stakes were driven into the ground around a property, then rope strung on them to mark the boundaries. In large landholdings, men had been known to move the markings around in order to gain extra land, or to avoid paying higher taxes.

A memory caused his hand to tighten around his mug. He vividly recalled how, while walking home from Lady Ahaneith's banquet with Raia, she'd told him her father had arranged a marriage with the neighbouring landholder so that they could consolidate their monopoly over Abdju's farmland. Such a thing in itself was not unusual. But coupled with the fact that Ra-hotep also married Userkare's betrothed – Raia's mother – right after Userkare was sent away and then took over his land… Makae wondered just how badly Ra-hotep might have wanted to get rid of Userkare.

"And were Userkare's claims looked in to?" Makae asked.

"They were. That's precisely why the palace scribes were in such an uproar. One of their own had been forced to produce records contradicting Userkare's statements. Userkare was found to be in the wrong and, as I recall, his claims dismissed as the ravings of a man recently returned from hardship. In any other case he would have simply been stripped of his lands and sent back into exile, but Queen Merneith was new to the throne and I believe she was unwilling to upset such an old family as Userkare's."

Makae leaned back on one elbow, blowing out a puff of air as he absorbed this new information.

"So," Ammon asked, sitting cross-legged and resting his elbows on his knees as he leaned forward. "Does this sound like a man with motive for a tomb robbing?"

Nodding, Makae said, "It does indeed. That is, if he maintained the belief all these years that he'd been wronged."

"Or if he had, in fact, been wronged." A half-smile played on Ammon's lips, as if there was more to tell.

"You think he was telling the truth?"

"I can't be sure. Like I said, it was all before my time. However, you've put me in mind of something. I *can* tell you that Ra-hotep's primary scribe is also the same man who records the landholdings and crop amounts for the farms that produce the food for the Land of the Dead. Just a few days ago he submitted a tax scroll showing that, shortly before he contracted the illness that killed him, Ra-hotep acquired *more* of Userkare's land."

"I don't understand. How could that have happened?"

"One of three ways." Ammon held up three fingers, curling them down as he counted off. "One, Ra-hotep could have purchased the land from Userkare. That seems unlikely, does it not? Given their history? Two, Lady Ahaneith could have granted it to him because Userkare was not competently managing it, and I can tell you that is not the case here. Whatever his state of mind may be, Userkare has been managing his lands just fine. Or three, Ra-hotep stole the land by moving the land markers without Userkare's knowledge. Just like Userkare accused him of doing ten years ago."

An hour or so later, Makae stood with his back to the little river – an offshoot of the great one that ran from the far lands of the south up through Kemet and into the northern sea. Before him lay a vast swath of farmland, its rich, dark silt as yet unturned for planting. In the distance beyond the farm lay the village of the Land of the Dead, the small huts almost invisible at such a length, and beyond that the great mountains that marked the entrance to the great desert.

Breathing in deep, Makae watched Raia's distinctive figure – a tall silhouette against the grey sky and beige cliffs – walking back and forth along the rope that marked the edge of her father's property. Something about the image of her solitary figure moving amidst such an enormous, empty landscape seemed indicative of who she was.

Despite her large family, she *was* a solitary woman, one who stood alone and above those around her. Older and more mature than the children she cared for, with more responsibility than most people carried in a lifetime, she bore it all with a straight back, chin held high.

It was a shame, he thought, that he'd only just begun to know her. He'd never met a woman he could imagine spending his life with, but he found Raia admirable in so many ways that he was sure that, given time, they'd find themselves more than compatible.

Furthermore, he hadn't quite realized how much he'd missed the bustle and noise of a big family until he'd broken his fast with Raia's children the morning after Lady Ahaneith's banquet. He'd sat back in silence mostly, letting the children talk over one another, asking him questions, calling one another names, jostling about in a pack, so very like the many brothers and sisters and cousins he'd grown up with, and would never see again. Raia had feared he'd find them all overwhelming, and it had been difficult to express just how comforting he'd found it, and difficult to express that he'd found her family just as appealing as he'd found her.

One more deep breath and he set forward, knowing what he had to say would likely cause her to shut him out of her world forever.

Lost in thought, Raia stared at the knotted rope strung between the stakes, wondering how it was that her father had acquired so many extra *khet* of land. He'd never mentioned anything to her, and yet his scribe had told her the other day that such was the case. That was why this year's taxes were higher than she'd anticipated. And so here she was, pacing the lengths of the land, trying to reconcile the numerals. As a small girl, she'd walked these lands with her father, picking out landmarks, counting her steps, sharing her sums and observations. Ten years had passed since she'd last traversed the full stretch of her father's land,

and her old milestones – trees, rock piles, and stone benches – had slipped away down the shadowy steps of time.

Furthermore, she herself had grown. Her legs were longer than those of her twelve-year-old, unmarried self. The numbers no longer added up like they used to, her gait was lengthier, and her feet larger. For some reason she found it more troubling that the figures she'd found such comfort in over the years had failed her somehow, rather than that her father had failed to mention the acquisition of land, something so critical. No, it was more troubling that all her childhood sums had become outdated, subjective to something as unaccountable as the length of her stride. The memories of her youth were skewed by the passage of time, as if she herself had somehow outgrown the land she'd grown up on.

"Raia," a rich voice murmured behind her, startling her.

Turning, she blinked at Makae, realizing he'd managed to walk all the way across the field from the little river without her noticing. Yet she smiled, clasping one of his hands in greeting. His hand was warm, and hers were chilled from standing outside so long, so she let him fold her fingers against his palm and keep them there.

"Hello," she said, feeling slightly awkward. She hadn't seen him since the night of the Horus Festival, when she'd been idiotically confused – mad at herself for wanting him to spend the night, but also mad at herself for being too proud to ask, and ultimately a little wretched that he hadn't offered.

Coming to her senses, she frowned. "What are you doing here? Has something happened? Did you learn something new about my *yet*'s tomb?"

Raia saw the hesitation in his parted lips and said shortly, "Just tell me. Whatever it is, get it over with."

"Why don't we walk? You're cold, and the walk will help warm you."

"Fine. Just please, do not spare me the details. I would like to know what's happened."

He nodded, his jaw tight. He tucked her hand into the crook of his arm and turned her towards the river. Makae proceeded to tell her that he'd met with one of the queen's officials that morning, and that the man was able to relate some of the history surrounding her father and Userkare. When he reached the part about Userkare blaming her father for his family's exile, she cut in, her fingers tightening on his arm.

"That's impossible. My *yet* would never do such a horrible thing just for some land. He had plenty of his own. I already told you he warned us away from Userkare. Clearly the man is unbalanced."

Makae placed a hand over hers, rubbing the back of it with his palm. "I know it sounds bad, and you are right to be loyal to your family. I am only telling you what happened. I am not accusing your father of anything." But she heard the unspoken 'yet' that hung in the air, even as he continued. "But you have to hear me out, Raia. Did you know Ra-hotep acquired some of Userkare's land before he passed away?"

She stiffened. "Yes. I just learned of it the other day. That's what I was doing out there today, counting the *khet*."

"Do you happen to know how he came by it?"

Raia stopped walking, pulling her hand from Makae's arm. "No, but I suppose you are about to tell me."

"No." He shook his head. "I don't know. I was hoping you would."

"I? Why would I know?"

His gaze remained steady, boring in to her. "You were his daughter. He left his land to you over Semer."

Although he hadn't said it as such, Raia felt Makae's words as an accusation. Why didn't she know? She should, shouldn't she? Why hadn't her father bothered to tell her?

"So?" She snapped. "I had my own property to manage. He probably wanted to spare me the worry."

She knew it was a lame excuse. A sick feeling grew in her belly, and her mind circled back on her earlier thoughts. They'd been a premonition, she realized, her beliefs falling apart around her, the walls and ceilings of her memories cracking and turning to dust, sifting away like the landmarks she'd counted her steps by. Once she'd married, her father stopped taking her on walks around his property. She'd told herself it was because he knew she was busy in her new life, but she'd felt it as a loss, missing the closeness they'd once shared. Now, she wondered if he'd been hiding something. He would've known that if he let her walk the property, as she had before she married, she'd count it and discover something was different. It wasn't just that her stride and her feet were much larger than they'd once been, but her father's land, growing ever larger over time…

"Raia, I'm very sorry to be the one to tell you all this, I am sure it is not pleasant to contemplate, but I need to ask you something. I went by Userkare's home earlier, and his manservant told me he was too unwell to see me. I didn't think it right to force my way into a dying man's home, but I thought he might be willing to see you. He *did* ask you to come and visit him again."

Raia glared at him for a moment, but looked away from the pity she saw in his eyes, as if he knew she was struggling. His implications infuriated her, but she was even angrier that she'd allowed him to plant doubt in her mind. That she already half-believed her father to be guilty made her feel like a traitor to all he'd taught her.

"Fine," she said, "I will speak with him. But only to prove he's raving mad."

"Rai," his voice was soft, though the admonition she heard in that single word made her stubbornly return his gaze.

"I *said* I would speak with him." Even she knew she sounded like a petulant child. No one had ever chastised her before, and she wasn't pleased to learn that Makae could accomplish it with little more than the tone of his voice.

"Fine," he sighed. Once again she sensed his hesitation as he looked off into the distance, to the craggy mountains edging the desert. Finally, he said, "There's more."

She closed her eyes, sick with foreboding. *Here comes the end*, she thought. The end of what, she wasn't sure, but she felt it deep in the pit of her belly.

"Your brother is being taken advantage of."

Raia's eyes snapped open. "What?"

"His huntsman is stealing from him."

"I don't understand what that has to do with anything."

But in a few minutes, she did understand. Too well.

"Get away from me," she said when he'd finished, her voice flat and hard as she held up a hand to ward him off.

"I'm sorry. I never wanted this to happen, I swear to Ba'al."

"Get. Away. From. Me." Her jaw was clenched tight. She didn't want to scream, didn't want him to see her emotions. She drew in a breath, trying to count the seconds of the inhalation, then the exhale, but failing both times.

Makae stepped back, waiting, watching her.

"No," she said when she recovered her voice. "First you imply my *yet* was a thief who brought his own desecration upon himself. But even before that, you suspected my brother of organizing the theft of our *yet*'s tomb. And rather than speak with me about it, you went behind my back. And now you want my help to sort it out? By the gods, what is next? You are worse than Apep, dragging chaos in your wake!"

"Raia, would you really have been open to discussing this with me before?" He didn't give her time to answer; they both knew the truth. "I promise I had no idea of all this the night we were together. That morning after, I wanted to find some way to make this work between us. I *still* want this to work, that's why I came to you, to tell you the truth. I do not want there to be any secrets between us." His palms were up, in a gesture of honesty.

"*This*? How would *this* have worked? We slept together one night. That is all. You are going back to Thinis. What is there to make work?"

"I'm not going back to Thinis."

She blinked at him. Her heart, racing with anger and a sense of betrayal, lurched and shifted pace. She hated herself for feeling something like hope, and tamped it down deep.

He repeated himself, his soft tone a mingled apology and appeal. "I do not think I will be going back to Thinis. Lady Ahaneith is petitioning Queen Merneith to have me stay. If she consents, I am to head the security here."

Somehow this knowledge hurt almost as much as all the other things he'd revealed to her. It was the final blow in a devastating trilogy of revelations. "It does not matter now, does it?" She said, more a cold statement than a question.

"If that's how you feel. It can be otherwise, if you wish it."

Raia snorted indelicately. "As if I have any choice in the matter."

He shook his head slowly, not even needing to speak for her to know he was reproaching her for simplifying the matter. For letting her stubborn loyalties outweigh her chance at happiness.

"Will you still speak with Userkare?" Makae asked after a few moments had passed.

"I cannot answer that right now. I need time to think. Please, just leave me alone." She couldn't look at him, knowing if she did the tears welling in the back of her throat would work their way up, and then she'd be lost. She'd never forgive herself for giving in to her emotions.

Makae hesitated, and she felt his scrutiny. She stared fixedly at the craggy entrance to the desert, willing him to go away. Finally, she saw him nod slightly out of the corner of her eye. Turning, he said over his shoulder, "If you change your mind, or if you need me, I'll still be at the palace for the next few days."

"I will not need you." She pushed out through clenched teeth. She would *never* run to him. *Never* show such weakness, never want him again. At least, that's what she told herself as she listened to his soft footsteps fade away. *Like the landmarks of my father's land, slipping down the steps of time…*

Raia stood there for some time, her unseeing eyes fixed in the distance, the chill air seeping deep under her skin, until she eventually realized she was shivering. The skies were growing dark as she turned and made her way towards the city, a hollow sensation gnawing at her chest.

Chapter 14 – Revelations

Batr kept his hands firm but gentle on Iset's shoulders as he watched her eyes flick around the room, taking in her surroundings. The fact that she was laying in his hut with him seated half on the bed next to her, still dressed as Dedi but without the scarf wrapped around her face, her unbound hair tumbling down around her in a reddish-black tidal wave, quickly worked its way into her consciousness.

Jaw clenched tight, she hissed through gritted teeth, "What am I doing here? What did you do?"

Well that was unexpected, he thought. "What, no 'thank you, Batr, for saving me from the burial chamber'?" He mimicked a woman's voice. "Or how about 'thank you, Batr, for waking me from a horrible dream during which I almost screamed your ears off'? Either of those would do much better than whatever you're thinking right now."

Although he made light of it, he was glad he was sitting down. The relief of her waking and seemingly unharmed was enough to weaken all the muscles in his body, rendering him light-headed and silly. He wanted to pull her bound chest to his and breathe in her jasmine scent, but given her current state he suspected she might still try to tear his eyes out. She'd been flailing quite a bit in her sleep, and had inadvertently smacked him upside the head a few times as he'd tried to wake her. She was deceptively strong for such a slight woman.

"I have no reason to thank you until you tell me what in the name of the gods I'm doing here. How are you involved in this?" She pulled from his grasp. Scrambling backwards until her back hit the wall behind the bed, she drew her knees up to her chest.

"Perhaps it would help if you told me what *this* is."

But she just glared mutinously at him and shook her head. She said, "You need to let me go. Ahmose is expecting me at home."

Of course it wouldn't be as easy as just asking her to tell him. Nothing with her was ever easy. Or simple. An exasperated noise escaped his throat. "I'm not exactly holding you hostage. And don't worry, I've already sent a messenger to him to tell him you're with me and going to be late. I asked the widow Neb-tawy to go sit with your *mewet* as well."

"You did what?! How dare you?"

"Nofret…" her eyes flashed at him for using the endearment and he quickly raised one hand to signal surrender, "Iset, please listen. I didn't *do* anything to you. I was on my way to Amunemhat's tomb, where you were working – where *Dedi* was working – to see if you – Dedi – whomever – wanted to walk home together. I saw a group of men leave the tomb, but I didn't see you. So I went inside looking for you."

At first he'd assumed they'd been having some sort of tomb robbers' meeting he wasn't privy to, and Iset was just hanging back. So he waited, too, thinking he'd catch her alone when the others were gone. Licking his lips, he recalled the fear that had spiked through him when he didn't find her inside the tomb immediately, thinking they'd done something horrible to her and then tossed her body into the underground chamber. He'd been terrified, *actually terrified*, at the thought. And it would be his fault because he hadn't pushed her to be truthful with him, because he'd known for almost a whole two days that she was Dedi and he hadn't put a stop to it.

He cleared his throat and said in a gruff voice. "I found you in the burial chamber. I couldn't wake you." By Ra that had been one of the worst moments of his life. Those few seconds of time when he thought she was dead, right before he found her pulse, beating strong. Since she was still wearing the scarf and bindings, he was fairly confident the other men didn't know she was masquerading as a boy and hadn't taken advantage of it. But knowing what he did about her nightmares, he had a pretty good idea that she hadn't chosen to go down there of her own volition. He'd desperately wanted to do violence to the men that had put her in the tomb. He still did.

Breathing heavily to calm his rage-filled thoughts, he continued. "I brought you here because I didn't think you'd want me to scare your brother and *mewet* by taking you home like that. I took off your scarf so that you could breathe better, but figured you'd be less than thankful if I tried to take off your... you know..." he gestured to her chest to indicate the bindings that flattened her breasts.

He couldn't quite keep his eyes from going to said breasts when her hands flew to cover her chest, as if to hide the physical reality of the bindings. Her expression had softened somewhat as he spoke, but now it took on a hunted look that called to mind the gazelle by the oasis pool.

"So you know," she whispered.

He frowned. "Know what?"

She croaked out, "That I'm – I am Dedi."

A smile curled the corners of his mouth as he let his eyes trail over her face and the hair that tumbled around her shoulders. "I would say that it is fairly obvious now."

"Did you know before?"

Her arms crossed over her chest, hands resting on opposite shoulders, her knees still drawn up. It was such a defensive position that Batr's heart ached for her. He took a chance and told her the truth. "I've known since the night we went to the House of Hent. Your scarf slipped off when you tripped and fell."

When the tears welled in her eyes he moved towards her, to take her in his arms. But she flinched away, putting one hand over her mouth and the other out to stop him. He sighed and pulled back, waiting.

She shook her head, dashing tears from her eyes before they fell. "And you still...? But the night of the festival you were so..."

He raised his eyebrows, wondering how she was going to describe him.

She must have noticed the look on his face, as she scowled and muttered, "Never mind."

He sighed. *At this rate we'll be at this all night and get nowhere.* He leaned forward and folded his big hands over her slender shoulders – gently, but firmly, as she tried to twist away. "Iset, listen, I *will not* hurt you. But you have to tell me how you got into the burial chamber."

Her voice was a whispered rasp, her tone accusatory. "Don't lie. You *know.* They said you worked with them. I heard them say they needed your arm to break through the stone. Then… then they were going to get rid of you."

"Ahhhh," he pulled back, understanding dawning. "I see." He passed a hand over his forehead and, with his palm against his eye, pressed on his cheekbone to massage away the tension building there. He couldn't tell her everything about who he was. He wasn't yet in a position to lay all his pieces on the game board, in case she didn't tell him all she knew. Furthermore, it might scare her off if she knew just what his purpose was in the Land of the Dead. And he didn't doubt for a minute she would think he'd been nice to her and her family solely to get information. Yes, it started out that way, but their relationship had become more than that, hadn't it?

"Would you believe me if I said I was trying to help you, Iset? I'm not in league with those men. Not really. I *want* to help you, but I don't know as much as I need to. I was a soldier, not just a seasonal conscript, but a full-time soldier. I know people. If you tell me who put you in there, I can protect you and your family. If you don't, I can't promise that whoever you're involved with won't do something like this to you – or your family – again."

A host of emotions flickered through her big, beautiful eyes, and he feared she'd turn mutinous again. He reached out to take up her small hands in his. Turning them over, he could see flecks of paint under her nails and in the creases of her palms and knuckles. She saw it too, and tried to pull them from his grip but he held on.

"Enough, Iset. Enough already." His voice was stern now. "Tell me how you're involved in all this. Why have you been dressing like a boy and working in the Land of the Dead?"

Iset finally gave way. What choice did she have? If he was asking her like this, he could very well be telling the truth. And she'd kept so much bottled up for so long, it came as a relief to have someone compel her to tell it all. Well, *almost* all.

Batr listened in silence for the next few minutes as she told him about how, a few months after her brother died, her father's debts intensified. She'd always known her father drank, but back then she didn't realize their increased debt was due to his growing gambling problem. She'd only discovered that delightful bit of information after he'd passed away. Needing to ensure her mother and brother had enough food, she'd had no choice but to find work in order to help support her family. Women's work paid less than men's, and when she'd gone to her father for advice he concocted the scheme for her to become Dedi. It was her own foresight to give Dedi an accident that would prevent her from having to speak. People tended not to ask questions of mutes.

Dedi was only meant to be a temporary relief. Enough to get them by until her father could catch up on his debts, until she could marry well, until Ahmose was old enough to take up work. All those things that she'd been hopeful would happen soon, but never did.

She scoffed, raking her hands through the thick, reddish-black waves of her hair. "Believe me; I know now how foolish it was. Once we started with the lies, it became impossible to extricate myself from them. If I were to get rid of Dedi somehow, or say that he left town, there would be all sorts of questions. And then what would I do for work? You've seen my *mewet*, she needs someone around all the time. And now that my *yet* is gone, it is impossible to get rid of Dedi. How else would we survive? I've been caught, and I haven't been able to figure out how to get out of this situation."

Batr spoke in a measured voice but she could see emotion, maybe anger, simmering in his eyes, as he asked, "But how did you manage to keep people believing in Dedi? I mean wouldn't they expect to see one or both of you together?"

She shook her head, elbows resting on her knees. "It's been exhausting. You saw, you were there at the House of Hent. My *yet* took me out – as Dedi – to the tavern once before. And now that he's gone, I've gone out a couple of times on my own to keep people from getting suspicious. And sometimes I go out as myself and visit women in the neighbourhood. At least as Iset people expect me to be home, taking care of my *mewet* and brother, so they're not as surprised they don't see me. But Dedi, well, people expect to see young men out and about. I couldn't have done it without my little brother though, he's been a great help. He's learned to bake… sort of." She smiled sadly and reached out to lightly trace the fading mark on the edge of Batr's hairline from the bread slab Dedi had pitched his way. "And he's a remarkably good liar for such an honest boy."

"How did you end up in the underground chamber, Iset?"

Where to begin? She wondered. His hands rested near hers on the bed, and she focused on them rather than look up at him. His were large and dark, hers small and pale in comparison, fragile even. Addressing their hands rather than look at him, she told him everything that had happened over the last couple of days.

Everything, that is, except the part about her father's involvement in the robbing of the nobleman's tomb. Since he hadn't mentioned it, he probably didn't know, and therefore couldn't be working too closely with the thieves. She simply couldn't tell him about what her father had done. It was too shameful, too awful, and *too dangerous*. Desecrating the tombs of the dead was a stain that flowed down the family line, tainting everyone in its wake. While a part of her instinctively trusted Batr, a part of her feared that he would despise her when he knew what kind of man had spawned her. Furthermore, if he planned to involve the authorities to catch the men who were robbing tombs, she couldn't implicate her father. She, her brother, and their mother might all be subject to punishment, and she couldn't allow that to happen to them.

Instead, she told Batr that the men simply believed her father had kept the plans to the tomb somewhere, or had left a mark to indicate where the entrance to the pharaoh's burial chamber was. They wanted her to find it and show them where to dig. They would need to break through the floor directly above the pharaoh's burial chamber, and without knowledge of exactly where that was, they'd need weeks' worth of night-time digging. There were over two hundred chambers surrounding the pharaoh's, taking up a vast swath of land.

As she spoke, Batr's expression grew tighter, and more impatient. "So they threatened you?" He growled.

She nodded. "Yes. Well, Dedi. They told me they would hurt Ahmose, and tell the authorities –" She caught herself just before she slipped and told him they threatened to reveal her father's involvement. "They said they would tell the authorities my *yet* had been involved, and that we would all be punished. They also… they also said they would come for me. Not Dedi, but me, Iset."

Iset shuddered, tears prickling her lids. Over the last few days she'd hardly given a thought to what it might be like if the men *had* come for her. She'd been more concerned about Ahmose and her mother. Now, a horrible vision of Addaya's angry face flashed through her mind, and the reality of his innuendos crashed over her like a ton of mud-bricks.

Batr's fingers tightened around hers, and there was urgency in his voice. "Iset, tell me who they are. Tell me and I'll stop them."

She told him what she'd been able to discern about the men. One was surely Addaya, and the others she described by their features – a crooked-nosed man she'd seen in the inventory hut, and then again speaking with Batr at the House of Hent, and the other with a mean, nasally voice.

And another man she didn't know anything about, except his build.

"Teos," Batr nodded.

"What, the scribe who keeps the inventory?" Satsobek frowned. "How do you know?"

"After. I'll tell you after. So that gives us Addaya, Teos, Pamiu – that's the one with the nasal voice – and the stone cutter with the crooked nose. Good. Give me a few minutes to sort this out. I've laid out a clean shenti for you and some water. Take your time freshening up."

"But wait! What will you do? I don't understand!"

Promising that he'd explain it all soon, he left her alone in the room.

Taking out a very small papyrus scroll, a brush, and a pot of black ochre paste, Batr dashed off a quick message in the language of his homeland. He was not in the least bit literate in the language of Kemet, although as a boy he'd learned to speak Kemeti fluently as his tribe traded with various other nomadic peoples, some of whom came from the western reaches of Kemet. Now, writing in a foreign language served an important purpose. He could write his brother with the names of the tomb robbers and orders to arrest them immediately and be reasonably assured that, even if the message was intercepted, nobody else would be able to read it.

Craning his head out the door, he spotted the boy he was looking for a ways down the street, talking to some friends. He'd enlisted the boy a few days back, when he'd first arrived in the Land of the Dead, as a messenger between himself and his brother.

Temer, a lanky youth about eleven or twelve years old, said goodbye to his friends and sauntered over to Batr's hut. Batr handed him the note and a sack of barley grains. The boy would be able to trade the grain at the market for other foodstuff, fabric, or trinkets without arousing suspicion. Batr always made sure that the boy was paid handsomely for his time – and his silence.

Batr breathed easier once the boy was on his way. He was confident that, within a few hours, Makae would send soldiers to round up the thieves and take them to Abdju's *hnrt* – the prison complex. Makae didn't need Batr to tell him to push them for information on other men who might be involved, and any other robberies they'd planned. Batr's brother was just as skilled as he in questioning prisoners and suspects, more so, sometimes, as his silent nature caused many people to incriminate themselves.

By this time the sun had set behind the cliffs and the horizon was a shade of purple-blue merging to near black. In his greeting room, while he waited for Iset, Batr lit some oil wicks and laid out barley bread and bowls of nuts and dried fruit on the table alongside a jug of wine and two mugs. Very similar to her own greeting room, the room was furnished with a padded stone bench, a stool, and a small rectangular table.

When she joined him a few minutes later, Batr had a speechless moment during which his eyes roved over her rather scantily clad figure. She'd crossed his shenti over her front, tying it up behind her neck. The style caused the front to flap open with each step, revealing a considerable amount of soft, pale inner thigh. The flickering lights reflected off the white of the fabric, emphasizing the red highlights in her inky hair, and casting a golden hue on her fawn-coloured skin.

His mouth went dry and he fumbled to pour wine into their mugs – a difficult task when he seemed unable to take his eyes from Iset's lithe form. It was no wonder half the men in the village wanted her.

Offering her a spot on the bench, he chose to stand instead. He was already restless in anticipation of what he planned to tell her, and knew he wouldn't be able to sit still. A plan had begun to form in his head, a plan that would enable him to protect Iset and her family for as long as he was alive, and he wanted to go about things the right way.

He leaned against the wall and crossed his arms over his chest.

Iset sipped her wine and watched Batr over the rim of her mug. Normally smooth and charming, he appeared uncomfortable now as he stood several paces from her. The guttering light of the oil wicks deepened the shadows of his lean, chiseled torso. The whites of his eyes and the flash of his teeth contrasted starkly with his dark skin.

"By tomorrow morning, the men that are after you should be in the hnrt," he said, "and you'll be safe."

"I don't understand. How is that possible?" It certainly didn't *seem* possible that it could be as simple as telling Batr who the men were and that, in the time it took her to wash the paint from her hands and change her shenti, he'd magically fixed her problems. Well, the most pressing problem at least. Even with the thieves in the hnrt, she would still be an impoverished, unmarried woman who dressed as a boy to support her sick mother and younger brother.

He shook his head, his hair casting his face into shadow, then light again. "I cannot discuss the particulars with you until it's all done. But they will be arrested tonight. That'll be the end of it."

"What? Just like that?"

"Yes."

"How can I trust that? If I don't have the answers they seek by tomorrow, they'll come for us." She wrapped her arms around her belly as fear and doubt gnawed at her.

"No." His stern tone cut through her thoughts. "I *will not* let anything happen to you." She looked up to meet his narrowed gaze. "I want to be clear on something. I'm about to tell you something about myself because I want you to believe me when I say that I'm going to help you, and I've already taken steps to do so. This is not something I disclose to others because it's nobody's affair but my own. But now I'm sharing a confidence in exchange for the one you've given me. Do you understand?"

"But what are you going to do?"

"I asked if you understood." Although his lids were lazy his words were hard.

Chastened, she answered curtly, "Yes. I understand."

He gave a short nod. "Good." He shifted and tucked his thumbs into the top of his shenti. The movement pushed the fabric down an inch, exposing more of his abdominals, making it absolutely clear to Iset that those sleek dark muscles extended all the way down under the top of his shenti, along with a trail of dark, softly curling hair.

She lifted her mug of wine and tried to focus on keeping her hand steady as she sipped it.

His words came out clipped, rougher than usual. "I was fifteen when my younger sister was arranged to marry into a neighbouring tribe. One of my brothers, my *mewet*, a couple of cousins, and myself travelled with my sister to take her to meet her husband, to leave her with her new family. My *yet* stayed with our people, along with my other brothers and sisters. There were thirteen of us children living at that time. My *yet* had two wives, you see, but they got along well enough, and when my second *mewet* died, my own *mewet* raised all the children as her own. I don't even recall now which of us all belonged to which woman. It didn't matter that much then…" His eyes narrowed, as if looking off into the distance.

"Anyway, our tribe had been warring off and on for some time with another for control of one of the oases. I think some of the men in my tribe wanted to begin to cultivate there. I don't even really know exactly what the issue was. I was young and didn't pay much attention to such things." He waved a dismissive hand. "But a few men were killed amidst the fighting and the raiding of one another's tribes. Amongst our tribes when someone is killed, the killer, or his family, is expected to pay a blood price to compensate. Otherwise the family of the dead man have a right to seek out the killer and kill him. If they can't find him, they may kill another man from his family instead."

He shrugged one shoulder in a nonchalant manner, but Iset could hear emotion thickening his voice. He began pacing in the small space of the living room as he continued.

"So we left on a journey of a few days to take my sister to her wedding. We were gone maybe ten days. On the way back we were caught in a windstorm and had to camp an extra night. One day after that we arrived back in our tribe's camp."

The roughly cast ceramic handle of the mug dug into Iset's palm, she was gripping it so tightly. Something horrible was about to come from Batr's mouth and she wasn't sure she wanted to know his secrets anymore. She swallowed, and her dry and tightly clenched throat produced a small noise of distress. Batr turned his dark, pain-wracked eyes to her at the sound and his gaze snagged on her face. For a moment, they stared at one another, and she tried to tell him she didn't need to know. She tried to push the words out, she got so far as opening her mouth, but couldn't get them past the lump in her throat.

Batr's eyes skittered away and he finished in a whoosh of air. "They were all dead. Every one of them. The other tribe raided the night before we'd returned. If we hadn't been caught in the storm, we would have been there with them when it happened. My brother and cousins and I buried them all that afternoon. My *mewet* was so upset she took her own life in the middle of the night." His gaze fixed on the wall across from him as he added, "I was on guard that night. I didn't think to check on her in her tent. I presumed she was sleeping."

Iset put her mug down and stood up. Batr didn't look at her, though. He leaned back against the wall, closing his eyes. He said, "There weren't even enough of us left to demand retribution or avenge our families. We had nowhere to go. My cousins joined some of their family in another tribe. My brother and I made our way north, to the great sea. At a tavern in some port city one night we met some men who were looking for two strong crew members. We lied about our abilities." He gave a derisive snore of laughter. "We'd never been to sea, but by the time we were out of the port it was too late to get rid of us. The man who captained that ship was Sekhrey Bey, the man who is now the head of the queen's royal guard."

His eyes opened for just a moment to slide over her face, gauging her reaction, before he closed them again. His nostrils flared slightly, his breathing laboured.

"So you see," his voice was rough. "I know people. I won't let anything happen to you. I *can't* let anything happen to you."

Several questions ran through Iset's head. The foremost one, though, was what in the name of the gods was Batr doing here in the Land of the Dead if he was part of the band of pirates under Sekhrey Bey? Being so far removed from the court and absorbed in her rather complicated life, stories rarely reached her of the goings-on of the nobility, but tales of the band of brigands had certainly made their way south. Sekhrey Bey and his men had been raiding the shores of the great northern sea for years, much to the awe and dismay of the Kemeti militias and merchants. When they were captured in a storm off the coast of Kemet they'd been offered well-paying positions in the militias, eventually leading to Bey's promotion to Captain of the Royal Guard.

All of the village boys, her little brother included, had been agog with the story for over a year now. The played often at being pirates, taking other boys hostage, and pretending to kidnap young girls from the village as booty. While their play finally died down somewhat, there'd been a time when a girl had to constantly be on alert for fear that she'd be turned into a bargaining tool by a neighbouring boy for her brother's rations of bread, a small piece of wood, or a pretty stone. Even a woman her age was not immune to their assaults. She herself had once or twice been attacked by a band of little boys, brandishing "knives" fashioned from switches of papyri stalks. She'd chased them off with threats to tell their mothers, but the inspiration for their actions left an imprint.

The spectacular fashion in which Bey had saved the queen from a tiger attack *and* a subsequent kidnapping attempt over a year ago was fodder for the boys for weeks on end. Not only that, several months back his second-in-command, Ebrium, also a former pirate, caught a group of men who'd actually murdered the high priest and priestess of the Temple of Mehyt in Thinis, the seat of the queen's power.

But she couldn't ask Batr about all that right now. Not after what he'd just told her about his family. His eyes were still closed, his arms crossed over his chiseled chest. Moving quietly, Iset came to stand in front of him and placed her hand on his forearm. He started, looking down at her as if surprised to see her there.

Her eyes roved over his face, wondering about the half-moon tattoos there, wondering what sorts of things he'd seen. Previously she'd wondered who he was and what kind of threat he was to her. But now she didn't just want to *know* him, she wanted to understand him, and what made him who he was. He was clearly a dangerous, yet capable man. She'd seen that in the way he handled Senebtawi and Addaya. But he was also the man who sat by her and made her eat when she was sick, the man who'd carried her little brother in his arms when he was sleepy, a man who'd bowed to her mother and made her feel like a lady. He was charming and kind and lethal at the same time. What sorts of experiences made a man like that?

As she studied him, he studied her back, waiting. His chest rose and fell gently with each breath but she could feel his pulse speed under her fingertips. Iset ran the palm of her hand up over the smooth ridge of his pectoral muscles, up to the thick column of his strong neck, taking a moment to marvel at the difference in their skin tone. Fascinating that two people could come from such different places – she from a village near a bustling city and he from a small tribe in the desert – and have such different lives, and yet have something so intimate and profound in common. She had endured great, crushing losses, and so had he.

"I'm sorry," she murmured. "I hope you don't blame yourself for it. Before I lost my older brother there was also a little brother and a sister, and several infant siblings. I cannot help but think if I had worked harder, prayed to the gods more, done something differently, they might still be with us. In my head I know it doesn't make sense to blame myself. But my heart still aches, wishing I could have done more."

She rested her hand on his cheek and felt his jaw clenching beneath her touch. So she pushed herself up onto the balls of her feet, keeping one hand on his arm for balance, and brushed his lips with hers. His spicy, heady scent filled her airways, cutting off any rational thoughts she might have had.

His arms stayed crossed as her lips brushed his again, then once more. She held her breath, wondering if – now that the truth about her and Dedi and her father was in the open between them – he was no longer interested in her.

As she pulled away in disappointment, his arms suddenly unfolded and he gripped her hips. He tugged her body against his length and kissed her with a fierce passion unlike anything she'd ever experienced. His mouth was bruising, insistent, claiming hers with an intensity she hadn't known could exist between two people. And she met his ferocity with her own abandonment, letting go of all her fears and doubts to lose herself in this one moment. Instinct told her that he was somehow safe – for now.

Pausing for breath, Batr rested his forehead against hers. Eyes closed, he whispered, "I was terrified something had happened to you in the tomb. I didn't see you when I came in. I thought they had done something to you, that you were…" his voice choked with emotion.

Iset's heart filled to almost bursting. That he would care enough to worry, to come find her.

She said, "But I'm not, thanks to you." Laying her palms against his face, she kissed him again. His large hands roved up her back, crushing her to him in his powerful embrace, mashing her breasts against his chest. Leaning against him, she felt his rigidness against her belly and was momentarily gratified and alarmed. She'd never been so close to a man's erection before and it felt impossibly hard and hot through their thin layers of linen.

Sensing her hesitation, Batr took her by the shoulders and gently pushed her back from him. His eyes were even darker than before, almost black, and his chest rose as he hauled in rapid breaths. Then a slow, sexy smile curved his lips and he gave her a lazy look through his long, thick lashes, right before he slipped a hand behind her knees and scooped her lightly up into his arms.

In a few short strides they were back in his bedroom and laid out on his bed. Batr's sinewy torso hovered over her, resting on his elbows. His warm, masculine scent comforted her, buoying her through unfamiliar territory, even as it was intoxicating, stealing away her ability to think. In her last moments of rational thought she was aware that she was losing herself, becoming a mindless writhing mass of limbs and lips full of hunger and yearning. Aching loneliness and desire overcame her instinct to maintain control.

When he bent his head to slant his lips over hers, his rigid cock grazed her thigh. Inexperienced as she was Iset's body seemed to know what to do, and she shifted to press her leg against him. His hips bucked in response and he groaned into her lips and swore.

"By the gods, Nofret," he whispered in her ear, his warm breath sending shivers out across her skin. "You will kill me like this." But his hips continued to rock against her.

"Mmmm," she smiled, thrilling at his desire, feeling powerful that she was able to illicit the same want in him that he did in her. Shifting once more, his hardness met the mound of her sex and it was her turn to gasp. She had no idea anything could feel so achingly, awe-inspiringly pleasurable. Iset moved against him, a raw and agonizing sensation radiating up and out. She needed *more*.

Only two thin strips of linen separated their bodies, and that reduced to one when Batr reached to untie her shenti, pushing it open on both sides to pool around her, baring her naked body to his gaze.

His breath came out in a soft puff of air. "Nofret, do you have any idea how beautiful you are?"

Iset shook her head. Not in denial of his compliments, but because hearing him say such things would only distract her. He'd be gone soon enough and she would be left to find a way to continue on with life, just as she had learned to do over the years. *Keep surviving.* But for tonight she wanted to feel his skin on hers, his body over hers, against hers, in hers.

She reached for him but he caught her wrists. She might not want to hear his compliments, but the way he was looking at her was more honest than mere words. Admiration, desire, and something almost worshipful burned in his hot gaze as his eyes raked her body. When he dipped his head to kiss her neck, her collarbone, the tops of her breasts, she twisted to pull her hands from his grip, but instead he pinned her to the bed, holding her wrists gently next to her shoulders.

A wicked smile crept over his face and she thrilled to see it. He shook his head. "No. I won't last if you touch me."

"But…" she licked her lips, biting down on the bottom one, unsure how to express what she wanted. Instead her hips moved beneath him, pressing against him in a small undulation.

He swore softly. "By the gods, do you have any idea what you do to me?"

She slowly released her bottom lip and pursed her mouth in a little smile. "No. Why don't you show me?"

Batr growled, dipping his head to the space between her breasts, dropping little kisses along their tops. Anticipation made her ache and squirm beneath him. When his warm breath preceded his moist mouth over her nipple, she couldn't help but arch into him. Like most women, Iset had explored her own body at one point or another. She was aware of which areas elicited pleasure, and she'd also heard stories from her friends. But nothing, nothing in her life prepared her for the exquisite, awe-inspiring moment when his tongue laved her sensitive bud before taking the rosy peak into his mouth.

As if of their own volition, Iset's hips ground upwards against Batr's, and against his rigidness. He groaned against her breasts, pausing in his ministrations to mutter, "Iset, if you keep this up I can't… I swear… I can't hold back."

Realizing he'd released her wrists, she slid a hand between them. Down the long hard muscles of his abdomen, her fingers playing over the dark curls that led a trail to the edge of his shenti, and reached for the ties that held up his skirt to free the last barrier between them.

Whispering against his ear, she urged him. "So don't hold back."

She only knew what to do based on things others had told her. But that didn't matter. Her body craved him and she let her instincts guide her. She relished the closeness of him. The feel of his strong, unyielding body against hers, the hushed rub of his skin, his hardness against her sex, the smell of him, and the way he manipulated her senses into forgetting everything her mind dreaded. Dissolute, she was drunk with a thirsty desire. She was safe and secure in his arms; he was a brace against the world.

Propped up on one elbow along her side, his free hand joined hers between them. While she tugged away his shenti and tossed it from them, he reached for the intimate space between her legs. His long, bold fingers slipped between the folds of her sex and she cried out as pleasure spiked through her. With a skilled caress, his fingers swirled over the bundle of nerves at the apex of her plush, silky flesh. Lost in the moment, she gave herself up to the sensations that swept through her body in shuddering waves.

She became aware of a voice, her own, murmuring, "Please, oh please," while Batr trailed his lips over her neck and jaw and she undulated against him, her fists bunched alternately in the sheets and over his thick shoulders. In a glorious moment of pulsing ecstasy, the sensations overwhelmed her. Every muscle, every fiber of her being, twisted and tightened and caught up until she couldn't take it anymore and the world behind her eyes exploded into a thousand stars of bright, joyous release.

By the gods he was ready for this woman. So ready that he was shaking. But somehow he managed to catch his breath and focus on her, rather than the visceral need throbbing through him. She was utterly incomparable in her pleasure.

The unadulterated way she abandoned herself up to it, *to him*, was superb. From the way her body moved against him and the way she clutched him to her, to the pleading whimpers escaping from her ripe lips and the way her drenched sex pulsed around his fingers, all of it made him feel incredibly powerful and in complete awe of her at the same time. She was stunning to watch, and he wanted to make her peak in his hand over and over.

While he still cupped her sex, she turned into him, panting, her hands curled against his chest, riding out the last of her climax. He kissed the top of her head, her forehead and, when she turned her face up to look at him, her cheeks. Finally, he brought his mouth down over hers. At first slow and decadent with an almost unbearable sweetness, as her slender fingers uncurled and smoothed over the skin of his shoulders and arms, increasing in urgency and hunger, their kisses worked him up to a feverish pitch. His hands slid over her, once again dipping in to her sex to feel the searing wet heat there. He groaned into her mouth and she shifted onto her back, pulling him over her. Batr nestled himself between her legs, nudging against her.

"You're incredible," he murmured into her ear.

She wiggled beneath him, pressing her slick entrance against him. In a haze of lust, Batr pushed the swollen head of his hardness into her. Iset let out a sharp cry, her head thrown back and he stopped abruptly.

"Iset, gods I'm sorry. Are you all right?" Eyes scrunched shut, jaw clenched, her face was a mask of pain.

Opening her eyes, she gave a shaky laugh. "I'd heard stories, but I didn't really know it would hurt quite so much the first time."

"Stories? What do you… for Ba'al's sake! You've never done this before?" Batr looked down to the place where they were joined, momentarily horrified, before pulling back slightly to alleviate the pressure on her. He swore. "Why didn't you tell me? I thought… I assumed…?"

Her mouth hitched in a half-smile, the fog of pain slowly clearing from her eyes as she wrapped a hand around his bicep and pulled, urging him closer. "Why did you assume?"

Uncomprehending, he let her tug his upper body towards her, but kept his hips immobile, terrified of hurting her again. He'd presumed her to be innocent, but more so when it came to flirting, not sex. He'd never imagined she was *that* innocent.

"Iset, you've been engaged twice. You're a beautiful woman. You seemed to know what you were doing just now. How could you *not* have done this before?" He was furious with himself. In his own callous haste he'd been far too rough with her.

Planting warm little kisses on his neck and shoulders, she wrapped her legs around his calves, as if to lock him in place. "I have only kissed one boy before. Once. Five years ago."

He shook his head in wonder. "Why didn't you tell me, Nofret? Gods, if I'd known, I'd have gone about things differently."

Her shy smile melted his exasperation, though, and any softening of his ardour was stoked right back by the gentle, welcoming rocking of her hips. "I'm not terribly experienced with this, Batr, but are we supposed to be talking the whole time?"

"I – by Ra!" He laughed, dipping his head to claim her mouth in a kiss full of bruising emotion. She was amazing. The most amazing thing he'd ever set eyes on. She was an utterly unpredictable, foreign creature and he was in love with her. It was that simple, he realized. He was madly in love with her.

Slowly, very slowly this time, Batr pressed forward to be enveloped by her snug, soft warmth. He kept his eyes fixed on her face, though, for signs of distress. But Iset held his gaze, biting her lower lip with an encouraging smile. As if he was a young man during his own first time. He almost laughed at the absurdity of it. Ironically, he was just as nervous and ready to spill as he had been back then. All thanks to her, this beautiful woman beneath him.

Light-headed, he'd been holding his breath, so intent on her, that when the moment came that they were fully joined a sense of other-worldly euphoria overwhelmed him. She murmured in his ear, entreating him in whispers to move, and he complied. With her soft thighs wrapped around him, holding him fast, the mounds of her beautiful breasts pressed against his chest, and delectable noises coming from her mouth, it took all his strength not to drive into her with the force of a quarry-man wielding a hammer against stone.

As their hips began to rock in time, the expressions that flickered across her face kept him mesmerized. The way her teeth sank down on the fullness of her lush lower lip, the glaze of pleasure in her eyes, the tilt of her head, her thick hair tumbling across his bed, he focused on these things rather than the sensation of her silken depths stretched around him. But when he reared up and palmed one of her breasts, rolling the hard pink peak between two fingers and she cried out in response, clenching around him and losing their rhythm as passion wracked her body, he knew he was close too.

Capturing her mouth once more before increasing his speed, soon they were both panting and moving against each other in desperation, a turbulent and rocky joining, rushing towards spectacular wreckage. When the moment finally arrived, too many sensations rose up and crashed over him. When his shudders had stilled, he collapsed onto his elbows overtop of her, both of them slick and heaving.

Chapter 15 – Missing

Iset ran her hands over Batr's hair, pushing it back as his braids tickled her breasts and stuck to her damp skin. His head rested on her chest as he gulped in air and muttered her name, shaking his head. She smiled, trailing her fingers over his forehead and the arch at the back of his neck, pleased to see that he was just as shattered as she was.

She was glad it had been him. Glad that her first time had been with a man who'd been so generous and so gentle with her. She hadn't told him at first because she didn't think it would matter so much, didn't think he would care that she'd never slept with a man before. Given her past history with men, she'd never expected her own feelings or experiences to be of much importance to him. That he'd actually been upset she hadn't told him came as a shock. Tingles ran across the surface of her skin, a physical manifestation of the deeper emotions coursing through her. Yes, given more time with him, she could see herself falling dangerously in love with him.

And that thought frightened her as much as any band of tomb-robbers ever could. She'd lost too many people she cared about all ready. If she allowed herself to care too much for him, knowing she'd lose him sooner or later, her heart might crack into a hundred pieces, like shards of limestone chipped from a sculptor's block.

With a nudge from her, Batr rolled to the side and up to standing. Iset pushed her back up to the wall, to a sitting position. He gave her a lazy smile. "Wait here."

Still unabashedly naked, he strutted out of the bedroom. Despite her sobering thoughts, watching his firm, naked backside in the shadowy light of the oil wicks made her smile. He was so confident, so unafraid of the world and all the dangers in it. She wished she could bask in the safety of his presence for eternity. But she couldn't. Because tomorrow, whether or not the threat of tomb robbers still loomed, she'd have to bind her breasts, don her father's old clothes, wrap her face in swaths of linen, and pretend to be someone she wasn't.

Suddenly her life seemed so much more unbearable than it had before. As if the weight of all she'd lost suddenly crashed down over her like the roof of a tomb, suffocating in its enormity. Choking back sobs, she stuffed the palm of her hand into her mouth, trying to breathe around the painful lump lodged in her throat.

"Oh nononono," entering into the room carrying a basin of water and linen rags, Batr rushed towards her. He put the basin on a small side table and, sitting next to her on the bed, gathered her in his arms. And just like that Iset let loose all the sadness and fear and emotion that she'd kept bottled inside for what felt like years.

"I'm sorry," she sobbed into Batr's strong neck while he rubbed her back. "I – I don't know why I'm crying."

"Oh gods, Nofret." The day-old stubble on his jaw rasped against her cheek. "I'm the one who should be sorry. I was too rough. I'm sorry, I should have been better. I just wanted you so much and…" He blew out a violent puff of air. "Gods I'm such a bastard. I'm sorry."

"No." Her voice was muffled as he mashed her harder against his chest. "It's not that. *That* was wonderful. You were wonderful. Maybe that's why I'm crying. I… it was just so *nice* to not have to think about things. I… I was hardly able to mourn the loss of Sharek last year when my *mewet* fell ill and then I had to become Dedi. I know it sounds silly. I'm sorry, I'm sure no man wants to hear that sex with him reminds a woman of all her problems but…"

His words were soothing, laced with understanding. "But all this time you've had to be strong for your *mewet* and brother, and there's been no one to be strong for you."

Nodding, she tried to wiggle a hand between them to wipe the dampness from her cheeks. Instead, holding her away from him, he cupped her face in his palms and swiped the tears away with his thumbs. *Gods* she was so embarrassed to be crying like this. She *never* cried and she hated this feeling of vulnerability. His tenderness made her feel even worse.

"Nofret, Iset," he smiled at her, his handsome face so beautiful and kind it was too painful for her to look at. Her eyes dropped away to the sheet wrapped over her lower half. "Look at me, beautiful. Listen, I want to ask you something."

Heart pounding, she blinked and looked up. A sense of foreboding gripped her. Somehow she knew what he was going to ask, she could see it in his dark, hopeful eyes, and she went rigid under his touch.

"Nofret, come with me. When this is over, come back to Thinis with me. I have a home near the queen's court. Ahmose and your *mewet* will be happy there. Ahmose can study and train whatever he likes, and we can do anything you want to help your *mewet*. Doctors, hekka, food, I know some good women there who would sit with her and keep her entertained, whatever she needs. I'll make sure you have anything and everything you want."

Iset didn't think it was possible since she'd already steeled herself against this, but her heart felt like it was breaking apart, cracking open and cutting her up inside with its sharp shards. "I can't." She whispered.

"Of course you can." Iset couldn't look at him even though he still cupped her face, tilting it up to his. To look would be to see the reflection of her own hopes dying in his eyes.

"Iset, do you understand what I'm asking? I want to make you happy. Come with me. You won't have to be Dedi again ever. I want to feed you all your favourite dishes, by hand if I have to," he chuckled and she remembered how he'd threatened to sit by her all night if she didn't eat a bowl of lentil mash. "I want to fatten you up – like the Widow Neb-tawy if it pleases you – and buy you the finest linen dresses and have servants wait on you. I just want you to be happy and not have to worry about anything ever again. Let me do that for you."

Shivers overtook her as she miserably shook her head side to side. She wanted so very desperately to say *yes*, even if it meant leaving the Land of the Dead. In truth, she didn't care if she never saw the village again. All her happy memories here were marred with the pain and fear she'd endured since her older brother died, and the losses even before that. Since Sharek had died and she'd become Dedi, since her life had taken a very different course than her friends, she'd grown apart from all those she'd once been close with.

No, it wasn't the leaving that was the problem. It was *her*. The stain on her family name, the things her father had done – things she hadn't told Batr about – made it impossible for her to say yes. Sooner or later it would come out that her father had helped rob a tomb. Sooner or later the shame of her family would come back to her, and she, her brother, and her mother would have to pay for the crime. She couldn't bring that on Batr as well. Not after all he'd done for her.

And she couldn't tell him about it now. Especially not if he was close with Sekhrey Bey and the men that worked directly under the queen. Or, as she was beginning to suspect, he himself was somehow working with Sekhrey Bey. If the stories she'd heard about the former pirates were true, they were mostly honourable men. Batr would be utterly disgraced by a wife whose family had defiled the sacred tombs of the dead. It would ruin his life. *She* would ruin his life.

Then she realized he hadn't told her in what capacity he wanted her to come with him. He hadn't specifically asked her to marry him. Was she to be a concubine, then? Somehow that seemed worse than dressing as Dedi every day; not only would she be ashamed for her brother and mother to know what she was doing, but to know that Batr might one day marry another and leave her…

Pulling back from him, Iset shook her head. "I'm sorry, Batr. I can't. I can't go with you. It won't work." For so many reasons, it couldn't possibly work. She moved to get up from the bed, but he grabbed her wrist.

"Iset, I can give you a better life than this. Tell me why not."

She shook him off. "No. It's simple. The answer is no." Reaching for her old clothes, she yanked them over her head. Smoothing her hair down, she turned away from him. "I have to get back to check on Ahmose and my *mewet.*"

In a haze, she moved towards the door. She was barely aware of him wrapping his shenti around his lean waist and tying a long knife over top. Somewhere in the back of her mind she wondered at that knife – why was he carrying it? But she decided it was too much to take in right now. She snatched at her head wrap, pulling her hair up into a topknot so she could wind the scarf around her head and face. It was an effort to force down the feelings of dread as she donned that wrap again. That symbol of the endlessly suffocating cycle of her wretched life.

In a hard, tight voice Batr said, "I'm going with you."

Shaking her head – she seemed to be doing a lot of that tonight – she argued weakly, "No, its fine. I'll be all right."

He growled in frustration. "Enough already. Just stop it."

So instead she nodded, waiting for him to finish while she stared at the ground, inspecting her bare toes on the reed mats laid out on his floor. He had every right to be mad at her. She wouldn't be surprised if he wanted to rage and yell at her. By rejecting his offer of kindness she'd done the stupidest, most ridiculous thing in all the living world.

Kindness. Because that's what it was. He hadn't said anything about love, not that she really expected that anyway. She'd almost married twice before without love. But she didn't want to just be a burden to Batr, a responsibility. Perhaps he'd offered for her because he felt guilty about losing his family, and protecting her was a means of assuaging his guilt. Eventually he'd come to dislike her for it. Worse, what if she was like her mother, and couldn't conceive without the child dying? At nineteen she was already getting older, she might not be able to provide Batr with children. He might turn to drink, as her father had.

And despite everything she'd told herself and how unrealistic the expectation, a small part of her *did* want there to be love between them. Silly of her. Childish, even, to think she could ever hope for such a thing.

Batr walked beside Iset, moving through the darkened streets of the village in silence. Only the sounds of their sandals slapping against the sand, hardened by thousands of feet over hundreds of years, accompanied them. The smell of dust and sand swirling up from the ground mingled with the smells of dinners cooking in clay ovens. The aromas of lentils, barley, fresh bread and, occasionally, a fowl or larger fare, wafted in the air, reminding Batr that he hadn't eaten despite laying out food for them earlier. They'd been too busy tangled in his bed, bodies blending, melding, in a wondrous coupling unlike any he'd ever shared with a woman.

Nevertheless he'd been a fool. He'd thought that telling Iset about his family would help her to trust him. And he'd hoped their love-making might somehow bond her to him, make her want to stay with him. Rather than satisfying any cravings for her, the gods knew it had made him covet her even more.

But something had gone wrong. He didn't expect her to feel the same depth of emotion he did, but he knew his offer couldn't be entirely repellent. Even if she didn't love him, she'd clearly felt some desire for him. It wasn't hubris that caused him to question why she'd rejected him. His pride could have accepted it if she'd turned away from him in distaste, though his heart would have suffered a mighty blow. But what he saw in her eyes was more like fear, reminding him of the moment when the gazelle across the oasis pool from him had been startled into flight. The magic – the hekka – of one the most beautiful moments of his existence had been broken then, just as now. Except this time, Batr was determined not to let Iset bolt out of his life like a frightened antelope.

She might be able to fool the village into thinking Dedi existed, but she wasn't a good enough liar to convince him she'd told him the whole truth about how she ended up in the burial chamber. She was holding something back, he was sure of it now, something that terrified her so much she couldn't even tell him *why* she wouldn't be with him. Batr was resolute, though, and not the type of man to so easily give up something he wanted. Once he discovered whatever had her so petrified, and done away with it, then he'd see how she *really* felt.

The shuffling sound of another set of sandals hurrying towards them drew his attention. A short, round figure emerged from the evening gloom, pale, naked skin and beige shenti glowing in the darkness.

"Dedi," breathless and urgent, the widow Neb-tawy flapped a hand at them. As they neared, Batr could see the older woman's eyes were wide with alarm. Panting, she stopped and dropped her hands onto her knees, hauling in shallow breaths.

"Neb-tawy, are you all right?" Batr moved to her side, wrapping a hand around her arm to help steady and comfort her. "What's the matter?"

Iset had pressed her hand over the fabric that masked her nose and mouth. He didn't doubt she was sick with fear, knowing that the widow was meant to be sitting with her mother and brother. Trepidation fluttered in his own gut, and he wondered if it was possible the tomb robbers had somehow intercepted his message to his brother. Or if they'd decided to take their threats one step further to prove their determination to get what they wanted.

Batr rubbed the old woman's broad back. "Take deep breaths, Neb-tawy. Tell us, is something wrong? Is someone hurt?"

The old lady shook her head, still hauling in air. "I – I don't know. I – I left Ankhesenamon in bed. She's fine. But Ahmose."

Behind her wrappings Iset made a little noise of alarm, her free hand now pressed to her chest between her bound breasts. He saw the tears well up in her eyes and cursed inwardly.

He urged the older woman. "Neb-tawy, what about Ahmose? Please. Tell us."

"I told you," she looked up at Iset, shaking her bald head. "He's always out with those boys, the stone-cutter's sons." The widow pulled herself up to full height and pointed a finger at Iset. "They came by the house earlier and asked him to come out. I told him to be back by dark, and that was hours ago. He missed dinner. He's probably busy getting in to trouble with those boys. And I have no idea where your cousin Iset is."

Batr let go of the old woman to clap a hand over Iset's shoulder. The rigid tension in her body and the roll of her eyes told him she might be in danger of swooning. He swore to himself again, realizing she hadn't touched the food he'd laid out, and the gods only knew the last time she'd eaten.

"Thank you, Neb-tawy." He inclined his head, tightening his grip on Iset's shoulder as she tried to pull from him. "Don't worry about Ahmose, Iset's probably found him by now and brought him home. We'll head back to the hut right now and check."

The old woman narrowed her eyes at Iset and said, "Ahmose needs a man to whip him into shape. Iset ought to marry and get Ahmose into a trade, instead of letting him mess around with those stone-cutter's sons. They're older than him, and I've heard they sneak out sometimes to the tombs and muck about out there with girls and such."

Batr could feel Iset practically vibrating with impatience under his fingers and, thanking the widow again, steered Iset quickly away in the direction of her hut. They didn't have far to go and within a few minutes she burst through the door, tugging at her face-wrap to loosen the fabric around her nose. A quick search of the rooms revealed only her groggy mother, who sat up when Iset peered into the room, Batr right behind her.

"Iset?" Ankhesenamon sat up in her bed. "Is that you? Oh, no. It's… wait… Dedi, right? And… you are…" She trailed off, looking Batr over in confusion. Then she smiled, like the morning sunlight cresting the edge of the eastern horizon. "Batr. The man Ahmose likes so much."

Batr blinked. Did the woman not even know her own daughter posed as a boy to support her? Gods, it was worse than he'd imagined.

"No, mewet, it is I, Isetnofret," Iset choked out. "I – I'm sorry to disturb you. Please, go back to sleep."

"Iset? But what are you doing in your *yet*'s old clothes?" The older woman looked Iset over.

"Don't worry yourself. Everything is fine. I made a mistake is all." Iset's words were soothing, but Batr could hear the exasperated impatience in them. Iset pressed her mother to lie back down and tucked the threadbare sheet around her before ushering him out of the room.

When they were in the greeting room she turned on him. "Where is my brother?!" She demanded.

Stunned into incredulity, Batr blinked at her. "I have no idea. He's probably just out messing around, doing what boys do."

"No. No. Ahmose *always* comes home on time." She paced for a moment, the air nearly crackling around her, her eyes flashing with fury as she stepped back up to him. "You did this." She stabbed a finger at his shoulder. "You distracted me so that the other men could take him. Nebtawy said he was out with the stone-cutter's sons and you yourself told me the stone-cutter is one of the men threatening me. How would you know that if you aren't involved with them? How did you know who *any* of them are?" Her voice, though still low so as not to disturb her mother, was becoming increasingly frantic.

"You came to our house looking for Dedi right after you'd come to the Land of the Dead. You pushed your way into our home, our lives, into my… my…" she was heaving in air now in gulps. Even in the dark room, lit only by threads of silvery moonlight seeping in the narrow window, Batr could see her face darkening with emotion. "Our *yet*… oh gods… he died in the cliffs by the tombs… if they've taken him there… Damn you! You distracted me and now they've taken my brother! Even if you're not involved with them, this wouldn't have happened if I was home with my family, where I *should* be." Her voice was thick with accusation and tears.

Seizing her hand, he pulled her to him, enfolding her in his arms. "Nofret, it's not like that." He murmured against the wrappings about her head, wishing he could get to her mouth to kiss her and show her how very little it was *like that.* But then, as if struck by an ice-cold tidal wave, he realized it *was* like that. He *had* tried to infiltrate their lives to get closer to her in order to get information. He'd even planned to charm her, to seduce her if necessary. If he hadn't actually been successful in his endeavours, she might have been home with her brother tonight, and none of this would've happened.

Then again, if the tomb robbers truly had taken Ahmose, and Iset had been with him, they'd probably have her right now also. His fingers tightened possessively around her.

But she twisted in his grip and smacked her palms against his chest. "Get away from me," she hissed.

"Iset, I'll help you find him. He might just be out playing somewhere. We'll look together. I won't let you go out alone."

Anger imbued her with surprising strength for such a slight woman, and when she lunged to shove him towards the door it knocked him slightly off balance. "You don't have a say in the matter, Batr. Stay away from me, or by the gods I will bring every curse I can think of down on you. Now get out get out get out!" She punctuated this command by slamming her hands on his chest and arms, propelling him towards the door, which she opened and pushed him through.

He could have stopped her, of course. Even in her rage it wouldn't have been hard to compel her to cease her assault. But to what end? She was frantic and furious and he didn't want to upset her further. And she was right, he *was* partly to blame. That didn't mean he would acquiesce to her orders, there was no chance he'd let her search for Ahmose alone. He'd just have to make sure she didn't know he was watching over her.

Batr followed Iset through the dark. Her robe-clad figure and beige head wrapping served as beacons against the blue-black backdrop of the night. It had been some time since he'd hunted in the desert, but the skills acquired from years of raiding and stalking in wide-open spaces served him well in the cramped streets of the village. Other people moved about the streets, on their way to visit friends, lounging in doorways watching neighbours go by, calling out to one another. Groups of women and girls, arm-in-arm, twittered together. The odd man hailed Iset, in her guise as Dedi, but she barely mustered a curt nod. Her movements were jerky and erratic as her head craned from side to side, peering down alleyways and into backyards while she hurried through the village.

Only once, when Iset ventured down an empty side street, did she stop and turn to look in his direction. He was trailing along at a distance, slipping into darkened doorways and the spaces between houses, when his sandal clipped a rock that skidded and hit the side of a building with a clatter. By the time she stopped and turned, he'd tucked himself around a corner, waiting for the sound of her sandals slapping the earth before leaving his hiding spot to resume his pursuit.

It was a frustrating business overall. He didn't know the village well enough to guess where a boy might steal off to with his friends, or where one might take a boy if one were so inclined to do so. In his message to his brother, Batr had given the locations of the tomb robber's homes based on the details he'd gleaned from the widow Neb-tawy, but it seemed unlikely they'd hide the boy in such obvious locales. Given the direction Iset was going, it appeared she thought so, too.

They were, in fact, heading towards the tombs. If the worst came to pass, if the thieves *had* taken Ahmose, and if

Makae didn't arrive soon with soldiers and aid, at the very least Batr had his long blade strapped to his side, and he wouldn't hesitate to use it.

Terror squeezed Iset's heart, clawing its way up her throat, tightening in her belly, making it impossible to breathe or think. Mindless with fear, she rushed through the streets of the village looking for her brother. Her numbed brain looped the same thoughts over and over, chastising her for allowing Batr to muddle her focus, for thinking it possible to rely on someone else for help. On the one hand she blamed him for pursuing her and for being so charming, but deep down she knew it was her own fault. She cursed herself for being weak, for wanting to let someone else take care of her problems. And look where it had gotten them. Even if Batr wasn't involved with the band of thieves, her feelings for him were nothing but a hindrance, something she'd have to cut out of her heart if she wanted to survive.

She paused near the house of the stone-cutter, hearing the sounds of people on the rooftop. Listening for Ahmose's voice, or that of children, she heard only adults talking and the booming laughter of a man. Near the square that served as a market-place during the daytime, on the edge of the village bordering the desert, she came across a group of boys and stopped to look. The boys had formed a ring, and above their heads she discerned sticks waving about in the centre of the circle. Cheering and jockeying for a more advantageous position, it was clear there were boys play-acting at fighting in the centre.

Hope flared between her breasts, and Iset moved towards them. *Please, dear Isis, please let Ahmose be there.* As luck would have it she was a slight bit taller than most of the boys, and so was able to see the heads of the fighters. Moonlight glanced off the tops of their bald pates, and as they whirled and lunged she tried to find Ahmose's braided side-lock either amongst the crowd or the boys with the sticks.

But no. While some of the boys looked her way, afraid an adult had come to break up their fun, none of the upturned faces belonged to Ahmose. The fighters broke apart when one managed to push through the others' defences and crack him on the shoulder. Admitting defeat, the sticks were passed along to new boys, neither of whom was her brother.

Tears welled in her eyes. If she were garbed as Iset she wouldn't hesitate to ask Ahmose's whereabouts of the boys, but as Dedi she was at a loss. Her mind raced to find a means of communication when a hand patted her arm and caused her to start.

Whirling to face the touch, Iset found a boy about ten or eleven years of age looking at her with wide eyes. Like many boys his age he was unabashedly naked, his gangly body sun-browned and awkward.

"Dedi?" The boy asked.

Iset was almost too surprised to nod in response. Her mind calmed enough to recognize the boy as a friend of Ahmose's, the grandson of one of her father's old friends.

"Are you looking for Ahmose?" The boy inclined his head. "I saw him not so long ago with Dejet, the stone-cutter's son, and Seret, the draughtsman's little brother. They were on their way to the creek on the other side of the village."

She managed a quick nod of thanks. *By the gods*, she was on the wrong side of town. The creek was at least twenty minutes away, while their home lay almost in the middle. Horrible images of her little brother lying face down in the creek flashed through her mind and Iset choked back a sob. Sandals smacking the hard earth, she hastened towards the stream where young boys were wont to fish and bath. She'd wasted valuable time following the widow Neb-tawy's notion that the boys had gone to the tombs, and she prayed now the mistake wouldn't cost her the person she held most dear.

Passing her hut several minutes later on her way to the stream, she opened the door and peered into the darkness. Determining Ahmose still hadn't returned, she hurried on, moving into the lusher area surrounding the narrow waterway. Trees loomed above her, and scraggly bushes spotted the ground, extending out into the pathway and forcing her to slow lest she trip on a root or scratch her ankles on the branches.

She was moving into the even gloomier darkness of the bushy area near the creek's edge, when she spied a figure limping along a pathway off to her side a ways. Stopping short, she steeled herself for fight or flight.

"Ahmose?" She called out.

"Iset?" A small voice called back.

"Oh!" She cried out, not even caring if others overheard her. Nothing else mattered as she rushed to her brother, throwing herself to her knees to wrap her arms around him, then pulling back to shake and scold him, then hugging him fiercely again. When she'd finally convinced herself he was whole, she pulled back to examine him, recalling he'd been limping.

"Ahmose! What happened?" His right eye was swollen almost shut, and he favoured his left leg. "Are you hurt? Who did this?" She dug her fingers into his thin shoulders as images of Ahmose fending off a group of tomb robbers flashed through her mind.

"S'all right, Iset." The boy sighed. "I got 'em. We were playing pirates down by the creek 'n' Seret said that Sekhrey Bey was the best pirate there ever was. 'N' then I said that I *knew* a real pirate and Dejet called me liar. I told him about Batr, how he was a pirate *and* a tribal warrior and how he could probably beat Sekhrey Bey any day, but Dejet didn't believe me. He just kept saying I was liar, and then he…" his voice caught. "Then he said our dad was a drunk and a gambler, and that he owed everyone and I was going to be just like him."

Ahmose lifted his chin defiantly, even if it *did* wobble a little bit. "So I hit him and we got into it. I know I shouldn't've, but I couldn't let him say that, could I, Iset? It isn't true, is it?"

"Oh, Ahmose," so many emotions washed over Iset she couldn't process them in that moment. She hugged her little brother and stroked his back. "Our *yet* was… not always as good as he should have been. But you won't be like that. You will be strong, and kind, and generous, and thoughtful. Do you know how I know that?"

He shook his head against her shoulder and she smiled.

"Because you are all of those things now. If you just continue to be exactly as you are, you will grow up to be the best of men, Ahmose. I promise."

"Except," she held him back from her by the shoulders, giving him a little shake, "if you ever disappear like that again, I will have no choice but to barricade you in your room until you *do* grow into a man. You have no idea how terrified I was. I should cuff you for doing that to me. I thought you'd gone out to the tombs and…" her voice hitched and it was his turn to hug her.

"I'm sorry, Iset. I really am. We just got into it and I should have just left it alone. But you didn't need to be so worried. Lots of boys go out at night. I just thought if the widow was watching our *mewet* it would be all right."

"Come, Ahmose. Let's get you home." She took her little brother's hand and helped him limp back to the house. Once inside she sent him right off to bed without dinner. A small punishment for not coming back when he was supposed to, and frightening her almost to death.

As she unwound the wrapping about her head, massaging her fingers through her hair, Iset recalled the feel of Batr's hands on her skin. The touch of his lips to hers, the ecstasy of their bodies blending. Bittersweet was the memory of his offer, a memory she would hold dear for the rest of her days even if it brought her great pain. She shook her head, trying to clear it of the jumble of emotions that overwhelmed her.

She'd accused him of terrible things, of being in league with thieves, plotting to seduce her in order to kidnap her brother, of making her problems worse, when all he'd done was try to help her. None of this had been his fault after all. He must think her a madwoman. She wouldn't be surprised if he never wanted to see her again. While she knew that would be for the best, it crushed her heart to think she'd lost him forever.

Outside, Batr leaned against the side of Iset's hut near the window of her bedroom, listening to her move about the room. Trying not to envision her undressing, he couldn't help but recall the first time he'd been inside her hut, how he'd peered into the darkened doorway of her room and thought of her smooth, olivine legs wrapped around his back. How he'd slip his hands up into her silken hair and capture her mouth with his, to nip and lick and suck her small, rosebud pink nipples while she rode him in his lap, driving them both to the highest peaks of pleasure. Those few stolen hours with her earlier tonight weren't nearly enough to satisfy his desire. A lifetime might not be sufficient. Knowing that she'd shared herself with him and no one else only flamed the fires of his need for her.

Of course he'd much rather be in her bed than standing in the chill night air outside her window. But it wouldn't help his cause to push her right now. Having overheard her conversation with Ahmose by the creek, he knew Iset could no longer hold him accountable for Ahmose's actions. She'd come around in her own time.

Or not. For the first time, a little voice of doubt niggled at the back of his mind. *What if whatever secret she's keeping is too great to bear?*

No, he decided. He wasn't one to back away from something he wanted. Whatever it was, he'd find out. And he wasn't leaving her alone tonight. Not until he was sure his brother and the soldiers scoured the town and dealt with the thieves. And even after that, he wasn't leaving the Land of the Dead until he was confident Iset would be safe. Whether she left with him or not was another matter.

Sighing, Batr crossed his arms over his chest, rested his head back against the wall, and prepared himself for a long night.

Chapter 16 – A Father Revealed

The next morning

Raia stood alone in the decaying hallway of Userkare's entranceway, waiting for his elderly manservant to return and let her know if her father's nemesis would grant her an audience or not. This time she didn't bother counting the cracks, or looking over the cobwebs that collected dust in the corners. She was far too exhausted to count. She'd slept little last night, quite possibly not at all. Her analytical brain worked busily, taking apart everything that transpired between her and Makae, from the moment they'd first met, to the moment she'd ejected him from her life. When it came to her brother and father, she compared her time with Makae to everything else she knew, all she'd said about them, and what he might have overheard.

In the end, she'd known what she needed to do. If she didn't find out for herself what had transpired all those years ago with her father, her mother, and Userkare, she'd never be easy. And so she'd dragged herself out of bed, waiting anxiously until the appropriate time to call on dying man and then hurrying to his home. Raia was not the sort to avoid unpleasant business, better to get it out into the open then leave it to fester and grow.

Finally, the elderly manservant returned. This time he did not lead her outside, but through the hallway, past a greeting room, and to a large room off to the right. There, reclining on a low, narrow bed, propped up against several cushions, sat Userkare. With a blanket drawn up over his lap, his long, bony hands rested atop the cover. Thin white linen curtains were tied back around the bed. Weak sunlight from the small window in the wall nearby filtered through the bunched curtains to reflect off the white coverlet, casting Userkare's skull-like face in an even more pallid hue.

"Raia," his expression lit up as she entered the room and he held out one hand for her to clasp. "You have returned."

Drawing a heavy wooden chair over, she sat near his bed. She couldn't help but notice the expensive wood, one that must have been imported from the far north, given that Kemet had no such strong wood for carving. Its finish was now chipped, the polish dull with decade of wear. Like everything else in Userkare's home, it was preparing for the other world.

Raia made small talk for a few moments, and she could see that Userkare had grown worse in the days since she last saw him, as evidenced by his inability to leave his bed today or the day before. Knowing that her time to question him was short, she brought the conversation around to asking him about her father, telling him what Makae had learned from Ahaneith's official.

"Ahhhh," the old man let out a slow gasp, his moist, flaccid lips parting and hanging open, as if too heavy to return to their resting state. His lids drooped over his eyes. For a moment, Raia feared his heart had given out, but he roused himself, lifting his head and saying, "So. It has come to this at last."

"What has, Userkare? Tell me." Raia leaned forward, her hands clutching her thighs.

Userkare fisted the cover in his lap. "I wanted to tell you the other day when you were here, but I did not know if you would want to know. I – I didn't think I could bear it if you didn't. You see, my great failing my entire life has been lack of courage. I am a weak man, Raia," he licked at a gob of spittle that had formed in the corner of his mouth. His next words came out an anguished whisper. "I am a horribly weak man. If I had been stronger, less afraid, things would have been different."

"Please, Userkare. Tell me what you mean." Growing frustrated with his roundabout speech, she drew her chair even closer.

He looked up sharply at her, meeting her steady gaze with his watery, jaundiced eyes. "Ra-hotep. It was all him.

When I returned I tried to claim you, but it was too much for me, I could not fight him." His voice turned ragged, phlegmy, but he continued. "I had lost *everything.* I had nothing to offer you. I was a broken man. I was weak." He broke into a coughing fit and reached for a square of linen folded on a table near his bed.

"Claim me? What do you…?" But dread grew in the pit of her stomach and, even as she tried to deny the thoughts that crowded into her head, she was already doing the math. Userkare was exiled twenty-three years ago; right before he'd been due to marry her mother. Raia herself was born shortly after her parents married, an early baby. A servant had once commented on how she'd been an abnormally large infant for one almost two months before their time.

Userkare's fingers tightened into a fist in his lap. Then he unclenched it, staring down at his pale palm. "I was too late. Your *mewet* had passed away long before, and you had just married. When I came home I wanted to see you, to tell you the truth. Ra-hotep refused to believe me. But I knew." He looked up at her, an intense, feverish light burning in his eyes. "He threatened me. He told me if I ever tried to contact you, he would have me sent back into exile."

"No, my *yet* would never have done such a thing. Why would he?" Raia couldn't believe the man who had raised her could be so awful as that, even as the world she knew crumbled around her like the mouldering walls of Userkare's family home. She told herself Userkare was not right in the head, that her father had been right to warn her away from him, but it felt hollow.

"Because he did not want anyone else to have credit for who you are. You are a bright, beautiful woman. One to make any man proud." He held up a finger when she would have asked him how he knew. "I have followed you over the years, even as isolated as I am," Userkare made a gesture to indicate the lonely, grey room in which they sat. "Ra-hotep disliked anyone who had something he did not. That's why he had us sent into exile. He wanted my land, and he wanted your *mewet.* And when I returned he was even more powerful than before. I wanted to fight him, but I had just returned, and had nothing. I would have had even less if I were forced into exile again." His hands still rested in his lap, and he turned them palm upwards, as if to show how empty they were.

"Most of my family died in exile, and while I was able to re-claim our home, and some of our lands, I had no wealth. Furthermore, I feared bringing the stain of exile on you and your children. Ahhh, Raia," his expression was anguished, "I have waited so long to meet with you. I thought it would never happen. I blamed myself every day for not knowing, for not taking your *mewet* – and you – with me."

Raia shook her head, still confused. "But how did you know? What made you think that you were…" She couldn't bring herself to say the words. She could never think of this wizened, defeated man as her father.

A coughing fit wracked Userkare's body, forcing Raia to wait for an answer. Finally, he gasped out, "I knew. I knew because we always said if we had a girl we would name her Raia, after a sister of mine who passed away as a little girl. Your *mewet* would never have named you Raia if you were not my child. I don't even think she knew it yet, but she must have been pregnant with you when I left, and I told her she could not come with me. I thought I was doing her a service, that it would be better for her. All our goods were stripped from us, and I had nothing to support her with. I did not know then that Ra-hotep wanted her, and that she would have no choice after I left."

Raia closed her eyes as Userkare dabbed at his now blood-flecked lips, her mind reeling.

"Wait," she said, lifting her chin. "What made you think my *yet* had you sent into exile? You came back and accused him of taking some of your land when you returned. And you were not surprised when I told you he had acquired more of it recently. Did you sell it to him to manage?"

"Mmmm." Shaking his head, Userkare wiped at his lips again, although right afterwards his greyish tongue slipped out to slide wetly over them. "He stole my land." The elderly man shrugged one shoulder, though his rheumy eyes burned with hate. "He knew when I returned from exile I would have little recourse. He moved the markers, and denied any change. I knew, though. Even though our records had been taken from us when we were sent away. I always counted my steps. I was gone fourteen years, but I still remembered how many steps it took to cross my land. One doesn't forget something like that."

Raia's breath escaped her in a pained gasp. In ten years *she* hadn't forgotten how many steps it was to traverse her father's land. Ra-hotep used to marvel at her ability to grasp numbers, and she'd always said it was because he'd been a good teacher, showing her how to count. Now she wondered if her affinity for numbers came from somewhere else.

The elderly man added, "I only learned he'd done it again a couple of weeks ago, when it came time to begin preparing my taxes." Userkare's breath was a rattling in his throat, and he began to ramble more. "It was his last chance to get the better of me, I suppose. He knew I was dying, and he hated me so much, he probably hoped it would kill me when I learned of it. I doubt he knew then he'd die before me. We'd been friends, once, you know, your *yet* and I. But my farms were doing well, and I was to marry your *mewet*. She was so beautiful, just like you. I didn't know how jealous he was until it was too late."

"But…" she held her hand over her belly, trying to understand. "The records indicated you were wrong. Back then, I mean. How could he move the land markers without the records proving otherwise? How could he have had you sent into exile?"

Userkare's head lolled back against the wall, his hands limp in his lap. But his eyes remained open, fixed beyond her shoulder, staring into the past. "It was so easy for a man with his sort of power," he panted. "So easy to bribe the right people, to have my family accused of the very crimes he'd committed. I was a fool to trust him as a friend."

"Who did he bribe?" A thought struck her. She'd been so absorbed in these new revelations that she'd forgotten to ask him about the very thing that had started this whole journey. "Userkare, do you know who robbed my *yet*'s tomb? Did you do it? Did you hire someone to desecrate his eternal peace?"

The old man's wispy white hair floated around his head as he rolled it from side to side against the wall in a negative gesture. "No, my child. I did not do it, though I do not blame you for suspecting me." He gave a grim smile. "Once again, I was too craven, too weak even to take my revenge on a dead man. But I believe I know who did."

"Who? Please, I need to know. I need to end this."

His eyes lighted on hers, and she saw sympathy in their yellowed depths. "Of course you do, my child. I have been selfish in my need to unburden myself to you. Of course." He nodded, and Raia bit down on her lips, resisting the urge to scream at this sickly man to tell her what she needed to know so she could be done with him and flee outside, into the open air.

In a series of rattling gasps, Userkare told her, "I believe the man who defiled Ra-hotep's grave is the same man who has helped him to steal from me all these years. The same man who helped write the documents that sent my family into exile. I summoned him to me after I learned your *yet* had stolen more of my land. I wanted to hear his explanation. He told me not to worry, that Ra-hotep had gotten what he deserved. He said your *yet* owed him for years' worth of work, and that he'd taken his vengeance. It wasn't until you came to see me a few days ago that I understood what he meant. That he was the one who robbed Ra-hotep's tomb."

"Userkare, please, who was it?"

"Why it was one of your *yet*'s scribes, of course. The same man he's had for twenty-five years. The one who keeps track of all the food for the workers in the Land of the Dead."

Chapter 17 – The Final Day

Donning her clothes for work that morning was one of the most loathsome tasks Iset had ever performed. She wanted nothing more than to stay curled up under her blankets on the rooftop, though the wan, grey skies above were dispiriting to say the least. The night had been cold, and she'd lain awake through most of it, turning over and over, not closing her eyes to sleep until Ra began to push the sun over the horizon. Even then, her sleep was fitful, as the birds began to chirp. Images circled in her mind over and over. Batr's face as they'd made love in his bed, then when she'd rejected his offer, and again when she'd pushed him from the hut and told him to stay away from her.

Intermingled with that was the fear that, having revealed almost all to Batr, she had exposed herself to worse danger. Perhaps the thieves would find out she'd told on them and come for her today at work. Batr had promised to keep her safe, and that the men would be apprehended, but then she'd accused him of terrible things. Perhaps he no longer cared what happened to her and her family. Perhaps by going to the tombs today she was putting herself directly in harm's way.

But what choice did she have except to carry on as before? Heaving a sigh, she'd forced herself to crawl out from under her blankets, as if battling against the ferocious winds of a desert sandstorm, and prepare for work. Furthermore, she was desperate for some shred of news about the thieves. If they'd been apprehended in the night word of it would spread through the tomb workers quickly. She'd likely hear about it by lunchtime, on the way home at the very latest.

Thankfully, Weni, her painting partner, had also decided to come in to work that day and she took some comfort in his silent company. With the flowers of Amunemhat's garden nearly complete, she took up mixing the ochre pigment to create the brownish-yellow colour required to paint the skin of his naked offspring. It was no small feat to avoid thinking of what Batr's future offspring might look like. Would they have his piercing, laughing eyes? His height, his skin colour? Would he want them to be tattooed like him? Even the girls? Would they have his sense of playfulness and mischief, and his bright smile?

Vain, foolish questions. The type of things a young girl in love might wonder about, not a pathetic woman who turned down a man's offer of protection after going willingly into his bed. She was trapped in this wretched, barren life as surely as if she'd been buried alive under the tomb itself, just as in her nightmares. Slipping a finger under the fabric around her nose, she tugged a little, just to let more air in, so she could breathe deeply. But the bindings across her breasts were too tight, even if she could draw air in through her nostrils.

Not long after they'd begun work, Weni cleared his throat, as if to speak, but was overtaken by a wracking coughing fit. One hand on his skinny knee, he held up the other to keep her attention. She waited, bowl of ochre paste in hand, for him to finish. Finally, the fit passed and he straightened, taking up his brush again and turning to the leaves of a tree on the wall near her.

"Teos weren't there this morning to hand out the supplies," Weni said in a scratchy voice.

Iset cocked her head, as if to ask him to continue. Her heart fluttered, hope flaring. She hadn't gone to the inventory hut that morning, as it was Weni's turn, so she hadn't known the man who managed the inventory was missing. If Teos hadn't come in to work today, did that mean the other thieves hadn't either?

"Dunno where he's at," Weni went on, stroking green malachite paste over the date palm outline on the wall. "The foreman were in his place instead, handing things out calm as you please. Wouldn't answer no questions, though." Weni grunted, reaching around to scratch at one cheek of his behind with his middle finger. "Imagine we'll hear more at lunch."

Iset nodded, turning back to her pastes in a daze. The rest of the morning passed slowly enough to drive her mad. When lunch was finally called she hurried to the lineup. Not because she was hungry. Not at all. In fact, her stomach revolted at the very thought of food. But she'd spent the morning praying to all the gods that the men had been taken, that she'd hear more of their fate at lunch, and that perhaps she'd even catch a glimpse of Batr.

It wasn't long before her prayers were answered. Even such a hardened group of men couldn't resist talking about how several people were taken from their homes in the middle of the night. Rumour had it that Teos, Addaya, the stone-cutter, and a security guard named Pamiu were arrested in their homes by men of Lady Ahaneith's sending. Their families had been taken along with them, someone had seen them standing in the street with a ring of soldiers around them.

Iset's hands shook as they gripped her bowl, and she had to set the food down to twist her fingers in the folds of her robe. *Safe safe safe* her mind chanted. *Safe safe safe.* It didn't seem real.

"What about that foreign fellow?" One of the men asked. "That new one with the things." He gestured with one gnarled, sun-darkened hand to his face, referring to Batr's tattoos. "He's not here today either. Did they take him, too? Anyone know what they all did to get themselves caught like that?"

The other men shook their heads. Nobody had heard about Batr. Their conversation turned to speculation about the men's activities, and she tuned them out. Where *was* Batr? Was it possible he'd left town already? He'd said he had a home in Thinis, so what had his purpose been here in the Land of the Dead? He'd told her he still had connections with Sekhrey Bey, and she had to wonder if the queen's guard was somehow involved in all this. Or, conversely, was Batr himself involved with the queen's guard?

Increasingly she began to fear that she'd return home to find soldiers waiting for her. What if they'd found out about the previous robbery that her father was entangled in? Last night, before she'd learned of Ahmose's disappearance, it had crossed her mind that Batr was somehow involved with the queen's guard. Now, Iset wondered if the queen had learned of the theft of the nobleman's tomb, and had sent Batr to investigate. She'd never heard of such a thing happening before, but if so, it would explain why he'd tried so hard to get to know her and Dedi. He hadn't been trying to *rob* a tomb; he'd been trying to *find* the robbers.

She wanted nothing more than to run home to check on Ahmose and her mother. She couldn't rest easy until she knew they were safe. But to leave work now, with all the speculation on the arrests, would only serve to cast suspicion on her. Without question she had to continue on as if nothing was wrong. After lunch she went back to mixing her pigments and painting the flesh of Amunemhat's children, but her hands trembled and she smudged outsides the lines more than once. The end of the day couldn't come fast enough.

As Iset scurried through the streets of the village she had to bite back a scream of frustration as, once again, the widow Neb-tawy delayed her. Could it be that some sort of hekka enabled the widow to know when Iset was most distraught, and the old woman sought to torment her?

"Dedi! Come here, boy." Neb-tawy flapped one hand while wiping sweat off her brow with the back of the other. "Dedi, did you find your cousin last night? What did I tell you about that stone-cutter and his sons? You know that man was arrested last night?"

Iset nodded, half-turned away from the older woman to indicate her need for haste, hardly aware of what Neb-tawy had to say, or her own responses. It wasn't until Neb-tawy mentioned Batr's name that Iset was called to attention.

"That man, the foreign one, has he offered for your cousin yet?" Neb-tawy waggled her fingers in the direction of Batr's hut.

Iset shrugged, slowly, shaking her head. She had no idea how to answer the widow. Even if Dedi could speak, there were no words to explain what had occurred.

"Mmmm," the older woman shook her head from side to side. "I thought for sure he'd ask you about it soon, he certainly seems to have an interest. He's a good man, that one, even with all that hair and the tattoos and such. I hope if he asks you'll let her accept. I saw him going back and forth through the village today several times. Wondered why he wasn't at work, but he said he didn't have much time today to talk. One time he was in such a rush he didn't even stop to say hello."

While the first revelation – that Neb-tawy thought Batr cared enough to offer for her – set Iset's thoughts into even more of a muddle, the latter one turned her back to her initial haste to return home and check on her family. Iset pretended to cough and made motions to her throat, indicating she couldn't speak and needed to take her leave. Neb-tawy finally released her and Iset hurried through the darkening streets. Bursting into her home, she tore off her head wrap and vest, while calling for Ahmose. Not receiving an immediate answer, she paused for a moment to listen. Faint voices could be heard coming from the back yard, and Iset dashed through the hut.

Behind the house she came upon a terrifying scene. Her mother, Ankhesenamon, sat on the ground, knees drawn up to her chest and hands bound behind her back with rope, a strip of linen tied around her mouth. Facing the doorway, Ankhesenamon's eyes widened as Iset gusted into the yard.

"By Isis and all the gods!" Iset cried out, rushing towards her mother. "What happened? Where's Ahmose?"

"Halt!" A deep voice boomed behind her, drawing her up short. She spun around and crouched, ready to defend herself and her mother.

"I said halt, ye daughter of a dog! I shall remove thy head from thy shoulders if ye take one more step towards that woman!" Her little brother brandished a stick at her. "I am the dreaded pirate Ahmose, and I claim this hut for mine own."

"What in the name of the gods are you doing, Ahmose!" Iset wanted to both hug and throttle her brother. Instead she scolded him. "You almost caused my heart to burst from my chest! Put that stick down right now. What have you done to our *mewet*?"

"Did I frighten you, Iset?" Ahmose asked eagerly, hurrying to pull at the knots that bound their mother's hands. "That's precisely what I'd hoped for!"

"For the love of the gods, Ahmose, you needn't sound so enthusiastic about nearly killing me." Iset's hand trembled as she reached behind her and found the wall, leaning against it for support.

Pulling at the linen over her mouth, Ankhesenamon smiled apologetically. "Sorry, darling. Ahmose asked if I would play pirates with him. I was meant to be a hostage. I didn't know it would frighten you like that."

Still overset by shock, this scene of playful normalcy seemed so utterly at odds with everything she'd endured over the past few days. She gave a shaky laugh at her reaction to her little brother, even as she squeezed her eyes tight against the sudden weakness that caused her legs to quiver and dark spots to overtake her vision. Absurd, she thought abstractedly, that her body would choose now of all times to seek unconsciousness. Now when relief should be the primary emotion, exhaustion beset her instead.

Using that excuse, she left her mother and brother in the yard to go to her room and change. She knew what she had to do. Not only had she accused Batr of terrible things last night, but she'd thought the worst of him today. All because she'd been in a state of near-hysteria, driven by fear and desperation. At some point it needed to end, this tumultuous existence was not at all sustainable. She'd drop before the week was out if it kept up. She needed to see Batr, to find out what happened last night, and if her family was still in danger. And regardless, she owed Batr an apology for her behaviour last night at the very least.

Iset took unusual pains to dress herself and apply some pigment. Green malachite for her eyelids, kohl to rim her lids, and a few smudges of red ochre for her lips and cheeks. She had one long-sleeved, full-length linen robe – grown a bit tight over the years as she'd developed, particularly around her bust, despite how thin she was – but it helped to ward off the cool night air. Over this she draped a plain shawl. Running her fingers through her thick hair to smooth it, she left it hanging loose and curling down her back.

She tried not to think about *why* she took such care with her appearance tonight. She tried to ignore the small and vain part of her that hoped Batr might ask her again to return to Thinis with him. *Foolish, foolish girl*, she thought, *tempting danger in such a way*. She well knew if he asked again she might not have the strength to refuse him. The thought of his strong, protective arms wrapped tight around her, his charming smile and low, delicious chuckle, all made her shiver, and she had to push such thoughts aside, focusing instead on keeping her hands steady and her chin up as she walked through the village to his hut.

Ra was pushing the sun behind the desert cliffs off to her left when she neared Batr's hut. The reddish-gold rays of light threw long shadows around her, turning the beige mud-brick huts pink with a cheery, auspicious glow that warmed her and gave her a small measure of hope that, gods willing, circumstances might yet turn for the better. And that's when, as she rounded a corner a distance down the lane from Batr's house, she saw him. With his broad shoulders, his incomparable height, his long braids, Batr's profile was unmistakable. He stood, arms crossed, outside the doorway of his hut, facing another woman. And what a woman it must be! Almost as tall as he, the tallest woman Iset had ever seen, and even cast in silhouette as she was by the sun, Iset was able to discern the strong lines of the woman's face, the bold curve of her breasts and abdomen, her softly flaring hips.

Slowing her pace, Iset ignored the other people on the lane that crossed her path. She couldn't take her eyes off the two figures engaged in what must be a deep discussion, given the closeness of their postures, the incline of their faces. Then the woman tilted her head towards him and he stepped closer, his big hands closing over her hips, drawing her to him, pressing her belly to his. His lips touched hers and Iset could feel the urgent hunger in their kiss all the way from the end of the lane.

Iset slumped against the wall of a nearby yard enclosure. A small noise of distress escaped her, and she slapped her hand over her mouth on instinct, as if she couldn't recall if she were Dedi or Iset. Transfixed, she watched as Batr put his arm around the woman's waist and drew her inside his hut, shutting the door behind them. For several moments she stared at the hut, all thought having flown from her head as shock surged through her, then slowly drained away.

No, she told herself. She had no right to be shocked. No right to even be upset. She'd known all along Batr was too charming, too perfect, but she'd allowed herself to hope. For all she knew, he kept a wife in Thinis along with his house, and when he'd asked her to return with him he meant for her to be just a concubine, or at best, a second wife. She'd never asked – only assumed – that he was unmarried. Perhaps his wife had come to join him and prevent him from marrying another, just like the last time she'd been engaged to marry.

Except in that case she'd been relieved to have the man's wife appear and put a stop to it all. *That* man had revolted her, with his rotten teeth, incessant smell of onions, and habit of reaching up under his shenti to scratch himself between his legs. This time, however, it felt like her heart had been torn out of her breast. Her stomach heaved, but she knew there was no sense in it. She'd eaten so little over the last few days that if she were to be sick there would be nothing to give up.

"Iset!" A voice from behind jolted her from her thoughts. Ahmose jogged towards her, anxiety written in his furrowed brow. *What now?* A voice inside her head cried out. *Will it never end?*

"Iset, I've been through half the village looking for you!" His voice was a fierce whisper as he neared. "A messenger came from Senebtawi just after you left. He's asked to see you or Dedi as soon as possible. I thought you'd want to know."

"I – yes. Thank you, darling. I – I suppose I should go over there right away." It seemed an age since she'd last seen Senebtawi – and argued with him over going to the festival with Batr – when in truth it had only been the day before yesterday. "Go on back home, Ahmose, and I'll be along for dinner shortly. I don't intend to be long at Senebtawi's."

Ahmose took off at a trot, and Iset forced herself to leave the lane leading to Batr's house. Several minutes later, with the sky darkening from its sanguine glow to a chill purple-blue, an unusually harried-looking servant threw open the door when Iset knocked and admitted her into the home before turning away, muttering absent-mindedly to himself.

The entranceway was a bustle of frenetic energy. Crates filled with linens, clay pots, and other items were stacked high against the walls, and servants hurried to and fro carrying bundles, jugs, and more crates of jewellery, furniture, and food. Iset looked around her in wonder. It seemed as though every item Senebtawi owned was being brought together in this one place. Almost all that she and her family possessed in the world would fit into just one of these crates, and would take no more than one person to pack it up within a few minutes. Yet Senebtawi's large entranceway was near full to bursting, and it appeared more was yet to come. As Iset surveyed the chaos, a cold, tingling sensation, a suspicion, grew within her belly. However, knowing she'd been so wrong about Batr last night, she didn't trust herself or her instincts anymore. She couldn't afford to alienate anyone else who might be helpful to her and her family.

Entering the room, the older man greeted her with surprise.

"Isetnofret!" He inclined his head to her, his braided and looped side-lock swinging forward. "The messenger said neither you nor Dedi were at home."

"No, Ahmose couldn't find Dedi, and I thought perhaps I could answer for him instead."

With narrowed eyes he assessed her. Appearing to resolve something in his mind, he clapped his hands once and rubbed them together. "Perhaps indeed." His lips stretched in a smile. "In fact, I believe you will do even better. Come, my dear, I need to speak with you in private in my work area."

"Is something the matter? Are you travelling?" The inclination to stay near the door beset her, but she fought the urge to flee. If Senebtawi knew something about the tomb robbers, if her family was still in danger, she needed to know. Her life was crashing down around her, and she needed some way to salvage the wreckage and piece it back together.

"No, no, nothing the matter, really. But yes, I will be travelling very soon. Tonight, in fact." He placed a hand on her lower back, urging her through the room and down a hall. "I wouldn't want them to overhear this. Nor would you, I think, when it is made known."

He ushered her into a room with a wall of scrolls on one side. A large desk of dark wood dominated the room, with several icons of various gods serving as scroll-weights to hold open sheets of papyri atop it. A few low stools were scattered about, and one large chair near the door. The room had one small, narrow window which, looking out into the murky, tree-lined courtyard behind the home, let in only a chill breeze and no light at all.

Senebtawi struck a light and lit an oil wick. The resulting glimmer lengthened his features, casting long, grotesque shadows along one side of his face.

"Isetnofret," he rubbed the side of his nose with the length of one finger, "there are matters which you must be made aware of. I dislike being the one to bear such bad news, but I believe your cousin Dedi has neglected to tell you some things of great importance."

"I'm sorry, Senebtawi, I don't know what you mean. But if you could come to the point, I'd appreciate it. My mother is well again today and I'd like to join her for dinner as soon as possible."

He nodded, his smile a little tight. "Iset, you may have heard by now that some men in the village, some of the tomb-workers, have been arrested. My friends amongst the court tell me it has to do with an incidence of tomb-robbing."

Frowning, she asked, "But what has Dedi to do with this?"

Senebtawi moved closer, at the same time blocking her quick access to the doorway. She hedged to the side, closer to the desk, wondering if her experiences in the tomb of Amunemhat had made her paranoid, or if she truly had cause for concern.

"I will be candid, Iset, in order to impress upon you the drastic measures required to salvage this situation. Your cousin and your *yet* were involved in the robbery. That necklace you found was stolen from a tomb a couple of months back."

To have Dedi's name connected with the robbery was an unexpected development. An image of her spending the rest of her days in a cell in the hnrt attempting to maintain the appearance of a scarred, mute boy flashed through her mind. Alternatively, if there was time, she could put out word that Dedi had fled the village after the arrests, and plead her family's innocence. Neither possibility would work in the long-term.

"No," she shook her head. "Dedi would never do that. My *yet*, perhaps. I have come to see that he was not always what he should be. But not Dedi. He couldn't."

Senebtawi scoffed. "Of course he could. I assure you, he and your *yet* both robbed a nobleman's tomb."

"But if Dedi was involved, then why wasn't he arrested with the others? How did you learn of this?"

The older man thrust his shoulders back and puffed his chest a little. "I told you, I have connections amongst the guard." A slight shifting of his eyes, however, gave her cause to suspect otherwise. "That is precisely the point I am making. You see, I've managed to keep Dedi's name out of this, to stop them from taking him as well, but it was at great cost to myself. I had to bribe several people to convince them Dedi and your *yet* had nothing to do with it."

Fear compelled Iset to place a hand over her chest. "Why?" The word escaped her as a whisper, but that cold, slithering sensation grew in her chest, tightening around her heart.

"Why?" Senebtawi repeated, moving closer still, forcing her to take another step back until she bumped the desk. "Is it not apparent, Isetnofret? I've made my intentions clear for some time to both you and your *yet*, before he passed away. I told him I wanted you, Isetnofret. And now I am the best person, *the only person,* to protect you and your family. With my connections at the court I can ensure you are not harmed by this."

He smoothed a hand over his pate and tugged at his braided side-lock. "And there is something else you should know, about that foreign one that has been hanging about you and Dedi. He is not at all what he seems. I have it on good authority that he's one of the queen's men, sent here to investigate this tomb-robbing. It was he who infiltrated the gang of thieves. His intentions towards you are not at all good. He has been seen much about Ahaneith's court with the daughter of the nobleman whose tomb was robbed. If they have their way, your whole family will end up under the ground, your names wiped from the tablets of history."

Iset's gaze shot up to Senebtawi's. How could it be possible for him to be at the court *and* in the village so often? Senebtawi didn't know just *how much* she'd seen Batr, but there was no way he could work in the Land of the Dead by day, be with her in the evenings, and still go back and forth to the court. There must be some mistake, there could be no two men like him in Kemet.

Then she remembered what Batr had told her last night, about having one surviving brother whom he travelled with. Could it be that this brother was somehow nearby also? That they were *both* sent to investigate the theft? Could it be possible that it wasn't Batr kissing that woman on the street, but his brother? Her heart dearly wanted to believe it. So much of Senebtawi's information was muddled that it was difficult to know what to think.

Mistaking her look of shock for something other than hope, Senebtawi pressed his point. "I only learned of it myself this afternoon. For your sake, out of concern for your well-being lest you be taken in by some trickery, I sent inquiries to men at Lady Ahaneith's court to discover his true identity. You see, Isetnofret, I am the only one who truly cares for you. I am the only one that can save you and your family from utter ruin. Marry me, Iset, and I will make sure you don't see the inside of the hnrt. Come with me tonight when I travel, I am going south for a time, to check on some business there, and I will keep you and your family safe there."

"No." The word came out so quiet even she didn't hear it at first.

"What?" Senebtawi cocked his head, leaning closer.

"No." Taking confidence from the conviction that Batr had been sincere in his desire for her, her voice strengthened. "Either your informant is wrong, or you are lying. Dedi did not rob anything, and whether Batr's initial interest in my family was for an investigation or not, it doesn't matter any longer."

"Isetnofret, don't be foolish." He closed his long fingers around her wrist, and while she couldn't shake his grip she resisted being pulled towards him. His voice hissed with anger. "Your *yet* and Dedi were certainly involved in the theft of the tomb, and were even planning to rob another one. Dedi was still planning to go ahead with it, until last night's arrests."

"No! You're lying." She twisted her wrist to no avail. He only held on tighter.

"What do you know of it?"

Suddenly an image came into her mind, a memory from the first time she'd been accosted by the tomb robbers. As she'd been forced down the ladder she'd looked up and caught a glimpse of the men.

"It was you!" She said in wonder. "You were the fifth man in the tomb that day."

Senebtawi's fingers dug into her wrist. "What are you talking about?"

"The day Dedi was first threatened in Amunemhat's tomb. There were five men." She couldn't believe she'd forgotten that important detail. "That's why you're hurrying to pack and leave town. You think they're coming for you, don't you? Only four were arrested last night. Addaya, Teos, a stone-cutter, and a security guard. You were the fifth. You were the one who named Ahmose when they threatened my family that first time."

"Dedi told you that?" His eyes narrowed, looking warily about him, as if to determine if anyone else might overhear them.

She snorted, anger making her bold and careless. "Dedi didn't tell me. I *am* Dedi." Only after she spoke did she comprehend just how much power she'd given him over her.

Even in the gloom of the ill-lit room Iset could see the emotions flit across Senebtawi's face. Amazement, dawning understanding, then contempt. "Your *yet*." He spat out. "That desperate fool. He had you pretend to be a boy for his own gain. If he'd just given you to me as I'd asked, you wouldn't have had to do it, you know. He refused. Even when his debts drove him to beg me for assistance. Why didn't you come to me, you silly girl? I could have put a stop to this all long ago."

Senebtawi gave up the pretense of being a benevolent saviour and Iset preferred it this way, with his intentions out in the open. At last she'd learned something of the origins of her recent troubles. Shifting against the desk behind her, an object dug into her hip and she reached for it. An icon, slightly larger than the length of her hand, she recognized it by touch alone. Ra, the sun god, was easily identifiable by his hawk-face and the sun disc on his head. On instinct, Iset's hand closed around the hard stone piece, even as she kept it hidden behind her backside.

Surprised to find herself calm in spite of Senebtawi's revelations, Iset pressed him, "Did you make my *yet* do it? Rob that tomb? Did you threaten him?"

"Tsst," Senebtawi clicked his tongue. "I only suggested if he wanted to pay his debts he was well-positioned to do so as one who knew the entrance ways to the many of the tombs. I merely offered my assistance and connections to help unload the items afterwards."

"What did you gain from all this? Surely you didn't put yourself and your own children at such great risk simply to help my *yet*." She found reassurance in the smooth curves of the cool stone tucked in her hand.

Senebtawi shrugged one shoulder. "Of course I could not put myself at risk without gaining some share of the profits. Your *yet* and the other men offered me my choice of the wealth. I helped move it out of Abdju and provided them with deben of grain they could use to barter with instead. Don't you see? I was only helping him."

"But he didn't do it, did he? Get rid of the items, I mean. My *yet* hid that necklace. Why would he do that?"

Sighing, Senebtawi turned his palms up, as if contemplating them. "Your *yet* had a – well let us say his conscience took a turn. It was too late to do anything about the authorities, if he were to be caught that would be the end of all. But he feared for his *ka,* his life force, in the afterlife, if he were to sell a dead man's wealth. He feared that he and all of you would be damned to wander in the underworld for eternity. So rather than sell his share he hid it. I had no idea where, I wasn't even sure that's what he did until you came to me and told me you'd found a necklace."

The knowledge that her father's conscience had assailed him did little to purge her anger at him, for it came too late to help any of them. Perhaps his ka was somewhat better off in the afterlife, but in the living world he'd still left his family in a terrible mess.

Tightening her hand around the statue of the god, Iset tilted her head to the side. "And Pharaoh Wadj's tomb? Did you try to involve him in that as well?" She had no doubt Senebtawi was downplaying his role in the whole affair. Her father was often guileless, and not a particularly crafty man. While he might have enjoyed drink and games of chance with men of questionable repute, she could never picture him organizing a crew of men such as the ones that threatened her.

Again Senebtawi lifted one shoulder, the light from the oil wick glinting off the wiry, dark hairs on his pale skin in a way that reminded her of a large, hairy spider. "I have no control over what those men choose to do."

"Did you kill him? I always wondered if his debts had something to do with the odd way he died. Was it because his conscience prevented him from going forward with more thefts?" It was the first time she'd given voice to the suspicion awoken early after her father's death, but her own boldness in asking it surprised her.

"Those were very bad men your *yet* involved himself with, Isetnofret. If they didn't like something he said, or didn't say, who is to know what they might do?" He'd stepped back from her when she'd revealed her identity as Dedi, but now Senebtawi moved towards her and she shifted to the side, intending to slip around the other side of the desk if he came closer.

But they were interrupted, the heavy wooden door banging open behind Senebtawi and causing Iset to start. Two young children, a boy and a girl, ran into the room, laughing and shrieking. Light from the hallway sliced in behind them.

"You two!" Senebtawi roared at the children, and immediately they stopped moving and stood, heads hanging. "Where is your sister? She is supposed to be watching you."

"Sorry, *yet*," the children mumbled. "We were just playing."

"Well out with you! You know you're not supposed to be in here when the door is closed."

"Yes, sir." The two left the room and Senebtawi pushed the door shut behind them, plunging the room back into near-darkness. In a quick motion with his hip, he also pushed a heavy chair in front of the door.

"That's not necessary," Iset reached for the chair, but Senebtawi moved in front of it.

"It is. They are ill-behaved and need a *mewet* to watch them." His tongue darted out, the resulting moisture on his thick lips caught the light from the oil wick and glistened. "Iset, it's a good thing all is clear between us now. We have a better understanding of where everything lies. You are in a very precarious position." Moving quickly for such a large man, he took hold of her upper arms, and gave her a little shake. "Marry me, Iset, and I will ensure that sneaking foreign filth never comes near you again. Marry me and I won't tell anyone you've been acting as a boy. I won't tell them about what your *yet* did."

"*You* won't tell?" Iset cried out, trying in vain to break his hold. "*You* are no innocent in this! Let me go and *I* won't tell what *you* have done."

"*Stupid girl,*" he hissed, leaning closer, his fingers like claws in her flesh. "I'm the one who knows people. That foreign one wants only to arrest you and destroy your family. All I've ever wanted to do was make you a part of my family and take care of you."

"Liar!" With that, she jabbed the thin stone disc of the god's icon into the soft flesh of his side. He let out a bark of pain, pulling back from her. But she pursued, poking him again. "Your son would be ashamed of you if he could see you now. And Batr is a better man than you'll ever be."

"That man won't protect you." With narrowed eyes he rounded her, avoiding the reach of the icon in her hand. "If he ever told you he would, it was only to bed you."

"Well then it seems you don't know everything, Senebtawi." She smirked even as she kept him at a distance, trying to move towards the door. "He offered for me even after I let him bed me."

Face twisted in rage, Senebtawi lunged forward, grabbing hold of her arm. Iset brought her other arm around and smacked him soundly on the head with the heavy bottom of the stone god, snapping his head back. He swore, but his grip tightened on her arm, wrenching it, and the pain caused her to cry out and drop the statue to scrabble at his fingers.

"Dammit, Iset, I wasn't going to hurt you but you leave me no choice." He rasped, his lips near her cheek.

"This *is* your choice!" She ground out, teeth clenched against the pain as he twisted her arm. When she brought her heel down on his foot he released her, but only long enough to deliver a blow to her face. Stars of light exploded behind her eyelids and her body went limp.

Chapter 18 – Reconciliation and Revelations

Earlier that afternoon

Raia sat in the main room of her home, late afternoon sunlight sifting through dust motes in the air. Despite the cheerful, rosy glow, her thoughts were in turmoil, her stomach roiling with anxiety. Abar had taken the children out to play by the little river, and the servants were in the detached kitchen behind the home. She was completely alone in eerie silence.

Raia was no longer sure who she wanted to claim as her father. It was difficult to claim Ra-hotep, now that she knew the truth about him and his awful schemes, but equally difficult to claim Userkare – a stranger, and a man who couldn't bring himself to fight for her even after Ra-hotep's death. She was only her mother's daughter, from a line of women with no fathers, a woman no man could lay claim to, and a woman beholden to no man.

She struggled with herself for a time, unable to decide how much to share with her family – or anyone for that matter. Ra-hotep's reputation would be ruined, though Raia was less concerned about him now and more about her brothers and sisters, for they were still her siblings, no matter who fathered them. She wondered how badly this would taint them, and if Abar's betrothed would still want her. It might be more difficult to find spouses for the others now.

In the end she decided that she had to tell them. Maybe not all at once, but Semer at least needed to know. She would need his assistance now more than ever.

With her elbows resting on her knees, she dropped her head into her hands, a puff of air escaping her. She'd have to tell Makae. It was a great blow to her pride that she'd been so wrong about everything, but it wasn't in her to be dishonest or shirk her troubles. Furthermore, she'd been cruel to Makae. Of all the men in her life, he was the only one who'd been honest with her, even knowing she'd be angry with him. She'd been too blind then to realize that he'd done it because he was a good, honest man. She wasn't at all sure he'd still want a future with her now, but if she wanted to have any chance with him she'd have to be honest, and hiding the truth would make her no better than either of her fathers. While it was too late to do anything about Ra-hotep's actions, his scribe must be penalized for his part in the theft of Userkare's land and – if Userkare was correct – in the desecration of Ra-hotep's tomb as well.

She set out in search of her younger brother, and found him at his father's home. When the manservant informed her that Semer had lain down for his afternoon slumber, she insisted the man wake him. The boy came into the greeting room several minutes later, not having bothered to adorn himself in his usual finery.

"What's this now, Rai?" Semer grumbled. "I'd just fallen asleep, and I have a busy night tonight. There is a post-festival celebration at Merinath's I intend to attend."

Stuffing down her irritation, Raia sat him down and laid bare to him everything that had transpired over the last several days, from the time Makae told her about the theft and desecration of Ra-hotep's tomb, to what she'd learned from Userkare that morning. Semer balked and argued when she told him that his huntsman was stealing from him, and even flung a few more insults at Makae for putting his nose where it didn't belong, but eventually he settled into acceptance. She also told him that, given the revelations of her lineage, it was all the more imperative that he learn to manage Ra-hotep's lands. Userkare intended to leave what remained of his lands to her, and there was no way she could possibly manage *three* farms on her own.

After his initial angry reaction, Semer sank into several long minutes of silence. He paced the room, his hands clasped behind his back, a look of intense concentration on his face. Recalling how Makae's silences endured her anger and forced her to calm herself, she gave Semer the time he needed to think.

Then Semer surprised her by sitting down abruptly next to her and asking in a shy, boyish voice she hadn't heard from him in years, "Will you still help me a little, Rai? Now and then, I mean? I know you don't owe me anything, and that *Yet* stole your *yet*'s lands, that he… he might have done a bad thing by separating your parents, but you know all of his affairs and I do not… And the children…" his face took on an almost comical look of horror. "Who will take care of them all?"

Raia put her arms around him and, after a moment of stiffness, he hugged her back. She smiled at the top of his head. "Of course I'll help you, Semer. I do not care to fight over a few extra *khet* of land, and you are still my brother, no matter what. The children can all stay with me, and please, I would prefer to tell them myself about all this, in my own time. But I do need you to put yourself forward, Semer, and manage your affairs now, like a man. Userkare plans to leave what's left of his lands to me, he has no one else, and I simply cannot manage all three farms alone. I will have to rent out his lands, or hire a manager. And right now I am exhausted and I need some time to resolve things."

When she finally left him, it was with the knowledge that some good might actually come of the situation. She and Semer had reconciled, and he appeared resigned – if not actually determined – to take over his responsibilities.

The sun's rays were long and low by the time she reached Lady Ahaneith's palace, stretching out across the tops of the white-washed walls. Upon inquiry, she was made to wait while a guard went to look for Makae. After several minutes, a young woman came into the courtyard where Raia was pacing and counting the etched stone columns along the length of the yard – thirty-six of them in total.

"Raia?" The young woman asked shyly.

Turning to look at her, Raia almost gasped. The girl was stunning. Long, silken dark-brown hair trailed down her back, her features were fine and delicate, and the most gorgeous, beaded blue necklace draped her slender neck.

Raia cleared her throat, her heart tripping in trepidation. "Yes, I am Raia. Where is Makae?"

Twisting her hands together in front of her, the girl said, "I – I'm sorry, he had to leave the palace." Anxiety tightened its grip on Raia's stomach, until the girl added, "He asked me to wait for you, in case you came. He didn't think you would, but he said just in case I was to stay here. Late last night he went into the village to see his brother in the Land of the Dead. He said it had something to do with your *yet*, and the tomb workers. Does that make sense to you?"

Raia placed her palm to her forehead, trying to take this all in. "Please forgive me, but who are you? How do you know all this?" This girl had intimate knowledge of her situation, and some familiarity with Makae. Jealousy, an unfamiliar emotion she despised as weakness, was taking hold of her, and she did not like the feeling of one bit.

"Oh, yes. You see, Makae helped me the other day. He… well he saved me from a bad situation and is helping me to find a means to live."

The gratitude and admiration shining in the girl's eyes made Raia's lips tighten into a straight line. She'd dreaded seeing Makae again after the way they'd parted, but a small part of her had nourished a hope that he might forgive her for the way she'd spoken to him. Gods, was it possible that she'd misunderstood Makae's intentions? He'd said he wanted things to work between them, but Raia could not foresee anything working if this beautiful young woman was in the midst of it. There was no chance of her sharing a man with another woman. Some might manage it – perhaps if there was a lack of love, or an incredible amount of it – but not her.

The girl must have seen the look on her face and rushed to explain. "Oh, it is not like *that*, please do not think poorly of him, although he found me in a tavern… in a bad place, he did not… it was not… I mean, he is an honourable man, I am certain of it."

The girl went on to explain how Makae had saved her from the House of Tiy and how she'd come to the palace the day before to seek him out. He'd asked her to stay until

Raia arrived, and until he could find a hut to settle her in. When Raia saw Makae yesterday and he'd told her about his visit to the tavern the huntsman frequented, he'd left out this part of the story – the part that made him look noble and heroic. It said much about his character that not only would he go out of his way to assist a poor young woman, but also that he wouldn't seek accolades for it.

"He bought something for you. He said it would match your skin tone. He didn't give it to you yesterday because he said the time was not right, but he wanted you to have it." The girl reached into a pouch tied about her waist, and pulled out a beautiful, red-beaded collar. Handing it to her, the girl said, "I make them, and he is trying to help me set up a business so that I might support myself. I…," the young woman paused, licking her lips and twisting her hands in her dress, "I would like to be like you, nebet-i. I would like to be a woman who runs her own household and does not need anyone else."

"Makae told you about me?" Raia frowned.

The young woman nodded, smiling. "He admires you very much. He… he didn't say that exactly, but it was very clear. He spoke a little about you before he left the palace to go to the village and arrest those men."

Raia closed her eyes, rubbing her temple with the palm of one hand. She'd made a terrible mistake driving Makae away. All because of her foolish pride. Pride that was, it seemed, unfounded, taught to her by a hypocritical man who had no right to it. A man who stole and cheated and lied to get what he wanted. She couldn't say that Ra-hotep deserved to have his tomb robbed – she wouldn't wish that on anyone – but his actions called in to question all his teachings.

"Wait," she started, looking up. "Makae went to arrest men? Who? Do you know who they are?"

"No, I'm sorry. He said they were tomb workers, though."

"Nothing about a scribe? And he hasn't returned yet?" Fear chilled her skin, turning it to gooseflesh. If he'd been gone since last night and hadn't returned, perhaps he was in danger. What if he didn't have the right men? Or if he'd missed one of them, the most dangerous of them all?

The girl shook her head, concern sparking in her eyes. "There is a messenger," she said. "One who came from the village. He is here at the palace. Perhaps he can tell you where to find Makae."

"Then we must find him, now!"

Not long afterwards, Raia was rushing through the city towards the Land of the Dead, a messenger boy trotting ahead of her to lead the way.

Makae sat with his brother in the greeting room of Batr's little hut in the village, discussing their next move. In the early morning hours they'd arrested four men and their families, and taken them to the prison on the edge of the city. Makae had found Batr and together they'd spent the better part of the day there, questioning the thieves and making arrangements to keep the families in custody in preparation for trial. So far, the men were unwilling to give up the name of their leader, but neither brother felt they would maintain their silence very long. Not once the questioning – and the punishments – grew more intense.

They had not been back in the Land of the Dead long when a knock sounded on the front door. Throwing one another a questioning look, each brother rested a hand on the knives at their belts before Batr moved to open the door.

Raia was the last person Makae expected to see there. Makae unfolded himself from the stone bench he was sitting on, moving swiftly towards the out-of-breath woman.

"Raia?" He frowned. "What are you doing here?"

Her eyes darted from him to his brother, confusion wrinkling her brow. "Makae? Are you all right?" Raia studied at him, as if she couldn't decide if it was truly him.

"Yes, of course." Stepping forward, he took her elbow and propelled her out the door, indicating with a jerk of his head to his brother that he'd be back in a moment.

Makae shut the door behind them and the two of them stood alone in the lane. Late afternoon sunlight slanted reddish-gold rays across the sky. Vibrant colour splashed across the sandy lane and beige, mud-brick huts contrasted with the long, dark shadows cast by the dying sun. People hurried to and fro along the lane, and only a few bothered to spare a glance at the unusually tall couple.

"Is something wrong, Raia? Why are you here?" Makae repeated, crossing his arms over his chest to prevent himself from reaching out to her. If she'd followed him all this way, there must be a reason beyond mere desire to see him.

"Makae," she stepped forward, closing the space between them. She spoke hurriedly, unlike her usual manner. "I went to the palace to see you, and heard you'd made some arrests. I had to be sure you were all right. I spoke with Userkare and Semer, and you were right. About everything. I'm sorry. I should never have spoken to you the way I did. I… I do not know where to go from here, but I wanted to tell you that you were right."

A smile played on the edges of his mouth. "You came all this way to tell me I was right?"

"I … you needn't look so smug about it. I said you were right. There's more, too…"

Make didn't let her finish. He stepped forward, placed his hands on her hips, and pulled her to him, capturing her mouth with his. With her hands sliding up his chest, she returned his kiss with an urgency and need that was particularly gratifying. More than anything, he wished them back in her room in Abdju, with nothing around them but a white linen sheet to ward off the chill air.

But that would have to wait. After a minute or two he pulled back and asked, "There's more?"

She nodded. "So much more, but it can wait. More importantly, did you arrest a scribe?"

His brow creased. "A scribe? No. Four tomb workers."

"Then this is very important. I think I know who organized the tomb robbing."

"Come, meet my brother and tell us both, then." Slipping his arm around her waist, Makae pushed open the door to Batr's hut and took her inside. Once he'd introduced her to Batr, he asked her to continue.

Looking between the two of them, she said, "I do not know who you arrested, but I am fairly certain the man who organized it is Ra-hotep's scribe. He manages the rations for the workers here, in the Land of the Dead. His name is Senebtawi, and he lives on the outskirts of the village."

"Senebtawi?" Batr repeated, panic flitting across his face as he jumped to his feet. "Son of a donkey's ass. Brother, we have to go. Now!"

Chapter 19 – Reaching an Understanding

The dark spots covering her vision prevented Iset from seeing the ground rise up to meet her after Senebtawi hit her across the face. But the older man's painful, claw-like grip on her arms kept her awake, pulling her upright when her legs refused to stay straight. She felt the edge of the desk bump into the back of her thighs again. It was all she could do to weakly push at his chest even as her legs kept trying to fold beneath her. The blow to her head, coupled with several sleepless nights and days with little to eat, made it impossible for her to make her limbs work the way she wanted them to.

And then she was spun around and her limp hands scattered papyri scrolls and stone icons. Her cheek hit the hard wood of the desk with enough force to jar her again, and she bit her tongue, tasting blood. She heard Senebtawi muttering angrily, but the roaring in her ears drowned out whatever he was saying. His thighs pressed against the backs of her legs.

Feebly stretching her hands out, seeking some sort of weapon, something sharp stabbed Iset's finger. Blinking against the dark spots in her vision, she saw the icon of Isis lying on its side, the goddess's face turned towards Iset. It lay near her hand, and without thinking Iset reached out to the goddess. Her own namesake, the goddess Isis had a tall throne carved atop her head to represent her close association with the pharaoh. It was the sharp top of the throne that had poked her finger. *Isetnofret. Isis is beautiful.* But Isis was also strong, a protector. It was she who had collected the parts of her husband Osiris's body and put them back together to resurrect him. It was she who bore his child, the Horus-god who took revenge on the brother who killed Osiris.

The tips of her fingers scrabbled at Isis's smooth body, catching just the edge of the base of the statue. Trying again, Iset managed to turn it over, but even as it turned it skittered back half a finger's width, slipping almost out of reach. Panic rose up in her breast but, she made her next attempt more deliberate, inching the goddess towards her.

The roaring in her ears became a shuffling noise, the sound of fabric swishing. Then she felt a pressure against her backside. It was Senebtawi, and she felt him shift, the pressure moving to one side as he reached down for the hem of her dress.

His voice finally broke through her haze, and she heard Senebtawi mumble, "I didn't want it to be this way, Isetnofret. I didn't want to have to hurt you. You made me do this." Fabric brushed her legs, bunching between her body and Senebtawi's.

Oh gods, please Isis, please help me. She stretched out until her whole arm was shaking, her fingers brushing the smooth stone statue, seeking purchase.

At the same time there was a pounding on the door to the room, the handle turning as someone tried to open it.

Senebtawi shouted, "I told you to go find your sister and stay out of here!"

The pounding on the door became more like thumping, rocking the large chair blocking the door. Senebtawi swore and released her dress, the pressure on her legs easing as he turned towards the door.

And that's when Iset snatched up the icon, reared up, snaked her arm around, and stabbed Senebtawi in the neck with the throne of Isis. The older man screamed, and blood seeped around the goddess's head and his clutching fingers, dripping down his neck. At the same time, he flailed out, the back of his hand coming in contact with the side of her head, hard. Iset's legs twisted beneath her. This time when the ground rushed up to meet her, there was nothing to break her fall and she succumbed to the darkness that welcomed her.

When Iset woke, the world was white all around her. Blinding white walls, thin white linen curtains over tall, narrow windows as well as curtains around the soft bed with white sheets, all reflecting white light back at her in a wide open room. All in contrast to the ever-shaded confines of her little hut. And a woman, unlike any she'd ever seen, with the palest white skin and fair hair, in a fine white robe. Sunlight glowed on her silky blonde braids as she stood whispering with Batr near a window on the far end of the white room.

Batr, whose smooth dark skin and long, braided hair were both unmistakable and unparalleled. How strong and beautiful and fierce he looked against the pure white backdrop. He'd appeared unusual and foreign in the Land of the Dead but here, in this room more elegant than any she'd ever imagined, he seemed perfectly natural and at home. For a moment she thought his glance flicked her way, but then he inclined his head to the woman at the window.

Iset decided this was the strangest dream she'd ever had, and wondered at its origin before falling back asleep.

When she woke some time later the setting sun bathed the room in a warm, rosy glow, while a cool evening breeze billowed out the curtains. She shivered against the cold and tried to pull herself into a sitting position, finding her whole body stiff and her throat as dry as the desert.

It hurt to move her head when she tried to survey the room, so instead she croaked out, "Hello?"

"Iset?" A hushed voice came from the other side of the room. And then a figure launched onto the bed, landing by her legs and wrapping itself around her torso. She cried out at the sudden stab of pain that jarred her whole body. The bundle on her bed jumped back and yelped, "Sorry! I'm sorry!"

A door near the bed slammed open, and her neck twinged as she twisted her head towards the sound.

"What's going on?!" A man thundered. Batr. And the figure now standing hunched and chastened next to the bed was her little brother. It was he who'd thrown himself at her.

"Is she hurt?" Her mother's voice piped in from behind Batr.

"Please," Iset put up a hand, "Could everyone stop yelling and jumping about?" She gingerly fingered her neck. "I – I think I've hurt myself and all this commotion isn't helping."

She waved off the ensuing apologies, asking instead for an explanation. What followed was even more commotion, albeit more quietly carried out. Batr left them to call for water and food, as well as water to be warmed for a bath. Nobody would tell her anything until she agreed to eat something. Even then, it was a struggle to get a straight story.

Batr did not return when the food came, and Iset was left with her little family to piece things together. Her mother knew so little of what had happened before Batr arrived on their doorstep carrying Iset's limp body in his arms. Ahmose knew a little more than her. In the end, Iset was able to determine that Batr and his brother had been the ones banging on the door to Senebtawi's work room. They'd gone to her house looking for her, and Ahmose had told them where she was. They'd broken through to find her on the floor, and Senebtawi bleeding profusely from the neck.

Senebtawi was now housed in the prison. Whether or not he survived the wound Iset inflicted with the god's icon was yet to be seen. If he lived, it would only be a matter of determining when and how he would be executed for his crimes.

Iset was shocked to discover that she had been unconscious for the better part of three days. After finding her at Senebtawi's, Batr had carried her home. Her mother had quickly inspected and bathed her and, finding no open wounds, they let her sleep for the rest of the night. When she couldn't be woken in the morning, Batr insisted on bringing her to the palace, wanting to ensure she had the best care possible. Over the last three days she'd been feverish, and they'd all taken pains – on Batr's orders – to make sure she ate, whether she wanted it or not. Iset had only vague memories of people coming and going.

"We thought..." Ahmose's lower lip trembled, but he quickly mastered himself. "You wouldn't wake up for so long."

"But I don't understand..." Iset's head ached. Apparently she'd hit her head when she lost consciousness at Senebtawi's. She could feel the bump near her temple. Her mother told her it had reduced in size, but it still hurt. "Lady Ahaneith. How is she okay with us being here so long? Why are we here?" *And why aren't we in the prison complex along with Senebtawi?* She held back the question that she really wanted to ask.

Her mother smiled. "Lady Ahaneith has been very generous. But she also wants to honour you, darling, for all that you've done."

"Honour me? That doesn't make any sense."

"No, it's okay, Iset." Ahmose nodded emphatically. "I gave Batr the necklace."

"You did what?!" Iset sat bolt upright, her aches and pains forgotten. "The one you found?" The one their father had stolen. The one that proved, without a doubt, that their father had been involved with a gang of thieves.

"Mmm hmmm. When you wouldn't wake up, I – I knew you had it in your room." Ahmose looked down at his hands, where they twisted the fabric of his shenti in his lap. "I was worried that Senebtawi had tried to do something to you because of the necklace. I... Iset I'm sorry, but I lied to you about how I found it. It wasn't by accident. I overheard *Yet* arguing with Senebtawi once before he died, I just didn't know then that it was about the necklace. He said 'I'm not getting rid of it. It's the wrong thing to do.' That's all I heard before he saw me and told me to get out of the house. But later that night I heard him in the back yard. I watched him through my window, and saw him bury something by the stone oven. I forgot all about it because *Yet* died shortly after that. Then you asked me to look for something he might have left behind and I remembered it."

"But why didn't you tell me when you gave it to me?"

Ahmose hung his head. "I thought you'd get mad at me for listening in when I ought not to, like *Yet* did. And I didn't think it meant anything."

Iset was having a hard time thinking clearly, but why they weren't all locked up was an absolute mystery to her. She tried to get more information from her mother and brother, but beyond learning that Batr did, indeed, have a brother – a twin at that – who was also at the court, they had nothing else to give. For the rest of the evening they were left alone, and despite her fears and confusion, Iset found that the cheerful attitudes of her mother and brother had an effect on her. Having to tend to Iset had given their mother some sense of purpose, and she appeared to have rallied to help care for her daughter.

They told Iset they'd been treated with kindness and consideration by Lady Ahaneith and her servants, and Batr had even arranged a room for them in the palace, so they could help nurse her. Surely, Iset thought, if they were all to be executed he wouldn't go about things in this fashion?

It wasn't until much later that night, while everyone else was sleeping, that she found some clarity to the story.

She'd woken from her usual nightmare to an empty room, lit only by a sliver of moonlight through the white curtains. She lay in the darkness for a time, regulating her breath, trying to put aside the images from her dream. No sounds of servants in the hallways or in the courtyard reached her ears, and she determined it was very late, or very early, in the morning. Unable to stay bed-ridden with her doubts and fears any longer, she found a robe and shawl laid over a chair for her, and slipped out of her room, wandering down the hallway until she came upon a door that led out into the back courtyard of the palace.

It was a clear night, and a slim crescent moon and stars lit the courtyard. Palm and sycamore trees swayed in a cool, winter breeze, and she drew her shawl tight over her shoulders. Jasmine bushes grew between the trees, their blooms dormant for the season but their foliage still glossy in the moonlight. Crickets chirped and, somewhere off in the distance, Iset could make out the echoing croak of frogs and toads. It was a funny, unfamiliar sound, one not often heard in the village near the Land of the Dead, and it made her lips quirk up in a smile.

Finding a bench nearby, she sat on the cold stone slab and breathed in deeply, inhaling the faint scent of lettuce leaves from the nearby gardens. She couldn't recall when last she'd had time to herself to sit and think in such a peaceful place.

And yet it was hard to find peace. Her fingers twisted the edges of the shawl in her lap. She was to meet with Lady Ahaneith tomorrow, and she had no idea what to expect. Batr had yet to speak to her, and she didn't know what to make of that, either. According to her mother and brother he'd been more than solicitous with them. When he wasn't at the prison questioning the tomb robbers, rounding up the last of the stolen goods, or in conference with his brother and Lady Ahaneith to deal with the southern raiders, he was taking Ahmose around the palace grounds to keep him entertained, even relieving her mother from time to time by sitting in Iset's room to wait for her to wake. And when she had awoken he'd been right outside the door, only to disappear moments later and not return.

A breeze rustled the leaves of the trees and she shivered. Her feet were bare, and she drew them up onto the bench now, tucking them under the edge of her robe and wrapping her arms around her knees.

"Cold?" A smooth, masculine voice drawled behind her.

She twisted on the bench, looking up to see Batr standing to the right of her, his face half-cloaked in shadow. Clothed in a long-sleeved tunic and a lion skin that emphasized his broad, muscular shoulders against the backdrop of a blue-black sky, his hands were clasped behind his back. His head tilted to the side in polite inquiry, but his expression was guarded. Having never seen him anything but open and cheerful, she didn't know what to make of him like this.

"Only a little," she said after a moment's hesitation. "I find it refreshing. I've spent too much time in that bed. I needed to move about a little." Remembering what had happened after she'd woken from a nightmare in his bed, heat rose to her cheeks.

If he also remembered it, he didn't say anything. Instead, with another nod of his head he indicated the bench she was sitting on. "May I?" He asked.

"Oh, yes. Please." With her feet still tucked under her dress, she shuffled over to make room, and he sat a measured distance from her – near to her, but not quite touching. She found herself regretting that, wishing their hands had bumped, or their thighs would brush one another. Anything to get over this awkward distance that seemed to have grown between them, even though this was the first time he'd spoken to her since she'd ejected him from her home.

Self-conscious, she smoothed her hands down over her hair. She'd left her room without bothering to look in the bronze looking plate. Her hair was unbound, falling loose down her back in waves, and she wore no makeup or jewellery. She felt out of place now under Batr's scrutiny. The brief glimpse she'd had of him yesterday when she'd woken had been enough to tell her he was clearly a part of this world, much more so than the world of the village. It had been one thing for her to think of him as a fellow labourer in the Land of the Dead, former pirate and soldier or not. It was another thing entirely to see him as a stately-looking man of the court, one powerful enough to bring her whole family to the palace of Abdju and have servants wait on her like a lady. She'd hardly known him in his former role, but this man she didn't know at all.

Batr studied Iset as her hands twisted the fabric draped over her knees, tugging her shawl tighter around her. He'd been unable to sleep, wondering how she was doing, and if her nightmares bothered her. Over the last few days, in her delirium, he'd heard her mutter things about her brother, the one who died in the tombs. Inevitably, her mother became aware of the extent of Iset's nightmares, and the older woman suffered great distress when Batr explained to her the many secrets Iset was labouring under. While it wasn't his place to interfere, Iset needed all the support she could get, she needed to eat, sleep, and rest. Even the healers he'd brought in agreed, although they continued to leave their potions and poultices and concoctions and sing their hekka. Thankfully, Ankhesenamon had put aside her own sufferings in order to care for her daughter.

Tonight, when he couldn't sleep, he'd strolled through the palace, walking past Iset's room out of habit. Seeing her door open and her room empty, he went in search of her, and found her curled on the bench in the courtyard. From a distance, with her long hair cascading down her back, bare feet tucked under her robe and arms around her knees, she looked younger than she was. More like the sweet, innocent girl she might have once been, and still deserved to be. Not a woman who had to sneak out at night to taverns, or stab nefarious tomb robbers in the neck to save herself.

That last thought made his chest swell. He wished he could strangle Senebtawi himself, but Iset's actions made him immeasurably proud. Perhaps he didn't want her so sweet and innocent after all.

She was certainly bold the other night in his bed, for even as he'd taken her for the first time she'd shown no virginal trepidation. Despite the cool night breeze his groin tightened in response to that memory, and visions of laying her down on the smooth stone bench flooded his thoughts. It was an effort to school himself to be polite, to remind himself that days had passed since they'd last spoken and she'd rejected his offer. He had no idea what – if anything – she wanted from him.

Now, sitting next to him, she was avoiding his gaze, giving him her profile. He watched the muscles of her delicate jawline clench and relax beneath her olivine skin, the slight flattening of her full lips as her luscious breasts rose and fell with her irregular breath. One bare foot rested atop the other on the bench, and she absently rubbed the ball of it over the toes of the other to warm them. Even her feet were elegant. He wanted to take them in his hands and warm them.

"Isetnofret," he said at the same time she said, "I suppose I should…"

They both stopped, Iset's face turned up to his, blinking owlishly. Then she rushed on, her grip on her knees tightening. "I should tell you I went to your house the other night, before everything happened with Senebtawi. I wanted to apologize for what I said to you. I acted like a madwoman. I was just so scared, and I thought – well it doesn't matter anymore, but I was wrong. It wasn't your fault. Ahmose got into a fight, that's all, and it had nothing to do with anything that's happened. Well, maybe a little bit, but only because he was fighting with his friends about pirates and he was convinced you would beat Sekhrey Bey in a battle, but you can't be blamed for that. Oh, I didn't mean *that*!" She covered her mouth with her hand, as if surprised by what she'd said.

His mouth hitched upwards in a slight smile. "Do you mean I can't be blamed for winning an imaginary brawl, or for Ahmose just thinking I might be able to? Sekhrey Bey *is* a rather large man, but I like to think I'd put up a bit of a fight if it came down to it."

"Will you please not tease? I'm trying to apologize. I *tried* to the other day, but when I got to your house after work I saw that you had company. I saw you, or a man that looked like you, and a woman, outside your hut and I thought…"

He was sure her cheeks were flushing a pretty shade of pink, and he wished it were daylight so he could see it better. "Ahhhh, I see." He smiled at her discomfort. "You saw my brother with Raia and thought it was me."

"So it wasn't you…" Iset sucked in her lips and squinted down at her toes. Batr knew it wasn't particularly kind of him to feel pleasure at her unhappiness, but the fact that she'd been upset by the thought of him with another woman kindled a spark of hope in his chest that had been barely flickering the last few days.

It wasn't as if he could hope for anything when he'd found her crumpled and unconscious on the floor of Senebtawi's work room, covered in blood. Much later he learned none of the blood was hers. But Senebtawi had put his bloody hands on her, and when he and Makae had finally managed to break past the door, the older man was kneeling on the ground next to her, blood spattered everywhere. Batr thought for sure they were too late. He'd kicked the older man out of the way and been shocked to find Iset still breathing. In the days since then she'd been horribly ill, as if her body had finally shut down from the stress and lack of nourishment she'd endured over the last several months. And for those few days the only thing he could hope for was for her to live. Anything beyond that didn't matter.

"I know about Ahmose," he told her. "I was there when you found him."

"You what? How?"

"I followed you that night to make sure you were safe. And I waited outside your home in case something else happened to you." His hand tightened into a fist on his thigh, thinking about how she'd almost died. Once again he'd failed someone he cared for, he could only thank the gods that he'd found her in time. "But I should have never left you. I had a man who was supposed to keep an eye on you, but he lost track of you when you went home and changed from Dedi to Iset. I'm so sorry, Iset. I should have stayed. I should have gone to work with you and made sure you were safe."

She took one of his hands in her small ones, gripping it for just a moment before releasing it. "No, it's not your fault. Please do not blame yourself. I… I didn't know you followed me that night, and I'm sorry. If I had only trusted you…" Iset's voice broke, then she cleared her throat and said, "You helped us, and you *did* save me. Again, that is. But I don't understand… Why haven't you arrested us yet?"

"What for?"

Iset looked up at him, disconcerted. "Ahmose told me you work for the queen, and Lady Ahaneith. You do, don't you? You're part of the queen's royal guard, along with Sekhrey Bey. Isn't that why you came to Abdju? To find the tomb robbers?"

Batr nodded. "Yes, that's why I came to Abdju. I think you know why I couldn't tell you that before. After all, you had a secret or two of your own, didn't you?" Even in the darkness he could see the tightening of her lips, the shuttering of her eyes as if he'd delivered a slight. He hadn't intended it as such; it was merely the truth.

He did, however, soften his voice when he asked, "But the tomb robbers have been caught, so why would I arrest you now?"

She searched his face, as though anticipating a trick. He kept his expression neutral. From the start, he'd wanted her to trust him. He willed her to do it now and be honest of her own volition.

A thick, curling lock of her hair had fallen forward to shield one side of her face, and she tucked it back behind her ear with a delicate motion. Her breasts rose and fell as she pulled and released a deep breath, tugging in one corner of her bottom lip to bite on it. He very much wanted to bury his fingers in her hair and let the soft strands sift over his hands, to turn her lips up to his and take her mouth by turns with sweet kisses and hard, needy ones. He wanted to pull her onto his lap so that her legs straddled his hips, and settle her onto him, to be enveloped by her, so that he could prove to himself and her that she was alive and well and that they could be happy together.

Instead he waited for her to answer his question. She broke his gaze by looking down at her toes again and, in a voice barely above a whisper, said, "Ahmose told me he gave you the necklace. You must know what it means."

"Tell me." He needed her to be the one who said the words first.

Her voice caught as she said, "Ahmose saw my *yet* hide it after he stole it from a nobleman's tomb. After he helped those men break in. My *yet* was a thief, just like Addaya and Senebtawi and the others you arrested. So why haven't you arrested us yet? You *know*." With that last anguished confession, she looked up again, moonlight glinting off the unshed tears that swelled in her eyes.

He nodded slightly. This was what he needed her to say. "Did you know your *yet* robbed the tomb? I mean before Senebtawi and his men threatened you?"

She blinked, confusion clouding her damp eyes and indignation tinging her voice. "Of course not."

He shrugged. "Then why would I arrest you?"

"Because my *yet* did something terrible. He committed a crime against maat, against the gods. He's dead now and can't be punished, but Ahmose and my *mewet* and I… we are his family."

Batr sighed. "Nofret, are you *asking* me to arrest you? Would that make you feel better?"

"What are you talking about?" Tears forgotten, she sat stiff-backed.

Curling one finger under her chin, he held her in place. "I realize you expect me to blame you for what your *yet* did, but I don't. Though I wish you would have trusted me from the start, I cannot blame you for keeping it a secret before. You thought I was involved with the thieves, didn't you?" She nodded her assent, her sad expression telling him that she regretted that assumption.

"So then the way I see it, Nofret, is that as soon as you learned of my status in the queen's guard, both you and your brother made a point of telling me your *yet* was involved in a tomb robbing. Do you see? Ahmose even provided evidence of the crime, and returned a valuable stolen item. And just now, you repeated it all, knowing I might arrest you. You risked your life to find out who those men were, and then you told me. If it weren't for your assistance, I might never have caught all the men involved. And for that Lady Ahaneith intends to honour you. I also expect that, in a day or two when the queen's messenger returns with her response to my missive, Queen Merneith will be in agreement. As for maat and the gods," he shrugged one shoulder, "who is to say what they will do? You are free of blame in this world. If your heart is judged in the underworld, Ammit will find only the weight of your own goodness. And *that* is a light weight to bear."

He watched Iset's large eyes shift from anger to shock to denial, and she tried to tug her face away but he caught her chin between his thumb and forefinger. She settled for shaking her head slightly. "No, that's not how it happened." She croaked. "I didn't report it right away. I didn't tell anyone when I learned my *yet* was involved in a theft."

"Because you didn't know who to tell. Or who to trust."

"Because I was afraid. Because I didn't want my family to be punished. I was wrong. Not my *mewet* and Ahmose, they didn't know. But I've done it all wrong." The tears were welling in her eyes again, threatening to spill over onto her cheeks.

"Iset," Batr dropped his hands to grip her shoulders and give her a little shake, while her feet slid off the bench. "Stop it. I'm not going to arrest you. You need to stop taking responsibility for other people's actions. You could have sold the necklace after you found it, but you didn't, even when you could have used the wealth for food. Is it really so hard to accept that someone might want to help you? Do you realize what it means that Lady Ahaneith plans to honour you? You will never have to go back to working in the Land of the Dead again, and your family will be safe. You can go anywhere you like. Accept it, Nofret. If not for you, then for your *mewet* and brother."

Iset pushed the palm of her hand hard against her mouth, willing herself to do what Batr said. It was still so hard to believe that she wasn't going to prison, that Batr had managed to see the story in a light that made her look not like a villain, but a brave woman. She couldn't speak, couldn't look at him. Instead, she stared miserably down at the space where their thighs – now angled towards one another – almost touched. She shook her head in disbelief.

"Gods, Nofret," Batr's tone was incredulous, "do you not see that you have done almost *everything? You* found all the men involved, and *you* almost killed Senebtawi. There was nothing left for me to do but take the information you found to Lady Ahaneith and the queen. You put me to shame. The queen ought to take you on as part of the royal guard to take my place."

Tears slipped over her lower lids, wetting her cheeks with cool moisture, and her reluctant bark of laughter at his absurd words resulted in a half-sob half-hiccup. She felt his deep, rumbling laugh in the vibration of his hands on her shoulders, and looked up at him. His hands slid up her arms, skimmed her shoulders, cupped her neck, and cradled her chin, forcing her to hold his gaze, as if he were afraid she'd bolt away.

"Just accept it, Iset," he whispered, his forehead tilting towards hers, his cheek near hers. She could feel his warm breath on her jawline. "You are amazing. I knew it from the moment I met you, and now other people know it, too."

Her breath caught and, absurdly, another little hiccup escaped her. Batr chuckled, but it didn't stop him from brushing his lips over hers in the barest whisper of a kiss, sending a surge of warmth through her chilled flesh, heating her core.

Batr hadn't intended to kiss her. Despite the wayward direction of his thoughts, he only wanted her to know that she was safe and would be taken care of. But her bare feet, tear-stained face, and charming hiccups were too much for him to resist. However, after the first sweep of his lips over hers, he drew back.

"Come," he said, pulling her to her feet and draping his lion skin over her shoulders. Ignoring the surprise in her eyes, he placed a hand in the small of her back to lead her from the courtyard. "Let's get you inside. You must be freezing."

He was certain he'd made his feelings clear, and he had told Iset she could go where she wished. He knew the Lady Ahaneith would reassure her tomorrow as well. The decision was Iset's to make, he wouldn't push her now. The next time they kissed, it would be because she made it happen.

Chapter 20 – First and Final Meetings

The next morning Iset sat anxiously on the edge of the bed in her room, waiting for Batr to escort her to meet with the pharaoh's second wife. The thought of meeting Lady Ahaneith chilled her more than the stone bench she'd sat on last night. Gods, what if she inadvertently slipped into the slang of the tomb workers, or did something terribly rude, without even realizing it?

Although she expected it, the knock on her door still startled her, and she tripped over the length of her new robe as she leaped from the bed. Stumbling to the door, she pulled it open in a flurry. There, bare-chested and leaning one shoulder against the doorjamb, stood Batr. Iset froze, once again struck by how at home he appeared here in the palace. Adorned as a man of the court, he wore a thick gold cuff on one wrist, and a gold chain over his bare chest. The long, dangerous-looking knife she'd seen him wear once before hung casually from his waist now, as if it had always been there.

The smooth, chestnut-toned muscles of his torso gleamed in contrast to his pure white shenti and the white-washed walls. His thumbs were tucked into the top of his shenti, pushing it down a little to reveal the dark trail of curls that led down, down into that hidden place she'd seen only once, and very much wished she could see again. His long dark hair was tied back, emphasizing his high cheekbones and laughing eyes. And mischievous they appeared, indeed, as their eyes met and she realized she'd been taking her time looking him over.

A flush rose to her cheeks, and her lips tightened, trying to conceal her reaction to him. Last night Batr hadn't asked her again to come to Thinis, but he *had* kissed her. *Sort of.* In a way, she was glad he hadn't asked. Sooner or later, he'd come to see their relationship as a mistake. The more Iset saw him the more she knew she did not belong in his world, and would only be a great encumbrance. At the same time, she'd ached for him to touch her again when they stood in the darkness in front of her room. One kiss, one little caress, and there would have been no chance of denying him anything. That he had done nothing left her more confused than ever.

She brushed past him into the hallway, her shoulder touching his, causing gooseflesh to rise along the surface of her skin.

Still leaning on the door, he scrutinized her, and his eyes narrowed a fraction. "Your hair is quite different today."

"Oh! Yes," self-conscious, she reached up to pat the elaborate braids piled atop her head. "A servant came to help me bathe and dress, and insisted on doing it. She did my make-up, also. I…" she gave a nervous laugh and spoke in a rush. "I felt utterly foolish. I've never had anyone do that, not since I was a child, and I think I got in her way more than anything. She told me to stop fidgeting."

In fact, Iset suspected the maid probably had more refinement than she, and had hardly been able to speak a word in case the girl went straight to Lady Ahaneith and told her what an ignorant village woman was staying in her palace.

"Does it look silly?" Iset asked, a part of her longing for the anonymity of the scarf and bindings she wore as Dedi.

Batr gave her a lazy smile. "You look beautiful. Lady Ahaneith will be pleased with you."

The wolfish look in his eyes set her heart pounding, and she ducked her head to avoid his gaze. Batr must have felt her hesitation, for he said, "I don't have to come with you, Iset. You can meet Lady Ahaneith on your own."

"No! I…" she clutched his forearm, "No, please. I'd like you to be there. I'm just nervous." She tried for a light-hearted smile. "It's not every day a woman like me meets the wife of a pharaoh."

He shook his head, an incredulous smile hovering on his lips. "Lady Ahaneith is not nearly as dangerous as some of the men you've faced. Or do you still think she will imprison you?"

Iset *did* think it still a possibility. While she'd believed Batr last night when he promised she was safe, a moonlit night has a way of cloaking the stark realities of day, and now she wasn't so sure anymore.

"Don't worry," Batr's tucked her hand into the crook of his arm and led her down the hallway. "I'll be by your side the whole time."

Iset was so grateful she could only squeeze his arm in thanks, turning her head to hide the tears that sprung to her eyes. She hated herself for being so emotional, but it seemed the last few months really had taken their toll on her, and she could no longer keep herself under control.

Soon, however, she learned that her fears were groundless. The Lady Ahaneith was all graciousness, a decent woman of understanding, and Iset recognised her as the golden-haired young woman she'd seen in her room when she'd woken the day before. She commended Iset, as well as her brother, for their bravery and commitment to Kemet. The lady did make a point, however, of telling Iset it was Batr who had brought them to her attention. Batr had ensured Lady Ahaneith knew just how much Iset had sacrificed, and the great risks she'd taken, in order to find the tomb robbers. Batr had insisted that it was mostly Iset's work that enabled him to catch all the men involved, and it was she that stopped Senebtawi from fleeing Abdju before they could catch him.

"It was truly an act of the gods, Hem-etj," Batr reminded Lady Ahaneith with an impudent grin, referring to the fact that Iset had stabbed Senebtawi with an icon of Isis.

"Of course," Ahaneith said after they'd spoken for a time, "I cannot publicly commend you in front of the court, as I might otherwise do. The situation is a delicate one. After all, your father *was* involved, and it would not do to draw too much attention to you and your family."

"No, of course, Hem-etj. I – I would never even wish for such a thing." She shrank from the very thought of a court full of nobles staring at her, judging her, knowing her history. It was enough that *she* knew it, never mind Batr and Lady Ahaneith.

Lady Ahaneith went on to confirm what Batr told her last night. Iset and her family were welcome to stay in the palace while Batr and Makae finished questioning the thieves and, once their sentences had been carried out, she could choose where she and her family would live and Ahaneith would furnish them with a house and enough to maintain them.

"When this matter comes to light, I imagine it would be preferable for you to settle outside of Abdju, someplace where you are not so well known." Lady Ahaneith gave a pointed look at Batr while she addressed Iset, a slight smile curving her lips, "Perhaps in Thinis, for example, where you know someone who can help you settle yourself."

"Thank you, Hem-etj, you are too kind." Iset ignored the lady's hint. When Lady Ahaneith dismissed them and Batr escorted her back to her room, she pled exhaustion. She knew he wanted to speak with her, she could sense his restless energy, but she needed to sort through her thoughts before she let her emotions dictate her actions.

Iset saw little of Batr over the next few days. He spent much of his time at the prison complex, finalizing the investigation into Senebtawi and the tomb robbers. When he wasn't there, he was in conference with his brother and Lady Ahaneith regarding the problems in the south, a situation Iset only heard of on her second day in the court. Iset also learned that, as a result of the southern raids, Batr's brother would be staying in Abdju. She knew Batr would miss his brother greatly; he'd said as much one evening when they were all dining together. He could hardly be upset with the reason, though, he said proudly. Makae was finally getting the recognition he deserved, and would likely marry Raia and acquire the large family he'd always longed for.

In his free time, Batr was often with his brother. When he wasn't with Makae, he spent time with her own little brother, answering his endless questions about court life, possible apprenticeship options, sailing, and soldiering. Iset's mother was also cheered by his company, and appeared to improve daily. Iset's nightmares began to recede, but the odd time she did wake from one, she stopped herself from venturing out into the courtyard. She was afraid of what foolish thing she might say or do if she found herself alone with Batr again.

Furthermore, she was much distracted when an envoy arrived from Queen Merneith in the form of Ebrium, Sekhrey Bey's second-in-command, who was sent to assist Batr and Makae with the investigation and trial of the tomb robbers. Ebrium, Ahmose reminded her in a state of awe, was the former pirate who had solved a double murder in one of Thinis's largest temples several months ago, along with the woman who was now his wife. Ebrium informed them his wife was heavily pregnant and unable to make the day-long journey to Abdju with him. He had, however, brought along his sister, Akshaka, and one of the queen's cousins, Penebui.

At first, Iset had been a little terrified to meet such esteemed people. Ebrium was even taller and broader than Batr and Makae, with the most unusual pale skin and blue eyes matched with thick black hair. While his sister bore his same exotic looks, Penebui was more like the Lady Ahaneith – blonde with blue eyes. They were the strangest group of people Iset had ever seen. However, the two teenaged girls greeted her with such chatty enthusiasm that it was near impossible to remain nervous around them. And once they learned how she masqueraded as a boy, and almost killed a man, their excitement was enough to rival that of Ahmose and ten boys like him.

"Was it very awful for you to have to stab him?" Penebui asked, her pretty blue eyes wide with concern.

Iset was helping the two women settle into their rooms in the palace the evening of their arrival. The girls had invited her to join them, as they wanted to ask her about the court of Abdju and her experiences. They'd talked Ebrium into bringing them along with him to Abdju, they informed her, as neither had been to Lady Ahaneith's court before. After a day spent travelling with them, it was clear Ebrium was more than happy to pass the voluble girls over into someone else's care. Passing a large hand over his weary-looking face, he'd thanked her for taking the girls out of his presence, stating the need for a strong mug of beer and several minutes of complete silence. Iset, however, found the girls delightful, if not a little intimidating, with their whirlwind questioning and conversation.

"I imagine it must have been a little satisfying?" Akshaka queried, bending down to place a folded linen dress into a basket next to her, her sleek, black braids swinging forward with the motion. "Sometimes when I am very angry with my brother Ebrium, he lets me hit him with a pillow, and I find it immensely gratifying."

"That is hardly the same, Akshaka," Penebui scolded.

"Of course not! But still… Oh," she put her hand over mouth, but a dimpled smile peeked out the side. "I'm sorry. I'm not being very sensitive, am I? I apologize. It's just that my brother and his friends often speak about fighting, and I watch them train sometimes. I have harassed my poor sister-in-law and Ebrium so many times to tell me how she helped fight off a group of attackers once. She kicked a man right between the legs and ruptured one of his… man parts. They say it was very serious. It was still swollen weeks later and he walked like he had a boulder tied to his waist and hanging down between his legs."

The beautiful girl imitated the bow-legged movements of a man in pain, blowing out her cheeks and crossing her eyes for effect. The two girls giggled, and Iset couldn't help but join in. Over the next few days she found their chatter to be soothing, in its own way. Through them she was able to experience what it was like to be a young woman without great worries, free to spend her time with friends, enjoying long walks along the river, shopping at the market, and taking extra care preparing her appearance for dinner at the palace. In doing so, she was able to shed some of her own worries and fears for the future. She began to familiarize herself with court manners, and become more comfortable in her new life, surreal as it all felt.

Akshaka, she learned, was not so different from herself. The girl was also low-born, even more so than Iset. Her father had been a gardener in a palace in a distant northern region, and they'd almost starved for years after his death. Her brother Ebrium had taken to the seas, like Batr and Makae, in order to help them survive. But over the last year or so, Akshaka and her brother had integrated into court life.

"Of course, it has not been an entirely seam-less incorporation," Akshaka assured her. "Ebrium still insists on swearing up a storm and stomping around every now and then when he's angry. Oh, and the way he cannot keep his hands off my sister-in-law Satsobek is practically scandalous. Even now that she's almost birthing, he simply will not stop kissing her in public. It's positively dreadful," Akshaka shook her head with mock sadness, a light of mischief glinting in her eyes. Iset smiled, her heart full to think that she might one day be friends with such kind, happy people.

And so it was that when her next challenge came, not long before her family was due to decide where they would go when they left the palace, she felt some small measure of confidence that she would not make a complete fool of herself. She couldn't be easy until she'd apologized in person to Raia, the daughter of the man whose tomb her father had robbed. Batr told her it wasn't necessary, that the necklace had been returned and Raia did not wish to pursue the matter, but Iset's conscience niggled at her, along with the remnants of other fears.

Batr offered to accompany her, stating that he would take the opportunity to visit Makae. She was aware it was more likely a kindness on his part, so that she might not have to be alone without support, and she gratefully accepted it. She was also grateful that he avoided more sensitive topics, such as her future, while they walked to Raia's home.

He told her that Senebtawi had recovered enough to stand trial, but it was unlikely he'd recover his voice. It would therefore be easier to keep her name – and that of her father – out of the records. They'd already learned from the other thieves that it was, indeed, Senebtawi who had ordered the murder of her father, out of fear that he might turn himself in and ruin the rest of them in the process. The trial was a mere formality at this point, a means of determining the extent of the punishment for the men and their families.

"I suppose there is some comfort," she murmured, "in knowing that my *yet* struggled with his conscience at the end." She didn't add that – horrible as it was – his death at the hands of the thieves was probably easier than what he would have suffered had he lived to go to trial. The shame of the ordeal would also have been much worse for her family, and their own punishment inevitable, had her father lived. She pitied the families of the other men, and hoped their lives would not be required to compensate for the disorder caused by the thieves.

"He also would not allow Senebtawi to marry you." Batr pointed out. "He knew what Senebtawi was, and must have cared enough to not want you to be tied to such a man."

Iset gave a small huff. "While that helps in some measure, had he never gotten himself in debt and involved in the first place none of this would have happened."

"But then you wouldn't have met me, and that would be a great shame, wouldn't it?" Batr took up her hand and placed it in the crook of his arm. The playful twinkle in his upturned eyes sent the blood rushing to her cheeks, and his words recalled the time she'd fallen unconscious in her hut and woken with her hand on his chest. Like then, she felt the warmth of his bare skin and the corded muscles of his forearm under her fingertips, and it made her want to feel his naked length over hers once more.

"Are you always so sure of yourself?" She asked, trying to keep her voice light.

"Is it always so difficult to make you smile?"

"Yes. I believe it is."

Batr threw his head back and laughed, and some of the tension she'd felt in his presence dissipated. He had a contrary way of setting her at ease while putting her on edge, making her tighten her fingers on his arm even as she tried to school her features to remain unreadable.

Once ushered into Raia's mansion, a home of even greater magnificence than Senebtawi's, they were met by Batr's brother. Makae spent most of his nights at Raia's, but Iset had spoken to him on a few occasions at the palace and found him to be a fascinating contrast to Batr. Although almost entirely alike in appearance, the brothers were near opposites in personality. Makae was quiet, his words measured, and Iset could never imagine him judging anything in haste. On the other hand, Batr was gregarious and brash, exuding a considerable amount of energy at odds with Makae's calm presence. While she found herself liking Makae very much, she realized that Batr's forward attitude served to push past barriers she'd set up to keep others at bay, barriers that might otherwise have remained intact for years to come. Over the course of a few days, he'd uncovered secrets she'd kept hidden from those who knew her best. It was a disconcerting revelation, but one that made her yearn for him all the more.

He asked her if she'd like him to remain while she met with Raia, rather than tour the grounds with his brother. But Iset wanted Batr to have every possible moment with his brother before he had to leave Abdju, and Makae had offered to take him around to see the gardens and to have a mug of beer.

"No, thank you," she declined, though she was indeed nervous. "I think I had best do this alone."

The men stayed with her until Raia joined them a few minutes later, along with a servant bearing a tray of warmed milk, a rare delicacy since milk never kept long in Kemet's heat. Once introductions were made the men took their leave, and Iset set about with her awkward apologies.

As she stammered out her story, Raia listened placidly, leaning back in a chair. Iset found it difficult to find the appropriate words. It wasn't just the awful deeds her father had inflicted on Raia's family, or that she was a noblewoman. Raia was an incredibly daunting woman in her own right. Iset was struck by the woman's regal bearing, a something in the lift of her chin, her height and broad shoulders, as well as her wide, strong cheekbones.

Iset also marveled at Raia's beauty. Her complexion was as smooth and pore-less as a polished, black river rock, worn by thousands of waves over hundreds of years. Her closely cropped, curly black hair emphasized her strong features and long neck, and Iset was sure she herself could never look half so attractive without her hair. Her lone decoration was the very same necklace her father had kept hidden; the one Ahmose had returned to Batr.

When Iset finished, Raia looked out the nearby window, fingering the necklace she wore before addressing Iset. Then she said, "I admit that when I first learned of the offense against my *yet*, I wanted everyone involved punished severely. I wanted to see their families suffer as I had suffered. I will not deny that, and I will not apologize for my sentiments at the time, which I believed then were justified."

Iset bit her lip, trying not to flinch at the tirade she feared would come next. But Raia surprised her. Leaning forward and resting her elbows on her knees in a casual manner, Raia said, "Since you have been direct with me about your circumstances, I'd like to tell you about mine. The necklace you returned to me belonged to my mother, not my *yet*. In fact, the man buried in that tomb is not my *yet* at all. And I know this because of what your family has done."

It was another ten minutes or so before Iset understood the whole of Raia's story, and when she did, she felt a great sense of relief.

"So you see," Raia said, "because of this whole situation I've learned that not everything in my life was as it seemed. Just as you were unaware of your father's actions, so I was unaware of things my father had done. Labouring under false pretenses, I did things my conscience otherwise would not condone. Sometimes when we exalt someone too much, it becomes difficult to see them as they really are. I find I prefer to know all, even the disagreeable, rather than live in ignorance. At least with everything out in the open, I can begin to find a way to move forward with my life."

Iset understood the sentiment. Now that her own past was in the open, ugly as it was, she must find a way past the wreckage of it all. Not only for her own sake, but for her mother's and her brother's.

She never would have imagined it possible that when Batr and Makae came to check on them a short while later that she would be deep in discussion with Raia about the difficulties of raising younger brothers. But it seemed that Raia's younger siblings and children were just as fascinated by Makae as Ahmose was by Batr. Raia even asked if Iset might come back again to share her tomb-raiding story with the children in order to add to their repertoire. Iset and Raia parted on better terms than she'd thought possible, and Iset's heart was much lighter. She was finally ready to talk to Batr about her future.

On their return to the palace, Batr led Iset to the courtyard and the same bench he'd found her on the night she'd woken up after stabbing Senebtawi. Like that night, the palm and sycamore trees swayed in a cool, winter breeze, but instead of crickets and frogs singing their nighttime song, sparrows and doves chirped and cooed in the branches. Batr sensed Iset's nervousness, but he also sensed that something had shifted for her. The wary tension she'd carried on her shoulders was dissipated.

Furthermore, her health seemed to have improved, as evidenced by the fresh glow in her fawn-toned cheeks. Her thin frame had also begun to fill out, emphasizing her curves in a way that made his fingers itch constantly to touch her. Though he'd promised himself he wouldn't push her, each day that passed without her in his arms was an agony of self-denial, a test of his will.

He asked her, "Are you tired? Akshaka and Penebui are taking their afternoon nap now."

She shook her head, raising one eyebrow. "No. It is a habit of the nobility I have yet to acquire. It is enough that I have begun to sleep through the nights."

"I am glad to hear it," he smiled down at her. Movement caught his eye and, in the distance, Batr spied Ahmose chasing a group of peacocks across the courtyard, Ankhesenamon trailing behind him. He chuckled, and said, "Court life suits Ahmose."

"Yes." A faint smile came to Iset's ripe lips as she watched her brother. "He is certainly enjoying the food, all the roasted meat and fish and such. Much more of this and I fear he will become rather stout. Which I suppose I shouldn't mind at all. He deserves it."

"And you also look as if you've been eating. Even without me sitting at your feet and forcing it upon you. I confess I find it quite agreeable on you."

Iset met his eyes for a moment and blushed prettily before ducking her head to avoid his gaze.

He asked, "And your *mewet*? She seems to find it agreeable as well."

Iset nodded. "I think she has found some purpose, having to take care of both of us these last two weeks." Iset picked at her fingernails, looking down. "It makes me wonder if somehow, deep down, she didn't know what was happening all along, and stayed in bed to avoid facing it. Instead she left us to deal with it. Oh!" She quickly covered her mouth with her hands. "I can't believe I said that. What an awful thing of me to think."

He shook his head. "No. Although I'm sure your *mewet* loves you, what you've been through was difficult and you can still be angry for a time. Be angry at the gods, be angry with your parents, be angry with me, if it makes you feel better. Just not for too long."

"Angry with you?! Why in the world should I be angry with you?" She finally looked at him, her long lashes blinking rapidly. He'd intended to provoke her to smile, but she seemed so serious he couldn't bring himself to tease her.

He shrugged one shoulder. "You've been avoiding me, and I assume it's because you're angry with me. Maybe because I didn't help you sooner. If I had, I could have prevented that scenario with Senebtawi, or when they forced you down into the tomb."

Iset shivered, and her fingers tightened around the edge of the bench. "I could never be angry with you, not after everything you've done for us." Her voice dropped to an emotional whisper. "I don't know what we would have done if you hadn't been there to help."

Taking a deep breath, Batr said, "My offer still stands, Iset. Come to Thinis with me."

For the briefest of moments, she hesitated, and he thought she might say yes. Then she smoothed her dress over her knees and said matter-of-factly, "I have been afraid to discuss this."

"Why? Are you hiding something else?" He didn't want to think it, but then again, with her, who knew? Or, perhaps even worse, he'd misread her signs and she simply did not want him at all.

She shook her head. "No, no more secrets. I abhor that I ever had to lie in the first place, and I won't keep anything from you. You deserve more than that from me. I suppose I thought that you would find us a great encumbrance, and wish to be rid of us."

"I… what?" Batr was rarely struck speechless, but he hadn't anticipated such a response. "Why in the name of Ba'al would I think such a thing?"

"Oh, I've no doubt Ahmose would behave himself and do as you tell him. He absolutely idolizes you. But you know what my *mewet* is like, and…"

Batr cut her off. "At least she isn't meddling and managing, like some. If she needs for anything, it is company and a life without so much strife. She seems to do well-enough when she feels she has a purpose. I imagine it might make her feel useful to live with us and help raise our children."

Her lips parted, as if on a silent gasp, but then her jaw squared and her fingers went back to twisting in her lap. "I thought I would be your biggest problem."

"You would?" Batr knew he was parroting her, but she continued to amaze him.

"Me." She turned her sad eyes up to him. "I'm not sure I belong in this sort of place." She gestured around the courtyard. "*You* do, but I don't. I'm just a girl from the village, and yes, I am a draughtsman's daughter, which isn't quite so low as a stone-cutter's daughter, or a… a water-carrier's daughter, but it is infinitely worse because of what my father did, and what I have done since. I don't know how I could ever go to court, or be in the presence of the queen, or any such thing. You would be shunned. And I… I hardly know how to behave half the time. Sometimes I feel all the servants here think me a great peasant. I couldn't bear to be a burden to you, to have people think you foolish for taking up with a girl like me, when you could have so much better, like a nobleman's daughter. Your brother and Ebrium have both found noblewomen, and so could you."

Batr stared at her in shock for a moment. Then he burst out laughing.

Iset's lips tightened in indignation while she waited for Batr to stop chuckling. It was one thing for her to pour her insecurities out to him, and quite another for him to laugh at her for it. She glared at him and said, "You know, I was trying to be considerate, but I have half a mind to accept your offer just to spite you and make your life more difficult."

He grinned. "Truly? Then I accept your terms. Now can I take you to my bed before Ahmose finds us and I am required to spend the next ten years answering all his questions?" He grabbed her hand and moved to stand.

"You… hold a moment!. I have not done yet." She tugged him back down.

"Please, no more! My friends and family will accept you no matter what."

"I'm beginning to see that now, but I didn't know it before. Akshaka and Penebui have been wonderful, and it helped very much to know Akshaka and Ebrium were commoners like me. Speaking to Raia today has also lifted a great burden. I… in truth I think I was still afraid she would want to see me punished."

It was more than that, too, Iset thought. Raia's forgiveness, while not indicative of the rest of the nobility in any way, had given her some hope that others might accept her one day as well.

Batr smiled down at her, and the tenderness she saw in his eyes quite took her breath away, causing her heart to stutter in her chest. He said, "I wish you'd told me this before, so I could tell you how foolish you were. But," he held up a hand to stop her indignant protest, grinning as he said, "truly you have nothing to fear. Both Akshaka and Penebui have already told me repeatedly how much they admire you. Akshaka told me if I do not marry you there is something irreparably wrong with my head, and Ebrium actually agreed with her for once. My brother warned me that I am growing older and will lose my handsome looks soon. So you see, you must marry me, or else I shall grow old alone, with no one to warm my bed."

"I should hope that is not the only reason!"

"Of course not, I am trying to assuage your fears. I also thought you too hard-hearted to listen to my love-talk and chose to appeal to your more practical side."

"Hard-hearted? I am no such thing." She had to admit, though, that she *had* tried very hard to harden her heart against him. She'd been terribly unsuccessful. He was, after all, a very charming, handsome man.

"No? In that case," he placed her palm against his chest so that she might feel the warmth there, "let me say that I would think it fairly obvious by now that I am madly in love with you, Nofret. You are the most beautiful woman I've ever met. You are smarter than you give yourself credit for, braver than the fiercest of soldiers, tougher than the most dangerous pirate on the great seas, more honest than a judge and jury altogether, and I desperately want to get you back in my bed so I can make love to you for days. I want to give you anything and everything that will make you happy. And you should know that I am generally not in the habit of proposing marriage to just any woman. I have a deadly fear of them taking me seriously and accepting. But in this case I assure you I am quite sincere."

"Is this a proposal then?" She felt amazingly light, like a soft, white, dandelion spore picked up and blown in a breeze.

"Of course. In case it wasn't clear before, I am asking you to marry me."

"You never asked the question."

"Haven't I?"

She shook her head, emotion rising in her throat, burbling out in a silly little giggle. "You asked me to come to Thinis, but you didn't say what for."

"Ah! I see. Stupid me. I warned you I'm not in the habit of this. Well then, Isetnofret, will you do me the great honour of coming to Thinis with me for the express purpose of becoming my wife? I'd like to spend my life with you by my side, and for you to bear my children, lots of them, by the way, if possible. Is that specific enough?"

Tears welled in her eyes and she bit down on her lips to keep from sobbing aloud. Instead, she nodded vigorously, even as he pulled her into his arms and her cheek squashed against his chest.

"Yes," she finally half-laughed, half-wept onto his linen robe. "Yes."

He squeezed her tighter, until she almost couldn't breathe, and she pushed off his chest a little to look up at him. She was amazed to see unshed tears shining in his eyes, and she smiled, reaching up to touch his cheek. Then she drew herself up to press her mouth to his, and his breath was sweet, like honey and carob tea. It was a slow, decadent kiss, a soft melding that sent delicious heat splicing bone-deep under her skin, melting tension and apprehension in its wake. He hooked one hand under her knees and drew her legs up over his lap so her feet rested on the other side of his thighs. Sliding one rough palm down to her ankles, he discovered her cold feet.

His head pulled back, placing one large hand over her bluish toes. "Your feet are like blocks of ice, Nofret. You ought to be back inside, where it's warm. My bed, by the way, is particularly snug."

"Mmmm," she smiled dreamily. Despite the sunlight, the day *was* rather chilly, but she'd hardly noticed it with the heat of his body so near hers. "I have never seen blocks of ice before. Do they look like feet?"

He snorted, rubbing his palm over her toes. "Now should we wait until your family returns to tell them, or can I take you to my bed right now? I should tell you that I already have your *mewet*'s blessing, she gave it to me days ago."

Iset laughed. "That sure of yourself, were you?"

"No," he shook his head. "But I was that hopeful."

"Then you'd best take me to bed now and we'll tell them at dinner. Because as soon as Ahmose finds out we're moving to Thinis you will have a million and one questions to answer."

Batr grinned even as he pulled her to her feet and ushered her towards the palace. More than anything, Iset couldn't wait to spend the night next to him and wake in the circle of his arms. She still had her doubts about joining the ranks of the nobility in Thinis, but she knew that with Batr by her side she could face the future with her head held high.

Taking her hand, he tugged her down the hallway behind him. Once in his room with the door closed behind them, he pressed her down on his bed, laying out beside her and capturing her mouth in a deep kiss. His calloused palm slid up under the edge of her robe, circling her slender calf before moving to the outside of her thigh, where his fingers made little circles near her hip. Her mouth pressed harder against his, her kisses growing more insistent, as his fingers played over the top of her thigh, towards her centre. Her legs parted slightly, granting him access to her most private of places, allowing him to slip his hand between her smooth thighs. "Yes," she gasped when the tips of his fingers brushed her soft curls, gliding down between the folds of her sex.

Her hands slipped from his neck to bunch in the fabric of his tunic. She murmured incoherencies against his mouth. He traced lazy circles over the sensitive tip at the apex of her sex, and her hips began to rock against him. His cadence increased, and soon her mound was pressing against the palm of his hand with urgency, her face tucked into his neck, whimpering her need with warm breaths and kisses on his bare skin. When he slipped one finger between her silky, molten folds she buried her cry of release in the curve of his collarbone.

After a few moments had passed and she'd regained her breath, Iset tugged at Batr so that he moved above her, even as he reached to pull the sheets up over them, trying to warm their chilled bodies. But she didn't need bedsheets. She needed the heat of his naked body against hers, to feel his skin on hers, and she hauled at the edges of his tunic, desperate to rip the fabric out of her way. He let her pull the tunic over his head and toss it aside, before reaching for her own robe, and she shimmied awkwardly out of it beneath him, giggling like a giddy girl as they twisted in the sheets.

And then there was just the two of them, stripped of their clothes and their secrets. With another tug, she flipped over to straddle his hips, sitting atop him while he lay prone beneath her, his large hands clenching her hips. Iset couldn't bring herself to say the words, words she was too afraid to say in case she woke up and he was gone, leaving the dark void in her life all the worse for she hadn't realized until now that it could be filled. Instead, she affirmed her affections with her caresses. Her fingers traced the ridges of his chest to tell him how much she admired him. She smoothed her palm over his abdomen to tell him that she appreciated everything he'd done for her. Soft kisses on his shoulders and neck were meant to whisper how much she prized his kindness. When her lips met the soft curls below his belly button, to travel further and tell him that she loved him with her mouth on his hardness, he caught her face in his hands.

"Not now," he growled. "I won't last. But definitely later."

With a quick motion, he had her on her back again, the dark skin of his muscled biceps bulging as he held himself above her, between her bent knees. She breathed deeply, taking in his heady, masculine scent, shivering as his warm mouth closed over her bared neck. She needed more than the ministrations of his fingers. She needed to feel alive with passion, with the burning intensity of urgent love-making. Shifting beneath him until the tip of his manhood was fitted against her, she tilted her hips insistently, and could feel his smile against her neck.

Ever so slowly, Batr began to push forward past her body's resistance, filling her with his thickness and heat. She reveled in the sight of his strong chest and shoulders over her, the weight of his body, the soft rub of his skin, his rich scent, and the sough of his breath near her ear. He flooded her senses, and there was nothing in the world she wanted more than to take all of him in. She breathed him, swallowed him, saw and heard only him.

Soon their bodies were moving together in a gentle, undulating wave, like the encroaching tide on a breezy day. Entwining her legs around his, her arms over his strong, broad back, their lips touched and parted, bodies rippling with pleasure and need. With every thrust of his smooth, firm hips he drove emotion up into her, sensations and feelings she'd held tight for so long. This closeness they shared unlocked hidden recesses of fear, love, and loneliness within her, until tears formed in the corners of her eyes and slipped down into her hair.

The swell of their movements intensified, surging upwards towards a final crescendo, a tidal wave that poured through her. She cried out, muffling the sound against his shoulder as he continued to surge within her, rocking her in a current, until he too jerked with his release, a deep, ragged noise tearing from his throat.

For several moments he lay over her, elbows by her ears, as they gasped for air. He murmured words of veneration and wonder. She let her hands and lips speak for her, hoping the way she nuzzled his neck, the way her fingers trailed over his sweat-dampened back, and the way she rubbed his thighs with hers, would suffice.

Batr collapsed to the side of her, his arm draped across her chest under her breasts, pulling her close to him. She lay that way for a few minutes, enjoying the heat of his body tucked against hers. When his breath began to even, to soften and grow heavy with sleep, she moved to slip out from under his hold. But he tightened his grip, his arm a solid beam of marble.

"Don't go yet," his sleep-slurred voice was hushed against the tangle of hair at the back of her neck. "For the second time since I met you I thought you'd died. Don't go yet."

Iset twisted to face him and saw a hint of grief in his sleepy, upturned eyes, eyes that normally held so much humour. Emotion welled in her breast again, as she realized how selfish she'd been. All along she'd been trying to protect herself from loss, when he'd experienced so much himself. She hadn't given a thought to how it must have been for him to twice come across her unconscious body. It must have brought back such horrible memories for him, memories of the time he'd returned to his tribe to find his entire family devastated.

Smiling gently, she stroked the back of her hand over his cheek. "I am only going to the House of the Morning," *the washroom*, "I will be right back."

Batr nodded, and when she returned a few moments later, she let him pull her back towards him. She molded her naked body to his, tangling their legs together, tucking her cheek against his chest and slipping one arm up around his shoulder.

He touched his forehead to hers in a tender gesture and whispered, "I cannot wait for you to see your new home, and to make you happy."

Moving her hand to rest on his cheek, she murmured, "You've already made me happier than you'll ever know."

With her heart full to bursting, Iset held him as much as he held her, until his breathing evened out. Perhaps, Iset thought as she fell into a light sleep, she could learn to enjoy napping in the afternoons after all.

Epilogue

Two weeks later

Iset leaned back against the warm planks of the large ship and closed her eyes, letting the sun warm her on one side and the wood on the other. The slow rocking was soothing, as was Penebui and Akshaka's chatter. She'd never been on a ship before and while it had taken her an hour or so to become accustomed to the movement, she was quickly learning to enjoy it.

Penebui gave a little clap of excitement as she said, "I cannot wait to get to Thinis, and for Iset to see the court and the palace. Oh, and Ahmose will find so much to do. It will be like your first time at court, Akshaka, when you first came to us two years ago."

Akshaka agreed, relating how overwhelming and wonderful it had been for her the evening of the banquet when she met the queen, and adding a funny story about how there had been a great confusion because of her poor language skills. Apparently, the queen had thought Akshaka and Sekhrey Bey were married, because Akshaka had confused the words "brother" and "husband," while all along the young woman had only meant to indicate that Bey was as good as a brother to her.

Iset appreciated that the girls didn't actually require her to participate in the conversation, and were happy enough to let her nod and smile as needed. Every chance spent with Akshaka and Penebui was an opportunity Iset was thankful for, one that taught her more of what to expect when they arrived in Thinis. It had taken longer than anticipated to wrap up Senebtawi's trial, and that of the other tomb robbers, and then Batr and Ebrium had taken a few extra days to spend with Makae before parting with him in Abdju.

Each day that passed Iset grew more comfortable with leaving her home for Thinis.

Opening her eyes a slit, her gaze swept the length of the large barge. Beyond the several benches of rowers, her little brother and mother were leaning over the railing of the stern. Ahmose was hopeful of seeing a crocodile, or even a hippopotamus, but Iset had noticed Batr and Ebrium sharing an amused and wary look when he'd expressed his deep desire. When she'd asked Batr about it, he'd led her out of earshot and told her he'd been present on the hunting trip that saw Pharaoh Wadj killed by crocodiles, and a visiting Sumerian prince attacked by an angry hippopotamus.

"It is a long story for another day, but perhaps one that Ahmose is not ready to hear yet." His lips had curved into a secretive smile, and she'd frowned in response. "Ahh," he'd drawled, "you think I'm being inappropriate and disrespectful. But that's only because *you* didn't know the pharaoh like I did. Trust me; you would not mourn his passing either." He'd grinned then as he'd pulled her flush with his taut body, and she'd let him kiss away thoughts of anything else but getting him alone in their home.

Their home. Even now, she flushed at the memory of the things they'd done last night in his room in the palace, and how he'd whispered soon enough they'd be doing them in their home. Never mind that their home included servants, and even a cook. *Thank the gods for that*, Iset smiled to herself, thinking of how Ahmose had almost taken off Batr's head the first day he showed up on their doorstep.

Iset blinked, and her gaze rested on Batr's strong back at the bow of the ship where he was scouting for obstructions. She watched the muscles in his back bunch as he rolled his shoulders. A wave of emotion washed over her, as warm as the sunshine and as powerful as the swift push of the ship up the great river. By the gods she was an incredibly lucky woman to have captured the attention of such a man.

"Of course I do not begrudge anyone their happiness," Penebui said, nudging Iset's arm.

Iset realized she'd lost the thread of their conversation. "Sorry?" Iset asked, turning to the girls.

Both Akshaka and Penebui grinned. Akshaka passed a hand over her thick black braids and said, "Penebui was just saying that all the exciting men to come to court in the last couple of years are now happily married."

Penebui shook her head, an exaggeratedly mournful expression in her bright blue eyes. "It's tragic, really. There is not a single eligible pirate left at court. Now who am I to marry? I am getting older by the day and there is no one left."

Akshaka tsk'd, "No, your father would never let you marry a pirate. Unless, of course, he is one of the nobility. Or perhaps a foreign noble, like Sekhrey Bey."

Iset ventured to tease her friend by saying, "Perhaps when we reach Thinis there will be a handsome desert prince waiting for you?"

"Ooooh, like a tribal warlord?" Penebui's eyes went wide with delight and she held her hands up, fingers splayed, as if examining a picture before her. "That sounds exhilarating! Just think of the adventures we could have together. I've always wanted to go out into the desert."

"It's not nearly as exciting as you think," Batr's voice boomed as he dropped down next to Iset. "And a woman such as yourself would find it a great hardship."

Penebui sniffed. "I will have you know that I am tougher than I look."

Batr just grinned and tucked his arm around Iset, pulling her along the bench towards him.

Akshaka rolled her eyes and hooked her arm into Penebui's, drawing her up with her. "Come, Penebui, let's go see if my brother can think of any more nobles we've missed. Clearly we are no longer wanted here."

Iset protested, but the girls giggled and winked before heading off towards the far end of the ship. She let Batr pull her a little tighter against him, and the heat of his skin warmed her far deeper than any ray of sunshine could. Iset rested her head against his shoulder, and he kissed the top of her head, breathing in her scent.

His voice rumbled in his chest near her ear as he asked, "Will you miss anything from Abdju?"

She snorted softly. “No, I don’t think so. I am ready to move on. I have everything I want in the world on this ship right now.”

“What about the widow Neb-tawy?” Iset heard the amusement in his tone, and shook her head gently.

“I still cannot believe she suspected I was Dedi all along.”

On one of their last days, Batr had accompanied Iset and her family back to the village so they could say their goodbyes. Given the shame that had fallen on their family, Iset had only gone to see a select few people, and Neb-tawy was one of them. Iset had hugged her and thanked her for looking after her mother and Ahmose. Neb-tawy whispered in her ear, “And I am glad you finally got rid of Dedi.”

Iset had pulled back and stuttered, “Well, Dedi went back to his people in the south and…” she stopped when Neb-tawy shook her head, smiling.

“No, girl, I mean you don’t have to pretend anymore.”

“How did you…?” Iset started to ask, but Neb-tawy held up a hand and said with a knowing grin, “I didn’t. I had my suspicions, but now I know for sure.” She’d turned to Batr and patted him on the arm before hunkering back down on her stool and splaying her bare toes out in the sand. She said to him, “I told you she’d take you. Even with all that hair and those things.” She’d waggled her fingers to indicate his tattoos, and Batr had laughed, leaning down to hug the old woman.

“Now that’s enough,” she’d slapped his arm. “People will start to talk, you know, and you only newly married. I won’t have it about the village that I’m a homewrecker.” She’d winked then and sent them on their way.

Now, Iset could feel Batr’s lips spread in a smile where they met the top of her head. He said, “I believe she knows far more than we give her credit for. She knew all along that I wanted to marry you, even before I did.”

“No!” Iset feigned shock. “I thought your intentions were always honourable. Never say you tried to bed me without the intention of marrying me.

A bark of laughter escaped Batr. "Ha! This from the woman who bedded me with no intentions of marriage."

Iset tilted her face up to his, about to protest even though a smile hovered in the corners of her lips. He stopped her with his mouth on hers, with a hungry kiss that sent heat spiraling out from her belly and through her limbs. Batr cupped her face with one palm, while his other hand trailed down her backside to the top of her curves, caressing her with a promise of things to come.

Whatever argument she'd intended to mount was forgotten within moments of their mouths joining. When they finally parted to draw breath, she couldn't think of a single thing to say, except for a whispered, "I love you." Batr's arm tightened around her, and he smiled, the answering words written clearly in his shining, upturned eyes.

She'd been practising those three words over the past few days. They came much easier now, and each time seemed to strip away some of the fear of saying them. She rested a hand on her abdomen, rubbing it absently. She stopped when she realized Batr was frowning.

"What is it?" he asked. "Are you ill?"

"No," she hesitated; unsure of how to answer, not knowing if there was even anything to tell.

"Then what? Tell me what's wrong, Nofret." Batr demanded, concern shadowing his features.

I… it's very early to know for sure… but there's a chance…," she licked her lips before finishing in a rush. "Well, would you mind very much if there were one more of us on board?"

"One more…? I don't…" Iset watched as realization dawned on his face, his gaze going from her belly to her eyes as if to assure himself. "Really?"

She shrugged. "Maybe? I would not have said anything yet, except that you asked and, well… my monthly course is three weeks late."

"Three weeks? That would mean… by the gods! The very first time!" A silly grin spread across his face.

"Well you needn't look so proud of yourself. Even *I* know such a thing isn't impossible."

He laughed, wrapping his arms around her and squeezing until her face was squashed against his chest and it became difficult to breathe. She struggled against him and even then he refused to release her, but only relaxed his grip and murmured, "Nofret, I will love you regardless, never fear. If you have ten or none at all, I will still be a happy man. But if it is a boy, we shall name him Makae, of course."

"Naturally," her voice was a mumble against his shoulder.

"And if it is a girl, we shall send her out to apprentice as a tomb painter, so she can be just like her mother."

Iset slapped a hand against his arm in mock protest. "That's quite enough out of you."

Finally, he let her go, adjusting her so that she was tucked in the crook of his arm against his flank. "So you *are* happy about it?" she asked. "It isn't too much at once? Taking in me and Ahmose and my mother, and now possibly a baby?"

Batr leaned his head back against the railing and closed his eyes, a faint smile on his lips. "No, Nofret. It isn't too much at all. It is precisely what I've always wanted."

It was precisely what she'd always wanted, too, and she couldn't be happier. Iset rested her head on his chest and watched the water of the great river rush past them as she sped towards her new life, leaving the Land of the Dead far, far behind.

Next in the Series!

Book #4 of the Ancient Egyptian Romance Series
Lady of the Caravan

Penebui is certain she'll fall madly in love with her new husband. Once she makes the long journey across the unfamiliar desert to meet him, that is. She knows her duty is to marry strategically, and the chief of one of the most powerful nomadic desert tribes could help save her beloved cousin's delicate regency. There are just a few small obstacles to overcome; Penebui has never stepped foot into the desert, the man chosen to lead her to her fate scorns her, and someone might be trying to kill her.

Menes has one last duty to fulfill before he can settle into his new life as the commander of an oasis outpost. All he needs to do is get the queen's cousin safely across the desert so that she can marry the head of his tribe, a simple enough task for an experienced caravan leader such as himself. Except the woman in his charge draws trouble with every step, and she refuses to listen to a thing he says.

Follow Penebui and Menes as they brave the dangers of the great desert to prevent a tribal war that threatens the peace of Kemet.

To stay up to date on publications, go to www.DanielleSLeBlanc.com and subscribe to my mailing list!

You'll also be eligible for free chapters, early notice of giveaways, and more.

Or follow me on Pinterest under **Danielle S. LeBlanc** to see some of the pictures that help influence my novels.

CPSIA information can be obtained
at www.ICGtesting.com
Printed in the USA
FSHW01n2019081018
52868FS

9 780994 975126